SILHOUETTE LOVE STORY COLLECTION

MIDSUMMER BRIDE

by
Mary Lewis

When Eva meets the handsome Swedish Count, Max von Stjerna, the two fall deeply in love. But he is forced to marry her cousin or the curse will fall again on Castle Rosenborg . . .

STORMY MASQUERADE

by
Anne Hampson

Karen Waring was an actress playing her most difficult role; a middle-aged housekeeper working for playwright Clint Fraser. Then, one night, Clint accidentally met the real Karen, and suddenly she didn't know who she was – or who she wanted to be.

SHADOW AND SUN

by
Mary Carroll

Britt is furious when Philippe, master of the historic Chateau de Laon, continues to avoid her. But when at last she meets him her anger dissolves under his sensuous, irresistible spell . . .

MIDSUMMER BRIDE © 1980 by Silhouette Books

STORMY MASQUERADE © 1980 by Anne Hampson

SHADOW AND SUN © 1980 by Silhouette Books

ISBN 0 340 26458 6

Printed and bound in Great Britain for the Leisure Circle Ltd by Richard Clay (The Chaucer Press) Ltd,
Bungay, Suffolk

MARY
LEWIS

Midsummer
Bride

Silhouette Romance
Library

Chapter One

There was a touch of magic in the forest that morning, Eve thought, as she pedaled her bicycle along the path beneath the towering spruce. The rays of sunlight slanted down through their branches as from the windows of a great cathedral, and the air was pungent with burgeoning spring. Close at hand the dark brown water of a small brook newly released from its winter ice gurgled importantly, and from somewhere off in the woods came the faint cry of a cuckoo.

She braked her bicycle to a stop on the narrow path, lifting her bright head attentively, trying to catch a repetition of the elusive sound. Wasn't there some superstition about it? She thought, but the memory eluded her and the cry did not come again, so after a few moments she biked on, breathing deeply of the pine-scented air. Nothing, she told herself, could be quite so heavenly as a Swedish forest in the spring.

Beneath the trees the ground was velvety with moss through which the lingonberry plants were pushing their stiff, glossy leaves, and in a few sheltered spots remnants of snow still lingered. Eve Tremaine was a small girl with a gamine face, large, very dark blue eyes, a broad mouth, and a mass of short, golden-brown curls. She had a happy face in which everything seemed to curve upward: the outer ends of her dark eyebrows, the corners of her mouth, even the tip of her small nose. Her chin was gently rounded with a slight cleft and she had the clear, unblemished skin of a young child with a sprinkling of freckles over her nose and

5

cheekbones. In her jeans and boy's shirt she looked closer to twelve than the twenty she actually was.

Glancing down at the watch on her left wrist, she saw that it was nearly nine o'clock. She had promised Camilla that she would be home in time to go shopping with her, but the lovely morning had beguiled her farther and farther off into the woods and she would have to hurry to make it back in time. She began to pedal faster and was soon racing along the path with all the speed the rather ancient bicycle would allow. She was not sure how far she was from the lane that led to the Trillings' house, but she was not worried about meeting any cars on it. Anyone driving in would take the paved road directly in from the highway; the old logging road was all but abandoned now.

She didn't see the lane until she was on it, the trees having hidden the approach to it, so she zoomed out, braking hard in order to make the left turn. At that moment a horse and rider, also moving with considerable speed, came dashing along the lane. It happened so quickly that Eve had no time to think. Automatically she veered sharply away from the horse, but the startled animal reared onto its hind legs, seemingly poised directly over her for a terrifying second, then twisted adroitly away and galloped madly onto the path from which she had just emerged. A low-hanging branch of one of the spruce trees struck the rider across the forehead, and when Eve was able to stop her bicycle, jump off, and run back, she saw to her horror that the rider was now lying prone at the edge of the path. She let out a frightened cry. Had she killed him?

Cautiously she approached to examine her victim. It was a man, a very tall one. He was lying on his back, not moving. He was wearing riding breeches and a sport shirt open at the neck. She went slowly onto her knees beside him and gazed into his face. It was an attractive face in spite of the ugly red mark on the

6

forehead. There was a long, narrow, aristocratic-looking nose, deep-set eyes under bushy black brows, and a beautifully shaped mouth with a full lower lip on which her eyes lingered contemplatively for a moment. He had a fair Scandinavian complexion with a touch of color glowing on the high cheekbones. The chin looked firm and possibly stubborn, she thought. The mouth was now slightly open, revealing the glint of strong white teeth. His hair, which looked soft and silky as a child's, was a dark reddish brown, and she felt an urge to brush back the curling lock that had fallen over his forehead.

Who could he be, riding with such abandon through the forest? It was private land and surely no one from town would ride there. Could it possibly be—her heart began to beat faster at the thought—the count himself? But he was in Stockholm attending to business, according to Camilla, and was not expected home for several days.

To her great relief he was breathing, and even as she knelt there studying his face and debating whether to go for help or to wait and see if he recovered, his arms came up in a flailing motion and he let out a groan. Then his eyes opened, and she felt something like a shock wave through her entire body at their impact. They were a curious color: light hazel flecked with green and brown, golden in effect, shading off into deeper gold ringed with brown at the outer edges of the iris. She stared into them as though hypnotized. For a moment they were blank, then memory seemed to return and he let out a stream of incomprehensible Swedish as he struggled to sit up.

She backed off, afraid to offer any assistance because of the fury in those tawny eyes. He got to his feet without much difficulty and his hand went to his forehead.

"I—I'm sorry," she faltered in English, her limited

7

knowledge of Swedish deserting her in the crisis. "I hope you're not badly hurt. I had no idea I'd meet anyone on the road—" Her voice trailed off under the glare from those eyes.

"Who are you?" he demanded, also in English. "What are you doing on my property? And"—he looked angrily around—"Where the hell is my horse?"

"I'm Eve Tremaine," she replied meekly. "I was just riding my bicycle around a bit, and your horse"— she pointed down the path—"went thataway."

"Oh." He seemed to be trying to control his temper. "You are the American cousin who has come for a visit. And I"—he drew himself up haughtily, "am Max von Stjerna. In the future please remember that we often ride here, and try to exercise more caution. You might have been killed if my horse had struck you." He drew his heels together, made her an angry little bow, and strode off down the path after his horse.

Eve stared after him, her own indignation mounting. He had a right to be annoyed, but he didn't have to be so damned stuffy about it! If he was a fair sample of Swedish aristocracy, give her a good, simple peasant any day! How did Camilla stand him? She reclaimed the bicycle and rode on down the lane. It wasn't far to the Trillings' house, which stood back in a grove of birch trees. It was a typical Värmland farmhouse with red siding and a tiled roof. There was a small, enclosed porch around the front door and a balcony above with a door into the upper hall. Most houses had such balconies and they were used almost exclusively for the airing of bedding.

Eve knew that the house her relatives lived in had once been the home of the manager of the vast estate known as Lyckan. The big estate house was long gone, burned to the ground, they had told her, and the forest had grown over its foundations and the lawns and gardens that had once surrounded it. The farmland that

8

had been part of the Lyckan holdings now belonged to Rosenborg, the neighboring estate owned by the Count von Stjerna. Just what misfortunes had overtaken the family Eve did not know, because the Trillings seemed rather reluctant to talk about it. Although whatever had happened had been long before their time: somewhere around the middle of the nineteenth century. Lyckan meant happiness, she knew, an ironic name for an estate that had come to such an unfortunate end.

All her life Eve had been fascinated by her Swedish heritage. Her mother had been a Trilling, and her grandfather had emigrated to the United States at the turn of the century with his wife and baby daughter. Eve's father, Peter, was not of Swedish ancestry, and her mother did not seem particularly interested in her past heritage, but Eve had tried to find out everything she could about her Swedish relatives and longed for the day when she could save enough money to visit them.

The family that was now living at Lyckan consisted of Martin Trilling—who was her mother's cousin—his wife, Olivia, and two daughters, Camilla and Blenda. There was an older son, Pelle, but he was married now and had moved to Göteborg. Camilla was the same age as Eve and Blenda was ten. Eve and Camilla had started to correspond when they were little girls. Since English was taught in Sweden from the third grade on, Camilla could write and speak it fairly well, and Eve had been studying Swedish on her own for a number of years.

As soon as she had graduated from the junior college in Chicago, where she had been born and raised, and had found a position as a medical secretary in a local clinic, Eve had started to save for a trip to Sweden. Now she was finally here with a six-week leave of absence from her job, and she meant to make the most of it. She planned to stay with the Trillings for four weeks and then take a bus tour of Sweden before returning home. Camilla had wanted her to come for the Midsummer festivities, especially since she was to be married on Midsummer Day, so Eve had come the last week of May. Camilla was engaged to Max von Stjerna, but Eve had not met him yet since he had been away—until her unfortunate encounter with him in the woods.

Although she had not been at Lyckan for quite a week, she was already very fond of the whole family and thought of them all rather vaguely as cousins. They had welcomed her with true Swedish hospitality. The one that interested her the most was Martin. From Camilla's letters she knew that he had recently retired from his job as accountant at the local steel mill because of ill health and that his hobby was collecting old legends of Värmland, the province in which they lived. She soon discovered that he was a clever, articulate man who could tell wonderful tales of the past. She was particularly interested in his stories from the 1820s—the Golden Age of Värmland—when iron ore had been discovered and landowners grew rich from their private charcoal foundries. Later large commercial foundries made the private ones obsolete and the money dwindled away, but it was a wonderful period while it lasted.

It was the time when the great estates flourished and permanent guests were brought to live on them—artists, writers, singers, and the like—to bring a touch of glamor into the owners' prosaic lives. Parties and entertaining went on constantly, with people traveling from one estate to another in their sleighs or carriages. Lyckan and Rosenborg had both been prosperous during that period. Such a marvelous time, Eve thought, when wolves and great bears and the terrible lynx had prowled the dark forests, and trolls, goblins, and witches had been all too real! Martin's stories made it seem like only yesterday.

His physical condition puzzled Eve. He looked so frail, so ethereal, somehow, as though he were wasting away. Yet she knew that the doctor had said he had a mild heart condition and needed to take things easier, but had assured the family that he would be all right, that it was not serious. It was obvious that the whole family adored Martin, and their lives seemed to revolve around him like planets around the sun.

Eve left her bicycle—actually it belonged to Camilla—at the side of the porch and went into the house. Like all the Swedish houses that she had seen so far, she found it charming with its light birch furniture, a few beautiful antiques with their painted designs, original oil paintings, and plants everywhere, as well as the lovely tiled stoves.

It was quite a large house with four bedrooms and a bath upstairs and four rooms down, with an upper hall almost as large as a regular room furnished with bookcases and a couch. The front door opened into a center hall with the kitchen at the back, a dining room and small study on the right. On the left, the living room ran the length of the house, with large windows at the back looking out into a birch grove and what was known as Big Mountain rising beyond.

The study was Martin's private domain. All his books and papers were there, as well as his desk and typewriter and old worn leather chair. When he was working, none of the family ever disturbed him, and even the lively little Blenda would tiptoe around. It was not that they were afraid of him, for his attitude toward them seemed to be always one of a sort of condescending benevolence. It seemed to be more an attitude of worship, and Eve did not quite approve. In her own family, she and her two younger brothers treated their

11

father with respect and love, yet never hesitated to stand up to him when they felt they were not being fairly treated or when they differed in points of view. The Trillings accepted Martin's every command with a meekness that Eve did not consider normal or wholesome.

When she entered the house it was a few minutes past nine and Camilla was coming down the stairs with her shopping bag over her arm. It was Saturday, and since the bank where she worked was not open that day, she usually drove into town and did the week's shopping for her mother. Camilla was tall and slender with long yellow hair falling straight nearly to her waist, wide light blue eyes, and the delicate features so many Swedish girls seemed to have. Eve had found her to be a serious, rather stubborn girl of a very domestic nature.

After her graduation from the local *realskol,* Camilla had not gone on to the *gymnasium,* but had instead gone to work as a teller at one of the local banks. Now that she was engaged and would be married on Midsummer Day, she was to quit her job the first of June. She was neatly dressed in a skirt and blouse and on one slender finger there gleamed the plain gold band that signified her engagement. When she married she would wear a second, identical gold band.

"There you are, Eve," Camilla said in Swedish. Although she knew English quite well, she seemed hesitant to use it. "I thought I might have to go without you."

"I had a bit of an accident," Eve explained. "I nearly rammed into your fiancé out in the woods. He was riding a horse and I came pelting out of a side path right in front of him."

"Max? Is he back?" Camilla stopped with one hand on the stair railing and regarded Eve with surprise.

12

"He's back all right. I hope I didn't do him any permanent damage!"

"Damage? What happened?"

"I scared his horse and it bolted and Max's head hit a branch and he fell off his horse. It knocked him out, but he came to right away He was pretty mad, though."

"Well, I imagine so! He prides himself on his horsemanship and you made him look foolish. He has quite a temper anyway."

She continued on to the door and Eve followed her. They walked around the house to where the family's Volvo was parked in what had once been a woodshed. Camilla did not speak again until she had backed out and was driving down the lane toward the highway.

"What did you think of him?" she asked.

Eve was cautious. She didn't want to hurt Cam's feelings. "I thought he was frightfully good-looking," she replied. "I hope he will forgive me in time. I'd hate to be on bad terms with your fiancé, especially since I'll be here for the wedding."

"Oh, he will," Camilla assured her. "He never stays angry very long."

From the beginning, Eve had been a bit puzzled about the girl's engagement. The letters she and Camilla had written over the years had been brief and factual. No girlish confidences or intimate confessions. She had tried a few times, but Camilla had simply not responded. Now that they were together the situation was about the same. Camilla seemed to like her and enjoy having her there, but there was no intimacy.

Eve did not think that Camilla behaved at all like a prospective bride. Max might have been her brother for all the emotion she displayed when she spoke of him. Nothing changed in her face or voice, no dreams shimmered behind the cool blue eyes. So why was she marrying him? Eve wondered. True, he was a good

13

catch with his wealth, his big estate, and his title, but Camilla did not strike her as being the mercenary type. And if she did not love Max, why did he want to marry her? Did he love her? She was a pretty, pleasant enough young woman, but hardly the type to enslave the passions of a sophisticated man like Count von Stjerna. She wanted to ask Camilla about it, but so far the girl's reserved attitude had put her off.

Now that she had met him, the urge to know more about their relationship became too strong to resist. She could not get those blazing golden eyes out of her mind. There was no tactful way to put the question, so she asked bluntly, "Are you in love with Max, Cam? You don't act as though you were."

Camilla did not reply immediately. She turned onto the highway and headed toward town. It was a drive that Eve always enjoyed, through the forest and along the bluffs above the river where the logs were floating down to the pulp mills or on to Lake Vänern. In the distance the sharply etched contours of the bluish-purple hills rose against the sky. The air was unbelievably clear and pure and smelled of pine.

Just when Eve was beginning to think that Camilla intended to ignore her question, the girl said, "It is a long story, Eve. Very complicated. No, I do not love Max, nor he me. We have known each other all our lives and we are more like a brother and sister. I do not think you would understand if I told you why we are going to be married."

Now Eve was really curious. "Try me!" she said. "Unless, of course, it is a deep, dark secret."

"Oh, it is no secret. Everyone in town knows about it. Part of it anyway. It started long ago, back in the middle of the last century, the period Papa is so fond of talking about. I think he has told you what a splendid estate Lyckan was in those days."

14

"Yes, he has. I'm fascinated by his stories."

"It was almost as big as Rosenborg. Well, it happened that one of the Trilling daughters, Katarina, was engaged to be married to the son of the owner of Rosenborg. The son's name was Max too. It is an old family name. They were to be married in the spring."

"But something happened?"

"Yes. Perhaps you know how it was the custom then to have permanent guests living on the estates. There were several such guests at Lyckan and one of them was a young composer named Mikael Svahn. He and Katarina fell in love and sometime toward the end of the winter she ran away with him. They were on horseback. A servant who had found out what they intended went to the count and he and his son Max pursued the couple in their sleigh."

"Did they catch them?"

"No. The lovers had crossed the river on ice that was beginning to break up, and when the sleigh attempted to follow them, it went through the ice and both men were drowned."

"How awful!"

"Yes, it was. That Max was an only son, just as the present one is. When the countess learned what had happened she became very ill—they called it brain fever in those days—"

"Did she die too?"

"No. She lived to be quite old, but she was never quite normal after that. Anyway, when she was ill and quite out of her head she sent for the Trillings, Katarina's parents, and said, 'You have killed my men, but you will suffer for it. Evil days will come to Lyckan and no head of the family will live past the age of my husband—until the day comes when a Trilling woman marries a von Stjerna of Rosenborg and the slate is wiped clean.'"

15

"How old was her husband?"

"He was fifty-four."

"But—good heavens, Camilla—surely nobody took it seriously!"

"Not at first, I shouldn't imagine, but Katarina's father died the following year at forty-seven, and within a few years they had lost most of their money and the big estate house burned down. They had to close down their foundry and sell most of their land to the von Stjernas."

"But that still doesn't—"

"And since that time all the Trilling men have died fairly young either from accidents or illness. And now my father—"

"Camilla!" Eve was horrified. "You can't really believe that your father is dying because of some crazy curse!"

"I don't know what I believe, Eve." Her face was set in hard, stubborn lines. "But Papa believes in it. He has always loved the old legends and superstitions and to him they are real. He is not an ignorant man—you know how clever and sensitive he is—but he believes there are forces in the universe that most people do not understand. He believes that he will die, and this past year he has grown much weaker. Max says that if someone believes strongly enough that he is going to die, then he will."

"You mean like a voodoo curse, where somebody sticks pins in a wax image? Oh, Camilla, it is all so ridiculous! Do you mean to say that you and Max are marrying just to remove that old curse?"

"It was more a prophecy than a curse. And I do believe that when I marry Max Papa will recover his health."

"Does he know why you're doing it?" Eve demanded.

"I have never discussed it with him, but he is very

happy about our marriage. He is looking much better since we announced our engagement. You should have seen him a few months ago!"

"And Max—why is he willing to go through with it if he doesn't love you? He can't be all that fond of Martin."

"Max is almost thirty-five and his mother insists that he must marry and produce an heir. He is an only child, and she does not want Rosenborg to go to distant cousins someday—as it did long ago when the old count and his son were both killed. I am a suitable choice. We may not be rich or titled, but our family goes back to ancient kings, and it is the bloodline that his mother is concerned about. She approves of me. Max and I talked it over and decided it was the best thing to do."

"But—isn't there anyone he loves, that he would prefer to marry?"

"No. Several years ago there was someone—a woman named Mitra Carsing. She was a café singer once, but then she married a rich Swedish industrialist who died soon after. I suppose she is very beautiful and glamorous. Max was madly in love with her and wanted to marry her, but his mother broke it up—or so I have heard. I have never asked Max about it. The countess did not consider her at all suitable, because she was a foreigner and had a rather unsavory past—before she married Herr Carsing."

"What nationality was she—this Mitra?"

"I'm not sure. One of those central European countries. I think Max still sees her when he goes to Stockholm."

Eve did not like the sound of that at all. It seemed to her that Camilla was involved in a very bad situation. "Does Max have to have his mother's consent to marry?" she asked.

"No, but he would not want to distress her."

17

"Oh, Camilla!" Eve said angrily. "Surely you don't want to marry a man who loves someone else! And what if you fall in love someday? Do you want to destroy all your chances for future happiness? You're still so young—"

"The only thing I want in this world," Camilla broke in forcefully, "is to see Papa well and strong again. I would give my life itself for that!"

It was obvious, Eve realized, that where Martin was concerned Camilla was a true fanatic. There was no point in arguing with her, and, anyway, it was not her affair. Suddenly the image of that lean, vital face with those penetrating golden eyes swam before her and a shiver went over her. It was wrong—terribly wrong—for Camilla to marry him. But what could she do about it?

She thought about Martin, the charming, idolized father. What was there—beneath the surface charm? Was he really about to die because of his belief in an old prophecy—or could it be that his decline was deliberately induced to trick Camilla into marrying the count? She had noticed that he ate practically nothing. He had spoken to her at times of a desire to travel and to improve what was left of the old Lyckan estate. How else could this be accomplished except by marrying off his daughter to a wealthy man? None of his adoring family would ever suspect . . .

"I told you you wouldn't understand." Camilla broke into her reverie.

"Oh, I understand why you're doing it, all right. I just don't approve."

"You Americans are so romantic—but love is not everything, Eve. Arranged marriages often work out much better. Well, here we are." She turned adroitly into a parking space at the shopping plaza. "Did I tell you that today is Blenda's name day?" She picked up the shopping bag from the seat. "We will have a little

18

party for her later in the afternoon and I must go to the bakery and pick up the torte that we ordered."

Eve forced her mind away from the story Camilla had told her. "You mean one of those fancy cakes with whipped cream and fruit on it that you had for me when I arrived?" she asked.

"Yes. Blenda is spending the day with her girl friend, but she will be home this afternoon."

They got out of the car. In Sweden, Eve had found, the main shopping area of any town or city was called Centrum. In Romeby the plaza was quite new and had been built some distance away from the old center of town where the mills were. It consisted of a large complex built around a central square with shops on the ground floor and apartments above them. Not far away was another complex of modern apartment buildings.

Eve noted that the older women here were much better groomed and smarter-looking than women in the markets at home. No curlers or sloppy jeans here! They all wore dresses or suits and usually hats. Eve felt a bit self-conscious in her jeans, although the young teenagers wore them.

The girls went up the stairs to the supermarkets, and Eve saw that the upper hall was crowded with shoppers busily chatting with friends they had encountered. Everyone in town seemed to gather at Centrum on Saturday mornings. Eve enjoyed following Camilla through one of the big stores, watching her make her selections. Camilla was a very serious shopper and considered each item carefully for price and quality. It was not so different, Eve thought, from the markets at home, except that some items she took for granted were unobtainable here and there were other things here that she had never seen before.

"Should I buy Blenda a present?" she asked.

"You can if you like, but it is not necessary. We will give her a few little gifts."

19

"What would she like?"

"Oh, anything. Some candy, perhaps. It is very expensive here and we seldom buy any."

Eve bought a little box of chocolates and discovered that they were, indeed, quite expensive.

"Doesn't your mother like to do her own shopping?" she asked.

"Papa used to bring her in every Saturday," Camilla explained, "but he doesn't drive anymore because of his heart and Mama cannot drive, so she turned the shopping over to me. She says that I am more clever at it than she. She only gives me a list of what she needs. It is getting more difficult with the prices so high."

"You'll make a very good housewife, Cam."

The girl frowned. "Yes, but with Max there will be no need to economize or to do any of the housework. The servants do it all."

Eve didn't see what she was complaining about. It sounded like a very happy arrangement to her!

They went down to the lower level again to the *Konditori* to pick up the torte, then drove home. When they carried the groceries into the kitchen at Lyckan, Olivia turned from the sink where she was peeling potatoes and said, "Max has been calling you, Camilla. I told him you would call back when you got home."

"All right, Mama," Camilla replied indifferently. "I will call. Shall I ask him to the party this afternoon?"

Olivia looked doubtful. "If you really think he would care for such a trivial affair—"

"Oh, Mama, you know he adores Blenda. I am sure he would like to come if he is not too busy." She left the bag of groceries on the kitchen table and went out to the telephone in the front hall.

Eve felt a curious sinking sensation in the pit of her stomach. She didn't want to see the count again—not this afternoon, not ever! The thought of having those

20

magnificent tawny eyes turned on her again made her heart pound and her knees tremble. It wasn't because he had been angry with her—other men had been just as angry at various times and she couldn't have cared less. So what made him different? Her feelings made no sense, except that she had an instinctive sense that the man was somehow dangerous to her. But since he was engaged to Camilla, it would be impossible to avoid him, so perhaps it was better to see him and get it over with—like going up in a plane immediately after a crash.

In the study next door she could hear Martin's typewriter clattering away. He was compiling a book out of all the old legends he had gathered and had told her that he hoped to have it published.

"Can I do anything to help?" she asked Olivia in her careful Swedish, trying not to listen to what Camilla was saying on the telephone.

"No, thank you, dear. Later, perhaps, you can set the table, but there is nothing I need help with now." She was a tall woman, big boned but well proportioned, with long blond hair, now partially gray, wound into a bun at the back of her head. Her wide blue eyes so much like Camilla's held a sweet, rather vague expression. To Eve it seemed that the woman was completely dominated by her husband. When she spoke she had the habit of letting a sentence trail off unfinished, then she would often draw a deep breath on the word *"Ja,"* which the Swedes seemed to like to say while inhaling rather than exhaling and let it hang in the air like a wisp of smoke.

Eve sat down at the table and thought about the amazing story that Camilla had told her. It was like something out of the Dark Ages. She had always heard that the Swedes were a mystical, brooding lot, especially here in Värmland, which had produced far more poets and writers over the years than any other province. Most of the Swedes she had met so far, however, were a more practical type, except for Martin, who doted on his ancient legends and superstitions. Did he really believe he would die if Camilla did not marry Max? She wondered what the girl's mother thought about it.

It wasn't easy for her to converse with Olivia because of her limited Swedish, but she tried. "I don't think Max likes me very well. I nearly ran into his horse with my bicycle this morning and the horse threw him. He was quite angry."

Olivia gave her a thoughtful glance. "I would not worry about it, my dear. At heart he is a kind man and will not stay angry with you for long. *Ja—*"

Eve thought that there was little kindness in the man's heart or anywhere else, but didn't want to say so.

"Do you approve of Camilla's marrying him?" she asked bluntly.

Olivia did not look around this time, but Eve noticed that she stopped working on the potatoes and became very still.

"*Ja*, it is good."

"Even if she doesn't love him?" Eve persisted.

When Olivia replied her voice was so low that Eve could barely hear her. "Love? But it is her father that she loves, more than anyone, and to her that is all that matters. She—"

Camilla came back into the room. "Max says he will come to Blenda's party," she told them.

"Did he—uh—say anything about me?" Eve asked.

"Yes." Camilla smiled at her. "He said, 'I will come if you promise to tie up your dangerous little cousin!' "

Eve's cheeks burned. "Did he really say that? I don't see how I can face him!"

"Oh, he won't eat you. He was only joking."

Eve wished fervently that she could stay in her room until the party was over, but she knew that would not be possible.

Chapter Two

That afternoon the table was set in the dining room with the best embroidered linen cloth, the best coffee service, and plates of cookies, tarts, jelly roll, sugar cake, and homemade pastries were set out. The torte was kept in the refrigerator for the final course. Eve wondered how Swedes managed to stay so slim when they were all so fond of goodies. Coffee parties seemed to be their favorite mode of entertaining.

The family gathered in the living room. Blenda was there with her girl friend, Maria, a charming little redhead. Blenda was a lively, sweet-tempered child with blond braids, a snub nose, and the big blue eyes that ran in the family. She usually wore slacks, but today she was sedately clad in a pretty blue dress with matching ribbons on her braids.

Martin sat in his favorite easy chair with Camilla on the floor at his feet. From time to time, Eve noticed, he would stroke the girl's hair—as though she were his pet dog, she thought resentfully. He was a tall man, at least six feet, and quite gaunt, his face sunken beneath prominent cheekbones. His hair was still thick and wavy, but had turned almost white, and his eyes were gray with the dreamy expression of one who looks inward rather than outward. He was a handsome man, with the pure esthetic features seen on old statues of saints, Eve thought, and it was easy to understand why his womanfolk adored him. She wondered how he had got along with his son, Pelle. When he spoke his beautifully modulated voice had an almost hypnotic quality.

"Well, what a pleasant gathering we have here today!" His smile included each one of them. "If only Pelle could have been here—but of course he lives too far away. However, we do have our charming little cousin from America—" He smiled at Eve and she smiled back. In spite of her nagging doubts about the man, it was hard to resist him. He had such a wistful, vulnerable quality—she could understand Camilla's urge to protect him.

The doorbell rang and Blenda jumped to her feet. "There's Max!" she cried. "I'll let him in!" And she ran out.

In a moment she came back, proudly leading Max by the hand. He had changed into light gray slacks with a yellow pullover sweater, and the only sign of his encounter with Eve was a purple swelling on his forehead. When she found herself once again gazing into those unsettling golden eyes, her heart seemed to miss a beat.

"Eve, this is Max von Stjerna," the child announced. "He brought me a present!" She held up a small beribboned box.

Max drew his heels together and gave her a formal bow.

"I have already had the pleasure of meeting Miss Tremaine," he said with a rueful smile, and his hand touched the bruise on his forehead.

Eve felt herself flushing with humiliation. "I hope you recovered your horse," she said stiffly.

"Yes, thank you. He had not gone far." His gaze flickered over her with amused contemplation, and Eve thought angrily that his present attitude was worse than his outburst of temper.

They soon convened to the dining room for their little feast. Everyone seemed to be in good spirits—except Eve—and Max kept them laughing at his quips, while Martin dispatched his ethereal charm. After they had eaten, Blenda opened the gifts she had received. Max's gift was a little charm bracelet, and she was ecstatic over it. He certainly knew how to handle women of all ages, Eve mused. Even Olivia expanded and grew more feminine when she was with him. But Eve wouldn't let herself be taken in by him, she vowed to herself. Both Max and Martin were dangerous men in their different ways, and she would remain on her guard.

She had been curious to see what sort of atmosphere Max and Camilla would generate when seen together, but she soon realized that their emotional climate was as calm as the pond over by the old mills. There was simply nothing there: no subtle exchange of glances, no electricity—nothing at all. Not even irritation, which would have been better than such a bland relationship. What kind of a marriage could they possibly have? Camilla deserved better than that. She was conscious of a sudden, unreasonable anger over a situation that was completely beyond her control and most certainly none of her business.

When he was about to leave, Max turned to Camilla and said: "My mother has asked me to invite you and Eve to lunch tomorrow at one. She wants to meet your American cousin."

Camilla glanced at Eve. "Is that all right with you?" she asked.

"Of course," Eve replied stiffly. It was the last thing she wanted to do, but there was no way she could avoid having some social intercourse with Max and his mother while she was at Lyckan.

He looked at Eve and a challenging light flickered in the depths of his eyes.

"Will you walk a little way with me, Miss Tremaine?" he said. "I want to talk to you."

Eve opened her mouth to refuse, but Camilla said quickly, "Yes, why don't you, Eve? You two ought to get better acquainted. I have to help Mama with the dishes."

"Why don't I help her and you go with Max?" Eve suggested. "After all—"

"But it is you I want to talk to," the count said, and his fingers closed over her arm. Against her will, she found herself walking out with him. When they were nearly to the lane he released her and gave her a quizzical smile.

"Are you waiting for me to apologize for the way I talked to you this morning?" he asked. "Is that why you have been giving me all those glowering looks this afternoon?"

Eve flushed. "Of course not. You had a right to be angry. You could have been seriously hurt, and I was careless. There is no reason for you to apologize."

"Well, I could not help wondering. First you try to kill me, then you act as though you can't bear to be in the same room with me! What have I done to merit such displeasure? Since you are staying with Camilla and we will be seeing a good deal of each other over the next few weeks, I wanted to get things straightened out between us—otherwise it will be rather awkward."

Eve hadn't realized that she had let her feelings show through so plainly. "I don't even know you, Herr *Greve*," she said coldly, using the Swedish word for count. "So how can I dislike you?"

"You do, though. Obviously. And for heaven's sake, call me Max! We no longer take titles very seriously in Sweden."

He turned off the lane onto a path that led into the woods.

"This is a shortcut to Rosenborg," he explained.

26

"You have not yet seen my home, but I will show it to you tomorrow."

"I've seen it from the highway," she told him. "It's quite imposing—almost a palace." She was trying to sound friendly and relaxed, even though every cell in her body was warning her to turn around and run.

"Now you must tell me why you do not like me," he said firmly. "Does it have something to do with my engagement to Camilla?"

He must have been reading her mind! "Yes," she replied, "since you insist on bringing it up—I don't approve of her marrying you at all!"

"Indeed? And just what makes you think I would be a bad husband for your cousin?"

"You don't love each other! I don't see how Camilla can possibly be happy with you."

"Ah, you Americans! So incurably romantic! In most countries marriages are arranged by the parents. Love is a youthful illusion at best, hardly necessary in the functioning of a successful marriage."

"I don't believe that!" she cried. "On the contrary, it is the most powerful force in existence. Your emotions can starve without it. And I can't believe that Martin will die if you don't marry! How can you go along with such a ridiculous fantasy? You sneer at my belief in love, yet you are encouraging a superstition that is far more incredible!"

He stopped on the path and turned to her. His eyes were veiled and somber now.

"You are new here, Eve," he said. "There are many things you do not understand. This is an ancient, legend-ridden land. Much stranger things than that have happened here. If Martin believes that he will die, then he will. You speak of love's being the most powerful force in the world—but there is another that is just as strong, and that is fear. Fear can kill. Any psychologist can tell you that. And it is a fact that not

27

one of the Trilling men who have lived at Lyckan have survived beyond the age of fifty-four."

"That doesn't prove anything. And while we're on the subject, I might as well tell you what I think, since I can't tell Camilla." She put her hands on her slender hips and faced him defiantly. "I think that Martin is faking his decline to make Camilla marry you!"

He stared at her in surprise. *"Herre Gud!* You have not even been here a week, and already you think you know more about us than we know about ourselves!"

"Perhaps I can see things more clearly than any of you, because·I am a stranger and not blinded by sentiment or superstition!"

He stepped closer and seized her wrist, his eyes blazing down into hers. "Then what does this great wisdom of yours inform you about me, may I ask? Why do you think I am marrying her?"

Eve was beyond all caution now. His grasp seemed to burn into her flesh with a fire that spread throughout her entire body.

"Camilla says it is because your mother insists that you marry and produce an heir!" she flung at him. "But I think you are marrying her to cover up your affair with a woman your mother won't let you marry!"

He turned pale with fury and leaned over until his face was so close she could feel his warm breath on her cheek.

"Now you are speaking of matters about which you know absolutely nothing," he said in a voice of cold contempt. "And I warn you, if you try to interfere in this matter in any way I will—"

She knew she had gone too far, but was beyond caring or caution. "Well, what will you do, Herr Greve?" she taunted.

"You will find out!" He pulled her roughly into his arms and she felt his slender yet powerful body hard against hers. His fingers gripped her hair and he pulled

28

her head back so that his mouth could find hers in a punishing, furious kiss. For a moment the earth seemed to tilt on its axis and she wanted to strike him, to beat him off in a fury.

But instead of fighting him she found herself holding him even closer, found herself responding to his kisses, as though their fierce anger had somehow been transmuted into another and even more dangerous emotion. Her knees seemed to give way beneath her and somehow she was lying in the grass beneath the sheltering branches of a tree, and Max was beside her, his arm beneath her head, his hand caressing her in a way that spread ripples of fire through her body. Never in her life had she felt so swift and violent a desire. He was speaking to her in Swedish now, a soft murmur that she could not understand, except that she knew he was no longer angry. His mouth was on hers again, shutting out the world. She moaned faintly and when his mouth left hers she cried, "Max—Max!" in a despairing sob.

But then a full realization of what she was doing swept over her and she managed to break away from him and stumble to her feet. Without another word or a backward glance she fled toward Lyckan as though the devil himself were after her.

Chapter Three

When she was sure that he was not pursuing her, she slowed her pace. Her heart was pounding and she was trembling violently. She couldn't go back to the house and face the family until she had herself under control. What on earth had possessed her to behave in such a way with a man she hardly knew? There was something about him that brought out a side of her nature that she hadn't known she possessed.

The things she had said to him—whether or not they were true, she had had no right to say them. What could she possibly hope to accomplish? She couldn't change the way anyone felt. She would only succeed in making everyone angry with her. But why had he kissed her like that when he was so angry with her? And why had she permitted it? One moment she had been furious with him, and the next—she had been willing to let him do anything he wanted. Fortunately her reason had returned in time. Her cheeks burned with shame at her vulnerability. All she could be sure of was that she had been right in her first reaction to him: the count was a dangerous man—to her. All she could do now for the rest of her visit would be to avoid him as much as possible.

Was there any way she could get out of going to Rosenborg for lunch the following day? She could say she had a bad headache, but then the countess would only change the invitation to another day. No, she would have to go and try to pretend that nothing had happened. He would have to do the same for his mother's sake as well as Camilla's. There seemed to be some sort of chemical reaction when they got together that brought out the worst in both of them!

Finally she rose to her feet and walked slowly on to the house, hoping that none of the emotional upheaval she had been going through would show in her face.

On Sunday mornings the Trillings usually went into Romeby to attend services at the Lutheran church that stood high on a hill surrounded by a cemetery, but this week Martin stated that he didn't feel up to it and would stay home. Eve immediately volunteered to stay with him and keep him company. She hoped that it might give her a chance to talk to him alone and perhaps allay some of the suspicions she entertained about him, which she did not really want to believe. The rest of the family drove away, and Eve and Martin went out to the kitchen for another cup of coffee.

Eve loved the big old kitchen with its painted wooden bench, the copper utensils hanging on the walls, and the iron stove that remained even though an electric one now stood beside it. They sat down at the long wooden table on which the family ate most of their meals, reserving the dining room for special occasions, and Eve poured coffee from the thermos flask that was always kept filled. There was a bowl of sugar lumps on the table and she got the triangular carton of real cream out of the refrigerator. Although there were many items lacking in the markets here that she was used to at home, Eve felt that the plentiful supply of cream more than compensated for them. The Swedes had not yet turned to the chemical concoctions used so freely by the Americans to whiten their coffee.

Looking into the gentle, intelligent gray eyes, Eve began to feel ashamed for the dark thoughts she had been harboring about him. Much as she hated to admit it, perhaps Max was right and she didn't understand the situation at Lyckan—or the people involved in it.

Martin picked up a lump of sugar, put it into his mouth, and sipped his coffee through it in the manner that seemed to be popular among the Swedes. *Kaffe på bit*, they called it. Then he smiled at her.

"My dear," he said, "I am afraid I have been very self-centered since your arrival and talked only of my own interests. It is not often, you see, that a fresh audience presents itself—and I get carried away by my passion for the past. However, I am really interested in hearing more about your family and my cousin Jane, about whom I know so little. Do you resemble her?"

"No, I take after my father's people, who are mixed French and English. Mother's eyes are a lighter blue

31

than mine, more like Camilla's, and her hair is blond, too. My two younger brothers are regular towheads." She went on talking about her family, telling him about the big old tree-shaded house in the suburb of Oak Park where she had been born and raised, about her father, who was a C.P.A. and had an office in the Loop, about her job at the clinic—all the prosaic facts that had gone to make up her happy but uneventful life.

"I decided not to go to the university," she explained, "because Dad has the boys to put through and I wasn't really yearning for a degree. I love my work at the clinic."

Martin listened as though he were really deeply interested in all that she said, nodding and smiling occasionally, but saying little.

"I understand there are many Swedes in that area," he remarked when she stopped to refill their cups.

"Oh, yes. Loads of them. We had a neighbor who spoke Swedish so I got him to give me lessons, then I went on studying by myself. I always meant to come over here as soon as I could earn enough money."

"It seems a bit odd that you should feel that way. Your mother never seemed to want to visit us."

"Oh, she would love to come, but she married right out of school and has been tied down ever since raising children—you know how it is. She and Dad plan to come over when the boys are a little older. I don't know why I felt that way—that I had to come, I mean. It was as though something were pulling at me." She stopped and frowned, unable to put her feelings into words. She had never really thought about it before; she had only known that she had to come.

Martin nodded understandingly. "You were born with the ancient heritage in your blood," he said, "stronger than most."

"I don't know. It was as though something were

32

waiting for me here," she said slowly. "But that doesn't make sense."

"Yes, it does. You are a mystic, Eve, like me. You feel things deeper than your mind can comprehend. At any rate, I am glad that you came, and you speak Swedish very well."

"Thank you. It was a little difficult at first, but I'm getting on to it, I think. The dialect is different here than what I learned at home."

"Yes, the Värmland dialect is closer to the Norwegian. We are quite close to the border here, you know. Camilla must drive you there someday. Do you think Sweden is beautiful?"

"Oh, yes! So different from the flat country where I come from, although I love our lake."

His dreamy eyes studied her. "How old are you, Eve?" he asked.

"Twenty, the same as Camilla."

"A wonderful age, but sometimes painful. Is there any special young man in your life?"

"I'm afraid not. Mother says I'm too picky. I date a lot, but even with the ones I like—well, there just seems to be something missing."

"Perhaps you are looking for something that does not exist except in fiction," he suggested.

"Maybe," she agreed. He had given her the opening she had been waiting for, so she went on. "Do you believe in romantic love, Cousin Martin?" At first it had puzzled her how to address Olivia and Martin. At home she would have called them by their first names, but the Swedes were more formal, so she'd decided to tack on the title of cousin. They seemed to approve.

Martin gave her a long, contemplative look. It was impossible to tell what was going on behind those veiled gray eyes.

"I would not go so far as to say it does not exist," he

33

replied finally, "because it certainly does. However, it is bound to be of a transient nature and therefore is a poor basis for marriage. It is better to get it out of your system early if you can, then marry someone you know well and respect."

Did he really believe that, she wondered, or was he trying to rationalize what Camilla was doing? In spite of her decision not to interfere, she felt impelled to go on.

"Camilla told me the story about your ancestors," she said. "I've been wondering about Katarina and Mikael—that must have been a great passion to make her abandon her fiancé and family and run off with him. Do you know what happened to them afterward?"

A look of distaste flickered for a moment in Martin's eyes. "Of course they had no further contact with the family," he said, "but I have heard that they went to Italy and were married there. Whether they were happy together or not no one knows. One can only hope so, after the terrible tragedy their actions caused." His voice was bitter, as though to him the event were quite recent. Obviously, she thought, he had no sympathy for the runaway lovers.

"Do you really believe that all the misfortunes that followed—the burning of your estate house and so on—was caused by that?" she asked. It was as far as she dared go; never could she ask him, "Do you think you are going to die because of the countess's prophecy?"

The gray eyes were unfathomable. "Eve, there is a great deal in life that we can never understand," he said slowly. "One can never quite separate reality from fantasy with any exactitude. Sometimes what the mind believes can have a physical impact on events. All superstitions are based on that fact. As for the burning of. Lyckan, I have always believed that it was a deliberate act of revenge by someone from
34

Rosenborg. Cause and effect, you see. Nothing supernatural."

So there it was, Eve thought. He denied believing in the old prophecy in a literal sense, yet still he was wasting away. Was it an act, as she had told Max, or was it from some deep subconscious belief that he was not aware of himself? Was he capable of deliberately sacrificing his daughter—either for material gain or to save his life? She found that hard to accept now that she was getting to know him better—and yet there was something about him that she could not understand or warm to.

His thin hand reached out to touch her arm. "Eve—you do not approve of Camilla's engagement to Max, do you? Isn't that why you are asking me these questions?"

She felt the flush mount to her cheeks. "They don't love each other," she said defensively.

"But it is a good match, a sensible one, and they made the decision themselves. Why should I interfere?"

It was not what she had hoped he would say. She had wanted him to say something like "If I thought they were doing it for me, I would put a stop to it at once." But he was too clever for that; he would shift the responsibility elsewhere.

"I believe it was his mother's suggestion," he went on. "She wants him to marry and have children. Don't concern yourself with it, Eve. They know what they're doing." There was something in his voice that almost made it sound like a warning, the second one she had received.

So either he really had no idea why Camilla was marrying Max, or he was being deliberately evasive. Either way, there was nothing she could do about it.

He still seemed to be reading her thoughts, because

35

he gave an odd little laugh and said, "Did you think she was doing it to save me from the ancient prophecy? A charming thought, but I am afraid they are much too modern and civilized to believe in that!"

Now she could say it—he had led up to it himself! "Do you believe that it will save you, Cousin Martin?" she demanded.

For a moment she saw something that was decidedly unfriendly glimmer in his eyes, but then it was gone and he let out another of his strange little laughs. "Save me? My dear child, the doctor assures me that if I take care of myself there is no reason why I cannot live a normal life span. I am afraid you are letting your imagination run away with you."

She saw now that any idea of appealing to Martin was useless. She was sure that he knew what was going on—but he would never admit it. And whatever his reasons for wanting Camilla to marry Max, he had managed to convince himself that it was all to her own advantage.

Eve was very nervous as the two girls started out on the walk to Rosenborg when the family returned from the church service. In Sweden no one ever used a car when it was possible to walk or ride a bicycle. Probably because of the high price of gas, Eve decided, or maybe the Swedes were just used to walking. It was only a scant kilometer on the path through the woods to the neighboring estate, so Camilla did not suggest driving. It was a sunny day but a bit on the cool side, so the girls wore suits instead of summer dresses.

Eve could not help thinking about the scene that had occurred on the path in the forest the evening before, and she dreaded having to face Max again, not to mention meeting his mother, whom she pictured as a rather formidable dowager.

"What is the countess like?" she asked Camilla.

36

"Oh, she is an intelligent, sensible woman and I am very fond of her," Camilla responded. "In spite of being a cripple, she is always cheerful and pleasant."

"What happened to her?"

"She and the count—her husband, I mean—were in an automobile accident about six years ago. He was killed and she was injured so badly that she will never walk again."

"How terrible."

"Yes, it was."

"I thought she might be something of a tyrant from what you said about her not letting Max marry that woman you told me about."

"No, she is not like that at all. It was simply that she knew that Mitra was not the right sort for him. Any mother would try to save her son from a bad marriage."

"Have you ever talked to her about it?"

"No, but Mitra's husband had relatives here and before he died they used to come here once in a while. I've heard people talk about her. They say she is vain and shallow and man-hungry."

"I wonder what Max saw in her!"

"I suppose she has a lot of sex appeal." Camilla's lips curled scornfully and she tossed back her golden hair that had a tendency to fall over her face. "Men are so stupid when it comes to women."

Eve decided she'd heard enough about Mitra. "Are you planning a church wedding, Cam?" she asked. It was a subject she couldn't seem to keep away from—the way one keeps biting on a sore tooth.

"Yes. It has to be in a church, but it will not be a large wedding. There is a little chapel on the Rosenborg grounds. It used to be the custom, you know, for a big estate to have its own and the pastor would give them private services. They don't do that anymore, but it has been kept in repair and all family weddings and

37

funerals and the like are held there. The countess wants us to be married there, of course, so that is what we will do. It is a small place, so there cannot be many guests—only family and our closest friends. But there will be a big reception in the afternoon for everyone."

"And it is to be on Midsummer."

"Yes, Midsummer Day. On Midsummer Eve it has always been the custom for the current count of Rosenborg to have a big celebration for all those who work for him on the estate. There is feasting and folk dancing and, of course, the raising of the pole. There will be too much going on that day for a wedding, so we will have it on the following day. That will be Saturday, the twenty-fourth of June. My best girl friend will be my attendant and Blenda will be my flower girl. If I had known sooner that you would be here, I would have had you—"

"No!" Eve was surprised by her own vehemence, which had been an involuntary reaction. "I'd rather just watch from the sidelines," she added a bit lamely, trying to play down her too emphatic response. The mere thought of walking down the aisle toward the altar where Max would be standing waiting for his bride was frightening. She could imagine his intent golden gaze. . . .

Camilla was regarding her a bit oddly. "You really are opposed to my marriage, aren't you?" she said.

"I just don't like the idea of marriage without love."

Camilla's pretty young face grew curiously wooden, as it always seemed to when they talked about love. "Love is usually nothing but infatuation," she said. "It is better to marry someone you know and respect."

Now she was quoting her father's words, Eve realized. The poor girl had been thoroughly brainwashed!

"Will you have a honeymoon?" she asked.

"Yes, we will fly down to Grand Canary for a few

38

weeks. They have a villa there, because the countess likes to get away for the coldest months."

How matter of fact she was about it, Eve thought wistfully. If a girl who really loved Max were marrying him, how ecstatic she would be over such prospects!

The woods thinned out, the path broadened, and soon they entered the grounds of the estate through a gate in a hedge. A formal rose garden had been planted there but it was too early for anything to be blooming. The big house could just barely be glimpsed through the trees. A brick walk led over to a flight of shallow steps down to a pool filled with water lilies, in the center of which was a charming statue of three dancing water nymphs.

"It's an original Milles," Camilla told her. "They have some of Christian Eriksson, too, and a Vigeland, I think, but most of the statuary is Italian. The old count used to bring them back from his travels. The rose garden here is quite famous and they bring tours in when it is blooming."

They walked around the pool and on through the rows of carefully clipped shrubs and beds of tulips that were nearly ready to bloom.

"This must be an enchanting place later in the summer," Eve commented.

"Yes—but I find the fields of wild flowers far more beautiful," Camilla replied. "The buttercups and bluebells and the wild roses that grow along the roads—"

There was a faraway look in her eyes and Eve wondered what she was thinking about. There was a great deal about Camilla she did not understand.

"What sort of life would you choose if you could have anything you wanted, Cam?" she asked curiously.

Camilla did not hesitate for a moment. "A stud farm," she said. "I would like to raise show horses." A flush of delicate pink stained her fair cheeks as she gazed wistfully off at some imagined place of happiness.

"Aren't there horses on Rosenborg?" Eve asked.

"Yes, of course, but not the sort of thing I mean. Rosenborg is so big—it's an experimental farm—Max hasn't much time to spend on the horses."

"What do you mean by experimental?"

"Well, the government is interested in developing types of grain that are hardier—we have such a short growing season, you know—and more disease-resistant. Max is experimenting with that. He is always going to Karlstad or Stockholm to confer with people in labs or government officials. He even won some kind of an award last year. He takes farming very seriously—much more so than his father, who left it all to his estate manager and was always off traveling somewhere.

"I don't know much about it. Ask Max if you're interested. He loves to tell people about his crops. He has a big dairy herd too. Rosenborg is quite an enterprise and Max has hundreds of people working for him."

Eve was surprised and intrigued. She had imagined that Max was just a rich playboy—she had not pictured him as a hard-working farmer.

They passed by another fountain and were approaching the broad stone terrace at the side of the house. From the glimpse she had had of it from the highway, Eve had thought it reminiscent of a southern plantation, with tall white pillars supporting a circular balcony, but that was not visible from here. She saw that the house was of yellow stucco with white trim around the windows and dark yellow awnings.

Then, to her consternation, Eve saw Max come around the house from the back regions. He was wearing his riding breeches and apparently had just left the stable. When he saw them he waved and smiled and came over to them.

40

"Hej!" he greeted them. "I've been riding and forgot the time." He kissed Camilla lightly on the cheek and nodded rather curtly to Eve. She was relieved to see that the swelling on his forehead had gone down and that the bruise was fading.

"We are early," Camilla said. "How is Skadi?"

"She had her foal last night—a mare. Would you like to see her?"

"I would love to!" Camilla looked more excited and alive than Eve had seen her since her arrival.

Max glanced at his watch. "Come, then. We still have a few minutes before Mother will expect us for lunch."

He turned back the way he had come and the girls followed him around the house and down a back path to the stable.

"We only keep our riding horses here now," Max told Eve, his manner polite yet withdrawn and cool. "The workhorses and dairy herd are on the farm run by my estate manager. Do you ride?"

She shook her head. "When I was a little girl I was sent away to camp for several summers and I learned to get on and off a horse without falling on my face, but I don't know if I could even do that much anymore."

He gave her a scornful glance. "I daresay such matters are not important in your country. Cam rides beautifully. Perhaps you should have some lessons so that you could go out with her."

There were a number of outbuildings behind the house: an old carriage house, a big red barn, and a long stone stable that looked to Eve as though it were several hundred years old. They entered it and she caught the intriguing odor of straw, leather, and horses.

Max stopped before one of the stalls. "Here are Skadi and her new offspring."

Cam ran forward with a little cry of pleasure at the sight of the dainty brown mare with a blond mane and the tiny, tottering colt at her side. The baby was just like her mother except for a white star on her forehead.

"Oh, Max! She is so beautiful!" Mindless of her best suit, she knelt and put her arms around the foal's neck. Skadi whinnied and nudged her anxiously. "What are you going to call her?"

"I thought you should name her, my dear. After all, Skadi is yours now."

She flushed with pleasure. "Well, I will have to think about it." She pushed the mare's nose away. "Stop it, Skadi. I am not hurting your baby." She stood up, brushing straw off her skirt, just as a young man came out of the next stall. Eve regarded him with interest. He was startlingly good-looking, with dark hair curling close to his head, smoldering brown eyes, and high Slavic cheekbones. She judged his age to be somewhere in the late twenties. He certainly did not look Scandinavian. When he saw the two girls he stopped and made them a slight bow.

"This is Marko Kardelj, our groom," Max told Eve. "Marko, this is Eve Tremaine from America. She may come over for a riding lesson someday." He turned to Eve. "Marko has only been with us for a few months," he explained, "and we were very fortunate to get him, since he knows a great deal about horses. He is from Yugoslavia and I believe he speaks a little English— don't you, Marko?"

"Yes, Herr Greve," Marko replied. He gave Eve another little bow, his eyes downcast. Then Eve saw his eyes lift slightly to meet Camilla's blue gaze. It was just the briefest of glances, and they both looked away almost at once, but a thrill of excitement passed over Eve. There was something between them—she was sure of it! She had felt the spark that had leapt from the dark eyes to the blue; there was everything that was lacking between Camilla and Max. How could Max miss it? she wondered, but he only went on talking calmly about horses. The two did not look at each other again, and then it was time to return to the house for lunch.

"I have been thinking of starting a stud farm," Max said on the way, "and if I do, I will make Marko the manager. He was working on one in Yugoslavia and I am sure he could handle it."

A stud farm! Eve remembered what Camilla had said on the way to Rosenborg and glanced at her curiously, but Camilla would not meet her eyes. Her cheeks were flushed.

"I'll go in the back way and get washed up a bit," Max said. "You girls go on around to the terrace. I think we are having lunch there. Tell Mother I will join you in a minute."

The terrace was of stone with a yellow awning to shelter it, and it was fairly warm there out of the wind. The countess was there now in her wheelchair, and Eve regarded her with interest. She was very attractive, with clear, smooth skin, almost unwrinkled except for the inevitable sagging around the chin, and a mass of wavy white hair twisted high on her head. Her eyes were very much like her son's, except that they were a shade or so darker—almost amber. She was wearing a smart embroidered jacket and had a lap robe over her knees. She smiled and held out her hands to the girls.

"Welcome!" she exclaimed. "I am so glad you were able to come today."

Cam went over to kiss her cheek. It was obvious the two were fond of each other.

"This is Eve Tremaine, Fru Grevinna," she said.

Eve took the cool white fingers in her own warm clasp.

"How wonderful that you have come all the way from America to visit your relatives," the countess said in English, which she spoke with a charming accent. "What do you think of Sweden, my dear?"

43

"It is very beautiful," Eve told her. "Especially Värmland. I had no idea it was so mountainous and had so many lakes."

"Yes, our province has a certain magic all its own. I hope you can see a good deal of it while you are here." She looked around with a slight frown. "I hope that naughty son of mine is not going to hold up lunch. When he gets out on his horse he forgets there is such a thing as time."

"Oh, he is here," Camilla assured her. "He is cleaning up. He just showed us Skadi's foal. Isn't she a love?"

The girls sat down on chairs near the countess, and Camilla went on talking animatedly about horses while Eve pursued her own thoughts. Somehow she had guessed a secret that none of the others knew—neither Camilla's family nor the countess nor Max—but there was nothing she could do about it. It was obvious that Camilla meant to marry Max in spite of what she might feel for the handsome foreigner. Besides her own fanatical regard for her father, she was surrounded by forces too strong for her to resist. It had been decided that she was to marry Max—and that was that!

No one but Eve had any desire to help her escape the destiny that was closing in—but what could she do? Talking was useless. Was there any chance that Marko might persudae her to run away with him—as her ancestress had done? Eve almost laughed at the thought of the consternation that would ensue if the ancient drama were reenacted! Not much chance of that, though. In this case, the bride-to-be was the one most determined to go through with the marriage. No matter what she might feel for Marko, Eve knew, Cam's love for her father was the strongest motivating force in her life.

Max joined them, having changed into gray flannel slacks and a white shirt. A table had been set on the terrace and now a maid in a crisp blue-and-white

44

uniform served them omelets, broiled fish, hashed brown potatoes, vegetable salad, with stewed fruit and cream for dessert.

"Well, Max," the countess said when they had finished their coffee and he had smoked one of his slender, aromatic cigars, "why don't you take Eve on a tour of the house? I want to discuss some matters concerning the wedding with Camilla."

Max rose and turned to Eve. "Would you like that?" There was a challenging glint in the tawny eyes.

Actually she didn't but there was no polite way of saying so. He slipped his hand under her elbow when she stumbled a little leaving the terrace, and as before his touch seemed to burn into her flesh like cold fire. It was inevitable under the circumstances that she would see a good deal of him during her stay here. How could she bear it? Somehow she had to try to get their relationship onto a more normal footing before the situation grew too awkward to handle—even if it meant humbling herself before this impossible, arrogant man.

"Max, I want to apologize for the things I said to you yesterday," she said stiffly. "You seem to have a strange effect on me. Of course I know nothing about you or your reasons for marrying Camilla."

He looked down at her, his elegant eyebrows slightly raised. "You certainly do not," he agreed coldly, "but for Camilla's sake we must try to be civilized with each other. There is no reason for us to be enemies, after all. Now come, I will show you my house."

It was obvious that he took great pride in it. It was old, going back to the late eighteenth century, with high ceilings, tall windows, elaborate cornices, and all the intricate workmanship that is lacking in modern houses, however expensive. It was furnished with a curiously effective mixture of old and new, Swedish and European, with even a touch of the Oriental. The floors were of highly polished parquet.

"My father and grandfather both traveled widely," he told her, "and brought back things from all over the world. There are Swedish antiques here as well as French and Italian, besides the modern pieces that Mother added."

"Do you like to travel?" she asked.

"Yes, my parents usually took me with them when I was small and I have been in most countries, but I do not want to make a career out of it. I feel that my place is here, working on the estate."

Eve found herself falling in love with the house as they wandered through the large rooms. Besides the drawing room there was a large, formal dining room, a well-stocked library, a breakfast room for more informal meals, a huge kitchen with modern equipment elbowing the old, a pantry, and quarters for the servants. Upstairs were six bedrooms, some modern bathrooms, and a lovely ballroom with crystal chandeliers, mirrored walls, and French windows opening onto a balcony. All the rooms contained a beautiful old tile stove or a fireplace.

"How romantic!" Eve exclaimed, whirling across the polished floor of the ballroom. "Do you use it much?"

A shadow crossed his handsome face. "Not anymore. My parents used to enjoy having big affairs here. It was built in the days when the estate owners were always giving parties and balls. Such gay times! People do not live like that anymore. Perhaps it is just as well."

She looked around, imagining that she could hear the echo of distant music, the sound of laughter and voices long stilled. Slowly she turned and walked out onto the balcony that overlooked the rose garden and stood with her hands on the balustrade, gazing down at the fountain. What would he say, she wondered, if she asked, "Do you know that Camilla is in love with Marko?" He would probably toss her off the balcony!

She could feel the tension mounting in her body that

was always there when she was near him. Did he feel it too? Was that why they always seemed to get angry with each other—because of that unbearable tension that had to be dispelled one way or another? Why had he kissed her yesterday in the forest? Why had she responded? What would she do if he kissed her again? Would she respond in the same way, all her defenses down, wanting only for him to make love to her?

She heard him coming up behind her and turned around. His eyes were on her, intent and unfathomable. She shivered. Was he remembering, too, what it had been like to be in each other's arms?

"Eve—" he said, and came closer.

Again the violent trembling seized her and she closed her eyes. She felt his arms closing around her, his hands against her back pressing her body to his, his mouth seeking hers.

Chapter Four

There was the clatter of steps in the empty ballroom and Camilla's voice calling: "Eve, Max! Where are you?"

Max released her abruptly and she opened her eyes. For a moment he held her gaze, his tawny eyes searching hers, then his mouth curled in a mocking smile as he turned away.

"Here we are!" Eve called, hoping that her cousin would not see her confusion or sense the electricity crackling in the air between them. But Camilla did not seem to be sensitive to emotional vibrations. She came over to the French windows and said cheerfully, "The countess thinks that since it is such a beautiful day, you might like to take us for a drive after lunch, Max."

"Of course," he replied formally. "We will show Eve some of the sights, eh? Mårbacka, perhaps, or Rottneros, the only estate grander than ours?"

Later that afternoon when Max had dropped them off at their door, Eve could not resist bringing up the subject of the handsome stable hand.

"Marko is awfully good-looking, isn't he?" she said carelessly. "Are there many Yugoslavians in Sweden?"

Camilla paused on the path leading to the house and gave Eve a quick glance, the pink mounting to her fair cheeks.

"Yes, there are people here from many European countries," she replied. "Marko is very good with horses. He used to work on a Lippizan stud farm near the Italian border in Yugoslavia before he came here."

"Oh, you mean those marvelous horses from the Spanish Riding Academy in Vienna? I didn't know they raised them in Yugoslavia."

"Well, they do. Marko used to train them."

"Then he must be very clever. It will be a break for him if Max starts a stud farm here and makes him manager. Isn't that funny—that's what you said you'd like to have!" she said guilelessly.

Camilla pressed her lips together and the pink deepened. "Well, I love horses too," she said shortly, and went on into the house.

Eve resolved to take Max up on his offer of riding lessons on the following day when Camilla was at work. She wanted to get to know Marko better. Accordingly, the next morning when Camilla had driven off to her job at the bank and Blenda had gone to school, Eve put on her jeans and a pullover sweater—it was a bit cloudy and rather chilly—and set out for Rosenborg. She found Marko in the stable currying one of the mares.

He looked rather surprised when he saw Eve. Suddenly she felt a bit shy under his dark, questioning gaze.

"Good morning, Marko. I came over to see if I could do a little riding this morning. Herr Greve said maybe you could give me some pointers. I haven't ridden for a long time."

"Certainly, Miss Tremaine," he said in careful English. "I will saddle Roskva for you. She is our gentlest mare."

Eve watched while he brought out a saddle and proceeded to put it on one of the pretty brown mares with a flowing blond mane.

"Camilla said you used to work on a Lippizan stud farm," she said.

The brown eyes flashed at her briefly. "Yes, Miss Tremaine."

He didn't seem very talkative, but Eve persisted. "They are beautiful horses, aren't they? I saw them perform once in Chicago when they were on tour."

"Yes, they are good horses. Very intelligent."

"Do you miss your home in Yugoslavia?"

"Sometimes—but there is more freedom here. I think that will do. Shall I help you mount?"

She hoped that he didn't think she had come over just because she wanted to flirt with him. With his looks, he must have had a lot of experience with that. But, then, what difference did it make what he thought? The main thing was to get to know him a little better, and coming over to ride was the only way she could manage that. No doubt that was how Camilla had got to know him.

With his help she climbed awkwardly into the saddle. It had looked like a small horse, but once she was on its back, it seemed awfully far to the ground, and she clutched the reins nervously. Marko gave her a pitying look and told her how she should sit and how to handle

49

the reins. Then he led the horse around the stable yard a few times until she got more confidence.

"Do you want to take her out on the path, or would you rather just walk her around in here today?" he asked doubtfully.

Eve's pride would not let her admit that she was afraid to be on her own, so she said, "Oh, I'll take her out for a little ride, I guess.".

Marko opened the gate and led the mare out to the beginning of a path that led back toward the woods.

"Just follow this path," he told her, "and you'll come out over by the fields beyond the patch of woods. That is probably as far as you should go today. Just take it easy and you will be all right."

"Thanks, Marko. Where did you learn to speak English so well?"

He stood looking up at her with the sunlight glinting on his dark curls and she thought he was the best-looking man she'd ever seen. There was something so different, so exotic about him—no wonder Camilla was smitten!

"I studied it in school," he told her, "and there were many American and English tourists who came to the farm. Sometimes I conducted tours around and I had to speak English."

"Well—here I go." She nudged Roskva with her heels and off they went down the path. She wondered if you said *whoa* in Swedish to stop a horse! She had forgotten to ask Marko. Well, she could just tug on the reins. It was very pleasant trotting along through the woods and her nervousness soon left. Those long-ago days at camp came back to her, and she thought that perhaps riding a horse was like riding a bicycle; you never really forgot how.

Suddenly she was out o the woods and at the edge of a field that had just been freshly plowed and harrowed. There seemed to be many acres of it stretching off toward the hills. In the distance she could see a tractor or some sort of farm machine moving along with a flock of gulls behind it. Gulls, she thought, so far inland? But then she remembered the river and all the lakes. Marko had suggested that she should not go any farther, but she didn't feel like going back yet.

The path led along the edge of the field, so she followed it until it crossed a wider road. Instead of continuing on the path, she turned onto the road. There was more room there, and, feeling rather daring, she urged the mare into a gallop. The horse seemed to be glad to stretch her legs a bit and Eve found it exciting to feel the wind blowing through her hair and to feel the strength and power of the animal beneath her, almost as though it were an extension of herself. Faster and faster ran the mare. Eve thought she heard someone call her name, but by now they had attained such a speed that she was afraid to look around or to try to rein in the horse. It was all she could do to stay in the saddle, and she could feel that one foot was dangerously near to coming out of the stirrup. She closed her eyes and grabbed onto the pommel of the saddle, hoping Roskva would slow down by herself.

Then she heard the sound of galloping hooves behind her and felt someone grab the reins. She opened her eyes to find Max on his beautiful black stallion, Sleipnir, beside her. He gradually slowed the horses down to a walk and looked at her with exasperation.

"Just what the hell do you think you are doing?" he demanded.

Her fright quickly gave way to anger. "I was doing fine until you came along!" she cried, pulling her reins from his grasp.

"You call that fine when you were practically falling off your horse? *Herre Gud*, you had even dropped the reins! And just look!" He pointed down the road. "This road leads into the pasture and you were almost

51

up to the gate. Roskva is not a trained jumper and would probably have balked when she reached it, and you would certainly have been thrown."

It didn't help her temper to find out he was right. "All right, I'm sorry," she muttered. "I'll never take your damned horse out again."

"Of course you will," he retorted. "You have to learn to ride properly. But next time follow instructions."

They turned the horses and started back toward the path. For a few minutes they rode in silence, then she gave him a sidelong glance. "By the way, Max," she inquired of his stern profile, "how do you say *whoa* in Swedish?"

"Whoa?"

"Yes, the word that means stop. I presume your horses only understand Swedish instructions."

"Oh, I see. The word is *ptroo*."

"That's not a word. That's what you say when you spit tobacco."

"Nevertheless, that is what you say to a Swedish horse."

"And when you want him to start?"

"Slap the reins and *tch, tch* at him."

Again they rode on in silence. Then he looked at her again and she could not read the expression in his tawny eyes. Then he said, "There is something I would like to show you, Eve, if you could bring yourself to spend a couple of hours in my company."

"What is it?" she asked.

"Something I am considering buying Camilla for a wedding present. I would like your opinion."

"I don't think my opinion is worth much," she said. "You know Cam a lot better than I do."

"But you are a woman."

"So is your mother. What does she think?"

"I haven't consulted her," he said impatiently. "I

just wanted to show this to you, and I thought you might enjoy a little outing. It's a lovely morning for a drive."

"It is?" She looked at the sky, which showed some signs of approaching rain.

"Yes, it is," he said firmly. "The sun will come out before long. I promise to have you back before *middag*."

She knew that the smartest thing she could do was to stay as far away from Max as possible. Being alone with him was like playing with matches around an open can of gasoline. He knew it as well as she did. Why didn't he just leave her alone? She opened her mouth to refuse, but to her horror found herself saying, "Well, all right. Do I need to change my clothes?"

"No, you are fine as you are," he said indifferently.

When they arrived back at the stable, Max turned the horses over to Marko and led Eve to the carriage house, now used as a garage. There were three cars in it: a beautiful, gleaming Rolls-Royce limousine, a trim Mercedes-Benz, and a battered Land-Rover.

"Mother likes to travel in style," he explained, when he saw her staring in awe at the limousine, "but where we are going the roads are bad, so, if you do not mind, we will take the Land-Rover."

"Why should I mind? You should see the car I drive at home!"

"We use the Land-Rover around the farm." He helped her in, then went around to the driver's side. As he backed out of the building, he told her, "There is an apartment upstairs here, and Marko lives there. We used to have a chauffeur, but when Otto died we never replaced him. Mother likes to have Marko drive her now, if he is not too busy. She does not go out much anymore—just to visit friends or an occasional shopping trip."

"She seems quite contented," Eve remarked.

53

"Yes, she has adjusted remarkably well to the drastic change in her life-style. She no longer cares to travel without my father, but she enjoys going to Grand Canary every winter with one of her friends."

"Camilla told me you were going there for your honeymoon."

"Yes." His lips tightened and she got the impression that he did not much care for that subject.

They drove out to the highway along the river, but Max soon turned off that onto another road that led away from the river into the forest. The road seemed to be rising and occasionally it would skirt a sheer, rocky cliff or pass between large boulders that looked as though they had been flung there by playful giants. Quite frequently a small lake would gleam briefly from among the trees as they drove past.

They drove on in silence for a few minutes. She felt his sideways glance slide over her before he surprisingly commented, "I like the way you wear your hair. It does not fall in your face all the time."

"Oh, it's too curly to do much with. I just hack it off with nail scissors. I couldn't stand to have it hanging around."

"I wish that Camilla would do hers up. It is always falling in her face and she is always pushing it back. It makes me nervous just to watch her. Why do girls do that?"

"I've never thought about it, Max. Maybe they need to keep busy with something in the same way some people are chain smokers. Or maybe they are shy and hide behind it."

"Camilla is not shy. And she always ties it back when she rides."

"Well, she's happy then," Eve said without thinking.

He frowned and looked at her sharply. "Meaning she is not happy the rest of the time?"

54

"No, I don't think she is, but we'd better not get onto that subject or we'll just have another fight."

"True." He gave her one of his quick, charming smiles. "We must not fight today."

For a while they came out into more open land with small farms scattered around. In other places the forest had been cut down by the lumber companies, leaving the hills pathetically bare.

"It seems a shame to destroy your beautiful forests," Eve commented.

"I agree, but the lumber is needed. The forests will be replanted."

"Martin thinks man will destroy the world for his own selfish needs."

"He may be right, but we cannot retreat back to the Stone Age."

"It must take a long time to grow a tree as tall as some of these spruce. Are there still animals in the woods?"

"Yes, quite a few. Moose and deer and all the small varieties such as fox, squirrels, rabbits, and so on. Even bears once in a while. There used to be a lot of them—as well as wolves."

"I've always loved Selma Lagerlöf's stories about this province. Such terrible creatures that used to live here: lynx, wolves, and the great bear that could only be killed with a silver bullet—"

"Not to mention the witches and devils and trolls! But you need not worry, they are all gone now."

"Are they? I'm not so sure. When I am alone in the forest I can feel a certain magic—"

They were back in the forest now, still going uphill, rising in places to a level above the trees, so that they could look down over their tops to a distant lake shimmering in the morning sun that had—as Max had predicted—broken through the clouds.

Where on earth was he taking her? Eve wondered. What could possibly be out here that Camilla might want? A horse on somebody's farm? But she didn't need another horse. When she married Max she'd have plenty of horses, but not, of course, the stud farm and Marko. . . .

Finally Max turned left onto a lane leading down toward the lake they had been driving along for the last few minutes. She saw now why he'd used the Land-Rover. It was one of the worst roads she'd ever been on, with tree roots and an occasional large rock jutting up in the way. It required skillful maneuvering even with the Land-Rover to get down the hill. At the bottom of the hill the road turned right along the lake.

"This is Visten," he told her, "one of the nicest lakes in our area. I often come here to fish."

The lane was even worse along the lake. In one place it came so close to the water that planks had been laid down on which to cross. There were a number of summer cottages scattered along the shore. Finally the lane petered out altogether in a little clearing. Above them, on a slight knoll, was a cottage with a path leading up to it through the pines.

"Here we are," Max said unnecessarily, and they got out and walked up the path, thickly covered with fallen pine needles. The cottage was nestled among the tall pines. The soil had all been eroded away in front of it, and there were only large flat rocks sloping down to the water's edge, where an old rowboat was tied to a small dock. The view of the quiet lake ringed with trees and the purple hills rising in the background was beautiful and peaceful.

Eve drew a long, happy breath. "It's lovely here, Max!" she exclaimed. "Is this your cottage?"

"Not yet, but I hope that it will be soon. It belongs to an elderly couple whose children are all grown and live too far away to use the cottage except for vacations.
56

The old couple can't drive anymore so they never come here and can't keep it in repair, and they have decided to sell. I thought Camilla might like to have it. Of course it is very primitive. Come, I will show you."

He took a key from his pocket and they went on up to the screened porch that ran the width of the cottage. There was a long table with two benches on the porch. Eve noticed that the screen was ripped in places and some of the boards were sagging.

"It will take a bit of work to get it in shape," Max said, "but it is basically sound."

He unlocked the front door and they stepped into the little living room. There was a small, wood-burning, pot-bellied stove and an assortment of the usual summer cottage type furniture, mostly discards from other homes.

"I intend to have a fireplace put in instead of the stove," Max told her, "and completely refurnish it, of course. I think it could be very charming."

"Yes, I'm sure it could," Eve agreed, and went on into the kitchen at the back. There was another old stove—a black iron wood-burning range—some cupboards filled with odds and ends of dishes, a table, and a low shelf to hold the water pail and basins.

"There is no plumbing or electricity," Max told her. "There is a pump out back for water and an outhouse, of course. For lighting they used kerosene lamps. I told you it was primitive."

"That doesn't matter," Eve assured him. "After all, it's only a summer cottage. I love it. How many bedrooms are there?"

"Two. They both have double bunks. It would be a nice place to bring one's children—" His voice trailed off and there was a wistful note in it that stirred Eve's heart.

"Yes, it would. I'm sure that the family who used to come here had many happy times. I can feel it somehow."

There was a curious pain in her heart when she thought of Max and Camilla coming here with their children. But why should she care, she told herself angrily. It had nothing to do with her!

After a quick look at the two tiny bedrooms, she went back to the porch, feeling that she did not dare to linger there with him. If she had known he was going to bring her to an isolated place like this, she thought, she would never have come. Had that been his intention all along—to get her here where they were totally alone with no danger of interruptions? She walked quickly over to the railing and looked out at the lake, her heart pounding so that she felt almost suffocated. He came to stand beside her.

"What do you think?" he asked. "Would Camilla like it?"

"You know her better than I do, Max. But it's obvious that you like it. Why don't you buy it for yourself?"

"You are right, of course. I love it here. My life is sometimes rather hectic and I need a place where I can get away from it all and just fish and relax."

Her hands gripped the railing. She was very conscious of Max's strong, lithe body beside her, his face so close that she could see the little lines at the corner of his eyes when he smiled. The air was filled with the scent of pines and the sunlight glimmered on the blue lake.

He took her hand and she felt an electric shock run up her arm. It was warm there out of the wind with the sun shining on them, and she was aware of something soft, languorous, and certainly dangerous stealing over her. Not violent this time, but sweet, gentle—and inevitable. His arm went about her shoulders and he drew her closer. For a moment his eyes looked deeply into hers and her whole body seemed to melt with a pure, sweet desire. He kissed
58

her, gently at first, then with increasing urgency. Yes, it had been madness for her to come, but a madness that she seemed unable to resist.

"Eve," he murmured, his mouth close to hers, "I have tried to fight the way I feel about you, but it is hopeless. I want you. I have wanted you from the moment I saw you, and I think you feel the same way. There is a sort of magic between us—" His hand was warm against her breast and he bent to kiss the hollow of her throat. "We can go inside—"

"This is why you brought me here, isn't it?" she whispered.

"Yes, this is why I brought you here, my little love. And you came, did you not?"

How could she fight this man? she thought despairingly. Did she even want to? "Camilla—" she managed to say.

"She does not love me. It does not matter to her what I do."

"I think it does, Max. She cares for you in her own way."

"She would mind only if I did something to threaten our marriage. That is all she is concerned about. How can it hurt her if we take a little happiness together now before it is too late?"

Her thoughts were in tumult. One part of her told her that he was right. Why shouldn't they take a moment's happiness when it was available? All her friends made love as casually as they played a set of tennis, but she had always held back, saving herself for—what? The knight in shining armor who would carry her away on his white charger to eternal bliss? Life wasn't like that. Life offered joys with one hand and took them away with the other. You had to take them quickly while you could. She wanted Max desperately—but there was the other part of her mind that was asking her if she could bear to go away and

59

leave him after they had become lovers. To never see him again, to know he was living with Camilla, that she was bearing his children—how could she bear that?

He was drawing her toward the door and she wanted to go inside with him, into the little bedroom, and lie with him on the narrow bed and become completely, irrevocably his, to feel his eager, demanding mouth on hers, his lean hands caressing her, his weight upon her—but how could she even consider this when he belonged to another woman?

"If you really loved me," she cried, "you'd break your engagement to Camilla—"

"You know I cannot do that."

She pulled away from him. "Then take me home, Max—please! Take me home!" The tears were running down her cheeks, but she made no effort to brush them away.

"Eve, do not do this to me! You are driving me out of my mind!" His voice was husky as he tried to draw her back into his arms, but she pushed him away and ran from the porch back to the car. When he caught up with her she was leaning against it, sobbing.

"I can't bear it!" she gasped. "If I had you, I couldn't give you up—ever!"

"Eve, I am sorry. I thought that girls of today—"

"I'm not like that. I want it to be—forever!"

"Nothing is forever," he said brusquely, and helped her into the car.

They drove home in almost complete silence. Her whole body ached with emotional fatigue and frustration, and the lump in her throat would not go away. It had been better, she thought, in the beginning, when she had believed that she hated him.

When she came into the house it smelled of *plätter*, the Swedish pancakes Olivia was so good at making. Eve loved them buttered and rolled up with lingonberry preserves. Olivia turned from the stove with a smile.

"Just in time for *middag*," she said. "Did you enjoy your horseback ride?"

Eve stared at her blankly for a moment, then remembered that she had left that morning to go riding.

"Oh, yes," she replied. "It was fun being on a horse again, but I've got a lot to learn." No point in mentioning her trip to Visten, she decided.

"You must go with Camilla someday. She is a very good rider. *Ja*—"

At that moment there was the sound of a car pulling in to the graveled parking area in front of the house and Eve felt the blood rush to her cheeks. Was it Max? But there was no earthly reason why he should come. . . .

"That is Camilla!" Olivia exclaimed with a frown. "She did not say she was coming home for lunch. I hope nothing is wrong—"

The front door slammed and Camilla came through the hall into the kitchen. Her cheeks were flushed and there was a stormy light in her usually calm eyes. For one awful moment Eve thought that Camilla knew what had happened between her and Max—but that was ridiculous! How could she possibly know? Camilla did not even look at Eve, but went straight to her mother.

"Mama!" she cried. "Mitra Carsing is here!"

Chapter Five

"Here?" Olivia looked around the kitchen in astonishment, as though she expected the woman to materialize out of nowhere. "What do you mean?"

"She came into the bank this morning and said dreadful things to me! Everyone heard her. I have never been so humiliated!" She put her hands over her face.

Olivia put her arms around her daughter's shoulders and led her over to a chair. "Come now. Sit down and tell me about it. What did she say to you?"

Camilla rubbed the tears from her cheeks with the back of her hand. "She came in to cash a check, but it was really to see me. She came right to my window and looked me up and down in the most insulting manner and said, 'So you are the girl the countess has selected for Max! But he will never go through with this farce of a marriage—I will see to that!' Then she took her money and walked out. Everyone heard her and they all looked at me—it was dreadful!"

"She must be crazy!" Olivia said angrily. "Max is not going to break his engagement to you because of that woman—he is much too sensible."

"He was crazy about her once. Maybe he still loves her. Maybe she has some hold over him—"

"Nonsense. He gave her up once because his mother did not approve of her—why would he change his mind now?"

"But Mama—I have never told you this, but there were rumors at the time that she had become interested in a young actor and so was willing to give up Max. I have never dared ask him the truth of the matter, but suppose—"

"There is nothing to suppose. Max is engaged to you and he will never break that engagement. He would not bring such dishonor to his name. Where is this woman staying?"

"They were talking about her at the bank after she left. I heard someone say she had checked into the Hotel Munken last night. Everyone tried to be kind to me, to laugh it off—but I could see the speculation in their eyes. They are all wondering what will happen now—"

"Nothing will happen," Olivia said firmly. She was more decisive than Eve had ever seen her. For the moment all her vagueness had gone.

"Was she very beautiful?" Eve had not meant to speak at all, but the words came out of their own volition. She felt a searing jealousy at the thought of this woman that Max had loved—perhaps still loved.

Camilla looked at her in surprise, as though she had just realized that Eve was there. "Oh, yes. Stunning. Tall and slender with black hair done up on top of her head with little curls over each ear. Big black eyes slanted at the corners and a sexy mouth. She was wearing a gorgeous blue wool suit with a gold-and-silver scarf and diamond earrings."

Eve thought wryly that Camilla had not been too overcome by shock to take a complete inventory of her rival.

"Do you think Max knows she is here?" Olivia asked.

"I don't know. I should think he would by now—everyone else in town knows," the girl said bitterly.

"I saw him at Rosenborg this morning," Eve said. "I don't think he knew then." He would hardly have taken her out to the cottage if he had known—would he?

"Well, she won't lose any time getting in touch with him, I'm sure," Camilla said angrily.

"What's all this?" Martin had appeared in the doorway. He was looking at his daughter with his usual whimsical smile, but Eve saw that his eyes were sharp and cold. "Has something happened between you and Max? A quarrel—"

"No, Papa!" she hastened to assure him. "It is just that Mitra Carsing has come back. You know—the woman he wanted to marry a few years ago. She seems to think she can stop him from marrying me."

Martin stood very still for a moment, staring at nothing. Eve felt a shiver run through her. Then he went over and put his hand on his daughter's shoulder.

"Do not worry, my love," he said softly. "There is nothing she can do. Max will marry you as planned."

Camilla looked up at him, her eyes filled with adoration. "How can you be so sure, Papa?" she asked.

"Because I know Max. He would never break his word. I think, if you are so troubled, the best thing to do would be to get Max over here and talk to him about it. Tell him that he must send this woman away because her presence is an embarrassment to you—to all of us. But first—it would be a shame to waste those elegant *plätter!* Come, let us have our *middag.*"

After they had eaten Martin convinced his daughter that she had to go back to work that afternoon in spite of her humiliation. It was necessary to show that her head was still high, that nothing had changed. He told her that he would call Max and ask him to come over when she got off work. Eve could see that Camilla dreaded the thought of facing her fellow employees again, but for her Martin's word was law, and she drove away.

She was restless when Camilla had gone and wandered outside. She couldn't stop thinking about Mitra and Max. Would he be angry with her for coming—or pleased—or worried? Was he still in love with her? Was there really any chance that he would abandon Camilla for her? Finally she mounted the old bicycle and pedaled off down the lane.

When she reached the highway that ran along the river she turned in the direction of the bridge. She had no conscious plan. Most of the way was downhill and she coasted swiftly along, knowing it would be a tiresome haul back. There was a sharp bend where the road came out of the woods and led down to the bridge, and there was the hotel, perched on its knoll, overlooking the river. It was built against a hillside and all the rooms were upstairs except the lobby. There was a small dress shop at ground level on one end, and a graveled parking space in front. Because of its location, the grounds were small, but there was a little grove of pines with a few wooden benches and a table. The dining room was upstairs and had an outside terrace with umbrella-covered tables.

Eve pulled off the road into the pine grove and leaned her bicycle against a tree. What was she doing there anyway? she asked herself ruefully. Was she hoping for a glimpse of the glamorous Mitra? That was highly unlikely. She walked around to the front of the hotel and looked at the parked cars. There were several of the small shiny sedans that one saw everywhere in Sweden, and among them—standing out like a peacock among ducks—was a low-slung, bright red sports car of what Eve supposed was some Italian make. Well, thought Eve, if she were a beautiful, rich, ex-café singer type, that was exactly the sort of car she would drive! So it had to be Mitra's. She was just walking over to take a closer look at it, when she heard another car coming around the curve. Instinctively she moved back into the pine grove and stood where a tree shielded her from the road. She heard the car pull off the road onto the parking area. Cautiously she moved up to where she could peer around the corner of the hotel. It was Max, just getting out of the Mercedes-Benz. She pulled back in alarm. Suppose he had seen her! He would think that she had come there to spy on him! She heard the car door slam, and then his footsteps as he went up the steps to the lobby. From her brief glimpse she had seen that his face looked grim and unsmiling.

Well, she thought, at least he had not worn the joyous expression of a man about to be reunited with his beloved! He was probably angry with Mitra for coming there so boldly, but perhaps if Mitra were very clever and he really loved her—she turned away angrily. What was the use of trying to guess what would go on between them? It wasn't any of her business anyway. She got on her bicycle and headed disconsolately for home.

When Camilla came home from work that afternoon, Martin told her that he had talked to Max and that he would be over to see her that evening.

"Did you say anything about Mitra?" Camilla asked him.

Martin tipped his head to one side and gave his daughter his whimsical little smile, but Eve noticed that his eyes held a hard glitter. "I did not have to, my love. He seemed to know all about it. Do not worry. I am sure he is quite capable of dealing with that woman."

Shortly after they had eaten their evening meal, they heard a car coming up the lane. Eve slipped quietly away and went up to her room. She didn't want to be around when he came in, and she certainly didn't want to hear what he and Camilla would say to each other. She closed her door and lay down on the bed. She had been given Pelle's old room, which had been empty since his marriage. It was not a large room, but it was cozy, and she liked it. There was a big old painted wardrobe, an alcove under the eaves where the bed stood, a desk where Pelle had done his homework, with some of his books still on a shelf he had built above it. She had not yet met Pelle, since he lived a good many miles away, but she knew he and his wife were coming for the wedding. From what the others had said, she gathered that he had been very fond of sports—soccer, ice hockey, cross-country skiing, and so on—not like Martin at all.

She lay on the narrow bed with her arms folded beneath her head and stared at the ceiling. There was no tile stove in this bedroom, but it had a small, grated opening in the floor in one corner to allow warm air to rise from the room below, which in this case was Martin's den. Quite often she fell asleep to the sound of his typewriter coming through the grate. Now as she lay there trying not to think about what Max might have to say, she heard the sound of a closing door and then voices coming through the grating. Camilla and Max! Apparently they had gone into the den for their little chat, not realizing that she was in her room and could hear everything they said!

She started to rise, then fell back, overcome by curiosity. It wasn't her fault, she rationalized, if they elected to hold their confrontation where she could hear them. She heard Camilla's voice rise in indignation.

"I have never been so humiliated, Max! She came right into the bank and said that our marriage would be a farce and that she didn't think you would go through with it! Everyone heard her!"

Eve's ear was now so attuned to the Värmland dialect that she had no trouble understanding anything that was said, although she was still a bit hesitant in speaking it. Max was always easy to understand because he had gone away to school and spoke very pure Swedish. When he replied his voice was composed and soothing.

"Now, Camilla, there is nothing to get so worked up about. I had no idea Mitra was coming here. Believe me, I had nothing to do with it. Of course there is no way she can prevent our marriage."

"You've got to make her go away, Max! What are you going to do about it?"

"I went to the hotel this afternoon to see her—"

"So now it will be all over town that you visited her at the hotel!"

"Well, I had to see her, didn't I?" He was beginning to sound impatient. "I told her that there was nothing to be gained by her staying here, that I intended to marry you, and that there was nothing she could do about it."

"And what did she say to that?"

Max hesitated for a moment and Eve could imagine his shrug. "She was angry. She said a lot of things that need not concern you."

"But did she agree to leave?"

"No. She seems determined to remain for a while. She is used to getting her own way and does not give up readily. I cannot force her to leave, Camilla, you know that, but I promise that I will not have any further contact with her."

"Max"—it sounded to Eve as though Camilla were pacing back and forth in the little room—" tell me the truth. Are you still in love with her?"

"Certainly not." His reply came quickly and emphatically. "I was younger when I first met her and was dazzled by her beauty and glamor. Now I know that it was only infatuation. Far from caring for her, I do not even like her now. She has a cruel, selfish streak that I could not see before, and it is obvious that she has taken to drinking too much."

"But I am afraid of her, Max!" Camilla cried. "There is no telling what she may do! I know she won't leave you alone."

68

"But when she finds out how futile her attempt is, then she will go away."

"I don't think she will! I think she will do something terrible to prevent our marriage!" Camilla sounded almost hysterical and Eve was puzzled. Why couldn't she just accept Max's word that he no longer cared for the woman and drop the subject? Apparently Max felt the same way, for he sounded irritated when he replied.

"What is the matter with you, Cam? There is nothing she can do. You are behaving like a silly little girl. You are not in love with me, so it cannot be jealousy. What is it, then?"

"I don't know! I have a feeling something will happen to prevent our marriage and Papa will die! I am worried about him—this is upsetting him, I can tell. He might have a setback, just when he was starting to get better—"

"Papa! That is all you care about. Have you no thought for anyone else? I am doing my best for him, but I cannot force Mitra to leave Romeby! Would you have me drive her away with a whip?"

It was turning into a full-fledged quarrel now and Eve buried her head in the pillow, wishing that she'd left the room when she'd had a chance. She didn't want to hear anymore. But apparently Camilla realized that she had gone too far. Her voice was muffled as though she were crying when she said, "I'm sorry, Max. I know it isn't your fault. I won't say any more about it."

"All right, Cam." His voice just sounded rather tired now. "Try to pull yourself together. Have you forgotten the rehearsal tonight? We should be there in a few minutes. If you don't appear, everyone will think we have quarreled over Mitra."

"Oh, dear, I had forgotten all about it! Of course we have to be there. I'll be down in ten minutes."

Eve heard Camilla running up the stairs. Then she heard her running water in the bathroom and could picture her splashing cold water on her face to remove the traces of tears. When she came out she tapped on Eve's door.

"Eve?" she called.

Eve opened her door. Camilla's face was set in its calm, almost wooden expression. No one would have suspected that she had just been through an emotional upheaval.

"Yes?" she said inquiringly.

"We have a rehearsal tonight. I had almost forgotten about it until Max reminded me. Would you like to go?"

"What sort of a rehearsal?"

"Oh, our folk dancing group. I told you about the Midsummer festival at Rosenborg. I have to be in it this year, because of my engagement to Max. I thought you might enjoy watching us rehearse."

"Why, yes, I would." She glanced down at her jeans. "Do I have to change?"

"No, we all wear jeans to practice in. I am on my way to put mine on now." She was still wearing the suit that she had worn to work. "You can go on down and talk to Max if you like."

"Did you get things straightened out about Mitra?" Eve asked. Obviously Camilla was not aware that she had overheard their conversation.

"Yes, it will be all right. I'll tell you about it later." She went on to her room to change.

Eve certainly had no desire for any little chat with Max at that point, so she went back into her room to apply fresh makeup and brush her hair. When Camilla was ready they went down together. Max was in the living room talking to Martin and Olivia and rose as they entered. She met his eyes fleetingly, but they revealed nothing.

"Well, then, we will go," he said. "I brought the car

over because I thought you might be tired, Camilla, after working all day."

When they started out to the car, Eve asked, "Are you in the dances, too, Max?"

He smiled. "Hardly, Eve. It is customary for the owner of Rosenborg to watch from the sidelines. However, it is also part of the tradition that he should start off the dances by doing one special number with his wife—or, as in this case, his fiancée. So Camilla and I will do that dance together."

When they arrived at Rosenborg, Max drove around back to the old barn. The big doors were open, and as they walked toward them Eve heard the sound of voices.

"My father converted the barn into a dance hall," Max explained, "so the affair could be held there in case of rain. Unfortunately it often is cold and rainy on Midsummer. We do our rehearsing in there, although we hope to be able to dance in the courtyard where the pole will be raised on Midsummer Eve."

Inside the barn Eve saw that the stalls had been removed, so that it was all one big room with a raised platform at one end for the musicians. There were tables and benches along the walls, and at one end a small kitchen and lavatories had been added. There were already about twenty young men and women there, standing around in groups chatting while the musicians tuned their instruments and conferred on the platform. There were several fiddlers and an accordionist.

Everyone stopped talking and turned to greet them as Max and the girls entered. He introduced Eve to the group in general without attempting to give her all the individual names. She had been a bit curious about the attitude his employees might take toward him, wondering if any of the old feudal atmosphere lingered on, but they seemed to accept him more or less as one of themselves—although they did address him respectfully as Herr Greve rather than Max. To her surprise, Eve saw that Marko was among the group. Of course he too was an employee, but he had not been there very long, and somehow she had not expected him to be one of the folk dancers.

Another man, who had been talking to the musicians, came over to join them. He looked to be in his early forties and was tall and thin with a clever, intelligent face and wore dark-rimmed glasses. His nose was long and rather pointed, there were deep grooves on either side of his mouth, and he had a funny little one-sided smile that Eve found very attractive.

"Eve, this is Kjell Segerstam," Max told her, "head of the Conservatory of Music over in Ransäter. He works with the historical society dancers and is kind enough to coach ours as well."

He took her hand and smiled down into her eyes. "So this is the little American cousin I have been hearing so much about," he said in English with a charming accent. Eve smiled back and knew instinctively that she had found a friend. "You must come and visit our school someday," he told her.

"Yes, I would like to, Herr Segerstam."

Soon the rehearsal was under way and Eve sat on one of the benches to watch. In a few minutes Max joined her. She was looking at Marko, who seemed to be Camilla's partner in the number they were rehearsing.

"He seems to have learned your dances very quickly," she said.

"Yes, Kjell says he is the best dancer we have. He danced with a group in Yugoslavia, and I suppose their dances are not so very much different, basically. Camilla thought it would be fun to dance with the group as well as doing the number with me, and we needed a partner for her, so I asked Marko. He was a

72

bit reluctant at first, but he finally agreed. I suppose he feels a bit of an outsider, and he is not very fluent in Swedish yet, but he is learning quickly. He is a very clever young man."

"And a very gorgeous one!" she murmured, noticing how all the young women of the ensemble were keeping their eyes on him.

Max shot her a quick, annoyed look. "Oh, yes, all the girls are after him," he said dryly.

"Has he picked out a special one?" she asked, trying to sound completely disinterested.

"Not to my knowledge," he told her a bit shortly.

She decided it was time to change the subject. "Midsummer is very important here, isn't it?" she said.

"Indeed it is, as much so as Christmas, I would say. In a way they are similar festivals—one to celebrate the longest day of the year, the other the shortest."

"But the church didn't adopt it as they did other pagan festivals, did they?"

"No, it is the only one they left alone, although they do acknowledge it to the extent of setting up a birch tree beside the altar."

"Why do they speak of raising a Maypole," Eve asked, "when the festival is in June?"

"May does not refer to the month," Max explained, "but to the goddess Maja, in whose honor the pole is raised."

"I suppose it's an ancient fertility rite."

"No doubt. There is usually a brass rooster atop the pole: one of the most common fertility symbols."

"But they have roosters on church steeples!" Eve exclaimed.

"Yes, many pagan symbols remain although people no longer remember their origin. At Christmas all the old fertility symbols are used in the decorations—roosters, bucks, pigs, and so on. At Easter toy witches are hung up, because that is the night they fly on their broomsticks to Blue Hill for their annual rendezvous with the devil."

"You're beginning to sound like Martin," Eve teased.

"He is not the only one interested in the ancient superstitions of our country. There has been quite a revival of interest the past few years all over Sweden, and folk dancing is once again becoming popular."

Eve watched Kjell Segerstam as he darted among the dancing couples, calling out suggestions and criticisms. She found the music, which had seemed so charming and gay at first, growing monotonous and rather shrill as it went on and on. It had been a long, confusing day, and she suddenly felt extremely tired and longed for the sanctuary of her room. She wondered if anyone would mind if she slipped quietly away and walked home by herself. Although it was nearly ten, it was still not quite dark out.

She was just about to speak to Max about it, when Kjell called him over to rehearse the dance he and Camilla were to do together before the others came on. She decided to stay and watch a little longer. Her heart twisted with unexpected pain when she saw Max and Camilla take their places on the floor. She had thought Marko was the best-looking man there, but beside Max's lean, aristocratic features he seemed to fade into insignificance. How graceful Max was, she thought, with his broad shoulders and slender waist, as he moved with Camilla into the rapid ryhthm of the gay little tune. What a perfect couple they made—and how right they looked together! Her heart was heavy as she watched, her eyes blurred with tears.

After that they broke for coffee, which the girls made in the little kitchen, and soon Eve found herself sitting at one of the tables between Max and Kjell, with Camilla and Marko across from them. There were plates of cookies and cake, furnished by the Rosenborg kitchen.

"How did you like the dancing?" Kjell asked her.

"They seemed very professional to me. Actually, your folk dances aren't too different from our square dances at home."

"Well, I suppose they were originally brought from England and Europe, were they not? It is too bad you did not come here soon enough to join our group."

"Oh, I'm not very good at that sort of thing," she protested quickly.

"You know, Kjell," Max said thoughtfully, "I think we ought to use Eve in one number—as an American guest star, you might say. How about in the opening number when Cam and I lead out with the Värmlandspolska? Eve and Marko could join us."

"It's a clever idea," Kjell agreed, "but doesn't it break with your family tradition? I mean, the count and his lady dance alone—"

"It is my family and my tradition," Max said coldly. "Surely I can break it if I want to."

"Of course," Kjell agreed. "I like the idea, Max. What do you think, Eve?"

"I'd rather not," she replied flatly. "Anyway, I don't have a costume."

"Oh, I am sure I could find one at the Conservatory that would fit you, and you'd only have to learn a few simple steps—"

"She will do it, of course," Max said, in his haughtiest lord-of-the-manor fashion.

Eve could hardly refuse after that without making herself appear stubborn and ungracious, but she seethed in silence. What right did he have to force her into something he knew she did not want? Why was he doing it? After that episode at the cottage—she looked across at Camilla who did not look especially pleased at the prospect herself. It was not the thought of dancing before a crowd of people that disturbed Eve; it was more the idea of the four of them—Marko, Camilla,

Max, and herself—being involved in anything together. In view of the complicated emotional currents swirling around them, how was it going to work out?

He ought to bring Mitra into it, too, she thought angrily. She could weave in and out as they danced, singing one of her café songs and maybe tossing flowers under their feet!

Chapter Six

Camilla had decided to work until the first of June, and it was now the last week of May. Her wedding gown was being made by the local seamstress, a Miss Karlsson, who—as she was the only seamstress of any ability in Romeby—was in great demand, especially as the month of brides approached. On the day following the rehearsal, Camilla had an appointment with her for a fitting after work.

It was another beautiful spring day, a bit chilly but sunny with a few billowy clouds piling up above the purple hills. Kjell had sent over a couple of costumes for Eve to try on, so that if the one she picked needed altering, Miss Karlsson could take it with her when she left after Camilla's fitting. The more Eve thought about it the less she liked the idea of participating in the dance. Why had Max suggested it? He was such a complicated man, it was impossible to guess what he was thinking or what he would do next. She was determined to avoid him as much as possible.

Just thinking about him made Eve feel too restless to sit quietly at home reading, and since she had no desire to chat with Martin, and since Olivia was busy ironing and wouldn't let her help, Eve once again went to the shed for Camilla's bicycle and took off along the lane. She had no particular destination in mind, but she turned on the highway that led past the front entrance to Rosenborg. When she reached the wrought-iron gate she found herself slowing down.

Always before she had gone to Rosenborg by the shortcut and had never examined the gate. It was an interesting work of art, supported by tall stone pillars. On one pillar was carved the Värmland crest and on the other was the family crest of the von Stjernas, which consisted of two strange-looking beasts apparently locked in battle with a banner over their heads and some sort of flowers at their feet. The gate was not locked, but she had no intention of going in.

The big estate house looked beautiful from there, with a long reflection pool in front of it, mirroring the graceful white pillars and circular balcony, with a line of dark cypress trees on either side. She gave it a long, contemplative, rather wistful gaze, then biked on. Across the highway from the estate was nothing but forest: tall spruce and pine with an occasional grove of birches. The last few days had been so warm that all the snow was gone now from under the trees and spring flowers were growing in the ditches along the road. After a while she came to a slight opening in the trees, a clearing from which a path ran back into the forest. She was nearly past it when her eye was caught by a gleam of red, and she saw that a car had been pulled off to one side of the clearing so that it was nearly hidden by a clump of bushes. It was a bright red foreign convertible—the same car she had seen parked in front of the hotel.

Was it Mitra's? Somehow she was sure that it was—but what on earth was it doing there? Was it possible that because the countess would never receive her at Rosenborg she was meeting Max secretly in the woods? But Max had promised Camilla that he would not see her again.

She crossed the road and leaned her bicycle against a tree while she took a closer look at the car. It was empty. Had she gone to some secret rendezvous with Max in spite of all his protestations that the woman no longer meant anything to him? A tight feeling came into her chest at the thought. If Max were capable of such behavior, then he was not the man she thought him to be—was not worth a moment of the pain she had felt because of him. She was flooded with a terrible urge to know the truth, no matter what the cost.

Her eye caught the glint of something shiny lying at the beginning of the path, and she went over to it. Only a bit of plastic torn from the top of a cigarette pack, but it was fresh, as though it had just been thrown there. Somehow without conscious volition she found herself walking cautiously along the path. Suppose she met Mitra face to face? But then she realized that Mitra had never seen her and would have no idea who she was. But if Max were with her . . . That didn't bear thinking about. He would probably accuse her of spying on him—which, of course, was exactly what she was doing.

After a hundred yards or so the path ended at the door of a small building. A sign on the door indicated that it was some sort of a target practice club. Behind the building in an open meadow she could see a target range. The low murmur of voices in the lodge caught her attention. She knew that she should get away from there, but curiosity was stronger than caution or ethics, so instead of leaving, she moved as silently as possible around the side of the building and peered cautiously into one of the windows.

The window was none too clean, and as it was rather dark inside the building, at first she couldn't see anything. Shading her eyes with her hands to cut the outside light, she was able to make out something of the interior. There was a big stone fireplace, a table, and some benches—and standing beside the table were two figures, a man and a woman. They were too engrossed in their conversation to notice Eve at the window, so she continued to stare in at them.

The woman was tall and slender with long black hair hanging over her shoulders. Her back was to the window, so Eve could not see her face, but she did not doubt for a moment that it was Mitra, even though she now wore her hair loose instead of done up as Camilla had described. After all, there weren't too many women with long black hair in Romeby. She was wearing a simple but expensive-looking green knit slack suit and held a cigarette in one hand with which she was gesticulating as she talked.

The man stood at the end of the table in profile to Eve. She had been so certain that it would be Max that it was with a profound shock of surprise that she recognized Marko. He was standing with his hands shoved in his pockets, regarding Mitra with an expression that was far from friendly. Their voices were certainly loud enough to hear from where she stood, but to her disappointment she found that they were speaking neither Swedish nor English, but some language she had never heard before—probably Yugoslavian, she decided. They seemed to be arguing. Mitra seemed to be trying to talk him into something, because he kept shaking his head and looking stubborn. Finally they were both talking at once and Marko took his hands out of his pockets and waved them in the air, shouting at her angrily.

Mitra changed her tactics then, lowering her voice and moving closer to him, speaking in a pleading, almost pathetic tone. Finally he seemed to relent, because he shrugged and Eve caught the word *"Da,"* which sounded as though it ought to mean yes. Mitra

79

put her arms around him triumphantly and kissed his cheek and murmured something that sounded like *"Dobar"* a couple of times. Marko pushed her away with an impatient gesture and walked rapidly out of the lodge. Eve had no time to get away, but she stayed close to the side of the building and Marko stalked off down the path without looking back. Eve wondered if he would notice her bicycle and tried to remember where she had left it. She thought she had placed it among the trees at the edge of the clearing, so it was possible that in his state of mind he would walk by without seeing it.

She turned back to the window to see if Mitra were also leaving. The woman had seated herself on the edge of the table and sat there with one slender leg swinging while she lit another cigarette. At this angle she was in profile to Eve: a very beautiful profile, Eve noted, with classic lines. She was smiling faintly as though satisfied with the outcome of the discussion. When she raised the cigarette to her full red lips, Eve caught the glitter of a large diamond. Since Mitra did not seem to be in a hurry to leave the lodge, Eve turned away and ran down the path to the clearing. Marko was nowhere in sight, so she took her bicycle from among the trees and turned back toward Lyckan, her mind churning with conjecture.

Marko and Mitra. What sort of relationship did they have? It seemed obvious that they had known each other before coming to Romeby—a fact which was much too curious to be a coincidence. And if it were not a coincidence, then what was it? She tried to assemble the facts in her mind. Mitra was a very rich woman who wanted to marry Max. She was the sort of woman who would stop at nothing to get her way. She knew he intended to marry Camilla. But suppose— suppose something could be done to discredit Camilla so completely that Max would no longer want to marry

80

her. If she were caught in an affair with his own stable hand—yes, that ought to do it!

A rich woman could somehow manage to have a handsome young man come to work in the neighborhood: someone new and exciting, someone to catch the fancy of a girl unable to fall in love with a man she had known all her life. Eve didn't know how she had managed to get him a job at Rosenborg, but somehow it had been accomplished. With Camilla coming over nearly every day to ride, the rest was easy. He had exerted his manly charms, and she had fallen in love with him.

So far so good. But then? What had they been arguing about? Was Marko balking and refusing to go any further with the plan? Camilla might have fallen for Marko, but Eve was almost sure it hadn't gone beyond that stage. The girl was too fanatically devoted to her father to jeopardize the marriage she believed would save his life. And it was possible that Marko had come to value his work with Max and that with the promise of being put in charge of a stud farm he was no longer interested in whatever bribe Mitra was offering. It was even possible that he had really come to care for Camilla. Of course, Eve told herself, this was all pure speculation, but it did make sense. The next question was, what should she do about it? Her first impulse was to warn Camilla as quickly as possible not to have anything more to do with Marko. But, then, if she were wrong in her interpretation of the scene in the lodge, she might get Marko in trouble and cause Camilla a lot of pain without accomplishing anything. No, she would have to wait and see what happened.

Poor Camilla, if she found out Marko had only been making love to her on Mitra's instructions! Of course Camilla had no intention of breaking off with Max to marry Marko, but even so she would be hurt to learn that he was just a pawn of Mitra's. Eve's head was

81

whirling with doubt and confusion. If only there were someone she could talk to, she thought, someone to advise her, but there was no one she knew who was not too deeply involved in the problem. And, of course, it was really none of her business, as she had been telling herself from the beginning. She ought to ignore the whole thing and let them work it out for themselves. If only—if only she didn't feel the way she did about Max! She too was now as much a part of the confusing emotional tangle as any of them.

When she got back to Lyckan and went up to her room, she saw the box of costumes on her bed that Kjell had sent over. Well, she thought, she might as well try them on so she would know what work needed to be done, if any. She opened the box and took out the two costumes. Even in Värmland the costumes were not all identical, but they did all consist of a wool striped skirt reaching to about midway on the calf, an apron, a laced bodice, and a long-sleeved white blouse. The first one Eve examined was obviously too big, so she laid it aside. The other was smaller so she tried it on. It was a bit loose in the waist and reached almost to the floor, but of course that could be altered. The blouse fit fairly well and the vest could be laced as tightly as she liked. On the whole, when she surveyed herself in the mirror over the dresser, she was quite pleased with her appearance.

Her golden-brown curls framed her flushed face and her dark blue eyes shone back at her with excitement. The costume was very becoming, she thought, much more becoming than her usual jeans and shirt. She looked so—so feminine and appealing. Perhaps it wouldn't be so bad after all appearing in the dance. When Max saw her . . .

Shaking the thought off impatiently, she lifted the skirt to avoid tripping and went downstairs to show

Olivia. She and Martin were in the kitchen drinking coffee, and when Eve came in their faces broke into delighted smiles.

"Charming!" Martin exclaimed. "A real Swedish lass!"

Olivia took hold of the skirt. "It needs taking in," she said. "If Froken Karlsson is too busy, I can do it myself."

"The other was much too big," Eve told her, "but this one will be all right when it's hemmed up."

"*Ja*—well, you look fine in it," Olivia told her. "Come have some coffee."

"I'd better get this costume off first. I wouldn't want to spill anything on it."

She was nearly to the stairs when there was a knock on the door. "I'll get it," she called, and went to open it. There stood Max. When he saw her a look of startled delight came into his golden eyes.

"Eve! I hardly knew you. How charming you look. Is that the costume Kjell got for you?"

"Yes." She stepped aside for him to enter. "It's a little too big, but we're going to have it altered." She had wanted him to see her in it, but now all she wanted was to run away from his admiring gaze. The hall seemed filled with his vibrant presence as he stood there casually dressed in slacks and jacket, his fair skin glowing from the fresh cool air, his silky brown hair falling over his forehead. There was a smell of the outdoors about him mingled with the delectable scent of the shaving lotion he used.

The corners of his eyes crinkled as he smiled. "You are such a tiny thing, Eve, I am surprised that he found one that fits you so well."

"Martin and Olivia are in the kitchen," she told him, and made her escape.

She changed into her jeans and a sweater. When she

went back down she found Max in the kitchen drinking coffee and chatting with her cousins. She sat down to join them.

"Max was just telling us that he is going to drive out to his dairy farm this morning," Olivia said. "Why don't you go with him, Eve? You haven't seen much of his estate, and this would be a nice little outing for you."

Eve looked at Max, expecting him to come up with some sort of an excuse why he couldn't take her, but he merely inclined his head and said politely: "Of course you may come if you like, Eve."

There was really nothing she could say without being rude, so she said: "All right. I would like to see more of the countryside."

When they reached the car she said unhappily: "Why didn't you make some excuse for not taking me? You know that we should avoid being alone together."

He opened the car door for her and replied with a shrug: "It is necessary that we maintain at least an outward appearance of friendship or the family will think something is wrong."

"Let them think we don't like each other—I don't care. It might be easier that way." She got into the car and he went around to his side and slid in beside her.

"Does everything have to be easy? I wanted you to see my estate, Eve."

So—he had come intending to pick her up, she thought, gazing stonily out the window. The estate house and grounds with all the outbuildings occupied about ten acres of land and was surrounded by woodlands. Beyond that were the fields where the grain crops were grown.

"This isn't all your land, is it?" she asked.

"Oh, no. The dairy farm is separate from the rest, on land retained just for that purpose. Centuries ago our holdings were larger, but that would not be practical today. We have what by your measurements I think would be roughly about five thousand acres, that is all."

It sounded like quite a lot to Eve, a city girl who knew little about farming.

"Some of it is in forest." He added, "It is not all cultivated." Throughout the drive he maintained a strictly casual, friendly attitude, explaining the workings of the estate and answering her questions at length, yet she could not help but be almost achingly aware of the lean, powerful body beside hers, the slender yet strong-looking hands on the steering wheel. The very timber of his voice had the power to stir her emotions. No, she thought, it was not really wise to spend time alone with this man, no matter how carefully they kept their feelings in check.

He pointed out a beautiful meadow just beyond a patch of woodland. "We are on estate land again," he told her. "That is where I plan to build the stud farm. It is an excellent location for horses."

"This Marko whom you intend to put in charge," she said cautiously, "just what do you know about him actually? Did he have any references?"

Max gave her a quizzical glance. "He had excellent references from the Lippizan stud farm. Aside from that I know nothing about him, except that he does good work and seems entirely trustworthy. What is your interest in him, Eve?"

For a moment she was tempted to tell Max about the scene in the shooting lodge, but she hated to get Marko in trouble without any more to go on.

"Oh, I guess I've read too many spy stories," she replied lightly. "I can't help thinking that anybody from an Iron Curtain country is some kind of a spy."

Max laughed. "Why would the communists be interested in my estate? Anyway, he is from Yugoslavia and they are far more liberal and independent there. It is true that we have had a few Russians around here posing as ordinary workers but actually in the government's pay, but I am sure that Marko is just what he appears to be."

"He left a good job, though, to come here."

"We get many Yugoslavians in Sweden who leave because they do not like communism. Marko does not seem to want to discuss such things, so I have never pressed him."

Eve was silent, not daring to say any more. The situation was too complicated to be handled carelessly. Max ought to be told that Marko was somehow connected with Mitra, but she couldn't do that without also involving Camilla. Until she knew definitely how involved her cousin had become with Marko, she couldn't say anything.

Shortly after that they reached the dairy farm, where Eve met the manager and his wife, an attractive young couple with several small children. Max conducted her through the barn and milking sheds and showed her some of the herd of sleek, sturdy-looking brown cows. He explained that at one time the estate had done its own processing of the milk, but that now it was sent on to a dairy company.

By the time Max had finished discussing his business with the manager it was well past noon, and the manager's wife insisted that they stay for *middag*. They enjoyed a hearty meal and started back home around two. This time Max took a different route and showed her more of the estate land and some of the tidy red farmhouses where the men who worked on it lived. By now she felt that she had a much better understanding of all that Rosenborg entailed and a deeper respect for the man who was responsible for all of it.

They left the farm country and turned into an area where the forest was dense with great spruce trees towering into the sky, interspersed with patches of silvery-white birch and lesser pines. The hills rose sharply here with great rocks wedged in among the trees, remnants of the last Ice Age, and they came to a place where a rugged cliff loomed above them, shutting out the sun. Max pulled off in a little cleared section beside the road.

Looking up at the cliff, he said almost as though speaking to himself, "In the old days the Vikings believed that if they died in bed they wouldn't reach Valhalla, so if one felt his end was near and he had not been fortunate enough to die in battle as a true Viking should, he would leap off a cliff such as this one." Then he turned to her abruptly. "I've thought of you constantly, Eve. Tormented thoughts. Do you ever think of me that way?"

She had known all along that she shouldn't have come with him. It was impossible for them to be together without the smoldering fires leaping into flame. She should have invented some excuse, any excuse. Women were always claiming to have headaches. Why hadn't she thought of it? Was it because she had wanted to come with him? She could feel the inner trembling begin that would soon spread to her whole body.

"Max, why are you doing this?" she said helplessly. "You know it can only end in agony and frustration for both of us."

"Sometimes the desire to be alone with you and hold you in my arms becomes so strong that I cannot bear it," he told her. "Even if that is all I can ever have, it is better than nothing. It gives me a little nourishment to go on. Oh, Eve—"

He drew her into his arms and looked down into her eyes, then gently traced the line of her nose, mouth, and chin with his forefinger. "I must memorize your face," he murmured, "for the days ahead when I will no longer see it."

Then she was sobbing and holding him, all restraints

87

momentarily lost. "Max, I can't bear it! I love you so—I need you—why does it have to be this way?"

"We met too late," he said angrily, stroking her hair, "and now I am trapped. I must be true to my heritage. I am like the Viking who jumped off the cliff—there are certain standards to which I must adhere, whatever the cost." He began to kiss her wet cheeks, her throat, her trembling lips. Gently his hand sought her body, which vibrated with instant, tumultuous response.

Why not? she thought wildly. Why not, whatever the cost? Wouldn't it be worth it to have a memory of love? Even a painful memory would be better than no memory at all. She had known when she came with him that this was what he wanted, that this was how it would end. Why had she come if she hadn't meant for it to happen? From the beginning she had known that it must happen.

"All right, Max," she whispered. "I can't fight it any longer."

"Not here," he said huskily, "not in the car like errant schoolchildren. We'll go into the forest where the moss is soft and the sunlight comes down through the trees as in a great cathedral—"

They got out of the car and hand in hand started along the trail that lead into the forest toward the great cliff. She felt light-headed, unreal, as though she were moving in a dream. Suddenly there was a shout of laughter, the sound of young voices, and around a curve in the trail came a group of teenagers dressed in blue jeans and sweaters—two boys and two girls. They were flushed and a bit grimy and in high spirits. One of the boys seemed to recognize Max.

"Good day, Herr Greve," he said. "We've been climbing the cliff. Great sport. Are you going to try it?" They all glanced curiously at Eve.

"No," replied Max. "No, I do not think so, Lars."

The group went on. Max turned to Eve, who was

standing at the side of the path gazing after the young people.

"I had forgotten that this is a favorite spot for hikers," he said.

"We have no place of our own," she said hopelessly. "No place to really be alone. This was madness, Max. As you pointed out, we aren't schoolchildren. We'd better go home."

He regarded her for a moment, but then, apparently sensing that for her at least the mood was irretrievably broken, he turned back to the car. . . .

Promptly at four that afternoon Froken Karlsson, a tiny, dried-up bird of a woman with stringy dark hair and a sharp beak of a nose and tightly compressed lips—perhaps from years of holding pins in her mouth—drove up to Lyckan in an old VW. She had Camilla's wedding dress with her, for she had been working on it at home. Eve went up to Camilla's room to watch while the seamstress tried on the dress, and Blenda joined them, her eyes wide with excitement and envy.

The dress had been cut and basted and now must be fitted to make sure it was ready for the final seams. It was a simple dress of white satin with long sleeves, a high neck, and a full skirt. The hem was not quite right and Froken Karlsson sat on the floor with the inevitable pins in her mouth making the necessary adjustments.

Eve tried to picture Camilla walking up the aisle to a waiting Max, but the thought was so painful she brushed it away. A bride, she thought, should go to her groom with eyes shining like stars, her heart filled with love and joy. And he should wait for her with pride, tenderness, and longing. There would be none of that for Camilla and Max and it was all so terribly wrong!

"Will you wear a long veil?" she asked Camilla.

Blenda answered before her sister had a chance.

"Oh, yes! It is beautiful! And the little gold crown. May I show her the crown, Camilla?"

"If you want to," Camilla said indifferently.

Blenda jumped off the bed and ran to Camilla's dresser. From the top drawer she took out a box and carried it over to Eve, then removed the lid to show a dainty golden crown resting on a bed of tissue paper.

"It isn't solid gold, of course," she explained, "but it is gold-plated and very expensive. Fru Grevinna gave it to Camilla. She wore it when she was married."

Eve picked up the dainty object and examined it with interest. "It's lovely!" she exclaimed. "Does it have a special meaning?"

Camilla looked at her with a faintly ironic smile. "The Crown Bride," she said. "Haven't you heard of that?"

"It sounds vaguely familiar, but I don't remember what I've read about it."

"It goes back a long way. In the olden days there was a special crown which the church kept locked up and loaned out to brides—if they qualified! They were really valuable gold crowns, sometimes with precious stones."

"Oh, I wish they still did that!" Blenda cried. "How I would like to wear one when I get married!"

"What did she have to do to qualify?" Eve asked.

"She had to be a virgin."

"Did they take her word for it?"

"No, of course not. She had to be examined by midwives."

Eve was shocked. "But that is barbaric!" she protested.

"Of course. That's why it was discontinued."

"What happened to her if she didn't pass?"

"Well, she couldn't wear the crown. I suppose it was quite a disgrace. Sometimes her fiancé wouldn't even go through with the wedding."

Froken Karlsson spoke up unexpectedly in her dry, thin voice. "It's a good thing they don't do that today, or nobody would ever get married."

Eve laughed. "Yes, I'm afraid virgins are rather an endangered species these days."

"I don't know why they go on imitating that old custom with these silly fake crowns," Froken Karlsson said scornfully. "It no longer means anything."

"I don't think the crowns are silly," Blenda protested. "I love them, and when I marry I shall be a virgin too, like in the old days!"

"Don't talk nonsense, Blenda," Camilla said sharply. "You don't even know what it means."

"I do too! Mama told me." She put the crown carefully back in the box and carried it over to the dresser.

Camilla turned away. Eve was not sure, but she thought she saw the glint of tears in the girl's eyes.

Chapter Seven

That evening Camilla attended a dinner with Max—some sort of an agricultural group, she explained to Eve—the *Lantmännens Förbund*. There would probably be a lot of dull speeches, she complained. It did not seem possible to Eve that anything would be dull if Max were there, but she didn't say so. After her own evening meal with the family, she decided to go for a walk.

It was a fine evening, a bit cool, but the sun shed its golden light over the river and forest and the air smelled of pine and spring. She followed a lane that led through a meadow sprinkled with buttercups and bluebells, then veered sharply down a hillside to a swinging bridge across the river. This was one of Eve's favorite places to walk. Above the bridge were numerous little islands, densely wooded, the great jagged rocks rose out of the rapids. She could hear the roar of the falls down below, but was not close enough to see them. She walked out to the middle of the bridge, liking the queer, shivery feel of it, and stopped to look down, as she always did, fascinated by the rush of dark, icy water. An excellent place to commit suicide, she thought grimly, and wondered if anyone had ever jumped from there.

On the opposite side of the river were buildings from the old days of the mill, some of which were now in disuse. This had once been the center of Romeby, with the big estate house overlooking the river, a hotel, and various shops in addition to the mills, but now the center had shifted to the new Centrum. While she stood there gazing into the rushing water, she felt the bridge quiver beneath her feet and looked up to see Kjell walking across it from the town side. He stopped when he reached her and gave her his attractive one-sided smile.

"Good evening, Eve. How nice to meet you here."

"Good evening. I didn't expect to see you—don't you live over at Ransäter near the Conservatory?"

"Yes, but I had an errand in town and decided to take a walk over here before going home. This place has a rather special meaning to me."

"It is beautiful here, but frightening, too. The rushing water is hypnotic. You can feel it pulling at you, making you want to jump in. I was wondering if there had been many suicides here."

"I wouldn't know. I've only lived here a few years. But I almost jumped off here myself once." He spoke so lightly that Eve thought he was joking until she saw the expression in his eyes.

"You, Kjell? I find that hard to believe. You seem such a happy, well-adjusted person."

"I have come to terms with life. When the worst thing that can happen to you does happen, then you know that nothing can ever hurt you again."

"Do you want to tell me about it, Kjell?" she asked softly.

"Yes, I think I would like to. It was when I lost my beloved wife, Dorli. We had just moved here and everything was going well—then suddenly she was ill and we were told that she had terminal cancer."

"Oh, Kjell! How terrible."

"I met Dorli in Vienna when I was studying music there many years ago. She was a student too, and hoped to play in light operas. I loved her the moment I saw her. Her parents were opposed to our marriage at first, because she was very young and I was a poor young nobody—and a foreigner at that. They soon had to give in, however, because—as Shakespeare so graphically put it—'clubs could not part us.'"

"Was she very beautiful?"

"Beautiful?" He said the word slowly as though it were somehow strange to him. "I don't think so. I never really thought about it. She was just—Dorli. She was sunshine and moonlight and laughter and magic. As a matter of fact, she looked rather like you, Eve. She had a mop of soft curly hair, dark blue eyes, and a wide mouth that seemed always to be laughing. She was a born comic. She was very clever at imitations. Such a dear, funny little girl—" His voice trailed off.

"I wish I had known her! Did you have any children?"

"No. I didn't care, I only wanted Dorli, but I think she grieved about it sometimes. We were very happy when I got the position here at the Conservatory—it is such a beautiful place. At that time we had been married for nineteen years."

93

"Did she ever go on the stage?"

"No, she gave up her ambitions when she married me. She would have been a marvelous comedienne. I tried to persuade her to resume her career, but she said she didn't want to. I know there is a great deal of cynicism now about marriage. People seem to feel that it kills romance and imposes too many restrictions—but that is nonsense. When two people really love each other, and are friends as well as lovers, marriage is wonderful."

"Oh, yes, that is what I believe, Kjell. That's why I don't think Max and Camilla should marry—they don't love each other. But Max doesn't believe in romantic love."

Kjell gave her a searching glance. "I think he does, really. I don't approve of that marriage either, but there isn't much we can do about it, is there?"

"I suppose not. Was it when your wife died that you almost jumped off this bridge?"

"Yes, the night after her funeral. She had suffered so and had been so brave—but there is no point in going into that." He stared down into the rushing dark water. "I can't tell you what I was feeling that night, but I think I was on the verge of madness."

"What stopped you from going through with it?" she asked a bit timidly.

"Dorli did. She was here—"

"You saw her?" Eve gasped.

"No, but she was here all the same. She stood beside me just as you are now and I heard her say, 'No, love, don't be so silly. Your work is important and it's only for a little while, then we'll be together again for always, I promise you.' So I went home. Oh, I know the psychologists would say I conjured her up out of my desperate need—but I know she was here."

"Has she ever come to you again?" She felt tears on

her cheeks and wiped them away with the back of her hand.

"Not like that, but she is always near like a guardian angel." He laughed softly. "Such a funny little angel! She could never be serious for long. I am so grateful for the years we had together—so much love, so much laughter—"

She put her hand on his. "Oh, Kjell, what can I say? Thank you for telling me all this."

He lifted her hand to his lips. "Thank you for listening. It helps sometimes to talk about it. Well, I must be off. I will see you soon at rehearsal. We must get you started on your dance."

Eve went home in a sad but curiously exalted mood. That night after everyone else was asleep, she sat by her window, arms folded on the sill, gazing out into the cool, dusky night. Although it was quite late it still did not seem really dark, and she remembered that in a few weeks would come the longest day of the year, when it would hardly be dark at all. She wondered what it would be like to go farther north to the land of the midnight sun. How strange it would be, she thought, to see the sun gleaming redly on the horizon at midnight.

She felt a strange excitement, as though all the ancient forces of her own Scandinavian heritage were coming to life within her, calling her to the forest, to the dancing and rejoicing, to the worship of the sun. She thought of Max, so much a part of this land, part of the mystic golden enchantment. A longing so intense it was like a pain swept through her. If he had appeared beneath her window at that moment and called to her, she would have gone without hesitation into his arms, off into the dark shadows of the forest. But of course he did not come and soon she began to tremble from the night's chill and went to seek the warmth and oblivion of her bed.

The following morning Eve decided to have another ride on Roskva. In spite of the near accident, she had enjoyed it and wanted to practice until she could ride without looking foolish. Besides, she wanted to see Marko again. Since there was no one else she could safely talk to, she had decided to find out from him just what was going on. If there really were some sort of a plot, she might be able to stop it before it ended in disaster.

It was cloudy and rather cold but she hoped to get her ride before it started to rain. Dressed in jeans and a warm pullover sweater, she biked to Rosenborg and went at once to the stable. As she had hoped, Marko was there alone, sitting in the stable yard polishing a saddle. He rose at once when he saw her and gave her a little bow.

"Good morning, Miss Tremaine. Have you come for another ride?" He always spoke English to her and seemed to have a good command of it.

"Good morning, Marko. Yes, I want to try again."

She followed him into the stable, and when he had led Roskva out of her stall, she said, "You dance very well, Marko. Do you enjoy that sort of thing?"

"Very much," he replied. "In Yugoslavia at the Lippizan farm there was an outdoor restaurant in the woods above the stables and during the tourist season there would be entertainment. They had an accordian player and a little dance group that wore native costumes and did folk dances. I joined that group, so it was not hard to learn the dances here."

"Well, you certainly do them better than most of the young people who were born here. Marko, if you aren't too busy, why don't you saddle a horse for yourself and ride with me for a little while. That way I won't get into trouble, and besides, there is something I want to talk to you about—privately."

He gave her a puzzled, wary look and hesitated for a

moment before he said, "Very well, Miss Tremaine. But only for a short time. I do have work that I must complete this morning."

While she watched him saddle the horses, Eve wondered wryly if he thought she was amusing herself by making a play for him. No doubt with his looks he had encountered a lot of that sort of thing from the tourists at the stud farm. Well, she would soon disillusion him on that score!

When the horses were ready, he helped her mount and they rode off along the road toward the forest.

"Do you think it's going to rain?" she asked.

He glanced at the sky. "Perhaps, but not right away."

He led the way along the edge of a pasture, through a patch of forest, and out into the open again onto a narrow road running close to the edge of the bluffs above the river. Down below she could see the logs floating along with an occasional jam in the shallow water near the shore. There were beaches of fine white sand, and across the river were scattered houses and thick stands of trees and meadows stretching up toward the distant line of the hills. It was a peaceful, lovely scene, but Eve's mind was too occupied with what she intended to say to Marko to enjoy it. She began to wonder if she were being wise to confide in him, but something had to be done. Perhaps he would deny everything, but at least he would have been warned. He walked his horse alongside hers and looked at her questioningly.

There was no easy way to broach the subject, so she said bluntly, "Marko, the other day I was out biking and I saw Mitra's car parked in the woods, so I followed the path and saw her talking to you in a shooting lodge."

He stared at her in consternation. "You spied on us?"

"I looked in the window. I'm sorry, Marko, but

97

I know that she is here to cause trouble for Camilla, so naturally I wondered what her connection was with you. It was obvious that you two are well acquainted."

His lips set in a straight, angry line. "Have you told anyone of this?"

"No, there wasn't anyone to tell—without causing a lot of trouble. I thought I should talk to you first and find out what it was all about. I might add that I've had a feeling from the beginning that there was something between you and Camilla. I couldn't help wondering if Mitra is paying you to make love to Camilla—in order to break up her engagement to Max. I have to know the truth, Marko, for Camilla's sake." She looked at him challengingly.

For a few minutes Marko rode in silence, staring straight ahead on the road, apparently trying to decide how to answer her accusation. Then he sighed deeply and said, "Yes, I have known Mitra for a long time. She is my cousin, and when her mother died my mother took Mitra to live with us. She was only six at the time. Her father was a performer in a little circus that came to town and then moved on. I don't think she even knew his name. She was always a beautiful child, but wild and hard to handle. When she was fifteen she ran off with some man from the city. But she kept in touch with us and would come home for a visit now and then. She became a singer, and eventually she married the wealthy Swede, Carsing."

"Was she responsible for your coming here?"

"Yes. A few months ago she visited me at the stud farm and told me that there was something she wanted me to do. She said if I would agree, she would buy me a farm of my own. Her husband had left her a lot of money. So I asked her what it was I must do, and she said the man she loved was going to marry some young girl he did not love and she wanted to prevent it. She
98

said she wanted me to make love to the girl. At the time it didn't seem such a terrible thing to do."

"If Camila really fell in love with you, didn't you realize how much she would be hurt to learn you had only done it for money?" Eve asked indignantly.

"I didn't expect her to really love me. I did not know Camilla then. I pictured her as a shallow, vain girl who wanted to marry the count for his money and position—a girl who might amuse herself on the side with an affair with a stable hand. I wanted the farm badly, and in Yugoslavia I could never get enough money to buy it on my own."

"How did you manage to get a job at Rosenborg?"

"That wasn't difficult. Mitra paid them to give me excellent references from the farm, and told me to come up here and apply for a job on the estate. She said that Herr Greve was always on the lookout for a man who was good with horses and she thought he would hire me. If he wouldn't, she was going to get me a job with the Carsings—her husband's people—but I was taken on at Rosenborg without any trouble."

"Then when Camilla came over to ride it was simple for you to get to know her."

"Yes—it was simple. But what I had not expected was that I would fall in love with her—or that I would enjoy my work on the estate so much or that Herr Greve planned to start a stud farm and make me manager."

"But if you were going to get one of your own—"

"I would much rather be a manager for Herr Greve than to be given a farm for doing a dirty job," he said bitterly.

They had come to a place where the river formed swirling rapids on either side of a little wooded island. Eve pulled up her horse.

"Let's stop here for a few minutes," she said. They dismounted and walked over to the edge of the cliff, where they could look down at the foaming water. "Just what were you supposed to do?" she asked.

"Mitra wanted me to get Camilla to come to my apartment, and eventually she would have a servant tip off to Herr Greve what was going on."

"What were you arguing about in the lodge?"

"Well, Mitra had come here to see how the affair was progressing, and she was angry when she found out that nothing had happened. I told her that I no longer wanted to go through with it and that in any event it was useless because although Camilla has admitted that she loves me, the only thing that really matters to her is saving her father. She is like a saint with a holy mission! She must marry Herr Greve, and she will not endanger that marriage by carrying on secretly with another man."

"So she has never been to your apartment?"

"Never. Only once did she let me take her in my arms and kiss her, and that was when she told me that she cared for me. But then she said that it must never happen again, that there was no hope for us."

"But you, Marko," Eve probed, "what do you really want of her now?"

"I would like to marry her, of course," he replied. Anger flamed suddenly in his dark eyes and he struck the palm of one hand with his other fist. "Damn it—it is all so wrong! She should not be marrying that man! Not that I do not admire him; he is a good man, but not for her. At heart she is a simple girl, a peasant, like me. We could be happy together—" He turned away.

Eve put her hand on his arm. "Oh, Marko, I'm sorry. I don't want her to marry him either. But what can we do about it?"

"Nothing. No one can do anything."

"You don't think you could persuade her to break her engagement and marry you instead? If she loves you—"

"It is impossible. She has that obsession about her father. You must have seen it. She thinks he will die unless she marries Herr Greve."

"Yes, I know. Sometimes I have the feeling her father is faking his decline to make her marry Max, but I can't be sure."

"I never thought of that," Marko said slowly, "but even if he were, no one could convince Camilla of it. No, it is hopeless. I think it will be better if I return to Yugoslavia."

"But what about Max's stud farm?"

"I cannot stay here and see her living at Rosenborg with Herr Greve, no matter how much I would like to have that position. I told Mitra that if I could win Camilla away from him I would take her away from here, but that I was sure that I could not succeed. She had to be satisfied with that."

"If you fail, do you think she will try anything more?"

He shrugged. "She is capable of any devilment. I was fond of her once when we were children, but she has changed, grown hard and mean. For one thing, she has taken to drinking a lot, which she never used to do. I would not trust her for a moment. Well, now you know the truth about me, Miss Tremaine. Do you feel that you should tell Camilla or Herr Greve?"

Eve regarded him with a worried frown. "I don't think that would do any good. Camilla would be hurt, and Max would probably fire you. If you are going to leave anyway, there is no point in it. The only thing—"

"Yes, Miss Tremaine?" he said when she hesitated.

"Well, I wonder. If Max knew that Camilla was in love with you, would he still want to marry her?"

He gave a short, angry laugh. "You forget that it is Camilla who is determined to marry him. The engagement has been formally announced, the banns are being read, and since Herr Greve believes that a

101

gentleman never goes back on his word, he will go through with it unless she should ask for her release—which she will never do—or be caught doing something to bring disgrace to the family, as Mitra wanted me to arrange. That might have worked if Camilla were not so determined to make a martyr of herself."

"Then I suppose you're right," she agreed sadly. "There is nothing to be done."

He looked at her curiously. "You have only been here a short time, Miss Tremaine," he said. "Why does it matter so much to you whom your cousin marries?"

She flushed and bit her lip. "I—I want her to be happy," she said lamely.

An expression of pity came into his eyes. "Can it be that you have fallen in love with him yourself?"

"No!" she cried. "He is arrogant and impossible and I—I—" She turned away to hide the tears that had filled her eyes.

He walked back toward their horses, and as he untied their reins from the branch of a tree, he said ironically, "I fear that we are both victims of the same fatal malady, Miss Tremaine."

They rode home in silence, urging the horses to a much faster pace than when they had gone out, and when they arrived at the stable Eve's cheeks were flushed by the wind, her curly hair disheveled. When Marko helped her to dismount he retained his grasp of her waist, and his dark eyes gazed probingly into hers.

"What a pity that we should both love such impossible people," he said. "Now if we could love each other—"

"But we don't!" She tried to pull away, but still he held her.

"You know how they fight a forest fire," he said, "by lighting smaller fires around the perimeter to contain it? We might do the same—" He leaned down and pressed his lips against hers, his arms tightening around

102

her waist. It was an angry, impersonal kiss, without tenderness, without even passion. She was too surprised to resist and remained passive in his arms. He released her so suddenly she nearly fell and she saw that he was staring over her shoulder. She turned around to meet the coldly furious gaze of Max, who was leading his stallion out of the stable.

"I see you are losing no time in taking advantage of the opportunities of my stables," he said in icy disdain.

"Max, I—"

"It is all my fault, Herr Greve," Marko began, but Max silenced him with one glance from his blazing golden eyes.

"Take care of the horses," he commanded. Marko caught up the reins of their mounts and started toward the stable without another word.

"Of course, it is none of my business how you conduct yourself," Max said to her in his haughtiest, most arrogant manner, "but if you must come here to amuse yourself with my stable hand, please do not do it on my time."

Anger began to replace her shock and dismay. What right did he have to condemn her, even if what he thought were true—a man who already had a fiancée and an ex-girl friend on the sidelines! Did he have to possess her too?

"You said he could give me riding lessons—" she began.

"Riding, yes, but that did not include other services!" He was very close now, his eyes burning her with their contempt. She gasped and struck him across the face with all her strength.

"I hate you!" she cried, her fury now matching his. "I wish I never had to see you again!"

He continued to hold her gaze for another moment, then he turned, mounted his horse, and galloped off without looking back.

103

Chapter Eight

That day was one of the most miserable Eve had ever spent. She wanted to pack up and leave Sweden forever, but that presented too many difficulties. She would have to explain why, and that was impossible. It was also impossible to stay and go on seeing Max. It started to rain shortly after noon, so she stayed in her room and brooded most of the afternoon, trying to decide what to do. The situation seemed to get more complicated every day. The sound of Martin's typewriter coming up through the grating began to get on her nerves, so finally she went downstairs. Camilla came home and the women went into the kitchen for coffee. Olivia turned to her daughter with a look of excitement.

"Fru Enqvist called me today," she said. "She is going to give a ball in a couple of weeks in honor of your coming wedding. You and Max will be the guests of honor."

"Oh?" Camilla looked mildly interested. "I suppose it will be formal. I really haven't anything suitable to wear."

"You must get something," her mother told her firmly. "You will need many evening gowns after you are married anyway, because of all the formal affairs Max has to go to. Your wardrobe is very inadequate, but you never seem to want to buy anything."

"I don't have enough money, Mama. Anyway, Max said I can get a new wardrobe in Paris before we go on down to Las Palmas."

"Max is very good to you. But you must have a new evening gown for the ball."

"Who is Fru Enqvist?" Eve asked.

"The wife of the superintendant of the mills," Camilla told her. "They live in that big estate house on the company grounds across the river. They are very important socially here, next to the von Stjernas."

"You are invited too, Eve," Olivia said.

"I didn't bring any formal clothes."

"You must both get new dresses. It will be a very important affair."

Camilla and Olivia went on chatting about the ball, but Eve drifted off into her own unhappy thoughts. She couldn't bear to face Max again, but how was she going to get out of it?

After a while Camilla said, "By the way, Eve, there's another rehearsal tonight. You'll have to start working on your number."

Eve stared at her blankly. "Tonight? Oh, Cam, I don't think I can go."

Camilla looked puzzled. "Why not? You aren't sick, are you? I must say, you do look a bit peaked."

"I have a bad headache," Eve said, grasping at any excuse that offered itself.

"That's too bad, but I have some pills that should fix you up. We won't stay very long. This is just for you and Marko and Max and me to practice our special number."

That was even worse! Max and Marko—the very thought made her head really begin to ache. "I don't think—" she began.

The telephone rang and Camilla went off to answer it. After a few minutes she came back and said, "That was Max. He wanted to make sure I remembered about the rehearsal, and he wants to speak to you Eve. I told him about your headache and that you might not come, and he said he wanted to speak to you."

Eve got up and went out to the hall. She was afraid to answer the call and afraid not to. She picked up the

105

receiver as gingerly as though it were a snake. "Hello?" she said feebly.

"Camilla tells me you might not come tonight."

"That's right. I have a headache—"

"Do not lie, Eve," he broke in coldly. "I know why you want to avoid seeing me. But the rehearsal is important and I insist that you come."

So, he insisted, did he! "And if I refuse—"

"Then I will come over and get you. Do you want to make a scene in front of your cousins?"

"You said some very horrible things to me—"

"Which you deserved. But we still have to keep up the pretense that nothing is wrong between us. Cannot we simply forget what happened? I know that Marko likes to make advances to pretty girls. If I am willing to overlook your indiscretion, you should not stay in your room sulking like a little girl."

The man was impossible. Simply impossible. She wanted to bang the receiver down, but she couldn't risk having him come over and drag her out as he had threatened. She answered as coldly and haughtily as she could.

"Very well, Max. I will come, although I think the whole idea of the special number is a mistake, and I wish I didn't have to be in it."

"Nonsense, Eve. You will do very well."

When she came back to the kitchen, Camilla gave her a questioning look.

"You and Max do not seem to get along well together," she said. "I am sorry—I had hoped you would be friends."

"Well, we do seem to irritate each other at times," Eve replied wryly, "but don't worry about it. We get along well enough."

"Of course he is used to having his own way, and he has a quick temper, but he is really a very nice person."

"I'm sure he is."

106

"Shall I get you the medicine for your headache?"

"Headache? Oh—never mind. I think I'll be all right."

By the time they had eaten supper the rain had stopped and the sun came out from behind the clouds, so they decided to walk over to Rosenborg.

"If it starts to rain again, Max can drive us home," Camilla said.

They found Marko alone at the barn, sitting outside on a bench smoking a cigarette. He got up and tossed it away when he saw them, and made his formal little bow.

"Good evening. Herr Greve is not here yet."

Camilla looked at him, her face smooth as a mask, her eyes blank. "Why don't we go in and go over the steps for Eve?" she suggested.

They went into the barn and switched on the overhead lights, for even with the sun partially out the old building was a gloomy place. On the musicians' platform there was a record player with a stack of records beside it. Camilla looked through them until she found the one she wanted.

"It is called a Värmlandspolska," she explained to Eve, "and was written by a man named Dahlgren who used to live in this area. It is the one always used by the Count von Stjerna at the Midsummer festival." She put the record on the turntable, pushed a switch, and gay, lilting music filled the big room. "We do what is called a Hambo Mazurka to it," she told Eve. "The first part is not much more than a fast walk. Watch our feet." She held out her hand to Marko and together they moved swiftly across the floor.

Eve watched and listened. A man was singing on the record, but she found it difficult to understand the words because it was in heavy Värmland dialect. It seemed to be something about a man who met a young girl on the road and immediately lost his heart to her.

107

"Å jänta, å jä—å jänta, å jä—"

Suddenly there was another voice joining in, and she felt herself caught from behind and whirled around to look into the glowing eyes of Herr Greve. He repeated the words for her in English.

"'And pretty as a light day she·was—I lost my heart then on the road!'"

She found herself moving with him across the barn floor behind Marko and Camilla.

"Now the second position," Max said. "Put your hands on my shoulders, Eve."

She did so a bit unwillingly and his arms encircled her waist. He showed her the step and again they were whirling around the floor.

"'My lass and I—my lass and I—and all on the Midsummer Wake—'"

They stopped finally and Eve stood panting, flushed, and inexplicably happy. Marko and Camilla barely glanced at each other, then moved quickly apart. Max continued to stand with his arms around her waist.

"It is a very touching little song," he said. "It goes on about how he steals a kiss, then they go to the church and are wed, and 'Never ever will we part, my little wife and I, until death comes down our road—'"

A stillness seemed to come over the room as the record ended and Max's words hung in the air. Then Eve moved away from him to stand beside Marko.

"I think," she said softly, "we had better try it again with the right partners."

Friday was Camilla's last day at the bank. The Enqvists' ball was to take place on Saturday of the following week, so something had to be done about getting the proper gowns to wear. Camilla went out with Max for a while that evening to celebrate quitting her job, and when she came home she knocked on the door of Eve's room, then came in looking rather excited.

"Max has to be in Stockholm on Monday," she said. "He has a business appointment and there is a banquet he has to attend, so he suggested that we go with him to buy our gowns and do a little sight-seeing. What do you think, Eve?"

Eve was doubtful. "Would he drive?"

"Yes, so you could see a bit of the country on the way. We can stay at his apartment. His parents had one and he kept it to stay in when he goes to Stockholm, which is quite often. I have never seen it. Mama would never permit me to go to Stockholm with him alone, but it would be all right if we both go. I think it would be a lot of fun, don't you?"

It didn't sound like a good idea to Eve at all. Not that she wasn't eager to see Stockholm, but to be cooped up in an apartment with Max . . .

"You know that Max and I don't get along very well," she pointed out.

"But we won't be seeing very much of him," Camilla said, "and it's a wonderful chance for you to see Stockholm. I have a girl friend who got married and moved to Spånga and I'm dying to see her again. Besides, we can get much nicer gowns there than here in Romeby. Please say you will go!"

Camilla looked so eager that Eve didn't have the heart to refuse. She agreed reluctantly, knowing that the more time she spent with Max, the more difficult the situation would become. At least Camilla looked happier than she had for some time.

Since Max had an appointment for Monday, they decided to leave early Sunday morning and take a leisurely drive along the most scenic route between Romeby and Stockholm. They could do their shopping on Monday, and on Tuesday Camilla could visit her

109

friend in Spånga. Max had to attend a banquet on Tuesday night, and they would return home Wednesday.

Saturday Eve packed the smaller of the two bags she had brought with the clothes she thought she would need for the short trip, and on Sunday morning, after Olivia had served them a big breakfast, Max drove up the lane in the Mercedes-Benz. He looked very cheerful and exceedingly handsome in casual slacks and a pullover sweater. It was a perfect spring morning and Eve couldn't help feeling excited and happy as they drove off. Perhaps, Eve reflected, they could shut out all thoughts of the future and simply enjoy themselves in the present.

"We will not be in any hurry," Max said as he turned onto the highway. "We can stop anywhere you like along the way. Do you have a camera, Eve?"

"Yes, my father loaned me his thirty-five-millimeter slide camera," she told him. "He wants me to bring back lots of slides, and of course Mother wants pictures of Romeby. I've already taken quite a few of Lyckan and the river. How far is it to Stockholm?"

"In your miles about two hundred forty, I think. We'll be there this afternoon in good time."

"Are there any particularly scenic places along the way?"

"All of Sweden is scenic, if it comes to that," Max assured her. "We will go through Karlstad. Then I think I will take E-18. It goes above the big lake Hjälmaren as well as Malaren, and we should reach Örebro about the right time for a lunch stop. There is a magnificent castle there going back to the sixteenth century that I think you would enjoy seeing."

"I do have a weakness for castles," Eve admitted. "Does it have a moat?"

"Yes. It is practically an island, surrounded by water. Its architecture is not like that of the English castles, you understand—there are no battlements—but it is impressive all the same."

They didn't stop in Karlstad, but Max told Eve a bit about it as they drove through and across a bridge to the highway. It was the capital of Värmland and quite a bustling, rapidly growing city with many parks and statues and impressive buildings.

"Back in the Middle Ages," he told her, "it was known as Tingvalla. The original town was on an island, actually, where two arms of the river join before merging with Lake Vänern. From time immemorial the people of Värmland have met here to hold their ceremonies, arms inspections, fairs, and so on. Now the city has grown so big it has spread out over the mainland."

Max was a good driver, quick of reflex, steady of hand and eye.

At first Eve had had the back seat to herself, but later Camilla had insisted that she ride up front with Max so that it would be easier for him to tell her about the things they were passing. She was very conscious of his nearness, the scent of his shaving lotion, the quick flash of his eyes when he glanced down at her. His personal aura enveloped her as it always did when he was near. It was hard not to think about the times he had held her, the feel of his lips on hers. Her whole body tingled with excitement and she could almost imagine that Camilla was not there and that they were going away alone together for a few enchanted days.

"Was there much trouble when you switched from left-hand to right-hand driving?" she asked, determined to keep her mind on mundane things and not let it wander to the forbidden.

"Not as much as you might think," he told her. "There were some accidents and a bit of confusion at first, but we adjusted quite well."

111

"I hate to think what would happen if we Americans had to switch to the left!" she said.

They made such good time that it was only a little after eleven when they reached Örebro. They decided to stop anyway and stretch their legs by walking around the castle before having lunch. Max drove to a parking place close to the castle and Eve caught her breath with delight at the sight of the massive old building. It was built in a rectangle with an inner courtyard and had a great round tower on each of the four corners. The tops of the towers were shaped something like helmets, Eve thought, with a spire in the center. It was built of grayish-brown stone and was surrounded by wide bodies of water with bridges over to it in the front and on one side. It had a rather Germanic appearance.

They spent about half an hour exploring, then Max took them to a little café with some tables outside under the spreading trees, where they ordered coffee and open-faced sandwiches. While they waited for their food, Eve gazed up at the ancient castle walls.

"It's so lovely here," she said wistfully. "I'm really going to miss Sweden when I go back to Chicago!" That was true, she realized. In spite of the turmoil and unhappiness she had felt since coming to Sweden, in spite of her frequent urges to pack up and flee for home, the country itself had taken a firm grip on her emotions, and her heart ached at the thought that she might never see it again. It was in her blood, in the depths of her being, the feeling that her roots were here, that this was where she belonged and should stay forever. Even the language seemed familiar now, as though she had been born speaking it. Max, however, always spoke to her in English for some reason. He spoke it fluently with a charming accent, and she loved to hear him.

After they had eaten, they drove on above Hjälmaren to go north of the great Lake Malaren.

"It is a bit longer this way," Max said, "but I wanted to show you the Viking mounds—the Anund-högarna—at Västerås."

They were about 110 kilometers from Örebro, and Eve was fascinated by the great mounds, as well as by the ship graves, made by placing stones on the ground to form the outlines of a Viking ship. Sometimes, Eve knew, the Viking chieftans had been buried in their ships, others in wooden burial chambers inside the mounds.

"Do you think these mounds are haunted?" she asked Max, half in jest, half in earnest.

"Perhaps." He regarded her with a teasing light in his tawny eyes.

There was a huge rune stone at the side, and Max took a picture with Eve's camera of the girls standing beside it.

"I wonder what it says?" Eve gazed up at it dreamily.

"Oh, they are not nearly as exciting as they look," Max told her. "Actually they are rather dull, factual accounts of the men in whose honor they were raised."

They drove on, but Eve continued to question Max about Viking remains in Sweden. He told her about the even older things, Bronze and Stone Age sites: the great rock piles under which the Stone Age people buried their dead, of the "King's Grave" near Kivik with its Egyptian-like hieroglyphics, built about the same time as the pyramids, and other fascinating discoveries. They became so engrossed in their discussion of ancient places and objects that they forgot all about Camilla in the back seat. When Eve finally glanced back, she saw that her cousin was asleep.

"Poor Cam," she said, "we've put her to sleep."

"She is tired, poor girl," Max said. "She works hard and she has been under a lot of tension lately."

"I guess we all have." She looked up at him with a whimsical smile. "At least we're not fighting today."

His hand went reminiscently to his cheek. "No, you have not wounded me for some time now. You must be mellowing!"

Eve flushed. "Well, so are you, then. You haven't said anything to infuriate me."

He reached out and touched her hand. "We fight because when the charge builds up between us we either have to fight or make love," he said softly. "Since we can't do the latter, it has to be the former. You know that."

She glanced back uneasily at Camilla, who was still sleeping peacefully.

"You shouldn't say such things," she murmured.

"But it is true. What a pity that things must be as they are." He drove on in silence and there was nothing she dared reply.

They arrived on the outskirts of Stockholm about three that afternoon. Since their route brought them in from the north through the suburb of Spånga, Camilla insisted that Max stop at a telephone kiosk so that she could call her friend, although he told her she could just as well call from the apartment. She came back to the car looking pleased and said that her friend, Anna-Lisa was anxious to see her, and she was invited to spend Tuesday with her. "You are invited, too, Eve," she said, "if you want to come."

Before Eve could reply, Max said, "I am sure your girlish reminiscences would be a bore to her. She should not waste the little time she has here in such a manner. I will take her sightseeing on Tuesday."

"Then that's settled," Camilla said carelessly.

"But I don't like to bother you—" Eve began to remonstrate, but Max cut her short.

"It is no bother. My business will be taken care of on Monday, and I am free Tuesday until the banquet in the

114

evening. I would enjoy showing you something of Stockholm."

They drove on into the city, taking Sveavägen part of the way, past the Central Station, then cutting through side streets to the bridge leading over to the Old City. Eve was inexpressibly thrilled by it all. There it lay—the magic city—glimmering in its archipelago. She had not realized there would be so much water or so many hills and trees.

"It's so beautiful," she said with a sigh, "and, compared to the cities at home, so very old."

"It has been our capital since the thirteenth century," Max told her, "but it is changing too rapidly now for my taste. In the downtown area they are constantly tearing down the old buildings and putting up new ones of steel and glass. They are attractive in their way, but I do not approve of the destruction of the old ones. My father felt the same way. That is why he chose an apartment in the Old City, and why I have kept it instead of getting something more modern. At least there we are trying to retain the flavor of the past."

As they drove across the bridge Eve could see the tower of the famous Town Hall with its glittering spire, built on the very edge of the water with steps leading down to it, suggestive of the lagoon in Venice. The harbor was filled with ships of all sizes and descriptions and the traffic in the city was as bad as that in Chicago. Max, however, worked his way skillfully through it.

"My apartment is on Skeppsbron," he told her, "near the Royal Palace. My father selected it for the view of the harbor."

He pulled up in front of an imposing stone building. It must have been very elegant at one time, Eve thought, and still was, although it was beginning to show its age. There was a uniformed doorman, who saluted them smartly, and a large lobby with a marble

115

floor, numerous potted palms, and big leather chairs. It looked more like a hotel than an apartment house to her. Beyond open French doors she saw a dining room that extended onto a stone terrace facing a charming little garden.

The man behind the desk came out and bowed to them, and after a flurry of finger snapping managed to summon an elderly bellboy to carry up their bags. The elevator was an open cage affair that rose so slowly and reluctantly that Eve almost despaired of its ever reaching its destination. Max's apartment was on the third floor.

"I usually walk up," he told them with a grimace. "You can see why."

His apartment had a large living room facing the bay, two bedrooms, a bath, and a tiny kitchenette that was really no more than an alcove hidden behind an ornate Chinese screen. The living room was spacious, high ceilinged, with a marble fireplace and a number of comfortable chairs and sofas. The large bedroom had twin beds and a balcony overlooking the garden. When Eve went out on it and looked down she could see a few spring flowers in bloom around a little fountain. The castle walls loomed only a short distance away. The other bedroom was tiny and had only a single bed.

"It was really supposed to be a dressing room," Max explained, "but when I was a child and my parents brought me to town with them, I slept there."

The bathroom was large and old-fashioned with a big tub and a marble sink. Eve was enchanted with the apartment and went around examining everything with great interest. Camilla, on the other hand, seemed a bit puzzled.

"It is more like a hotel suite than an apartment, isn't it, Max?" she said.

"Well, this is a residential hotel," he replied. "The people who stay here are either elderly retired couples
116

who do not care to do their own cooking or people like me who use them when they come to town."

"Where do you have your meals?"

"There is a good dining room downstairs, or, of course, one can go out."

"I think it's a fascinating place," Eve said, thinking how wonderful it would be to live in such luxury, free from all household drudgery. She had never been particularly domestic. It had always seemed to her that there were many more interesting things to do than keep house. Somehow she felt more at home in this apartment than she had ever felt before in a strange place. It seemed to reach out and embrace her, whispering, "Welcome home, Eve!" For a moment she met Max's intent gaze, and his eyes seemed to be saying the same thing.

Chapter Nine

They rested for a while and then drove over to Skansen. Eve loved the big park, which seemed to be a sort of combination outdoor museum, zoo, and amusement park. They had dinner on the terrace of a beautiful restaurant overlooking a small lake where swans glided by, and later they sat on a bench under the trees and listened to a Straus concert played by a group from the Stockholm symphony orchestra.

Eve gave an involuntary sigh of delight when the strains of "The Waltz Dream" filled the evening air. "That's Oscar Straus, isn't it?" she asked Max. "It's one of my favorites. Those old waltzes make me feel—oh, it's hard to describe: happy and sad and full

117

of a poignant longing for something that probably doesn't even exist."

Max gave her a long, thoughtful look. "They affect me the same way," he admitted.

So! Eve thought. And this from the man who claimed he didn't believe in romantic love!

Eve lay awake for a long time that night in the bed next to Camilla's. Her cousin slept peacefully, but Eve tossed and turned, too stimulated to sleep. For some reason "The Waltz Dream" kept running through her mind and she was achingly aware of Max sleeping in the little room next to theirs. Was he sleeping or was he lying awake, too? If so, what was he thinking about?

She could hear the traffic of the city through the open window: the Old City with all its ghosts of the far past. Big, massive buildings, narrow, cobbled streets, ancient churches, and the castle with all its treasures. She was eager to go out and explore it. Finally she dropped off into a restless, dreamfilled slumber.

They rose early the next morning and had breakfast on the terrace of the apartment building, where audacious sparrows came and practically walked into their plates looking for crumbs. Max looked very elegant that morning, Eve thought, in a dove-gray flannel suit with a vest, a blue and silver tie, and his sometimes unruly hair carefully parted and combed.

"You must be going to the castle to see the king," Eve teased.

"No, that will not be until tomorrow night. This morning I have an appointment with the Jordbruksminister—what you would call the Minister of Agriculture."

"Really?" Eve was impressed.

"The government is interested in our grain experiments," he told her, and went on to explain a bit more about it.

118

When they started into town, Camilla said, "You might take us to NK, Max. That's where I usually buy clothes when we come here."

"Not today," Max replied. "I am turning you over to my mother's designer, Madame Sophie. I am sure she will have something suitable for the ball."

"But, Max, I can't afford her," Camilla protested.

"This is a gift—for both of you."

"I couldn't accept a gown from you," Eve told him stiffly. "It's very kind of you, but, no."

He knit his brows and replied coldly, "It is not kindness, I assure you. It is simply that it is necessary for you to be properly attired. Americans seem to have no sense of style. Older women tourists wear slacks on the streets—and you go around most of the time in those atrocious jeans—"

"I wasn't planning on wearing them to the ball!" Eve said furiously.

"I daresay not. But you will both be dressed by Madame Sophie for the occasion. I wish to hear no more about it." When he put on that lord-of-the-manor expression, Eve knew that it was futile to argue with him.

He let them off in front of an exclusive-looking little shop on a side street not far from the Opera House.

"Have them put it on Mother's account," he told Camilla. "I do not know when I will be back at the apartment, but I am sure you girls can amuse yourselves in town today. I will take you to dinner this evening."

"All right, Max. Thank you." Camilla kissed his cheek and he drove off.

The girls looked at the shop, which had one exquisite gown in the window. "I'm almost afraid to go in," Camilla admitted wryly.

Eve took her arm. "As Max's wife you must get used to such things," she said firmly. "Just act as though you

119

know what you're doing and no one will know that you don't. At least that's always been my system."

They went in and found themselves in a small reception room with velvet hangings, a big vase of roses on a desk, and no dresses in sight. A young woman came up to them.

"May I help you?" She was very chic, with careful makeup, blond hair in a high, intricate hairdo, and a black dress. She looked the girls over with a slightly dubious expression.

Since Camilla hesitated, Eve replied in careful Swedish, "We want to look at evening gowns. We were sent here by the Countess von Stjerna. This is the count's fiancée." That ought to do it, she thought, and it did! The young woman's attitude changed immediately from faintly supercilious to deferential.

"Oh, but of course! Come this way, if you please. Madame Sophie will be right with you."

They followed her into another room that was somewhat larger and had a number of velvet-covered chairs, a low table, and mirrored walls. They sat down and a maid brought in a tray of coffee, little cakes, and a box of cigarettes. Eve winked encouragingly at Camilla, who still looked uneasy. Very soon a woman came in wearing a professional, welcoming smile. She was tall and rather heavy, although well corseted, with carefully coiffured mauve hair, blue eye shadow, and rather full lips painted a bright red. She too wore a plain black dress with a string of pearls around her rather thick neck. She was probably Russian, Eve thought.

"Good morning, young ladies." She spoke Swedish with a heavy accent. "Do I understand correctly that you are the fiancée of Count von Stjerna?" For some reason she looked at Eve.

Camilla lifted her head and for the first time assumed an air of authority. "I am his fiancée," she stated

120

firmly. "I am Camilla Trilling and this is my American cousin, Eve Tremaine. We need gowns for a ball that will be held soon."

"Wonderful! I am sure that we can please you." She clapped her hands and a young woman came in wearing a flowing violet chiffon. There were two models, both very thin—one blond, with long, flowing hair, the other brunette, with a short curly hairdo. They seemed to be adept at quick changes, because they took turns walking in and out with various gowns. Most of them had full overblouses and many had matching shawls.

"What do you think of them, Eve?" Camilla asked her in English, perhaps hoping that Madame Sophie would not understand.

"They are very chic, and almost any of them would look good on you, but they are designed for tall Swedes. I'm afraid they wouldn't look right on me."

Madame Sophie gave Eve's slight figure a rather disparaging glance and said, also in English, which she spoke with as heavy an accent as she did Swedish: "Perhaps we can find something designed a bit differently for you, Miss Tremaine." Then she turned her full attention to Camilla, who, after all, was the one who mattered.

Camilla was rather taken by one in a lovely shade of blue, the exact color of her eyes, with a matching fringed shawl embroidered with gayly colored butterflies. When she tried it on, it fit quite well, only needing a few minor alterations.

"We can take care of them today," Madame Sophie assured her, "and have it at your hotel by tomorrow morning."

"Do you like this one, Eve?" Camilla asked, preening a bit before the big mirrors.

"Yes, dear, it's lovely on you. You're tall enough to wear that style," Eve assured her.

121

When Camilla went back to the dressing room to remove the gown, Madame Sophie turned to Eve.

"Is there any particular style you have in mind?" she inquired.

Eve poured some coffee and thought about it. "Something quite simple, I think," she said. "Fitted instead of having a loose overblouse. I'm too short for that style, popular though it may be. Do you have anything like that?"

Madam Sophie hesitated. "I might have. Let me see." She went out and Eve heard her voice in a back room speaking to someone in what sounded like Russian.

Camilla came back looking radiant. "It's such a lovely dress!" she exclaimed. "I've never had anything as nice as that. I hope Max will approve."

"Oh, I'm sure he will. You look stunning in it," Eve assured her.

Finally Madame Sophie came in carrying a gown over her arm. "We just happen to have this one," she said, "that was especially designed for an English girl who was visiting the Embassy last winter. A small girl, like yourself. She was to attend a reception at the Royal Castle, but got sick and was flown home, leaving us with the gown." She held it up. "It is too small for any of my models, but you could try it on, if it is what you have in mind."

Eve's eyes lighted up at the sight of it. It was a darling dress, she thought: honey colored chiffon with a fitted bodice, narrow, rhinestone straps, and a full swirling skirt. It would look wonderful with her hair.

"I'd like to try it on," she agreed.

When she came out of the fitting room, Camilla clasped her hands and exclaimed, "Oh, Eve, it's perfect! You look like a little doll!"

Eve whirled before the big mirrors, regarding herself with delight. She looked so feminine—entirely differ-

122

ent from the casual, little-boy look she usually affected. Perhaps Max had a point about those blue jeans!

"How much is it?" she asked.

Madame Sophie looked offended. That was a question her clients never asked openly. In her shop it was rather a matter of "If you have to ask, you can't afford it." She named a price in an impersonal tone.

Eve frowned, making rapid mental calculations. "That's a little more than I expected," she said ruefully. "Do you think you could come down a little? After all, you probably won't find another buyer for it, and it's a last year's model."

"But, Eve," Camilla broke in. "Max said—"

"Never mind that," Eve told her. "I couldn't accept such an expensive gift from him." She turned to Madame Sophie. "I'll give you a thousand kroner for it," she offered.

Madame Sophie stared at her. Eve could almost see the battle going on in her mind. After all, she was stuck with the gown. And, after all, the Countess von Stjerna was one of her most important customers. Perhaps it would be worth taking a loss to do her a favor.

"Very well," Madame Sophie said resignedly. "You may have it for that."

It took almost all the travelers checks Eve had with her to pay for the gown—money that she had planned to spend on a tour of Sweden—but it had to be done. She could not accept the gown as a gift from Max.

"Max will not be pleased when he finds out you paid for it yourself," Camilla told her as they left the shop.

"That's his problem," Eve replied shortly. She would not be bullied by the man.

"Let's go over to NK now," Camilla suggested. "There are a lot of things I need, and that is my favorite store."

The girls spent a happy morning wandering through

123

the main shopping center of Stockholm, and Eve picked up a number of gifts to take home to her family.

They had lunch in a busy restaurant and returned to the apartment by bus in the late afternoon, where they stretched out on their beds to rest their weary feet. Max arrived an hour or so later and they went down to the terrace for coffee.

"How did it go?" he inquired. "Did you get your gowns?"

"Oh, yes!" Camilla exclaimed. "They are really beautiful. Eve was wonderful! She actually talked Madame Sophie into lowering her price on the one she wanted."

Max looked at Eve in angry astonishment. "I told you I did not care what you paid for them—" he began.

"And I told you that I would pay for it myself," she interrupted. "Don't worry, you won't be ashamed of me. It is a lovely gown."

He stared at her crossly for another moment, and then his lips twitched in a smile. "You are a stubborn young woman," he said.

The following morning Camilla was eager to be off to visit her friend in Spånga. "I can take a bus," she told Max. "You don't have to bother driving me."

"How late do you plan on staying?" he asked. "You know that I have to attend a banquet."

"That's all right. I can get home by myself." She looked at Eve. "Are you sure you don't mind being alone this evening? I'll probably stay there for dinner."

"I don't mind at all," Eve assured her. "I'll eat here in the dining room. Stay as late as you like."

When she was gone Max said, "Is there anything in particular you would like to see?"

"Everything! But I'll leave that up to you."

"Perhaps we could start by driving to Millesgården.

Have you ever heard of Carl Milles, our famous sculptor?"

"Yes. Don't you have something of his at Rosenborg?"

"Yes, the statue at the end of the reflection pond is his. At Millesgården you will see his home and gardens as well as a superb collection of his works and others, including a Greek and German classical collection. If you are interested in sculpture it is well worth a visit."

"I don't know anything about sculpture, but I enjoy looking at it. I'd love to go there, Max."

It was a beautiful, sunny day with a brisk wind off the sea. They drove through the city across the Lidingöbron to the large island where the park was located on rocky cliffs just across the water from Stockholm. The entrance to the gardens from Carl Milles Väg was through a marble portal.

Inside was a delightful little courtyard and Max pointed out a charming bronze fountain called *The Little Naiad*. She read the inscription and translated it aloud: " '—I help you to forget how gloomy life can be.' Oh, Max, how lovely!"

He smiled at her and took her hand. Together they wandered through the extensive grounds and buildings. Perched as it was on the cliffs above the sea, there was a magnificent view of the city from there. The slopes had been transformed into an exquisite flower garden with dark junipers contrasting with the gayer colors. Many long flights of steps led to the various levels.

Eve was entranced by Milles's work; it seemed somehow part of a different, exotic world of the imagination, peopled by naiads, mermaids, gods, centaurs, and strange-looking humans. The gigantic statues seeming to ignore the laws of gravity soared upward toward the blue heavens. All the statues appeared to be frozen in a moment of violent activity—as though at

125

any moment they would again take flight or resume their interrupted dances. The whole place had an atmosphere of Nordic dreaminess and fantasy that made her dizzy with delight and what was almost fear.

She tried to explain some of what she was feeling to Max, and he nodded in understanding.

"Yes, there is no place in the world like it, if you have the soul to see and to feel something of what Milles was trying to express."

He took her to a spot on the eastern wall of the lower terrace and read her the words cut there in stone.

"From foreign lands come home to Lidingö
To sun and flowers—
To song of birds and summer nights—
To pine and birch and juniper and ash—
To waves of Värtan mirroring the moon—"

It was so beautiful that tears came into her eyes. "This is the soul of Sweden!" she whispered. "I can feel it around me with its awesome force—all the past terrors and beauty—"

He put his hands on her shoulders and turned her to face him. He seemed to be deeply moved. "Eve," he said. "Oh, Eve—"

A party of chattering tourists came along and the spell was broken. What would it be like, Eve wondered, to be alone in this place at twilight, the most dangerous time of day? To be there with Max, lost in enchantment . . .

He took her arm and they walked on, but she sensed that something had changed between them. They seemed to have taken a step beyond the stage of angry flirtation they had been engaged in up to now.

After they left the island, he took her to see the warship *Wasa*, which had been salvaged from the sea and set up as an exhibit. Built in 1625, she must have

126

been a magnificent sight with her great sails and strange, fierce carvings, but instead of sailing grandly out to sea, she had foundered and sunk into the ooze of Stockholm harbor. It had been a formidable task to get her up and restore her to some semblance of her former appearance, but it had been done.

Eve was particularly interested in the museum of relics salvaged from the warship. The exhibit that touched her most was one that showed the clothes of one of the seamen that had been taken from his mud-filled sea chest and carefully cleaned and pre-served. They were worn and shabby and spoke elo-quently of a difficult struggle for existence.

"Look, Max," she said. "See the patches on those trousers? They were sewn on with such neat, careful stitches! Perhaps he was just a young boy, leaving home for the first time, and his mother prepared his clothes for the great journey with loving care. How proud she must have been that he had been chosen to sail on such a fine, new ship! She must have wanted him to look his best in spite of his shabby old clothes. But I think she was frightened, too, thinking of the dangers he would encounter. I can almost see her, sitting by a window sewing her son's clothes with mingled fear and pride. Just think what she must have felt when she heard that the ship had gone down with all hands! Or perhaps it was a young wife—"

For a curious moment she felt very close to that woman, whoever she might have been, and to all women down through the ages who had sat and sewn and hoped while their men dreamed of glory and adventure.

Again Max looked at her with that new expression in his eyes. "Do you know," he said, "I have seen this exhibit several times, but I never noticed those patches, or thought about them if I did. Being with you is like going into a new world, seeing familiar things in a new

127

light, feeling things I have been too busy or distracted to feel before."

They drove back to the Old City and had lunch in a little garden café surrounded by a high brick wall covered with vines, with trees sheltering them from the sun, and a fine display of tulips bordering an old stone fountain. There were not many people there, for it was well past the usual lunch hour, and they sat in a secluded corner where the sound of falling water shut them off from the surrounding noises of the city. Max seemed to be in a pensive mood; he ate little and did not talk much. Finally he pushed aside his plate, lit one of his thin, aromatic cigars, and turned his compelling golden gaze on Eve.

"I have known Camilla all her life," he said abruptly, "and I have always been fond of her. She is an intelligent, warmhearted girl, and I thought she would make me an excellent wife. It has taken this intimate little time together to show me how incompatible we really are—and what I will be missing when I marry her."

Eve started to speak, but he silenced her with a gesture. "Please hear me out, Eve. There are some things I must say to you. Camilla is a very domestic girl. I daresay she can learn to lead the sort of life she will have to as my wife, but I am not sure that she will ever really enjoy it. Actually she should marry some worthy young man who will give her a nice little house or an apartment to keep. As my wife she will have to learn how to dress and talk to important people and attend governmental affairs. She will have to take over the running of Rosenborg, because my Mother is growing old and no longer feels up to it. That is one reason she was so anxious that I get married. You were right when you said that my engagement to Camilla was wrong. I suppose you could see it more objectively."

128

"I only thought you shouldn't marry without love," she broke in. "I didn't know about all the rest—"

"Love!" He grimaced as from a sudden pain. "I thought because of my infatuation for Mitra that love was a delusion, but knowing you I see how wrong I was—"

"Max," she said, her eyes intent on his face, "I think while we are having things out, you might tell me a bit more about Mitra. Were you really in love with her and did your mother break it up? Do you still care for her?"

"*Herre Gud,* no, Eve! I met Mitra at a susceptible age, I suppose—when I was ready for romance. She was the most beautiful and glamorous woman I had ever known and I thought I was in love with her. I thought she loved me. I wanted to marry her, but when I discussed it with Mother she told me that she felt it was only an infatuation and that Mitra would be totally unsuitable as a wife—although she didn't expect me to see that in the state I was in at the moment. She asked me to wait a year, and said that if at the end of that time Mitra and I still wished to marry, she would withdraw her objections. It seemed a reasonable request to me, so I agreed to wait."

"How did Mitra react to that?"

He shrugged. "She did not like it, but there was nothing she could do about it."

"And by the time the year was up, you no longer wanted to marry her?"

"It did not take that long—only a few months. Mitra and I had nothing in common, and I soon tired of her tantrums, her jealous rages over nothing."

"Was she angry when you broke off with her?"

"Actually I did not have to. While I was trying to find a tactful way to do it, she solved the problem by going off on a cruise with a handsome young actor for whom she had developed an infatuation. I was delighted, I assure you."

Eve was astonished. "Camilla told me your mother broke up your romance."

"I have never discussed the situation with Camilla. I suppose that is what she thought happened."

"But, Max—then I don't understand why Mitra is here now, trying to break off your engagement to Camilla. It doesn't make sense."

"No, it doesn't. I do not like to say this, but I am afraid she is slightly deranged. Perhaps she is drinking too much or on drugs—I do not know. But she has somehow convinced herself that we are still in love and that it is she I really wish to marry."

"Is she still at the hotel?"

"No, she moved in with her late husband's relatives, who live across the river from us."

"Are you worried about what she might do?"

"Not really. What could she do? I will take precautions to see that she is kept away from our wedding."

"Then you still intend to marry Cam, even knowing how incompatible you are?" she demanded.

"That is what I was trying to explain to you, Eve," he said, "to plead for your understanding. With you I have caught a glimpse of what love could be—'the singing and the gold—,' but it is too late. I have promised to marry Camilla and I cannot go back on my word."

"But if Camilla doesn't want to marry you, either—" Eve broke in furiously.

"But she does. Have you forgotten Martin? She is convinced that it is the only way to save him, and she would never give me my freedom. And I in turn cannot break my word to her. Please try to understand."

"Well, I can't!" She was angry now. "You and Camilla are just being martyrs for no good reason. Martin is faking his illness—I'm sure of it. It's no better than blackmail!".

"No, Eve, I am sure he is not faking. It may be psychosomatic, but to him it is real."

"But, Max, I asked him outright if he believed that the old curse was killing him, and he said it was nonsense and that all of you were too civilized to believe in anything like that."

"Of course he would say that. The belief is deeply buried in his subconscious, but it could kill him all the same."

All the old frustration and anger boiled up in her again. What was the use of talking? No one would listen to her. She tried a different approach. "Martin said it was your mother's suggestion that you marry Camilla. Is that true? How did you become engaged, anyway?"

He frowned, trying to remember. "No, it was not Mother's idea," he replied slowly. "She often discussed marriage, but had no one specific in mind. Actually I think it was Martin who started it. Not long after he retired because of his health, he made some apparently half-joking remark to Camilla about the curse starting to work on him, and he supposed he was doomed— unless, of course, she could fulfill the prophecy and marry me. They laughed about it at first, but then he began to fail, and he made a few more references to it until finally she came to me in tears and told me what he had been saying."

"You see!" Eve cried triumphantly. "It was all his doing—he didn't tell me the truth."

"He probably forgot just how it did start. Anyway, I asked Cam if she was proposing to me, and she said that in a way she was, and did I find the idea repulsive. I told her that of course I didn't, but that I must have time to think about it. It was then that I discussed it with Mother, and she said that Camilla would be an excellent selection. I was certainly ready for marriage—it is not easy for a man to live without a woman—and my experience with Mitra had left me cynical about romantic love, so I told Camilla I would

131

be honored to be her husband. Everyone was delighted and it has gone on now to the point where I cannot with honor go back on my word. Can't you see that, Eve?"

"Even if—" She had started to say, "Even if you both love someone else," but choked back the words. Even now, desperate as she was, she couldn't betray Camilla's secret, especially since she couldn't be sure whether Marko really loved her or was simply doing what Mitra had asked. What an utter humiliation it would be to Camilla if she were jilted by her fiancé and abandoned by the man she loved at the same time! No, she couldn't do that to her, whatever the cost to herself.

"Even if what?" Max asked gently.

She shook her head. "I was going to say, 'Even if you loved someone else,' but that's no good, is it? You don't care enough about me to create all the furor of a broken engagement."

He put his hand over hers, and his eyes were sad. "Darling, Eve, it is not a question of how much I care about you. I simply cannot hurt so many innocent people or go back on my word."

"Even at the price of an unhappy, unsuitable marriage?"

"We will not be unhappy, Eve. We are fond of each other and we will adjust. It will all work out—and you will be happier in your own country with some nice young American. Forgive me, Eve, but that is the way it must be."

She drew her hand away and fiercely willed away the tears that wanted to fall. She must not let him see how desperately hurt she was. They had talked it all out—there was nothing more to say. He had spelled it out plainly enough. Somehow she would have to get through the next few weeks without showing her torment.

"All right, Max," she said. "We'll never talk about this again."

132

He drew a deep breath and seemed to force animation back into his voice. "And now—shall we go to the castle and look at the crown jewels?"

When they finally got back to his apartment, she was exhausted physically and emotionally. She fell onto her bed and went to sleep. Sometime later she awoke to the sound of the shower running in the bathroom. She felt calm now, almost at peace, the anger and frustration drained away. She got up, tidied her hair, and went out to the living room. The morning paper was on the coffee table and she picked it up and tried to read it, but the words made little sense. When he finally came out of his room she looked up and almost gasped when she saw him.

"Max! You look absolutely gorgeous!" He was in completely formal evening dress, white tie and tails, and even had some sort of ribbon across his chest. He was carrying white gloves and an opera hat.

He made a rueful grimace. "This is necessary, you know. I am attending a banquet at the royal castle. Will you be all right? You can get your dinner downstairs—"

"Of course I'll be all right. Do you mean to say you are actually going to dine with the king?"

"Yes, we are good friends. He is about my age, you know. A charming fellow."

"Didn't he marry a commoner?"

"Yes, a German girl, a very accomplished young woman. They have an adorable baby daughter."

She couldn't take her eyes off him. "You look like something out of a Victor Herbert operetta," she said. "I expect you to burst into song any moment!"

He laughed. "I wish you could come with me. You would no doubt be amused by all the old-fashioned splendor."

"I would love it! Well, run along, Max, and have a good time."

He came over and stood beside the couch where she was sitting.

"We will try to get off around eight in the morning," he said. "I am sorry you do not have more time here—"

"I'm sorry, too, but thank you, Max, for a wonderful day. It really was, in spite of everything. I loved it."

The golden eyes gazed into her with sorrow and tenderness. "So did I. At least we will always have this day to remember. You see? I am really beginning to talk like a character in one of those operettas!" He leaned down, brushed her cheek lightly with his lips, and went away.

Eve took off her rumpled clothes, showered, and put on a fresh suit. There was no use sitting and brooding alone in the apartment all evening, she told herself. Camilla probably wouldn't be back until late. She hadn't seen much of the Old City—only the bit of walking she had done with Max after they had visited the castle—and this was her last chance. She went downstairs and out into the golden evening.

The Old City—Gamla Stan—was as it had always been: narrow, twisting, cobblestone streets and fascinating little shops that sold antiques, leather goods, and copper. There time seemed to slow down and memories drifted like evening mist from the Baltic.

With Max it would have been exciting and fun, but alone she felt depressed, weighted down by the centuries past that hung like a miasma over the Old City. She turned back toward the apartment building. Some of the guests were having dinner on the terrace, so she decided to join them, even though she did not feel hungry. At least it was something to do and put off the moment when she must return to the empty apartment and her thoughts.

She found a little table near the steps leading down into the garden. The waiter came quickly and was very attentive, very helpful, and she knew it was because of her association with Herr Greve. Looking up toward the massive walls of the castle, she thought of Max in his elegant clothes moving among royalty. How absurd she had been to think for a moment that he would have considered marrying her, a foreigner, who knew so little of this fascinating little country and its people. Compatible or not, Camilla would be more suitable, and no doubt she was young enough to adjust to the life she would have to lead. At least that was what she tried to tell herself, even though something inside her kept crying, "No! Max and I belong together—"

Finally, when she could not put it off any longer, she went upstairs to the apartment. It was not as lonely as she had expected. Again it seemed to reach out and welcome her. She undressed, changing into her night-gown and robe, and curled up on the comfortable sofa with a paperback book she had brought. In a few minutes the telephone rang. A bit startled, she went to answer it. Probably someone wanting Max, she thought.

"Eve?" It was Camilla. "I tried to get you before but you were out. Did you have a nice day?"

"Lovely," Eve assured her.

"That's good. I suppose Max has gone to his banquet?"

"Yes, long ago. He looked so beautiful in his dress suit!"

"I know. I've seen him in it. I suppose he'll be late getting back. Those affairs usually drag on and on. Look, Eve—Anna-Lisa is having a little party for me tonight—just a few couples in—and she thinks it would be better if I stayed here tonight instead of going home on the bus late at night. They only have one bedroom, but I can sleep on the couch. Would that be all right with you?"

"And leave me here with Max—unchaperoned?"

135

Eve said, trying to make it sound like a joke, but her heart was pounding with sudden excitement.

Camilla laughed. "I never even thought of that. I was more concerned about whether or not you'd be lonely there by yourself all evening."

"Goodness, no. I'm very cozy, and I'll probably go to bed in a little while. We must have walked miles today. But the thing is, Max wants to start home around eight tomorrow morning."

"That's all right. I'll get up when Anna-Lisa and her husband do—they both work—and get a ride part way with them. Anna-Lisa took today off to spend with me, but she has to work tomorrow. If you're sure you don't mind—"

"Of course not, Cam. Have fun, and I'll see you in the morning."

She stared at the telephone for a few minutes after she had hung up, but she was not seeing it. Her heart was still beating uncomfortably fast. When Max came home . . . But she was being ridiculous. She would be in bed asleep by then and he wouldn't even know that Camilla hadn't come back. She went back to the couch, but couldn't settle down to the book, so she decided to turn on the television set and see if there was anything worth watching. She found that they were running an American movie—*African Queen*—which she dearly loved, so she settled down to watch it. The subtitles were annoying, but at least there were no commercials.

After a while she grew drowsy, and finally she fell asleep with the television still going. Much later she awoke to find Max standing beside the couch gazing down at her, his eyes glowing with tenderness and desire. For a moment she was completely disoriented and stared up at him as though he were a stranger. Then memory and feeling flowed back into her along with a tide of longing to match the look in his eyes Without volition she lifted her arms to him and he knelt

136

beside her, his arms resting on the pillow on either side of her head, his eyes gazing into hers.

"Max—" she murmured sleepily, and slid her arms around his neck.

"Where is Camilla?" he asked. "I just got in—it's nearly one—isn't she back yet?"

"She called to say she's spending the night in Spånga," she told him. Her heart was pounding so hard that she could barely breathe.

Gently his hand caressed her cheek, her throat, then moved slowly along her body while his lips met hers. She began to tremble with the violence of sudden desire, and she could feel herself falling, falling into a vortex of a passion unlike anything she had experienced before. They belonged to each other—it had to be. He couldn't marry Camilla. They would be together, now and forever. . . .

His lips touched her eyelids, her shoulders, the hollow between her breasts. Her arms tightened around his neck, pulling him closer, closer.

"Max, Max—I love you!" she murmured. She felt his arms slide beneath her knees, the other around her shoulders. He was lifting her . . .

The doorbell rang.

Chapter Ten

For a moment neither of them moved or spoke, locked in consternation, willing whoever was out there to go away. It rang again, a long, imperious peal. Max muttered something that Eve could not translate, released her, and started for the door. Eve fled to her bedroom and sank trembling onto her bed. She heard

Max say, "Camilla! I thought you weren't coming back tonight."

"Well, I wasn't, only one of the couples at the party lives over this way and they offered to drive me home. I wasn't too keen on sleeping on the couch, so I decided to take them up on it. Did you just get in? What's the matter, you look sort of funny."

"It was probably the wine."

"Oh. Well, we'd better get to bed if you want to start early in the morning. Goodnight, Max."

Eve threw off her robe and got into bed. When Camilla came in she pretended to be asleep. She did not trust herself to say a single word. Suppose Camilla had arrived ten minutes later? There was enough light coming in through the open window for Camilla to undress, find her nightgown, and get into bed without turning on the light. She seemed to fall asleep immediately, but for Eve it was not that simple. She lay awake for a long time, too miserable and keyed up to sleep.

Was she glad or sorry about Camilla's unexpected return? If they had not been interrupted, would it have changed anything really? Probably not. Max had to marry Camilla, and nothing could change that, so it was no doubt a good thing that nothing had happened. And yet she was filled with a suffocating sense of rage and frustration.

What could she do about the situation? One scheme after another flashed through her troubled mind, only to be rejected. She couldn't tell Max that Camilla loved Marko—or tell Camilla that she and Max loved each other. Could she go to Martin and tell him everything and plead for him to stop the marriage? No, he would only accuse her of trying to start trouble, to get Max away from Camilla for herself. It was a tangled web and there was no magic word that would miraculously untangle it. The people involved had to set themselves free. Her only hope was that Marko might succeed in persuading Camilla to break with Max, but that was a forlorn hope indeed in view of her fanaticism where Martin was concerned.

She was relieved that in all the hurrying around the next morning to get off, she didn't see Max alone. Only once briefly, while Camilla was in the bedroom trying to squeeze the new clothes she had bought into her small suitcase, did they speak privately.

"Eve, I am sorry about last night," Max said in a low voice. "It should never have happened, and I promise you it won't again. I—"

"Please, Max, let's not talk about it. It's over. I'll be going home soon and we'll never see each other again, so let's just forget it."

A spasm of pain crossed his face. "No, Eve, I will never forget you. Knowing you has been—"

Camilla came out to the living room, saying cheerfully, "Well, I had to sit on it, but I did get it closed. I'm ready to go down now."

She seemed to be in very good spirits all through their rather hurried breakfast and told them all about the party and Anna-Lisa's apartment, which, it seemed, had a simply marvelous kitchen. She didn't seem to notice that neither Eve nor Max said very much. The drive home took considerably less time than the drive there, since they did not stop except for lunch.

They did not see much of Max for the next several days, except for one evening at a dance rehearsal. Since Camilla was not working now, she wanted to ride every morning, and Eve went with her. Her skill had greatly improved and she enjoyed it. However, it occurred to her that if Camilla and Marko were ever to see each other alone, she should stay home some morning. So on Friday, when Camilla suggested their usual ride, Eve told her she thought she would stay home and do some laundry. Something flickered in Cam's eyes for a

139

moment, but was gone before Eve could put a label on it.

"If you don't mind, then," she said, "I'll go alone."

"Of course not—run along."

When Camilla was gone, Eve gathered up a pile of clothes and washed them in the bathroom sink. When she had hung her clothes in the backyard, Eve got out the bicycle and took off down the road. She never tired of biking around the countryside. She knew that Camilla's favorite route by horse was on the road along the bluff overlooking the river, and she took it now, almost without volition. She tried to keep her thoughts away from Max, but it was impossible. Sometimes she longed just for a sight of him so intensely that it was a physical pain. Now she understood why people in love got some sort of consolation just out of walking past the house of the beloved. It had seemed silly to her before, but now she sometimes found herself biking past the entrance of Rosenborg, just for the dubious pleasure of gazing at the big estate house.

She had gone about a mile along the river when she saw Skadi and another of the horses from Max's stable tied to a tree in a grove of birches near the edge of the bluff. So it was Marko who had gone riding with Camilla, not Max, who always rode his black stallion, Sleipner. She stopped, parked her bike among the trees, and looked over the edge of the bluff. There was a path leading down to a beach of soft white sand in a secluded little cove, and there she saw Marko and Camilla standing by the river. They seemed to be arguing, and she heard Marko's voice rise in what sounded like anger.

"—just to please your father!" he said in his heavily accented Swedish. "In the old days a man had a right to sell his daughter to the highest bidder, but now—"

"It is not to please him, it is to save him!" Camilla cried resentfully, "And it was my decision, not his!"

"You may think that, but it was your father who skillfully guided you into making that decision! How can you be so blind? He isn't going to die—it's the money and title he wants. He has you completely brainwashed!"

So, thought Eve, he was using some of the weapons she had given him!

"You have no right to say such things!" Camilla cried passionately and pounded his chest with her fists, but he caught her wrists in his hands and drew her against him. Releasing her wrists, his arms went around her waist, and his mouth came down on hers in what looked to Eve to be a very well executed kiss. Ashamed of herself for spying, she turned away, but not before she saw Camilla's arms go around the young man's neck, and heard him say, "Yes, I have the right to say what I wish, because I love you and I think you love me!"

She rode away, a core of hope burning within her breast. If only he could talk Camilla into breaking off with Max! But knowing how Camilla felt about her father, it would not do to hope too much.

Although the preparations for the coming wedding were occupying a good deal of Olivia's and Camilla's time, for the next few days discussion of the coming ball took precedence. Camilla had told Eve that since there were to be about a hundred guests, it would take place partly outdoors, unless the weather made that impossible. The superintendant's estate house was not as large as Rosenborg and had no formal ballroom, but the large drawing room would be cleared for dancing, which would extend to the terrace, and little tables would be set up out in the flower garden, where people could sit with their drinks.

141

"There is a lovely view of the river from their garden," Camilla told her, "They have had other big affairs, but this is the first one we've been invited to—because I'm marrying Max, of course. We weren't considered important enough before." There was an edge of bitterness in her voice. "A long time ago there were balls given at Lyckan as fine as any in the province, but that was when our family still had the big house and were wealthy. People forget about that now. Papa has always dreamed that someday he might rebuild it, but there wasn't much chance of that, until—" She broke off suddenly, as though remembering Marko's accusations.

Yes, thought Eve, there were many reasons why Martin would want his daughter to marry Max.

All of the family, even Blenda, had been invited to the ball, and she too had a pretty new dress, long and ruffled. It was arranged that Max and his mother would pick them up in the Rolls-Royce to drive to the Enqvists' on the night of the big affair. Max came over the evening before to discuss the arrangements. Blenda's dress had just been completed and she was trying it on when he arrived. He admired her extravagantly and gave her a kiss.

"I am sure my women will be the most beautiful ones there," he said, and included Eve in his smile. She looked quickly away, unable to bear meeting his direct gaze. Since that night in Stockholm she had avoided him whenever possible and they had never been alone together.

"Even some of our staff will be there," he told them. "The Enqvists couldn't get enough help so Mother is loaning them some maids to work in the kitchen, and Marko will be tending bar—dressed in the provincial costume he wears in the dances. Fru Enqvist intends to have all the help wearing costumes. It should be quite colorful."

142

"Well, I'm glad she didn't want everybody to wear costumes," Camilla said. "I'd much rather wear my new gown from Madame Sophie's."

"Ah, yes!" Max laughed. "Poor Madame Sophie! She certainly met her match in Eve."

The following evening turned out to be warm and sunny, much to everyone's relief. The family arrayed themselves in their finery and sat in the living room waiting for the car to arrive. Olivia had refused to buy a new dress, saying that the one she had bought for Pelle's wedding was good enough. It was a dinner gown of dull blue satin and had a matching jacket with gold braid edging the collar and lapels. She had had her hair waved and looked very handsome. The girls had washed and set their own hair. Eve had talked Camilla into letting her set her fine straight hair in large rollers, so that it fell in soft golden curls about her shoulders. In her elegant new gown she looked beautiful. She had also set Blenda's hair, and the child was thrilled with the effect. Her own hair, however, was so short and curly she never did anything with it except wash it and dry it in the sun.

Eve was the last to come down. When she had put on the gown that she had sacrificed a tour of Sweden to buy, she looked at herself critically in the less-than-adequate mirror in Pelle's old dresser. Had it been worth it? She saw a small but beautifully proportioned young woman with flushed cheeks and a short mass of gleaming amber curls. The dark blue eyes had a wistful glow and somehow she looked older to herself than she had at the time of her arrival. Had falling in love done that to her? Yet she knew that she was far more attractive now than she had ever been with her new maturity—a woman now, no longer the gamine child.

Madame Sophie's gown was perfect on her, displaying her slight curves to their best advantage. The rhinestone straps glittered against her smooth white

143

shoulders and the full skirt swirled around her slender feet. She had bought a pair of gold sandals to wear with it and a lacy stole to throw around her shoulders against the inevitable chill of the night. Slowly she turned before the mirror, studying herself from all angles. She knew that she looked better at that moment than she ever had before—or perhaps ever would again. Except as a bride—but would she ever be a bride? She could not imagine wanting to marry anyone else after loving Max. She turned from the mirror with an impatient sigh, picked up her evening bag and gloves, and went slowly down the stairs.

They heard the car pulling up in front of the house soon after, and they went out to join the von Stjernas. Max was driving, since Marko was already at the Enqvist's. He got out of the car and looked at them admiringly.

"Herre Gud! What a gorgeous bunch!" he exclaimed. He kissed Camilla's cheek. "I have never seen you look so lovely, my dear," he told her, and she flushed with pleasure. His gaze slid to Eve and she turned away from the dazzling golden gaze. "Madame Sophie would be proud of you!" he said.

"I doubt it," she replied dryly, and went over to the car to greet the countess.

She too was wearing one of Madame Sophie's creations. It was of stiff yellow lace the color of her eyes and had a matching mantilla. With it she wore a magnificent necklace of emeralds and diamonds and other beautiful stones flashed from her aging fingers. Her hair had been freshly waved and piled high on her head, and she wore a discreet amount of makeup.

"How lovely you look, Fru Grevinna," Eve exclaimed, holding the thin fingers in her own sturdy clasp.

"So do you, my child. Come, sit beside me."

Max and Martin were wearing white dinner jackets,
144

and Eve thought Max looked as distinguished in that as he did in tails. Max had brought corsages for all the women, even Blenda. Eve's was a spray of white orchids, and she carefully pinned it to the base of a strap. They were leaving a bit early because the Enqvists wanted them to stand with them in the receiving line. Although it was past eight o'clock, the sun was still shining brightly as they drove off. There would be a buffet supper at eleven, and then the older people and children who wished to leave could do so, while the younger couples danced on.

They drove along the river and down to the bridge, then over into the old part of town. The old estate house had been built on a lovely site overlooking the river where it formed rapids before its plunge over the falls. The grounds were not extensive but were well tended with many tall trees and colorful beds of flowers. They followed a winding drive up to the house, which was of white frame with pillars supporting a large balcony. They stopped beneath a porte cochere, where an attendant in native costume opened the car door. Max got out his mother's folding wheelchair, and he and the attendant lifted her into it and carried her up the broad, shallow steps to the entrance.

They went in to be greeted by the Enqvists, whom Eve had never met: an imposing, middle-aged couple, both tall, fairly heavyset, with graying blond hair. They greeted the Trillings graciously, but Eve noticed that Fru Enqvist was especially effusive over the countess and Max. The large entrance hall had been decorated with flowers and potted palms, and beyond it Eve glimpsed other rooms equally bedecked. Obviously the Enqvists had gone to a great deal of expense and work to make this affair a gala one. The other guests soon started to arrive, and Eve stood there with the Trillings for what seemed like a long time, being introduced to

145

so many people that the faces soon became a blur and her hand grew tired from being shaken.

The countess was in her glory, greeting old friends and talking to people she had not seen for a while, and Max was smiling and charming to all. Camilla was unusually vivacious, her cheeks flushed, her eyes bright with excitement, talking to the guests with a gracious lady-of-the-manor air as though she were already slipping into her future role of Fru Grevinna. She was learning. She would be all right, Eve thought with a pang. She was the perfect example of a happy bride-to-be—and yet Eve noticed that from time to time her eyes would stray into the room beyond. Martin too was in his element. They had placed a chair for him next to the countess, and a stranger would have thought that he was the host from the way he was greeting the guests. Perhaps, Eve thought, he was imagining himself in a restored Lyckan. Finally the guests began to thin out—everyone had been extraordinarily prompt in arriving—and then there were no more in sight.

"I think they are all here," Fru Enqvist murmured with a sigh of relief. "We can go into the drawing room now."

Max was just reaching for his mother's chair, when Camilla gave a little cry of consternation. The others turned around to see what had happened. Another car had just driven up, and stepping out of it were the Carsings and Mitra. She looked absolutely stunning in gleaming red satin cut very low in the bodice to reveal her voluptuous breasts. In her sleek black hair she wore a glittering tiara and a matching necklace of what looked like real diamonds. Her head was held high and there was a defiant gleam in her dark eyes. She swept up the steps, followed rather timidly and apologetically by the elderly Carsings, a colorless, inconspicuous pair.

"Oh, no!" Fru Enqvist murmured despairingly. Eve could see that in her hostess's eyes her whole carefully,

146

expensively planned evening was collapsing around her in ruins. Anger blazed in Camilla's eyes.

"How dare she!" she hissed.

Quickly Eve glanced from face to face, assessing their reactions. The countess's eyes were cold, her face a frozen mask. Olivia looked frightened and Martin was staring at the woman with an unguarded look of pure hatred. But Max, who was her main concern, was regarding Mitra with a sort of grudging admiration and a rueful amusement.

Mitra barely nodded to her hosts, then swept on to Max, seizing both his hands and kissing his cheek.

"Darling!" she exclaimed in her heavily accented Swedish. "How lovely to see you again!"

The Carsings shook hands cautiously with their wooden-faced hosts, and Fru Carsing murmured apologetically, "Mitra is our houseguest and she insisted on coming. I do hope you don't mind!"

Fru Enqvist made an almost inaudible reply and the Carsings and Mitra moved on into the drawing room.

"I invited the Carsings weeks ago," Fru Enqvist told the countess, "long before that—that woman came to stay with them. It simply never occurred to me that they would bring her—" She was almost in tears. The countess reached out and patted her arm reassuringly.

"Don't fret about it, Elin," she said. "It isn't your fault, or the Carsings' either. Mitra is only making one of her gestures, so we will simply behave as though nothing has happened. After all, what can she do?" She looked at Max, who smiled reassuringly.

"You must not be concerned, any of you," he said easily. "She is my responsibility and I will see that she does not cause any trouble. Come now."

He got his mother and Camilla's parents settled in a comfortable corner where they could talk to their many friends, who were affectionately surrounding them. Max slipped his arms through those of the two girls.

147

"Shall we take a little stroll?" he asked.

Camilla was still flushed with anger. "I'd like a drink, Max," she said. "I think I need one!"

Max raised his eyebrows, but started toward the bar. Eve knew that Camilla practically never touched anything stronger than beer, but she understood the girl's desire to let Marko see her in all her finery.

"Of course," Max said, "I could do with one myself. But please do not let Mitra upset you. She only wants to cause a distraction, but she is harmless, really."

"As harmless as a Bengal tiger!" Camilla retorted, but she was beginning to look more cheerful.

The drawing room had been emptied of furniture except for chairs and sofas around the walls. Here too were flowers and potted palms. It was a large room with paneled walls and high ceilings. On one side French windows opened onto a wide stone terrace that had been strung with Japanese lanterns. There were more lanterns along the garden paths and in the trees—a very festive sight, glowing like colored fireflies in the approaching twilight.

At one end of the room there was a small orchestra, all the members of which were dressed in the provincial costume. The bar was at the other end next to the door into the dining room, which was filled with long tables covered with snowy linen, exotic flower arrangements, gold candlesticks, and the finest of place settings. Marko was at the bar with two other young men in costumes.

When he saw Camilla approaching, Eve saw a look of passionate longing gleam in his eyes for a moment, but then—his face again carefully blank—he was smiling politely and opening a bottle of champagne.

"You both look exceedingly lovely tonight," he told the girls as he filled their glasses.

"Thank you." Camilla stared at him for a moment, then picked up her glass and turned away.

148

Max lifted his glass and smiled at them. "To my lovely ladies!" he said. "May your every wish be granted!"

"That," said Eve, "is a very dangerous toast."

The orchestra had been playing waltzes for some time, and Eve saw Mitra dancing with a good-looking young man. She would certainly never lack for partners, Eve reflected, sipping her champagne.

"The Merry Widow," she murmured, and Max gave her an amused glance.

"Yes, indeed. You must admit that it took a lot of—what is that charming expression you Americans use?"

"Guts?"

He laughed. "Yes—guts for her to come here tonight."

"I never thought she was lacking in them," Eve retorted.

She glanced at Marko again and saw that he too was following the progress of his cousin around the floor with an expression of apprehension. One slip, Eve realized, one little indication from Mitra that she and Marko were not strangers, and everything would be lost to him. Indeed, there were many dark undercurrents following the woman in the scarlet gown!

They finished their drinks and Max turned to Camilla.

"I think, if Eve will excuse us, that we should have a dance now," he said. "People will expect it, and we must show that all is well between us."

"Of course," said Eve, and Camilla moved into his arms. When Eve moved away from the bar, she felt someone touch her arm. It was Kjell.

"Would you dance with me, Beautiful Lady?" he asked in English.

She accepted gratefully and smiled up at him. There was a wicked twinkle in his eyes. "We have many little surprises here tonight," he remarked. "What do you think of the glamorous Mitra?"

"I was just thinking that if she were found murdered in the garden, there would be many suspects," she told him.

He laughed. "How true! Whom would you favor? Surely not Max. In spite of his temper, he is not vicious."

"He has the least motive, anyway," Eve agreed. "Only one who is determined that he shall marry Camilla and sees Mitra as a threat—"

"What an imagination! We should collaborate on an opera. Can't you just hear Mitra singing an impassioned aria to the lover who has abandoned her? But who shall we have murder her?"

"Martin," Eve said quickly, then bit her lip. Perhaps she was going too far!

But Kjell only laughed again, admiringly. "Perfect! You have noticed it too—his obsession over this marriage. I do believe he would stop at nothing to have it consummated."

Eve was elated. Here was the first person who agreed with her suspicions.

"Kjell, do you think Martin is capable of faking his illness to get Camilla to marry Max?" she asked.

"Of course. He is a sly fellow, that one, and very ambitious."

"But if that is so, what can be done to stop them?"

Kjell raised his eyebrows. "Must they be stopped, my dear?"

"But if they don't love each other and are only marrying to save Martin—"

"Well, it is their own affair, I'm afraid."

"You told me once you didn't think they should marry either."

"Being a romantic I would prefer to see them marry for love, but since they seem so determined to marry
150

each other, we will just have to accept it, I suppose."

She wondered what he would say if she told him that she and Max were in love, but she didn't dare go that far. That was a secret no one could share. She knew she should give up and accept the inevitable, as Kjell said, and yet she felt that something dangerous and unpredictable—like an electrical storm, when one feels the charge crackling around him in the atmosphere— was building up and that she was the only one who was aware of it or who could try to prevent it.

"I really feel sorry for the Carsings," Kjell went on, "having Mitra forced on them this way. They never liked her, but had to tolerate her for Karl's sake—that was her husband, Mr. Carsing's brother. They used to come here sometimes when Karl was alive. That was when she and Max first met, and I think she had designs on him even then."

"Did their affair start while she was still married?" Eve asked in dismay.

"Oh, no, Max is too conservative for that. But after Karl died Max started seeing her in Stockholm. She and Karl had a big house on one of the islands near the city. She still lives in it. Many people think that Max gave her up because his mother asked him to, but I happen to know that Mitra jilted him for a young actor she'd taken a fancy to."

"He wanted to break off with her anyway," Eve said.

"That may well be. Anyway, the thing with the actor broke up long ago, and now Mitra seems to think she can get Max back. I suppose she believes her power over men to be limitless."

"If the Carsings don't like her, why do they let her stay with them, and why did they bring her here tonight?"

"I've heard that they owed Karl money. The two brothers inherited money from their father, but Karl

151

was clever and ran his into a fortune, while Einar lost most of his in bad investments. Now he owes the money to Mitra, and she holds that over his head, I suppose, when she wants something from them."

Kjell seemed to be a perfect mine of information, she thought—probably because people wanted to tell him their troubles. "Why did she go to the hotel at first, then," she asked, "instead of to the Carsings?"

"Oh, I imagine she thought the hotel would be a snug little rendezvous for her and Max, but when that didn't come off, she moved in with the Carsings. She's still trying, though. She's not the sort to give up easily."

The music ended and Kjell released her. "Look!" he mumured. "Our opera plot is beginning to thicken!"

She turned and saw Mitra approaching Max, where he was standing with Camilla near the edge of the room. When she reached him, she put her hand possessively on his arm and smiled up at him with a flash of her perfect white teeth.

"Well, Max," she said loudly, "aren't you going to ask me to dance?"

"*Oj, oj!*" Kjell exclaimed. "What will our hero do now?"

Eve could almost see the thoughts flashing through Max's mind in the few seconds that passed before he responded: if he turned her down, she would certainly create a scene—wouldn't it be better to treat it as a matter of no importance? Yes, even at the risk of causing a few raised eyebrows and annoying Camilla. He smiled, took Mitra into his arms, and swept her away to the strains of—by coincidence—the "Merry Widow Waltz."

"Excuse me, I had better take care of Camilla," Kjell murmured, and moved quickly toward the girl, who was staring after the couple, her blue eyes flashing angry sparks. Without even speaking to her, Kjell took her into his arms and led her off, and as they passed

152

her, Eve heard him say, "Act as though nothing has happened, my dear. It's all very silly, anyway. You know that Max cares nothing about that woman now."

A young man whose name Eve could not remember came up and asked her to dance and she accepted gratefully. As they moved around the room she tried to keep her eye on Max and Mitra, but it was very crowded and she found it difficult.

When the dance ended, she was relieved to see that he went back to Camilla at once, and that Mitra was immediately surrounded by a group of admiring males. To her surprise she found that she herself was in demand as a partner and was no sooner released by one man than several more were waiting to take his place. It was all fun, and she glowed under the many compliments her partners bestowed upon her. Camilla too as the guest of honor, was constantly beseiged with men wanting to dance with her, and Eve saw that she was now laughing and happy.

An hour or so passed in a happy blur. Eve danced, talked, and sipped champagne or punch until she began to feel dizzy. Then she heard the orchestra begin a medley of tunes from "The Waltz Dream" and a wave of exquisite pain swept over her. She automatically put her hand into that of the man who had just asked her to dance, but before they could begin, Max was there, not smiling now, but looking at her with an intent expression in his eyes that made her heart leap painfully.

"Excuse me," he said to her partner, "but I would like to claim this dance with the young lady." The other man backed off, made her a little bow, and disappeared. Max's eyes did not leave hers as he took her into his arms.

"I asked them to play this for us, Eve," he said. "I hope you don't mind."

"No," she said faintly. "No, Max, I don't mind." She felt as though she were moving in a dream. They might

153

have been alone; the crowd of laughing, chatting people around them did not exist. There was only Max—and the wistful, heart-breaking music. He held her close and laid his cheek against her hair. He didn't talk, but simply held her against his strong, hard body, and she could feel his heart pounding against her cheek. Her whole body seemed to throb to the rhythm of the music and she ached with a sadness that she had never felt before—not only for herself, but for the people all down the years who had loved and dreamed and grasped for an elusive happiness.

He began to sing then, very softly, for her ears alone:

"One chance—one dream—and all too soon it's gone.

Goodbye, my love, goodbye—"

She closed her eyes and shivered with the poignancy of her emotion. *No matter how long I live,* she thought, *whenever I hear "The Waltz Dream," I will die a little because once a long time ago in a faraway land I loved a count with golden eyes.*

The music ended. He lifted her hand to his lips and she saw the bitter unhappiness in his eyes.

"Eve—" he said. "Oh God, Eve—" And then he was gone.

The rest of the evening passed in a blur. She went on dancing and drank more champagne, and went for a walk in the garden with Kjell, Camilla, and Max, and they were all very gay and had a spirited discussion about something she could not remember afterward. Later they had an elegant supper in the dining room. Everyone was relieved when Mitra—after spending a great deal of time at the bar—disappeared with one of the young men who had been pursuing her. Apparently the countess had been right, and Mitra had simply been making one of her gestures.

However, Eve was sure that, as in any battle, the woman had fallen back temporarily to gather her resources in preparation for the big attack. There had been all the elements present that night for real trouble, Eve reflected later that night after she was home and in bed: Mitra and Max, the smoldering dark eyes of Marko watching Camilla and his cousin, even Max and herself. Yet nothing had happened. Somehow she sensed that the storm clouds she had felt gathering there for a while were not really dissipated. The storm would strike when it was ready.

Chapter Eleven

Now that the ball was out of the way, preparations for the wedding took precedence over everything else. There were other parties on a more modest scale and Eve was invited to them all. She was glad that the Trilling household was busy and that she could share in it, because it was agony to be idle and find her thoughts drifting to Max. He was also busy, getting his affairs in order so that he could get away for a few weeks on their honeymoon to Grand Canary.

Eve watched Camilla closely, but if Camilla was unhappy she managed to hide it. Martin was blooming these days. He was putting on weight again and seemed to be stronger. He spent less time alone in his den working and seemed to enjoy chatting with friends who were constantly dropping in to see them. Eve found herself resenting his improvement. At times when she was depressed she thought of him as a vampire, taking his sustenance out of the happiness of others, and yet she knew that she was not being fair. She had condemned him on instinct alone, and it was possible that she was wrong. Or the truth could be somewhere in

155

between and he might not be consciously aware of what he had done. Certainly the gay, infectious charm he was displaying these days was hard to resist.

Camilla had told Eve that the countess had insisted on taking full charge of the wedding and its expenses, since she wanted it done on a much grander scale than the Trillings could afford. The wedding itself, since it would be in the private chapel, would be attended only by the family and a few of their closest friends. Afterward, however, on the afternoon of Midsummer Day, there would be a large reception in the ballroom of Rosenborg to which several hundred people had been invited. Naturally an affair such as that required a great deal of planning, and the Trillings had to help.

On the Saturday morning after the ball Max showed up in the Land-Rover and told Camilla that there was something he wanted to show her—his wedding present. Eve knew what that was, of course, and felt a stab of pain when she thought about that lovely, quiet place on the lake.

"Come with us, Eve," Max said. Something in his eyes told her that he didn't want to be alone with Camilla when he showed her the cottage, so she agreed, although she didn't want to go.

It was another golden day, and they drove off to the blue lake that lay among the hills and forests. When Camilla made some reference to their approaching trip to Grand Canary, Eve asked, "What is it like there, Max? I've been fascinated by it ever since I read Cronin's book *Grand Canary* years ago."

"It is a very picturesque place," he told her, "and is very popular with the Scandinavians, you know. They go down there in droves every winter. My parents bought an apartment in a Swedish development down the coast a bit from Las Palmas. I haven't been there more than a few times myself, but·Mother goes every year to get away from the dark and the cold."

156

"It seemed to be a very strange, mysterious place from his book," Eve said.

He shrugged. "But that was fiction. It is very Spanish in atmosphere with a lot of rugged mountains and the climate is mild, never extremely hot or cold. There is a good beach of yellow sand at Las Palmas protected by a reef so that the swimming is excellent. In the evening when the sun goes down everything turns a lovely shade of mauve. The southern tip is almost like a desert—after all, the Sahara is not far away. Let me see—what else can I tell you?"

"Are there jungles there?"

"No jungles. They were barren, volcanic islands originally. Most of what grows there now was brought in. For instance, the pine trees on Tenerife came from California."

"Well, even if it isn't quite as Cronin described it, I would still like to see it."

When they reached the cottage, Camilla exclaimed, "This is the old Werle place. Pelle has a chum whose family owns the cottage just beyond it and we used to come down here a lot when we were children on our bicycles."

"I thought that I might buy it for us to come to on weekends," Max told her. "As you know, the swimming and fishing are good here."

"That would be very nice, Max," Camilla agreed. "Let's take a look inside."

They went up the steps and Max produced a key for the front door. Camilla wandered around examining everything.

"Of course it lacks all the modern conveniences," Max said, "but if I buy it, I'll have it remodeled to a certain extent."

"That's all right, Max, I know there isn't any electricity out here. The stove might be a little difficult to cook on—"

157

"You would not have to cook here," he assured her. "We would bring food from home."

"Oh, but I like to cook—" she began, then broke off when she saw his expression. "A gasoline stove, perhaps, for coffee," she said hastily. "It's very nice, Max."

Eve could tell that he was hurt that Camilla was not more enthusiastic about it. "Do you want me to buy it or not?" he asked rather curtly.

"Oh, yes, of course, Max. I think it will be a lot of fun to have a place out here."

She went to the door and looked out on the lake. "Look, there's a boat! *Hej!* It's Per and his wife—that's Pelle's old chum. I suppose they came out for the weekend."

She went out and ran down to the dock waving and calling, and the boat turned and started to come toward her. Max turned to Eve with a wry smile.

"I got the impression that she was not overwhelmed with delight over the cottage," he said. "What do you think? Perhaps I should forget about buying it."

"Of course she likes it, Max," Eve protested. "And you certainly ought to buy it, if only because you like it so much yourself."

"If only it were for you and me—" He reached out as though to touch her, but she moved away.

"Stop it, Max!" she said angrily. "What's the good of torturing ourselves?"

She went on out to the porch and saw Camilla coming up over the smooth rocks looking happy and excited.

"They want us to come over to their cottage for coffee," she called. When she reached the porch she slipped her arm through Max's and smiled up at him.

"It will be lovely having a place next door to them," she said. "Come on, let's go over to their cottage." She
158

pulled him toward the steps and Eve followed reluctantly, wishing that she hadn't come. The beauty of the lake shimmered before her eyes, the tall pines filled the air with their delicious fragrance, and the birds sang—but none of it was for her. She was a stranger, soon to go away forever and never see this lovely place again.

Besides the wedding preparations there were also intensified rehearsals for the Midsummer Eve celebration. Max had workers come in to clean and repaint the interior of the barn where part of the program would be held. It seemed that all of Rosenborg—the house, the grounds, and the outbuildings—were being refurbished for this momentous occasion. Even the little chapel was getting a new coat of paint.

"It is the first time that I can remember," the countess said one day when the girls stopped in for a little visit during a rehearsal, "that we have combined a Midsummer celebration with a wedding. I must not forget to have someone cut a little birch tree to put beside the altar in the chapel."

"What does that signify?" Eve asked. "I thought that birch branches were part of the pagan festivities."

"So they are, my dear, but in Sweden the pagan symbols have become so mingled with the Christian that no one can sort them out."

That night when they walked home from Rosenborg Camilla was unusually quiet. When Eve spoke to her she answered automatically, absently, as though her thoughts were far away. It must be hard for her, Eve thought, to be with Marko at the rehearsals, just as it was hard for her to see Max. She wondered if Camilla had seen him alone many times since that episode by the river.

"Why is it," Eve asked her, "that no Trilling woman has married a von Stjerna until now? You live so close

159

together, and if your ancestors really believed in the curse, it seems they would have tried to unite the families."

Camilla shrugged. "For a long time no von Stjerna would so much as speak to a Trilling. Then, when the Lyckan estate house was burned, the Trillings suspected that someone from the von Stjerna estate had done it. So there was what you might call a feud between the families for a number of generations. It has only been in more recent times that they have been friends again."

"So if you were to jilt Max now, I suppose it would start all over again!"

"I couldn't do that! It would be terrible." The blue eyes were somber.

When they reached the house the girls said a brief goodnight and went on to their own rooms. Eve got into bed but found that she could not sleep. She had been suffering a good deal from insomnia the last few weeks. No matter how tired she was, when she went to bed thoughts would begin to churn through her mind and it was impossible to fall asleep.

Over and over the same tired thoughts. Was Martin bluffing, or would he really die if Camilla didn't marry Max? Was there any chance Marko would succeed in persuading Camilla to jilt Max for him? And if she did, would she be any happier with him than with Max? And how was she, herself, going to stand a lifetime of exile from this beautiful country and the man she loved? Would she ever be able to love anyone again? And how was she going to get through the wedding day without breaking down?

She tried to break up the endless circle of thoughts by thinking instead of her life at home that she would soon be going back to: the comfortable old house in Oak Park, her work at the clinic that until now had been so absorbing, her many friends, and all the familiar

160

activities—but none of it seemed real to her anymore. It was as though it belonged to another lifetime. Perhaps, she told herself wearily, when she went back to it, it would be this life—Rosenborg, Max, the brooding forests, and glittering lakes—that would be the dream. A waltz dream. The strains of the music seemed to echo in her ears and again she heard Max singing softly, "Goodbye, my love, goodbye—"

She turned restlessly in her bed. Always her thoughts came back to Max. She loved him, she wanted him. She thought of his tawny eyes demanding her kisses, his eager mouth on hers, his strong hands claiming her body against his—how could she go thousands of miles away and never see him again? Suddenly, in the midst of her anguish, she heard the creak of a floorboard, the sound of Camilla's door being slowly opened. So—she could not sleep either! Well, it was no wonder. Her problems were the same as Eve's, except that she would not have to go far away from everything that she loved.

She heard the cautious footsteps going down the stairs. She was probably going down to the kitchen to heat a cup of coffee, or maybe some milk. Why shouldn't she join her? Maybe they could talk things out—not that it would do any good. They always came to the same impasse: Martin. But at least it would be better than tossing around in bed.

She slipped out of bed, put on her robe, and went quietly out of her room and down the stairs after Camilla. She had just reached the landing when she heard the front door close gently. She stopped in amazement. Camilla wasn't going to the kitchen after all—she had gone out! Where? For a walk? At this hour? Well, it was only a little after midnight and wasn't even totally dark out, because it didn't really get dark anymore. She went on down the stairs and opened the front door. Camilla wasn't in sight, so she stepped out onto the little porch. Then she saw the girl, fully

161

dressed, walking across the lawn toward the path that led through the woods to Rosenborg. Her heart began to pound with excitement. A midnight rendezvous! With Marko? Who else? Certainly not Max. It was hard to believe that Cam would do something so risky at this stage, but perhaps she was desperate for a few last moments with the man she really loved.

She felt a brief stab of apprehension. Suppose the things Marko had said to her were lies and he really had been making love to Camilla for the reward Mitra had promised him. Suppose Camilla were walking into a trap—a setup—of the sort Marko had described to her! After all, she had only his word to go on, and he could have been lying to keep her from exposing him. There had been a lot at stake. She remembered the way he had kissed her—no doubt believing her to be a vulnerable female. Marko was an unknown quality, a stranger—perhaps he had fooled them all. Should she run after Camilla to warn her? Should she tell her what she had found out about Marko? She took a few tentative steps, but then stopped. Something was holding her back—she wasn't sure what.

Was it her subconscious telling her to stay out of it—because actually she wanted Camilla to walk into a trap, wanted the engagement to be broken? She felt an enormous sense of guilt, and yet she could not bring herself to run after Camilla and stop her.

Slowly she went into the house and up the stairs to her bed. Now, of course, sleep was more impossible than ever. She knew that she would simply lie there wide awake until she heard Camilla come back. Camilla must indeed have been desperate to take such a chance, she reflected. Suppose Martin caught her? She lay there, her thoughts in a turmoil of mingled guilt and hope and something else—could it be envy? Envy because Camilla had the courage to do what she herself could not?

She had expected a long wait, but to her surprise it was barely half an hour later that she heard the front door open and footsteps coming up the stairs. What had happened? She had a bitter feeling of anticlimax when she realized that Camilla probably had just gone for a walk after all. She lay tense and listening. There were slight sounds as the girl moved around her room, then a creak when she got into bed. Then—the muffled but unmistakable sound of sobbing. Camilla was crying as though her heart were broken, apparently with her face in the pillow to stifle the sounds.

What had happened? Eve lay there for a few more minutes wondering what she should do. The sobbing continued unabated. Finally when she couldn't stand it any longer, she got out of bed once more and went quietly next door, hoping that none of the others would hear them. She didn't bother to knock, but walked right in.

The girl's clothes were strewn haphazardly around the room where she had flung them off, and Camilla, in rumpled pajamas, was lying face down on the bed, sobbing into her pillow. Eve went over and sat on the edge of the bed and put her arm around the girl's shoulders.

"What is it, Cam?" she asked softly. "Can I help?"

Camilla shook her head without looking up. "Nobody can help," she murmured into the pillow. "I've been a terrible fool, that's all."

"Tell me about it," Eve urged. "You went to Marko, didn't you?"

Camilla rolled over and looked at her in surprise. She looked like a little girl with her face screwed up in misery and tears running down her cheeks. "How did you know that? Did you follow me?" she demanded.

"No, of course not. But I'm not blind—I know you're in love with him. I was awake and saw you going

163

toward Rosenborg, so I assumed that was where you were headed. Did you see him?"

"No. He wasn't there. There was a light in his apartment, but his bed hadn't been slept in. He was probably at the stable. Jennie was due to foal any day. I should never have gone there!" She struck the wet pillow with her fist in an angry gesture of frustration.

Eve was puzzled. Surely the fact that she hadn't found him home hadn't upset her like this. "Why did you go?" she asked.

"Because I wanted to have something to remember in all the years ahead of me without him," Camilla said bitterly. "It seemed so futile—saving myself as a virgin bride for Max, when he doesn't even care."

"You didn't go to ask Marko to take you away with him?"

"*Herre Gud,* no! You know I can't do that. I have to marry Max. But I thought I was entitled to a few moments of happiness with Marko before—oh, God, how naïve and gullible I've been! I actually believed Marko when he said he loved me!" She started to sob again and put her hands over her face.

"What makes you think he doesn't?" Eve asked.

Camilla struggled to speak over the sobs that were choking her. "I stayed a few minutes. I thought he might come back. I was—a little nosey, I guess. I looked at some of his things—just because they were his. They made feel closer—can you understand that?"

"Of course, Cam." She thought of herself, biking futilely past the gates of Rosenborg.

"There was a picture in the top drawer of his dresser—a family group. I took it out to look at it, because I wanted to see what his family was like, and what he looked like as a little boy. It was taken when he was about ten, I guess. He was so sweet—his parents were nice-looking, too. They were standing outside a small house with plastered walls and a tiled roof. There were flowers growing beside it. Besides Marko there was a younger boy and a baby girl, about two, and one more—an older girl. She looked about sixteen. I recognized her instantly. She's a lot older and more sophisticated now, but the face was unmistakable—"

"Mitra?"

Camilla stared at her blankly. "How did you know? It seems to me you know a lot more about all this than you should."

"Yes, I do know quite a bit, Cam, and I'll tell you everything. But first—what did you think when you recognized her?"

"What could I think? She must be his sister and somehow she got him here to break up my engagement to Max. I guess he was supposed to make love to me. So none of it was real—all the things he said—" She buried her face in the pillow again.

"Cam, listen to me," Eve said. "I'm sure that he is really in love with you. Shortly after I came here I caught him and Mitra together. They didn't see me at the time, but I talked to him about it later and he told me all about it. You're right, she did ask him to come here and bribed him with the promise of a horse farm of his own. She's his cousin, by the way, not his sister. Her mother died and Marko's parents raised her. Marko was supposed to get you up to his apartment and then someone would tip off Max and he'd catch you together—a thoroughly nasty business. Marko didn't like it, but he didn't know you then and he wanted the farm. He told me that he thought you were just some mercenary creature who was marrying Max for his money and position. But then he met you and fell in love with you. He told Mitra he wasn't going to compromise you, but that if he could persuade you to break with Max and marry him, he would. I believed him, Cam. I still do. There is nothing for you to be so unhappy about. You have no intention of giving up Max

165

for him, so it is Marko who has the right to be unhappy—and believe me, he is!"

Camilla sat up and stared out the window for a few minutes without speaking. Then she said slowly, "He never asked me to come to his apartment, so what you say must be true. He only wanted me to break my engagement."

"You see? Mitra's scheme has failed. I believed Marko, as I said, so I didn't tell Max about his connection with Mitra. I didn't want to get him fired."

Camilla drew a long quivering breath. "I won't tell him either. I won't even tell Marko I know. I just won't see him alone anymore before the wedding. I know that what I was going to do tonight was wrong. It wasn't fair to Max or Marko or anybody. But I was so desperate—" She looked at Eve with a pathetic little smile. "Can you understand? Have you ever felt like that about anyone?"

Now was the moment to tell Camilla about herself and Max. Would it make any difference to the girl if she knew that they were just as unhappy over the marriage as she was? The sure knowledge came to her then that nothing would make any difference. The girl's fanatical determination knew no bounds. She was the type who—in the past—would have gone to the stake rather than renounce a belief. And Martin was just as bad; he would let her go to the stake for him. She had never encountered such a group of misguided, stubborn people in her life! There was Max, with his ideas of family honor . . .

"Yes," she replied, "I have felt that way, and I do understand, only I think you're crazy to give up your happiness for—oh, never mind. There's no use talking about it, I guess."

"No, there isn't." The fanatical gleam was back in her eyes. "I know what I have to do."

"Well, we might as well get some sleep." Eve got off

166

the bed with a sigh. "Don't cry anymore. Marko does love you, I'm sure—for what good that does."

"Thank you for coming in, Eve. I won't cry anymore." Her face was wooden again, drained of emotion. "Everything will work out for the best."

It would work out, all right, Eve thought as she went back to her room, but was it for the best? Camilla and Max would get married and fly off to Grand Canary—and she would go home and never see any of them again.

Chapter Twelve

After that the days slipped by with alarming rapidity until it was June 23—Midsummer Eve. It was a beautiful, sunny day, so rare for that season in Sweden when it was often cold and rainy. Eve had almost hoped that it would rain. Somehow it would have been easier to have nature match her mood instead of all this—what was it Max had spoken of?—"The singing and the gold!"

Everyone got up very early at Lyckan and Olivia prepared a festive breakfast, which Eve could not eat. She was so numb with misery over the thought of the wedding on the following day that she was not even nervous about the dance she had to do that evening. She knew it perfectly now. Her costume had been altered and she knew she looked her best in it, so there was really nothing to be nervous about.

The celebration was to start at five that afternoon. It would begin in the courtyard of Rosenborg with the pole-raising ceremony, and then there would be the folk dancing. A buffet supper would be served on tables set up in the grounds between the barn and the house, unless it rained, in which case it would be served in the converted barn. After the meal and a period of socializing, a general dance would be held in the barn. According to the ancient custom, a Midsummer Wake would be held, which meant that everyone would stay up to watch for the return of the sun after its brief disappearance.

Since this was a private celebration for the Rosenborg estate, only the employees and their families would be there. Their friends and relatives would come the following day for the reception in the ballroom, and a select few for the wedding itself. Pelle and his wife would be there, of course, but would not arrive until the following morning. There would also be some of the von Stjerna relatives coming down from Stockholm to stay at Rosenborg.

After breakfast Blenda said, "I want to go over to Rosenborg to watch them decorate the pole. Max said they would do it this morning."

"You might be in the way," her mother objected.

"No, I won't. Max said I could come."

"Eve and I can go with her," Camilla said. "I'll keep an eye on her. There might be something we can do to help, and, anyway, I want to show Eve the wedding presents."

They set out with Blenda skipping ahead. The child was quite wild with excitement from all the wonderful things happening at once. The meadows were a dazzle of blue and yellow flowers, the colors of the Swedish flag.

"Are you all right, Camilla?" Eve asked.

Camilla shrugged. "Yes, I suppose so. I no longer feel anything."

"The Rites of Spring," Eve said wryly, "with you as the sacrificial virgin!"

Camilla frowned and gave her a sharp glance. "I don't feel that I am being sacrificed," she said.

"But you are, you know, with your father as the high priest—"

"Stop it, Eve! You are talking nonsense!" Red spots of color glowed on her cheeks.

"I'm sorry. I know it's much too late to change anything now. Have you seen Marko lately?"

"No," Camilla replied coldly. "He will be leaving soon anyway. Max told me he is going back to Yugoslavia."

"Then he won't be managing the stud farm?"

"No. He told Max he wanted to return to his own country, but I suppose he doesn't want to stay here after Max and I are married. He probably never intended to stay anyway," she said bitterly.

At Rosenborg they found a group of men behind the barn in the process of decorating a long pole and Eve watched with interest. It was a full-grown tree—about thirty feet long—well smoothed down, and they were winding long garlands of birch leaves around it. A crossbar had been fastened on near the top, from which hung two large rings, which would also be wound with leaves and flowers. On the very top was fastened a large metal rooster that gleamed in the morning sunlight. Some blue and gold streamers lay on the ground to be attached later. Max was there, supervising the job, and they went to stand beside him.

"What do you think of it?" he asked Eve.

"It's going to be very impressive. I suppose the rooster is a fertility symbol. What about the rings?"

He looked at her and frowned, then gave an embarrassed laugh. "Do you know, I have no idea! They have always been used, as far back as I can remember, but their significance seems to have been lost in the mists of antiquity."

169

"Maybe they represent the bodies they used to hang on their sacred trees," she suggested.

"Herre Gud, Eve! What a cheerful thought!"

Camilla glanced at them uneasily. "Is there anything we can do to help?" she asked, as though trying to change the subject.

"I don't know, Cam. You'll have to ask Mother. We have extra help in, but there is a lot to do. Perhaps you could help with the flowers. She has a stack of them that have to be put into vases."

Blenda slipped her small hand into his. "I want to stay with you, Max, and watch them finish the pole," she said.

"Of course, little one. You can help them if you like."

The two older girls walked away, leaving Blenda happily twining garlands. When they reached the house, Camilla said, "Before we start working, come up to the ballroom. I want to show you the wedding presents."

"I thought you'd been getting them at Lyckan."

"Those are from my friends and relatives. These are from Max's."

The ballroom was still being decorated. Great satin streamers of blue and gold were being looped from the crystal chandelier to various points around the room. Along one wall long tables had been set up, covered with the finest linen, gold candelabras, and crystal punch bowls.

"The flowers will all be blue and yellow, too," Camilla said, "but they won't finish decorating in here until tomorrow morning. Right now they have to concentrate on tonight's festivities. Look, here are the presents." She led Eve over to another long table at the far end of the room that was covered with literally hundreds of beautiful things: linens, crystal, pewter ware, silver—everything imaginable.

170

"Merciful heavens!" Eve gasped.

Camilla gazed at the display with an almost sullen expression. "They are all from important people that the von Stjernas know. I don't feel that they have any connection with me. They belong to Rosenborg."

"But you will be the mistress of Rosenborg, Cam," Eve reminded her. "You'll be the one to use these things."

"Not really. I'd rather be in my own kitchen—" She shook her head impatiently. "Never mind. Look—this is from the king, Eve. Can you imagine?"

She pointed to an exquisite gold coffee service, prominently displayed in the center of the table. "It must be worth a fortune. I'll be afraid to use it!"

Eve studied the beautifully engraved card with the royal crest on it. "They aren't coming to the wedding, are they?" she asked.

"Oh, no! I'd die if they were! But we are invited to some kind of reception at the castle next fall. I'm terrified. What can you say to a king and queen?"

"Oh, they're just like anyone else, I should imagine," Eve said carelessly. "Ask them about their little girl, Vickie."

There were many things to do around the house that morning, and the girls kept busy until lunch. The countess asked them to stay and they all had a light meal of sandwiches and fruit on the terrace.

When they had finished the countess said, "I think we should all take a long nap this afternoon in preparation for the festivities tonight—otherwise we will be exhausted for the wedding tomorrow. Oh, not you, Max—I know you are too restless to sleep in the afternoon—but all us females. Both you girls are looking a bit peaked. By the way, Camilla, before you go I want you to come upstairs with me for a few minutes. There is something I want to give you to wear tomorrow."

Eve could not help feeling a stab of pain as she watched Camilla wheel the older woman away toward the little elevator in the hall that had been installed after her accident. Blenda ran on home without waiting for the others, but Eve remained to walk home with Camilla. Max rose from the table and stood looking down at her.

"Would you like to see the chapel?" he asked. "The tree has been installed, although the flowers will not be taken over until tomorrow morning."

"I'd really rather not, Max," she told him frankly. She had not attended the brief rehearsal that they had held the day before and she hated the thought of setting foot in the chapel.

"Please, Eve," he said, in a curiously humble voice for him. "I just—somehow want to be there with you for a few minutes, alone. It may be our last time together. I have to leave for the airport in a few minutes to pick up some relatives that are flying in from Stockholm, and from now on there will be people around us constantly."

She got up against her will and went with him across the lawn toward the little chapel. "There is really nothing left that we can say to each other," she told him.

They went through the pine grove and down the flagstone path to the chapel. It was very peaceful there with birds calling overhead and the sunlight filtering down through the trees. Borders of small, colorful flowers lined the walk. The interior had obviously just been cleaned because there was still a strong odor of furniture polish and wax. They walked down the aisle, where garlands of birch leaves had been draped along the pews. Beside the altar stood a splendid young tree. They stopped and gazed up at it.

"There it is," she murmured, "the sacred tree and the sacrificial altar waiting for the virgin!"

172

"Eve—"

The tree stirred something deep and primitive in her and for a moment she was strangely frightened. She turned as though to leave. "I don't like it!" she said sharply. "This is supposed to be a Christian church, but it is pure pagan—"

Max caught her by the shoulders. "Yes, we are still a pagan race in our hearts, but you are one of us, you know, and you cannot escape it. Eve—look at me!"

She lifted her head to gaze into the glowing golden eyes.

"I love you, Eve. You know that. It is you who should be standing by this altar with me tomorrow, not Camilla."

He looked so white and unhappy that her heart ached for him. She thought about the great estate house—all the work and money and preparations that had gone into making the wedding a thing of beauty. She thought of the wedding presents in the ballroom— even one from the king of Sweden. She thought of the countess and her intense family pride, and of Camilla and Martin and the other Trillings and of all the humiliation they would suffer if Max backed out now. She thought about Max himself and his high position in the community and what such a scandal would do to him.

She put her hands over his, where they rested on her shoulders.

"Yes, Max," she said, "I finally do understand. I know you have to go through with it."

He pulled her close and for a moment she allowed herself the bittersweet luxury of putting her arms around his waist and laying her cheek against his chest, where she could hear his heart pounding.

"Goodbye, my love," he said. "I will never forget you."

173

"Goodbye, Max. I will never forget you, either."

They kissed gently, then she drew away from him. "We'd better go now." She took one last, almost furtive glance at the tree beside the altar before she turned and walked out of the chapel.

In spite of her emotional turmoil, Eve fell asleep when she got home and slept for a couple of hours, probably because she was so utterly exhausted. It was a haunted sleep, disturbed by strange dreams, almost nightmares. She dreamed she was searching for Max in a dark forest where shadowy things dogged her footsteps. Then she found him, hanging from a tall tree in a clearing, and there were also dead animals hanging there. She awoke with a cry of horror, trembling and drenched with sweat. She felt completely disoriented and for a moment didn't know where she was. Then she heard water running in the bathroom and realized the family were starting their baths before dressing for the evening. She would have to wait her turn.

She turned restlessly onto her back and stared at the ceiling. If only she could just go back to sleep and stay asleep until this night and the following day were over! Even the nightmares were better than the reality. Well, at least it would all be over by the following night. She had made reservations to fly home on Monday. All she wanted now was to get far away from there and try to pick up the threads of her old life.

In her letters to her family she had never mentioned a word of what she was going through. She told them about the things she had seen and how interesting it all was, and how wonderful it would be to see a Midsummer celebration and wedding before she left. So now all she had to do was to go home and pretend that nothing had happened, and no one there would ever know. Was it possible to hide a broken heart? Well, she would try.

174

Finally she got her turn in the bathroom, and after a quick shower she put on the costume that Kjell had loaned her. It was still a little loose because she had lost weight the last week or so, she thought, regarding herself in the mirror. She did look a bit peaked, as the countess had commented, but still the costume was becoming. With makeup judiciously applied, no one would notice how pale she was. Finally she gathered up the little cap that she would put on later, her purse, and a light wrap in case it got cold—which it always did at night there—and went downstairs.

Olivia was hurrying around, doing some last-minute chores, while Martin, resplendent in a new suit, looked on benignly.

"Does anyone want a bite to eat before we go?" Olivia asked. "It will be quite a while before our buffet supper."

"Some coffee, perhaps, my dear," Martin said. "Nothing more. We are all too keyed up for food."

Camilla went over and put her hand on his shoulder. She looked beautiful in her costume, but there was a haunted look in her wide blue eyes.

"Are you sure you won't get too tired, Papa?" she asked him.

He laughed indulgently and patted her hand. "No my love, I shall be fine. I am feeling much better these days, you know. Just think—by this time tomorrow our little girl will be a countess!"

"Yes, Papa," said Camilla without expression.

He gave her an annoyed glance. "What's the matter with you, girl? You should be radiant with joy. Instead you look more as though it were going to be your funeral tomorrow instead of your wedding."

"I'm just tired, Papa. So many things going on. I'll be all right." She gave him a bright, artificial smile.

"Yes, of course you will." For just a moment Eve caught an uneasy flicker of doubt in his eyes. Was he,

175

perhaps, beginning to doubt the wisdom of the course he had chosen for his daughter?

"Girls always get this way before their wedding, Martin," Olivia told him firmly. "It is such a big step they are taking."

"Of course, of course." The gaiety returned to his eyes. "I understand—the prewedding jitters—"

Blenda danced into the room, her face alight with happiness. "Look at me, Eve!" she cried. She also had a provincial costume, and looked adorable in it. She was going to take part in a little "children's dance" around the pole with some of the other youngsters from the estate. There was at present a wide revival of interest in the old costumes and folk lore. Sweden had grown too rapidly from the old ways into a bustling modern industrial country and was now beginning to react by indulging in nostalgia.

"You're beautiful, darling," Eve told her, and thought wistfully how wonderful it would be if they all felt as happy as she did.

"So are you, Eve." Blenda hugged her. "I wish you weren't going home next week. I wish you would stay all summer. It will be so lonely here with both you and Cam gone." A shadow blurred the joy in her eyes.

"Oh, I'll only be next door," Camilla assured her quickly. "We won't be away long, and I'll be coming over here all the time."

Blenda's face brightened. "And maybe by next summer you'll have a dear little baby and I will be its aunt and help you take care of it!"

A sick pain lurched through Eve at the thought of Camilla's bearing Max's child. Thank God she wouldn't be here when that happened! She wondered how Camilla felt about it. The girl's expression did not change, except to grow a bit more wooden.

"Yes, maybe I will," she said.

176

By five o'clock a large group had gathered in the courtyard between the stable and the barn. Eve had not realized that there were so many people involved in the running of the Rosenborg estate. There seemed to be at least a hundred adults and about as many children. They were a fine-looking bunch of people—rural Sweden at its best. A good many of them were in costume. Eve saw two little girls, apparently sisters, wearing wreaths of entwined buttercups and bluebells. She was very busy with her slide camera, wanting to take home a full record of the festival for her family.

Everyone was·in a festive mood and stood around in groups, talking and laughing with their friends. Max went from group to group, being his most charming. Eve thought she had never seen him look so breathtakingly handsome as he did in his native costume. He wore dark knickers that fastened just below the knee, white stockings, a full-sleeved white shirt, and a scarlet vest with gold embroidery that hung open with no fastenings. His soft brown hair gleamed in the sun and framed his lean, tanned face in soft waves. He looked every inch the Count von Stjerna, Eve thought. While everyone seemed to like him and would laugh and joke with him, they still treated him with deference, she noticed. He was the Herr Greve, and no mistake. His mother sat in her wheelchair as though it were a throne, graciously receiving their guests. The chair had been decorated with garlands of flowers and she herself also wore a provincial costume, with a little cap perched on her pile of soft white hair.

In America, Eve.reflected, people tended to think of Sweden as a welfare state, a prime example of modern socialism—but that was superficial. All the old ways, their love of the aristocracy and their royal family, even the pagan superstitions were still there just beneath the surface, as alive as ever.

177

At a few minutes past five Max made a little speech welcoming them to the annual festival, thanking them for their good work and cooperation over the past year, and speaking briefly about the significance of the ancient ceremony they were about to witness. While he was speaking, Eve took some pictures of him standing there with one hand on the back of his mother's chair. At least, she thought, she would have something to remember him by. Then he stepped back and from behind the barn came the sound of fiddles playing the lively, rhythmic, and rather monotonous tune that accompanied the raising of the pole.

She saw the men—about half a dozen of them, all in native costume—come marching around the corner of the barn sawing away on their fiddles. Behind them came another group of costumed men and teenaged boys bearing the symbolic pole. A standard had been set up in the courtyard to receive it, and while the fiddlers stood in a semicircle playing away for dear life, the others went about the business of raising the pole by the skillful manipulation of long forked poles and a great deal of determined heaving. Finally it stood—tall, straight, and beautiful—a symbol of ancient gods and rites now only dimly remembered. Eve felt tears come into her eyes as the audience applauded the successful raising. There was a timeless quality to the ritual. She felt the presence of all the preceding generations and those yet to come.

"Quite impressive, isn't it!" Kjell had come to stand beside her while she watched.

"Oh, yes! I feel as though time didn't exist, and all the past, present, and future were merged into one."

"To me," he said soberly, "it is always remarkable how down through the ages man has managed to retain his gaiety and hope for the future in spite of all the calamities that have happened to him—wars, pestilence, famine, and inevitable death."

178

"There is a force in man stronger than despair," she said. A curious exultation filled her heart, and she knew that no matter what happened now she could face it.

The fiddlers began to play the children's dance, and a woman led out her little troupe of children to dance around the pole, with Blenda among them. While they were dancing, the adult group gathered inside the barn to await their turn. Eve left her camera with Martin, instructing him to take some more pictures for her, and joined the others. Marko stood somewhat apart from them. He too looked remarkably handsome in his costume, but his face was expressionless, his dark eyes somber. She knew what he must be feeling. He looked up and caught her eye and gave her a brief smile. She moved over to stand beside him, slipping her hand into his.

"It will soon be over," she murmured.

"Yes, and I will be gone. I have given my notice."

"Do you really feel that you should leave, Marko? Max offered you such a good position as manager of his stud farm."

"I know, but I cannot stay here after Camilla becomes his wife."

She understood only too well how he felt. She could not endure it either. "Has Mitra gone back to Stockholm yet, Marko?"

"No, she is still at the Carsings'. She is furious with me because I failed to break up the engagement."

"Do you think she will try to cause any trouble tomorrow at the wedding?"

"That will be impossible. There are detectives here now to guard the wedding presents, and I have heard that they will also be on hand at the chapel tomorrow to make sure that no one but the invited guests can approach it. The maids have told me that Mitra has been calling Herr Greve and making threats, so he is taking no chances. She is drinking too much and her character seems to be deteriorating. Believe me, she was not always like this."

"I'm sorry, Marko. I know this is all very difficult for you."

When the children finished their dances and received their well-earned applause, it was time for the special opening number of the adult group. The fiddlers had now been joined by the accordionists and she heard the familiar strains of the Värmlands Polka. Max came in and took Camilla's hand and nodded to her and Marko, and they went running out to the courtyard. Her mind was a blank and she went through the dance like an automaton, hardly aware of what she was doing. The faces surrounding them were blurred.

Max and Camilla looked incredibly handsome together. They belonged, she thought, as she never could. She was an outsider. She and Marko. He too seemed to be going through the number automatically, his face expressionless. When they whirled around the courtyard with her hands on his shoulders and his arms about her waist, she felt as though they were moving into some strange, timeless void from which they would never return. Then it was over, the audience was applauding with great enthusiasm, and, after taking their bows, she and Max joined the Trillings to watch the rest of the dances, while Camilla and Marko rejoined the group.

"You did beautifully, Eve," Max told her. "Not a single mistake."

"Thank you." She gave him a polite smile. Perhaps, she thought, if she pretended to be very ill in the morning, she could stay in bed and not attend the wedding. But then, of course, that would upset the family and she didn't want to do that. She felt like a little animal who, caught in the steel jaws of a trap, sees the enemy approaching with his club.

180

When the dances ended, everyone joined hands in a circle to move around the pole. After that came a social hour during which Max introduced her to many of his employees, and she shook hands and talked in her hesitant Swedish and smiled until she felt that she could never smile again.

Later a lavish buffet supper was served on the tables that had been set up on the lawn. It was a beautiful spot for it, with trees and flowers surrounding them and a fountain tinkling nearby. The sun shone and the birds sang while everyone ate prodigiously of the omelets, cold meats, lobster salad, and all the other delicacies provided. There was ample beer, and soft drinks and coffee afterward, with cakes decorated with a Midsummer pole. Eve had eaten practically nothing all day, and now she found, to her surprise, that in spite of everything she was very hungry, and ate a good meal.

She tried to pretend that it was she Max was marrying the next day. What unbelievable heaven that would be! She watched him listening to a voluble old woman, his head bent attentively, a smile on his lips, and a wave of such tenderness swept over her that she had to close her eyes for a moment. How wonderful it would be to share this life with him and all the obligations that would be a joy to fulfill.

The children ran about the spacious lawn, shouting and laughing. A baby fell into the fountain and had to be rescued. Servants came out and started to clean up the litter on the tables. Finally everyone drifted back to the barn for the dancing. Some of the couples with small children and some of the older people went home, but most remained for the Midsummer Wake. The musicians had taken up their position on the dais and couples began to move about the floor. This time the music was more modern.

Kjell asked Eve to dance, and as they stepped out

181

onto the floor she said, "I wonder what has happened to Marko. He seems to have disappeared."

"Yes, he left as soon as the folk dancing was over. I understand he is leaving the country soon. I'll be sorry to see him go. I rather like him."

"So do I. I'm leaving Monday myself."

"So soon?" He looked distressed. "I'll really miss you, Eve."

"I'll miss you, too—and everyone."

The evening went on in a blur of color and movement. The sun had set, but twilight lingered on. More drinks were set out on the tables along the walls. Some of the guests were partaking a bit too freely, perhaps, but everyone was happy and good-natured.

Eve found herself dancing with Max, who had cut in on the slightly inebriated young farmer who had been her partner.

"If it gets a bit too rough for you later on," he said, "let me know and I'll take you home."

"Nonsense. It can't be any worse than some of the bashes I go to in Chicago." She looked over to where Olivia and Martin and the countess were sitting, happily chatting with friends. "Do you think Martin will want to stay all night?"

"I really couldn't say, Eve. He looks lively enough, doesn't he? This is the first time they have attended our festival, you know, because it is only for Rosenborg employees. This year they are here, of course, because of Camilla. Mother will probably want to retire in a little while, although she does enjoy these affairs."

"What time will the sun come up?"

"Around two-thirty."

"I want to see that happen, at least."

"In the old days," he told her, "people would hike out and climb to the top of a mountain to watch the sunrise."

"Oh, yes! I would love to do that!"

"But it is—" He paused, frowning, and she saw that he was looking toward the doorway.

"What is it, Max?"

"There seems to be some sort of a disturbance. I had better go see what it is."

Before he had taken more than a few steps, Eve saw Mitra come into the barn, pushing a young man who had tried to detain her at the entrance. She seemed to be drunk and staggered a bit as she came across the floor. She was wearing a flowered slack suit and her hair hung down in an untidy mass over her shoulders. Max swore under his breath. The other dancers fell back in alarm as she pushed her way toward Max.

"Where are your detectives?" Eve asked.

"In the house watching the presents. I never thought—but I can handle this myself."

She stopped a few feet away from Max and stood there swaying a little and staring at him with wild, dark eyes.

"So—there he is!" she exclaimed. "The great Count von Stjerna!"

The musicians stopped playing and everyone stood as though frozen in their places, watching the little drama. Eve looked at Camilla, who was not far away, and saw that her face was a mask of consternation.

"Mitra—" Max began.

"You are a fool, Max!" the woman cried. "You know that we love each other! How can you toss me aside for a simpering, stupid child? But I have a noble, forgiving heart, Max, and I have come to save you from your folly! Just look at her—" She pointed at Camilla. "Your virgin bride! Did you know that she has been seeing my cousin Marko behind your back? I sent him here to show her up for what she is! Ask her, Max. Ask her, if you do not believe me! Ask her if they have not become lovers!"

Max looked at Camilla in astonishment and disbelief, and the girl broke into tears.

"Yes, I love Marko. I couldn't help it, Max, but we were never lovers and it's all over now, I swear to you!"

"She's lying!" Mitra said scornfully. "Of course they were lovers. Marko told me so."

Martin was now coming toward them, his face contorted with fury. "She is the one who is lying, Max! Get that drunken slut out of here!"

Max drew himself up to his full height and his golden eyes shot sparks of anger. "Enough of this!" he said coldly. "You are making a fool of yourself, Mitra. I am afraid that you have had too much to drink. Come—I will take you home."

Mitra glared at him in a fury greater than his own and broke into a wild diatribe in Yugoslavian that, fortunately, nobody could understand. Then from the pocket of her jacket she drew a small, pearl-handled revolver.

"Put that toy away, Mitra!" Max commanded. "Have you gone completely mad?"

She lifted her arm to its full length with the pistol pointing directly at his heart.

"If I cannot have you, Max, then nobody can!" she proclaimed dramatically, and pulled the trigger.

Chapter Thirteen

Eve had been watching with the same frozen horror everyone else seemed to be feeling. It was all so wildly melodramatic it didn't seem real; it couldn't be happening. Her mind was blank, but her physical reflexes were still working. When she saw Mitra's finger tighten on

184

the trigger, she did not consciously think, "I must save him!" Without any awareness of what she was doing, she simply sprang in front of him, crying, "No!" At the same instant the pistol went off and she fell into a swirling void.

From time to time she was conscious of vague movement, subdued voices, lights, and pain, but then she would sink once more into the void. She had no idea how much time had passed when she finally opened her eyes to find herself in a cool white room. The blinds were drawn and she smelled antiseptic and roses. When she turned her head, she saw a big bouquet of them on a dresser. She tried to remember what had happened, but it was all rather dim. A nurse came toward her and put her fingers on Eve's wrist. She was smiling.

"You are conscious now," she said in Swedish. "Good! How do you feel?"

"I'm not sure," Eve said faintly. She put her hand to her head, which seemed to be swathed in bandages. Her head hurt. "Is this a hospital?" she asked.

"Yes, this is a hospital. You were shot, Froken, but you are going to be all right now."

Shot. It was beginning to come back now. Midsummer Eve—Mitra—the little pistol aimed at Max's heart . . .

"Is Max all right?" she cried.

"Yes, Froken. He is waiting outside now. If you feel strong enough, I will let you see him for a few minutes, but then you must have another injection and sleep again."

"Yes, please let me see him."

The nurse went out and Max came in. He looked pale and disheveled and he needed a shave. He came and leaned over her and kissed her cheek, his golden eyes gazing into hers.

185

"Eve! Thank God you are finally conscious! It has been such hell—"

"Tell me what happened," she said. "It's all rather a blur." There was an I.V. attached to her arm and she shifted it irritably as he pulled over a chair and sat beside the bed.

"Darling, lie still," he said, "or they will make me leave. I am not to excite you."

"I'm not excited, Max, I just want to know what happened. I remember that Mitra was going to shoot you and I think I got in the way."

He clasped her free hand. "You did indeed, and probably saved my life. The bullet was aimed at my heart, but since you are so small it grazed your skull. Thank God it did not enter the brain, but there was a fracture and you have been unconscious for nearly a week. The doctor will give you all the medical details if you are interested, but they have assured me you will be all right now. You saved my life, darling. What can I say? You were willing to give your life for mine—"

"Not really," she protested. "I didn't even think. I just jumped."

"I realize that. It was the fact that it was a reflex action that showed me the true depth of your feelings. Would you have reacted that way for anyone else?"

"Well—not just any old Tom, Dick, or Harry, I guess." She made a wry grimace. "Have I really been here nearly a week? Then I missed my plane. Did anybody cancel my reservation?"

He sighed. "Really, Eve! How could anyone have thought of a silly thing like that?"

"Is this the hospital in Romeby?"

"No, you were there first, but their facilities are limited, so you were taken to Karlstad for the surgery."

"Surgery? What surgery?"

"There was a portion of skull pressing on your

brain—but you don't want to talk about that now, do you, darling?"

"Not really. Oh, my goodness, Max! The wedding! You should be on your honeymoon now!"

"*Herre Gud,* Eve, what do you take me for? There will be no wedding or honeymoon. At least not with Camilla."

"But you have to marry her—"

"No, I don't. That is all over. When I caught you in my arms as you fell, I knew that I had been a terrible fool. You were my love, my only love, and whether you lived or died I could marry no one but you."

"But, Max—"

"There are no buts. We held a conference while you were unconscious—the Trillings, Marko, my mother, and I—and everything was brought out into the open as it should have been long ago. It is all settled now. Marko admitted that he had been sent here by Mitra to break the engagement, but he said that he really loves Camilla and she seems to love him, so that is all right. They are to be married soon and Marko will run a stud farm for me, and I will build them a house—"

"With a big kitchen, I hope?" Eve said weakly.

He grinned. "The biggest and finest kitchen that money can buy I assure you, love. And as soon as you are strong enough, we will take off for Grand Canary."

She couldn't quite take it all in. Her head was swirling. "What about Mitra?" she asked. "What has happened to her?"

"Kjell grabbed her before she could fire again. She was arrested, but she is in a mental hospital now. She seems to have cracked up completely. By the way, darling, your parents are here. I called them the night this happened and they flew right over. A charming couple. They are in the cafeteria now, I believe, having breakfast. You can see them later."

She stared at him stupidly. "My parents are here?"

187

"They certainly are, and since they did come, they might as well stay on for the wedding, don't you think? The doctor says—"

"But, Max," she interrupted, "what about Martin?"

"Oh, yes. Martin. It is strange, but Mother was the only one who grasped an essential fact that the rest of us missed. During our conference when I told Camilla I could not marry her because I loved you, she said, 'But what about Papa? If he should die—' And Mother interrupted her, saying, 'Has it not occurred to you, my dear, that if Max marries Eve the conditions of the old prophecy will be fulfilled just as surely as if he marries you? Eve is, after all, as much a Trilling as you. Her mother is a direct descendant of the Trilling line.' Which is quite true—you are a Trilling. Martin was angry, I could see that—I'm afraid you were right about him all along—but he couldn't say anything."

Eve closed her eyes. "It's too much—I can't take it all in!" she murmured.

"Do not try my love. Rest now and we will talk more later." She felt his lips gently brush her eyelids. "I was so blind—but in that one moment when you took the bullet that was meant for me, I realized that nothing in the world mattered except our love for each other."

"I always knew that," she said drowsily, before her smiling lips met his.

STORMY MASQUERADE

"*Finished, is it?*"

The vibration in his voice was like the guttural warning of a jungle cat about to attack. Before she had time to move, her wrist was caught in a vice-like grip, as his sensuous mouth crushed hers in brutal, dominating savagery.

She was captive in his arms, for even his cruelty drew her, his magnetism far too strong. . . . She found herself swept irresistibly into the maelstrom of an all-consuming passion equal to his own. . . .

At last, breathing heavily, he held her from him, a sneering lift of triumph to his mouth as he saw the dark and dreamy glaze that covered her eyes.

"Well, Karen," he said in some amusement, "it wasn't finished was it? But it is now, because I say so. . . ."

ANNE HAMPSON
has the same impetuous streak as her heroines. It often lands her in the middle of a new country, a new adventure—and a new book. Her first-hand knowledge of her settings and her lively characters have combined to delight her readers throughout the world.

ANNE HAMPSON

Stormy Masquerade

Chapter One

The curtain fell to a deafening round of applause from a loyal and enthusiastic audience. It was another triumph for the Parkside Amateur Dramatic Society, and especially for Karen Waring and her friend Meryl Dempster.

'Just listen to that!' Automatically Meryl flicked a hand toward the lowered curtain. 'Gratifying, isn't it?'

Karen nodded, but before she had time to say anything the curtain was rising again and the entire cast was bowing to the audience.

'You were marvelous, as usual,' Karen was saying a few minutes later when they were in the dressing room they shared. 'If you're serious about making acting your career you'll be a star one day.' Having removed a long sleeky blond wig, Karen was busy taking off the makeup which added over ten years to her age. 'Most of the applause was for you,' she added sincerely. 'The author of the play would be delighted with your performance if only he could see it.'

6

'Thank you,' murmured Meryl from her place at the other dressing table. 'But, Karen, you know very well that you are just as popular with our supporters as I. They loved your performance.'

'I little thought,' mused Karen, 'when I let you persuade me to join the company, that I'd ever be anything more than an extra, yet here I am, the bitch par excellence!' She turned her dark head and laughed. 'No wonder I never find a boy friend!'

'Don't you ever get fed up with being the nasty piece of work all the time?' Meryl was dabbing her face with a pad of cotton wool soaked in *eau de Cologne*. 'I'm sure I should.'

'No; I enjoy the role I slipped into. Maybe I'm basically the bitchy type of girl and that's the secret of my success.'

'Hello . . . fishing for compliments,' teased Meryl, and they both laughed.

However, a frown soon appeared on Karen's brow, and her big gray-green eyes were shadowed. Meryl, noticing the change as she caught her friend's expression through the mirror, swiveled round on her stool to ask anxiously what was wrong.

'I'm restless,' admitted Karen with a little impatient sigh. 'I'm undecided about staying with Brown and Forsythe when my boss retires. I've been told that it's almost a certainty that I shall have to go to John Lacey, whose secretary's leaving to get married.'

Meryl grimaced.

'He's not a nice man, from what you've told me.'

'No one likes him. He's surly, bad-tempered and faultfinding. Dorothy told me she wouldn't have stuck it out this long if she hadn't been getting married and knew she'd be leaving soon. She's been a saint to put up with him as long as she has.'

'Are jobs easy to get?' asked Meryl, troubled.

'I don't really know. But in any case, I've had itchy feet ever since my sister got that job in Barbados. As you know, she works as a receptionist in an hotel. I wish I could land a job that would take me abroad.' Karen shrugged her shoulders resignedly. 'I'd never be as lucky as Jean. She got to know the manager of the Vervain Hotel when he was in London. He was staying at the hotel where she worked. Before he left he asked her if she'd be interested in working for him, on the island of Barbados. Naturally she jumped at the chance since, like me, she's no ties.'

Meryl nodded. Having finished removing her makeup she rose from the stool and stood for a moment looking at her friend through the mirror, noting the rare, classical beauty of her features—the high cheekbones with the transparent, alabaster skin stretched tightly over them, those unusual widely spaced eyes that always seemed to have a dewy look about them, the full, generous mouth and firm, pointed chin which gave her face an oval shape. Her hair, mid-brown touched with tawny-gold, was long and straight, flicked up at the ends and with a half-fringe falling enchantingly on to the high, intelligent forehead. Meryl's own beauty was fair and deceptively fragile; Karen's was of a darker, stronger kind which, to Meryl, seemed to possess the sort of delightful witchery that would appeal to any man. And yet, at twenty-two, Karen had not yet become interested enough in the opposite sex to offer encouragement to any of those men who, at various times, would have liked to go steady with her.

She had taken off the last of the heavy makeup and Meryl could not help but compare this unsophisticated beauty with what Karen had been like only twenty minutes ago. The bitch par excellence was no understatement!

'You fascinate me the way you make yourself up so expertly.' Meryl was thinking about George, their special makeup man who had been somewhat resentful when Karen decided to try doing it herself. But he had since admitted that Karen was a master hand. 'There's no doubt,' went on Meryl, speaking her thoughts aloud, 'that if you wanted to disguise yourself you'd have no difficulty at all. I'm sure you could deceive anyone—even me—if you wanted to.'

Karen laughed, recalling her first attempts, one evening when George was pushed for time, having arrived late owing to his car breaking down. To her own surprise she had been more than satisfied with her attempts and, with the practice she had had since, she mentally agreed that she would have no trouble in adopting an efficient disguise.

'I don't know about deceiving you,' she returned doubtfully. 'And as I've no criminal leanings I can't imagine a situation where I'd want to disguise myself.'

But how little she knew . . .

When, a week later, the final curtain came down on Clint Fraser's play, *One Stolen Hour*, there was not one among the cast who was not keyed up with anticipation, for the playwright had not only been in the audience, but he was to attend the party at the Sandiway Hotel which the company was throwing afterward, as this was the final week of the present season.

'I never imagined I'd ever have the honour of meeting the famous Clint Fraser!' Phil Armstrong had exclaimed a few days previously when the cast had been told that the author was to do them the honour of attending the last performance. Phil played the lead, mostly, and he, like Meryl, was keen to make acting a career. 'I wonder if he's coming as a scout?'

'He'd not bother his head about anything like that,' returned Leonard Holt, who had taken the part of the villain in the play. 'It's just interest, I expect, to see what a mess the amateurs can make of his play.'

Karen had said nothing; she had seen the playwright interviewed on television, and while admitting that his looks were extraordinarily attractive, and that there was something strikingly powerful and arresting about his tall, immaculately clad figure, she had found herself denouncing him as an arrogant, conceited man who was far too conscious of his position as one of the world's most talented playwrights.

However, on hearing that he was willing to come to a small theatre to see amateurs performing his play, and then to attend their party afterward, Karen was ready to revise her opinion of him and begin all over again.

As the cast was not changing until after the party, it was as the sleeky, blond-haired villainess that Karen was introduced to Clint Fraser by Jake Sheridan, their producer.

'How do you do?' Clint's handshake hurt; his pewter-gray eyes below straight black brows seemed to look through her rather than at her, and she knew for sure that he had not even taken the trouble to memorize her name. She colored when his eyes moved, to make a cursory examination of the sexy svelte figure revealed by the slinky satin dress she wore. She was glad to move away to allow Jake to introduce Meryl.

'He's a real he-man!' Meryl was exclaiming later when she and Karen were at the buffet table, plates in hands. 'And did you notice how handsome he is? And that attractive quality in his voice—stern, sort of, and yet you had the impression that he could be very kind. Did *you* notice that tone in his voice, Karen?'

'I noticed his arrogance,' was Karen's sardonic rejoinder as she helped herself to a slice of chicken from a dish. 'He's full of his own importance, if you ask me.'

Meryl laughed, her blue eyes alight.

'Your opinion of him matches that of most of the females in the cast. He seems not to be interested. But me—' She broke off and wagged a teasing forefinger. 'I, my bitchy one, am different! He congratulated me on my performance and said the kindest thing!'

'Good for you,' she said sarcastically as Karen stabbed a piece of meat pie with her fork. 'And what was this eloquent and flattering distinction he accorded you?'

Meryl laughed heartily.

'Don't be catty! And you're not on the stage now so you needn't speak like that! He said I ought to make acting my career.'

Karen swung around, sincerely interested now.

'He did? I'm so glad, Meryl. You're going to take his advice?'

'I think so, but later. Mum needs my money at present, just until the twins leave school and start work. If only Dad hadn't gone off and left us. . . .' Her voice trailed, and silence fell between the two girls, each busy with her own thoughts—Meryl dwelling on the misfortune that had befallen her family when her father went off with a girl of nineteen, and Karen reflecting on the untimely death of her parents in a railway accident four years ago, when Karen and her sister were left with no one else in the world.

'I'm getting morbid!' declared Meryl, and instantly became herself again. 'Gosh, I'm ready for this food! Where shall we sit?'

'Here,' from Josie Barlow who was with two other members of the company. 'We can easily make room at our table.'

The five chatted while they ate and then Karen and Meryl were alone again as the other three moved off. But they were soon joined by Phil, to whom Meryl said instantly, 'I saw you talking to our star guest.' She looked at him questioningly, wanting to learn something about the playwright.

'He was saying he's writing his next play on a boat. Jake was telling me earlier that he has a fabulous luxury cabin cruiser which he's going to moor at Barbados. He's going there in a fortnight or three weeks time. Jake asked how long the play would take to write and he said about six months. Imagine having six months in the Caribbean! I wish I could write plays!'

Karen glanced toward the man being discussed. Lean of build and strikingly handsome, he possessed the unmistakable attributes of culture and good breeding. His confidence obviously stemmed from the success of achievement; his air of distinction marked him an aristocrat, and Karen recalled that in the television interview it was revealed that he was connected with one of the most noble families in the country. He was in conversation with Jake, whose entire interest he was holding, when Sylvia Dawson, one of the cast, intruded into the conversation, and Karen saw that Clint hardly glanced at her before turning his head and resuming his discourse with the producer. Karen set her mouth, wishing she had the opportunity of telling him what she thought of his rudeness.

'Barbados?' Meryl's voice broke into Karen's train of thought and she put the objectionable Clint Fraser from her mind. 'Karen's sister lives there.'

'Yes, I know. Karen told me.' Phil continued to talk about the playwright for a few minutes, then looked up to see Jake approaching their table.

'And how do you like our Mr. Fraser?' Jake spoke pleasantly, his smile a little reserved. He was a thin, balding man with polished manners that always seemed at variance with the casual way he dressed, usually in denims and a roll-neck sweater. 'A charming fellow, don't you think?'

Meryl nodded but laughed as she saw her friend's expression.

'I like him well enough,' she said, 'but Karen wasn't all that impressed.'

'He's rather aloof at times.' Jake glanced around and

added, 'Let me get myself a few eats and I'll be right back.'

'Phil says he's writing his next play on a boat,' said Meryl when Jake returned and took a seat at the table.

'Where is his home?' Karen was trying to remember if it had been mentioned in the television interview.

'On the island of Grenada—the Spice Island.'

'But he's going to live on his boat? I wonder why?'

'He was saying that it's an experiment because he wants to get right away from everyone—servants, friends, the lot. He'll have almost total isolation on his boat.'

Karen became thoughtful, wondering how far Clint's boat would be from the hotel in which her sister worked.

'You're not your usual bright self,' observed Jake on suddenly noticing Karen's serious expression. 'Anything wrong?'

'It's nothing,' she said, and would have changed the subject but Meryl broke in to say, 'Karen's not happy about her job. As you know, her boss is leaving and she might have to work for a man she doesn't like.'

'I might try for a job that involves travel,' mused Karen.

Jake's eyes flickered over her.

'If you'd been older you could have had a job on Clint Fraser's boat.'

'I could?' Karen's eyes automatically slid to the man in question. His gaze met hers, stony and indifferent before he glanced away again. 'What doing?' Karen added without much interest. 'You just said he wanted to be alone.'

'He needs a woman to do for him. A sort of Girl Friday, from what I gather.'

'A Girl Friday,' from Meryl interestedly. 'Why must she be older?'

'I suspect it's because the young ones forget the real reason why they're there,' laughed Jake.

'You mean—?' began Karen, then stopped, colouring slightly.

'Yes, that's what I mean. A handsome man on a boat with a pretty girl—and the romantic setting of the Caribbean. . . . Well, I ask you?'

'He actually said that girls run after him?' Karen's eyes reflected contempt, but Jake was shaking his head even before her last word was out.

'Not at all, Karen. Don't be bitchy offstage,' he admonished with a mock severity. 'I gathered this myself—I'm very astute you know,' he added laughing. 'But he did say that he was having someone older because he was intending to write, not to pander to the whims of some female avid for romance.'

Karen gasped.

'The pompous, opinionated creature!' she exclaimed. 'Some female ought to teach him a lesson!'

Jake merely shrugged and laughed.

'How old has this woman to be?' Meryl wanted to know, her fork poised half-way to her mouth.

'Over forty-five. He's advertising in the newspapers sometime this week—at least, I think that was what he said.'

'I doubt if a woman over forty-five would want to be a Girl Friday,' said Karen. 'What are the duties?'

'He wants someone to cook and clean, and to wash

his clothes. He wasn't all that communicative,' Jake went on to add, a faintly bored note creeping into his voice, as if he were no longer interested in the subject. 'The woman will have a great deal of time off, from what I can gather.'

He left soon afterward and to Karen's surprise the playwright sauntered over to them. His movements were languid, with an almost uncanny grace about them that could not fail to attract attention. Karen noticed that several pairs of feminine eyes were following him as he crossed the room.

'May I join you?' Polite the voice, finely modulated and cultured. 'The heroine and villainess, eh?' He threw Karen a cursory glance before giving his whole attention to Meryl. She wore a little makeup, so that her prettiness came through, whereas Karen was heavily made up; as the bitch in the play she was thirty-five years of age and, therefore, totally different in appearance from her natural self.

'We thoroughly enjoyed acting in your play,' Meryl was saying enthusiastically, appearing to be perfectly at her ease with the man who, leaning back in his chair, was idly tapping the arm; and to Karen's critical mind even this small movement was irritating, because she regarded it as a sign of arrogance. 'Did you enjoy writing it, Mr. Fraser?'

'Yes, I enjoy all my plays.'

'All?' interposed Karen in surprise. 'You never write one you have difficulty with?'

'We weren't speaking of difficulty—' He paused as if trying to recall her name. Karen merely waited, determinedly refraining from offering it. 'We were speaking of enjoyment. Naturally I sometimes have difficulty, but I still enjoy writing the plays. If I found I wasn't enjoying a play then I'd scrap it at once, because it's my firm conviciton that anything which becomes a chore is bound to be inferior on completion.'

'There's a great deal of logic in that,' Karen was forced to admit, albeit grudgingly. Clint's pewter-gray eyes were cynical and it was patently clear that he had guessed she had made the admission reluctantly.

After staying with them—talking mainly to Meryl—he moved on. Meryl turned to Karen, eyeing her curiously.

'You were using your bitchy voice,' she said. 'Why?'

Karen shrugged. She could not have answered the question because she did not know what had prompted her to use the husky, sexy voice she had used on stage.

'It was good enough for him,' was all she said and was relieved when Meryl merely laughed and changed the subject.

'I think we ought to be socialising,' Meryl said after a while and Karen nodded in agreement. But she was finding the room stifling and after a few minutes she went outside for a breath of fresh air.

She was sitting on a dimly lit patio when Clint Fraser came out and she shrank back instinctively but realised he had seen her. She stood up without knowing why. He did not speak and for Karen the moment was charged with tension. She wondered if it was the dislike each felt for the other that was creeping into the atmosphere.

At last he spoke, saying casually, 'It was becoming rather warm in there. You obviously thought so, too.'

'Yes, I did find it a little overpowering.' Like you, she added, but silently. He was towering over her, regarding her in a way that gave her a feeling of having been stripped and, colouring, she took a swift step away from him.

'Your friend Miss Dempster has talent,' he remarked conversationally after a while. 'I've advised her to consider acting as a career.'

'Yes, she told me. Meryl's very keen on acting; it was she who persuaded me to join the company.' She was still using her stage voice, and he looked at her oddly, as if debating whether or not this was also her natural voice. However, he wasn't interested enough to inquire about it and another silence fell between them. Karen said, driven by some impulse she could neither understand nor control, because the last thing she desired was to open a conversation with him, 'Jake was saying that you're writing your next play on a boat.'

'That's correct.'

'It's to be moored at Barbados. That's a beautiful island.' She was about to mention Jean but refrained, deciding he would not be in the least interested in the fact that her sister worked on the island.

'It is beautiful, yes.'

'But you don't live there.'

'No, I prefer Grenada, mainly because it's not so touristy. It doesn't have as much to offer the visitor as Barbados.'

'It must be nice to live on a boat.' Karen's eyes were suddenly dreamy as she added, 'You'll have just the right atmosphere there. Jake says you want to be alone.'

'I do.' He sounded bored, she thought, and was not surprised when he excused himself and left her.

She walked from the patio onto the grounds, finding a dark path among the shrubs and proceeding slowly along it. Then she stopped on hearing voices from the other side of the hedge. Clint Fraser was with Sally Haworth, one of the older members of the company. Sally had obviously asked a question because Clint was saying, 'Yes, his acting was excellent for an amateur.'

'Meryl, the heroine, she's always very good too.'

'Excellent.'

'And the bitch. She—'

'Lacks finesse,' interrupted the playwright disparagingly. 'That girl couldn't act if she put everything she had into it.'

Karen gasped, the hot colour rising in her cheeks as anger and humiliation fought for supremacy. For him to have said a thing like that to one of her fellow actors! But he had been equally outspoken in that television interview, she recalled, obviously he was a man who always spoke his mind.

If only she could show him whether she could act or not! But the way she felt at the moment it would give her far more satisfaction to do him a physical injury. . . .

Chapter Two

Karen was back in her own office after having been called into the Managing Director's room to be told that, from the beginning of the following month, she would be working as private secretary to John Lacey.

'I hope you'll be as happy with him as you have been with Mr. French,' he smiled.

Out of politeness Karen was obliged to say, 'I think I will be, Mr. Smythe,' but her heart was heavy as she left the room.

At lunch time she bought a newspaper, deciding she would look for another post. And as she scanned the "Situations Vacant" column one advertisement, a square window-frame advertisement, stood out, the words dancing before her eyes. When she focused she read, "Wanted for a period of approximately six months, woman of forty-five or over for light duties on a luxury, ocean-going cabin cruiser. Duties include some cooking, cleaning, etc. Telephone for interview." The number followed. Karen read the advertisement again, then scanned the rest of the column, but her eyes returned over and over again to the advertisement put in by Clint Fraser, and inevitably she was hearing his deristve criticism of her acting.

She found herself studying the advertisement with concentrated attention as an idea was conceived. Why not apply for the post? After all, she had nothing to lose. And if she should happen to be fortunate enough to obtain the job, what a satisfying revenge she would have when, in six months time, she could confound him by revealing her true identity. He would be forced to eat those words about her inability to act!

The interview was to take place in a small private room at the Savoy Hotel in London where the playwright was staying while in England, and Karen had known a tense and breathless moment when, having rung the number and heard Clint Fraser's voice, she had given him her name—though omitting her Christian name—saying she was applying for the post.

'Miss Waring,' he had repeated, then given his own name and Karen had breathed freely again. Just as she had suspected, Clint Fraser had not bothered to memorise her name when given it by Jake when he had introduced them at the party.

The interview was for eleven o'clock the following Saturday morning and Karen rose early so as to give herself ample time to effect the transformation in her appearance. And when at last she was ready she felt just about as confident as it was possible to be. For the face and figure which she saw in the long, gilt-framed mirror faultlessly portrayed those of a woman in her mid-forties. She had dry, graying hair taken severely back from her furrowed brow; her face was pale, the lips almost colourless. The eyes alone had caused Karen some concern, but she had soon solved this problem by the use of horn-rimmed spectacles with clear glass in them. The dress, of a dull gray linen-type material, hung loosely, hiding the seductive curves beneath its austere folds and the shapely legs within its length. Only at the neck was it tight, fastened up high, to give an added severity to the face above it.

'Hmm. . . .' approved Karen with a satisfied smile as she picked up a heavy velour coat she borrowed from an elderly neighbor in the flat next door. 'Yes, you've done a most excellent job, Miss Karen Waring! I congratulate you!'

She was congratulating herself again an hour later when, having entered the room at the Savoy Hotel, she saw no sign of recognition on the face of the man standing there with his back to the window.

'Miss Waring.' The pewter-gray eyes ran over her figure indifferently before returning to her face, to settle there. He seemed to frown, as if he deplored women who used cosmetics too freely. However, as his interest was in her suitability as a servant rather than in her looks, he began briskly to ask the relevant questions. These were answered, but sometimes the answers were gone into a little more deeply as, for instance, when he asked why she should want to leave a perfectly good post as private secretary to take on something that was to last only six months.

'I want a complete change,' she replied frankly. 'I

know I can get another, similar post at the end of the six months.'

'You're sure?' His firm, finely modulated voice held a trace of anxiety. 'You're no longer young, remember, and so you might have difficulty. Secretarial posts are not so plentiful as they were a few years ago.'

'I'm willing to take the risk,' she said, looking away to hide her expression. 'I've always wanted to travel, and when you said on the telephone that your boat was to be moored at Barbados, that was an added incentive because, you see, my young sister lives there, and if I did get the post we'd be able to see one another regularly, which would be nice for us both, as we haven't any other relatives at all.' Karen held her breath, aware that for one vital moment she had forgotten to use her "mature" voice. But there was no sign that Clint Fraser had noticed, and in fact, he was looking rather bored, as if he were wishing the interview were at an end.

'You've had no experience in the kind of work I should expect you to do.' It was a statement but he looked at her, expecting a comment.

'Only that I look after myself in my flat,' returned Karen. 'And I think I'm a fairly good cook,' she added, watching his face intently, trying to find some clue as to whether or not he was favourably impressed. But she read nothing; his dark face was inscrutable, like a mask.

However, his next words were heartening, to say the least.

'I'm interested in the fact that you have a sister on the island whom you could see regularly. When I'm working on a play I work solidly for the whole day and, therefore, I should not want to see or hear you from the time you serve my breakfast at eight o'clock in the morning, until you bring in my dinner at nine in the evening.' He paused, giving her an opportunity to speak but she said nothing, merely waiting for him to continue. 'I have a small suite at one end of the boat, and this consists of a study, a small sitting room, a bathroom and a very small galley where I can make myself coffee when I want it. You would prepare me a snack lunch and leave it there. You would clean up the suite while I'm at breakfast, and be out of it by the time I'd finished.' Another pause, and this time Karen did speak, to ask what other accommodations the cruiser had.

'There is a dining room, I suppose, and a galley,' she said, 'but what about the cabins? I'd scarcely be able to clean the rest of the boat without making a sound.'

'My suite's right at one end and the galley's at the other. Your work would mainly be in there—the preparation of the food and the washing—' He stopped, frowning at her as if he considered the discussions of such things to be beneath him. 'As for the other cleaning—' he shrugged offhandedly, '—well, you'd have to do it either very early in the morning or late at night.'

'Yes. . . .' She nodded automatically.

'You'll have gathered,' he went on briskly, 'that you will have most of the day free. I'd prefer that you leave the boat as soon as possible and not return until it's time for you to prepare my evening meal. I like to know I'm entirely alone when I'm working. At home I have servants around and also gardeners. There are altogether too many distractions and it's because I'm trying to get away from these distractions that I've decided to use my boat.' He went on to say that the boat would be moored at the private jetty of the Smuggler's Cove Hotel, which was owned by a friend of his. The jetty was situated at an isolated part of the beach not accessible to the hotel guests, and so he could be sure of both privacy and quietness—the notice "No Guests Beyond This Point" usually being effective.

When Clint Fraser said that she would be expected to leave the boat for more than eight hours each day, Karen had wondered what on earth she would do with herself all that time. But on hearing him mention the Smuggler's Cove Hotel she could scarcely believe her ears, for it was right next to the Vervain Hotel in which her sister worked, and as Jean had a small bungalow on the hotel grounds, one of several provided for the more privileged on the staff, Karen could go there, using it as a second home, as it were. Yes, that would be fine, because, once she arrived at the bungalow she could get rid of her disguise for the next eight hours or so. She could don a bikini and sunbathe. It would be like a prolonged holiday! She had not thought of taking any clothes other than would be suitable to her "mature" age, just in case, by some mischance, Clint Fraser should see them. But now she could take what she liked, and leave them at her sister's.

'I've one or two more people to interview,' Clint was saying a short while later, 'but I'll let you know, by letter, not later than Tuesday.'

'Thank you, Mr. Fraser.' Karen rose from the chair. He opened the door for her and stood to one side.

'If I decide to employ you,' he said as she made to pass him, 'I should want you a fortnight today. I shall be flying to my home in Grenada on Thursday week and you would follow two days later. My boat's at Grenada and we shall sail with a crew from there to Barbados where the boat will be moored for about six months. The crew will then leave; they've already been hired by a South American family who are cruising the Caribbean for several months.'

The letter came three days later.

She had gotten the job!

There was her notice to give in and, fortunately for her, her boss put in a good word for her and she was able to leave without giving the customary one month notice. There was the rushing around, the handing over of her flat to an estate agent who would let it for her. There were clothes to buy, friends to see, and a final dinner at a small hotel to which Karen invited Meryl and two other friends. During the meal they all wanted to know everything, and Helen, Karen's friend from school days, was especially enthusiastic, simply because the masquerade appealed to her sense of adventure. Glenda, the other friend, foretold all sorts of snags and risks, and finally, the sack.

'He'll see through the disguise eventually,' she sighed. 'Karen, you must be crazy to have given up your excellent job for this. I wouldn't be in your shoes when he finds out!'

'What can he do?' shrugged Karen. 'As you say, he

can send me packing, and probably raise the roof at being deceived, but he can't do me any physical injury.'

'Well. . . .'

'You carry on,' enthused Helen. 'I'll book a holiday in Barbados and come and see you.'

'Have you thought what it's going to be like with that stuff on your face all day?' asked Glenda dismally.

'It won't be on all day.' Karen went on to explain what she had been told by Clint Fraser at the interview.

'You'll have the whole day to yourself!' exclaimed Meryl enviously. 'Good lord, that's not a job, it's a picnic!'

'So you'll be able to wash your makeup off until it's time to return to the boat?' interposed Helen. 'You'll be able to do it at your sister's, of course?'

'Yes. It'll be a relief, I must admit, because it isn't at all comfortable, wearing it too long.'

'Nor will it be comfortable wearing drab clothes,' added Glenda with a doleful shake of her head.

'It's to be hoped,' said Meryl thoughtfully, 'that Mr. Fraser doesn't ever want you in the night—'

'In the night? Why should he?'

'If he took ill, or anything. You'd not have time for making yourself up, and so the cat would really be out of the bag.'

'It's not an impossibility that he'd need me in the night,' Karen admitted, but added that she was not going to let a thing like that worry her. 'He seems so strong that I can't imagine him sick!' said she, reflecting on his healthy bronzed colouring and superb physique.

'You're going to get yourself into such a tangle,' warned Glenda woefully.

'Your sister'll be staggered when she knows what you've done,' laughed Meryl. 'Oh, but I do think you're adventurous, Karen!'

'Not adventurous but foolhardy,' from Glenda with a sigh.

'Oh, shut up, Glenda, you old pessimist,' chided Helen. 'I only wish I could have done something like this. Not only is Karen going to travel, but she's going to have fun as well, hoodwinking that horrid Clint Fraser.'

The following day Karen flew to Grenada, being met at the airport by Clint Fraser himself who took her by car to his home, a lovely modern villa set in extensive grounds overlooking the Caribbean Sea. Everything about the villa and gardens spelled luxury and good taste. The house had high airy rooms beautifully furnished, the grounds were immaculately kept with smooth velvet lawns, flowerbeds and borders, two fountains cascading into ornamental pools; statuary and terraces and sunken rose gardens, and towering over it all, graceful palms of many varieties, and royal poincianas and frangipani trees. Karen was enchanted with it and on one occasion had almost forgotten her role and would have exclaimed in her natural voice but she pulled herself up just in time. After that she was very guarded, assuming the kind of reserve that would be expected of a mature woman of forty-five years of age. She stayed the night at his home and the following day they sailed to Barbados where the crew was dismissed.

The *Fair Mermaid* had been moored at Barbados for over a week, and Karen had fallen into a pleasant routine where, donning an apron, she would prepare her employer's breakfast and take it in to him precisely at eight o'clock every morning. While he was eating it she would rush around with duster and vacuum cleaner, tidying up Clint's suite, but taking care to replace, exactly as she found it, anything on his desk. After breakfast she would clear away the dishes, wash them up, tidy the dining room for the evening, and then she would go off the boat and make for Jean's bungalow, where, after taking off her makeup, she would bathe and change—having already taken her clothes there—and if Jean was not too busy at reception, they would have a chat over morning coffee and Karen would then take a book on to the hotel's private beach. Jean came off duty at six in the evening, so the sisters had about an hour together before Karen began to change her personality in preparation for returning to the boat.

'It's wonderful, seeing so much of you!' Jean had said more than once during the past week. 'It was the greatest piece of luck that you landed a job like that!'

'I know it. I've scarcely anything to do. I have Mr. Fraser's washing and ironing, and my own, of course, but I manage to do that before I serve his breakfast, as I'm up at half-past six. It leaves me all this time to myself.' Already she had acquired a lovely honey-peach tan, and the front of her hair was becoming attractively lighter where the sun had begun to bleach it.

'You get prettier all the time,' Jean told her, watching as she began to unscrew several bottles in preparation for putting on her new face. 'Aren't you afraid of damaging your skin?' she asked, a frown creasing her brow.

'I admit I don't like having all this on my face for too long, but it's a case of having to when I'm on the boat—except at night, of course.'

'The risk seems so great,' mused Jean. 'He could find you out, you know.'

'I'm not going to let myself worry about it,' returned Karen carelessly.

'You've more courage than I!'

'Rubbish! Look at the way you threw up your job to take this one you have here—just because it was in the Caribbean.'

'And you threw up yours for a similar reason. But at least I can be myself all the time. How you manage not to give yourself away I don't know. Are you sure you never inadvertently use your natural voice?'

'I scarcely ever speak to the man,' returned Karen ruefully. 'He says good morning and I reply, and then he might say he'd like something done that's extra to my normal jobs and I'll answer. The other day he sent me shopping and I naturally spoke to him a little then, and at night when I serve him his dinner we might exchange civilities, but that's the limit of my need to converse so it isn't difficult to remember to use my assumed voice.'

This routine continued for another month and then two changes took place almost at once. First, Karen received a letter from Helen to say that she was coming over for a holiday, flying from London in less than a week's time.

'I know it's not giving you much notice, Karen,' Helen went on, 'but as it's not the busy season over there I'm sure you can get me accommodations. I made up my mind suddenly because one of my colleagues at work asked me to change holidays with her, as her mother was to go into the hospital in August and she wants to be off work at that time, so I obliged, taking my holidays now. I'm coming over for three weeks.'

Karen went at once and rented an apartment on the grounds of the Coral Court Hotel, paying the money for the three weeks. But the day after the arrival of Helen's letter Jean was told she was being temporarily transferred to one of the company's hotels on the island of St Lucia.

'Helen can have my bungalow,' Jean offered.

'She'll be delighted,' returned Karen, fully aware that she could not get the money back for the apartment but surmising that Helen would be more comfortable in Jean's bungalow. 'But are you sure you don't mind?'

'Quite sure; I know Helen well enough. Besides, I'd feel better if someone were in the bungalow at night.'

As Karen had prophesied, Helen was thrilled at the idea of having Jean's bungalow for the three weeks of her stay, although naturally she paid Karen for the apartment. Karen hired a taxi and met her at the airport, saying she was taking her straight back to the bungalow, from which Jean had departed two days previously.

'I go to the bungalow each day,' Karen said. 'It'll be in the evenings that you might feel lonely, but if you dine at the hotel that'll take care of a couple of hours.'

'Don't worry about me, Karen. You know me well enough to be sure I'll find plenty to do.'

'I'm usually at the bungalow by about ten to eleven o'clock.'

'And we've all day together?'

'Yes, until about seven, then I have to leave in order to be back to prepare Mr. Fraser's dinner.' They were entering the long, tree-lined drive to the hotel and Helen began to enthuse about the flowers and the smells and the white sandy shore seen through the exotic vegetation of the grounds. The bungalows were away from the hotel, delightfully set in a secluded spot with private access to the beach.

After Helen had settled in—Karen showed her to the bedroom and helped her unpack her two suitcases—the girls went out through a tapestry of exotic color, across two wide lawns, to the terrace of the hotel where they had a buffet lunch washed down with a fruity white wine. Helen kept asking questions about Karen's job, about her sister's job, and about the island generally. Karen answered, and a pleasant hour was spent over the buffet.

'You lucky blighter,' sighed Helen leaning back in her chair and staring out to where a graceful white-sailed luxury yacht rode its languid path over the waves. 'You'll never want to come back to England.'

'I might try for another post here when this one folds up.'

'Jean might be able to help.'

Karen nodded.

'I've thought about an hotel,' she admitted. 'I've met Jean's boss, the manager here, and I'm sure he'd be interested in offering me something.'

'Mr. Fraser could just want to keep you on, when he writes his next play.'

'I wouldn't stay, Helen. It's a super post, I admit, but the life I live isn't natural.'

'The dual personality, you mean?'

'Yes. I couldn't keep it up indefinitely.'

'But it's worth it for the six months?'

'Of course.'

'How is the play progressing?'

'I've no idea. Mr. Fraser's the most uncommunicative man I've ever met. He'd never mention his work to a mere underling.'

'I'd like to see his face when he sees yours!' said Helen, laughing heartily. 'When it's all over and you unmask and let him know he's been duped.'

'I'm looking forward to that!'

At half-past six Karen began to put on her makeup and at seven o'clock she was ready to leave the bungalow. Helen could only stare in admiration at the change in Karen's appearance.

'You'd have deceived even me!' she exclaimed and meant it.

When Karen met her friend the following morning she said delightedly, 'Mr. Fraser says I can have the whole day off. He's dining out this evening so you and

I can go somewhere for dinner.' It would be a little trying tonight, thought Karen, having to come to the bungalow, perhaps very late, put on her disguise, and then go to the boat. However, it would be worth it, and it had nothing to do with her employer what time she came in so long as she did not disturb him.

'There's a dinner dance at a place called Sam Lord's Castle tonight,' said Helen. 'It's advertised in the lobby of the Vervain Hotel.'

'Shall we go?' Karen was excited. This would be the first time she had been out at night since leaving England. 'I'd love to wear a long dress and really look myself!'

'Fine. I wanted to go but wouldn't have gone on my own.'

'It should be fun. What time does it start?'

'Dinner's at nine. Will we have to book?' Karen nodded her head and Helen went on, 'I'll phone from the hotel then,' and she went off to do it. A few hours later Karen was saying, 'I wish I'd brought all my clothes with me.' She and Helen were in their bikinis after having lunched at the hotel. 'My evening dresses are still in my cabin, and I've been meaning to bring them here but never really expected to have evenings off. It was only an afterthought that I brought a couple of long dresses. It would have saved me putting on the disguise again.' She was frowning, wondering how she could have come to overlook the fact that there was no need for her to return to the boat, seeing that her employer did not require dinner.

'What time will he be leaving? You could perhaps avoid the necessity of the disguise if you timed your return correctly.'

It was risky but Karen decided to take a chance.

'I'll leave it as late as I can,' she said, aware that the quickly falling darkness would be an aid to her slipping on to the boat unseen. And she happened to be lucky, because when she was a fair distance away she saw him come out on deck and she dodged behind a tree, watching as he came swiftly down the gangway, a tall, impressive figure immaculately clad in pearl-gray slacks and draped-line jacket, his shirt gleaming white against his burnt sienna throat. Karen caught her breath . . . what a superlatively handsome man he was!

Sam Lord's Castle was an hotel today, but it had a dark and bloodthirsty past, the legend of Sam Lord being that he caused ships to be wrecked by hanging lanterns in the trees. These swayed about in the wind and appeared to be the lights of Carlisle Harbour which misled the ships' crews and so caused the wrecks. The cargoes were raided and taken ashore to add their value to the coffers of the infamous Samuel Lord, the man who was reputed to have imprisoned his wife in the castle dungeon, from which she managed to escape to England by bribing her slave jailer with jewels. But this evening there was no sign of its grim past. On the contrary, the atmosphere was one of gaiety, where the women in their evening dresses and the men in casual but elegant suits, gathered to socialize in the lounge, glasses in their hands.

The restaurant, subtly lit by candles and lamps hidden in the thick green foliage of plants growing in huge pots, was large, with tables placed round a centre dancing space. Karen and Helen had a table well away from this dance space, and next to them was another table occupied by two young men who were obviously on holiday on the island. One smiled at Karen and then Helen, and within minutes the four were chatting as they began the first course. By the time the second course arrived the two tables had been joined to make a table for four. Names were exchanged, and Bill got up to dance with Karen while his friend, Derek, danced with Helen. And it was when they were just about to come from the floor that Karen gave a little gasp and stared at the tall, distinguished figure of her employer. He was guiding his partner to a table where six other people were sitting, his hand beneath the girl's elbow, and on his face a smile which was a revelation to Karen. What a difference in his appearance! He was actually laughing now, she noticed, and his dark pewter-gray eyes were laughing, too, as they looked into his partner's upturned face.

'Anything wrong?' asked Bill, a trifle concerned. 'You look as if you've seen a ghost.'

A ghost. . . . No, a man very much alive, a vital personality, a man obviously admired by his companions because every one of them looked up to smile when he reached the table. He was, decided Karen, the most distinguished man in the room.

'No, it's nothing,' she said to Bill, but a moment later she was saying softly to her friend, 'That's my boss—the famous Clint Fraser. It never dawned on me that this is where he'd be dining.'

Helen followed the direction of her eyes and gave a laugh.

'Wouldn't it be a lark if he asked you to dance with him?'

Karen's eyes twinkled. It would certainly add a little spice, she agreed.

Watching him in the company of others, Karen was so fascinated by the change that she could not take her eyes off him for very long at a time, so it was inevitable that he should in the end become conscious of her concentrated stare. His eyes met hers; she coloured and lowered her lashes.

She determinedly kept her eyes away for the duration of the meal, which was a pleasant, leisurely one and it was only to be expected that, while they chatted, the men should ask questions about the two girls. Helen had no difficulties; she told them she was on holiday and staying at the house of a friend. Karen, already having anticipated the question, also had an answer ready.

'No, I'm not on holiday, I work part-time and have been spending the rest of my time with my sister, who lives here. My job's one I can't talk about,' she added and there was the sort of firmness in her voice that instantly precluded any further questions from the men.

They were staying at the Coral Gables and had hired a car for the fortnight. They had already had one week, and they suggested the girls go about with them for the second week. This Karen had no intention of doing, and neither had Helen. So when the invitation came it was politely rejected, the men taking it in good part, with Bill saying good humoredly, 'Fair enough, Karen. But you won't cut us if we happen to meet again?'

'Of course not,' she assured him. She offered no explanations for being reticent about her work, but she felt that as her life—which could have been complicated—was running smoothly, she ought not to run any risks. It was improbable, but by no means impossible, that her employer would require more from her than he was getting at present. If, for instance, he decided to take a break from his writing it might be that he would entertain, and it would fall to her to do all the work involved. She had never expected this present state of affairs to continue unbroken for six months.

When the meal was over some of the guests went outside, while others congregated in the lounge, to spend the rest of the evening drinking and socializing. Karen and Helen went to a handsomely decorated room which Sam Lord had embellished with late Georgian woodwork and delicate plaster work on the ceiling, done by an artist who had worked on Windsor Castle. Here at one end was a raised dais on which a steel band was playing. On the polished floor several couples danced. It was an "excuse me" and Helen said, 'I dare you to dance with him, Karen.'

Karen turned, her eyes gleaming with mischief as they wandered from her friend's challenging stare to the couple dancing close together on the edge of the floor.

'I accept your dare,' she returned with a toss of her head and went forward resolutely to tap her employer on the shoulder. She received a scowling glance from the girl and a frowning one from her partner.

'Excuse me,' she said politely in her normal low-toned voice and Clint had no alternative but to leave his glamorous partner and allow Karen to slip into his arms.

She was recalling what he had said about not intending to pander to the whim of some female avid for romance and, an imp of mischief suddenly entering into her, she decided to flirt with him, just as a matter of interest, to see how he would react. She leaned away, fluttering her lashes as she said, her voice at its sweetest, 'Are you on holiday here?'

'No,' briefly and curtly, 'I am not.'

That was enough to put any girl off, thought Karen chuckling to herself.

'Working, then?' No answer and she added, quite undaunted by his manner, 'It's a lovely island, isn't it? So romantic. . . .' Her voice trailed away to a seductive silence; she was acting a part she had once played, the part of a scheming woman determined to get her man. 'Yes, so romantic. Don't you agree?'

He held her from him, his grip on her arms tightening ruthlessly.

'All islands in the Caribbean are romantic.'

'They are? You've been to them all?'

He pulled her to him again, forced to the action in order to avoid collision with another couple.

'Not all,' he replied curtly.

He was angry, she thought, amusement rippling through her. That imp of mischief impelled her to say, 'It's rather hot in here, don't you think? Shall we go outside into the cool for a little while?' That would disconcert her phlegmatic employer, she thought, peeping up at him through her lashes. His mouth was set, his jaw flexed. She had the greatest difficulty in suppressing laughter, but she did manage it and her voice was husky and coaxing as she added, curling her fingers against his shoulders and then deliberately allowing them to touch his nape in a sexy little caress. 'There's a full moon, and stars. And the air's scented by flowers. Let's go out,' she urged. 'Just for five minutes?'

He looked down contemptuously.

'Five minutes?' with a fractional lift of his brows. 'You don't give yourself much time, do you?'

'A kiss doesn't take very long.'

'It just depends on who's doing the kissing,' he returned unexpectedly and a certain quality in his voice set her pulses tingling. But before she had time to respond the music stopped and without so much as a word he left her to make her own way back to the table. Bill and Derek were still standing on the edge of the dance space, chatting to the two girls with whom they had been dancing.

'What happened?' Helen wanted to know. 'You look ready to burst with laughter.'

'I tried to flirt with him.'

'That shouldn't have caused you any difficulty, not with your experience as the bitchy one.'

'I asked him to go out to the garden with me.'

At that Helen's eyes widened to their fullest extent.

'That was rather risky, wasn't it? I mean, it's all very well in a play but—' She broke off, shaking her head as her eyes sought the object of their discussion across the room. 'I'd not like to trust that one in the dark!'

'Oh, I knew he'd not take me up on it,' returned Karen airily. 'Don't forget, I know him well, being his housekeeper. That man might write plays but he hasn't an ounce of romance in him. I told you why he didn't want a young woman for his housekeeper, didn't I?'

'You did, but what about this girl he's with now?' Helen was thoughtful as she continued to stare at the handsome profile of Karen's employer. 'I'm no real judge of the opposite sex but I've had my moments, and I'd never believe he's cold—at least, not when he gets going.'

'Gets going?' laughed Karen. 'What on earth do you mean by that?'

'I'll bet he can be as ardent as the rest.'

Karen fell silent, reflecting on how he was on the boat, totally absorbed in his work. She would have said he was as cold as stone but, watching him with that girl, she was beginning to wonder if she had made a mistake.

Chapter Three

As the evening progressed Karen became restless for some reason which she could not understand. All she knew was that her eyes would repeatedly wander toward Clint Fraser and his party, and especially to the glamourous girl who seemed to be coming in for more than her share of his attention. He sometimes caught Karen's eye and she noticed that he would frown. Obviously he believed she was attracted by him and the knowledge vexed her so much that, in the end, she politely excused herself and left the other three to wander out onto the moonlit grounds where the air was balmy and the grassy lawns cushion-soft beneath her feet. She walked on, among some of the loveliest trees and shrubs and exotic flowers she had ever seen. There were flamboyants and casuarinas, the beautiful pride of India, the frangipani and the pink poui and the delightful African tulip tree. It was too much! Her whole being was affected by the sheer

beauty around her. One or two people were strolling,
like herself, and stopping now and then to admire
particularly beautiful flowers, highlighted by the
lanterns in the trees above their heads. Karen, her
senses a little drugged by it all, could quite easily
create pictures of Sam Lord's lamps in the coconut
trees on the coast of Long Bay, swaying in the strong
tropical breeze, guiding ships to what should have
been a haven but was in reality the treacherous reef,
where they floundered, a prey to Sam Lord's slaves
who would then set out and capture the cargoes for
their master.

Karen had to smile at her mind wanderings. The
stories of Sam Lord's wickedness were legendary,
anyway, so it was quite possible that they were, in the
main, untrue.

She found herself leaving the more sophisticated
part of the grounds and entering a rougher, wilder
region where the Atlantic rollers, sweeping into the
shore, had ruthlessly killed the vegetation, leaving
only the gaunt and twisted skeletons of what had once
been a forest of beautiful trees. She stopped, her
slender figure outlined against the arc of the sky
where it touched the horizon, when suddenly she
heard the snapping of a dead branch beneath someone's foot and she swung around, nerves alert. Clint
Fraser! He saw her and halted, then turned abruptly
to retrace his steps, swiftly and determinedly as if he
were obeying an angry urge to put distance between
him and Karen in as little time as possible.

She shrugged and smiled to herself, yet at the same
time she was aware of confused thoughts through

which emerged a vague sense of disappointment. What was wrong with her tonight? She had felt on top of the world a few hours ago at the idea of coming to this function, dressing up for the occasion in a long flowing evening gown of midnight blue cotton, gossamer fine, like silk. Low cut at the neck, it was rather more revealing than any other dress she owned, but she loved the way the bodice fitted snugly to her curves and waist, and the way the intricate folds swayed when she walked and danced. Yes, she had been very happy a few hours ago, but now. . . .

Shrugging off the tinge of dejection which she could not understand anyway, and, with the intention of returning to the hotel, but not by the route chosen by her employer, she turned inland, only to discover that she was making things difficult for herself, as the ground was littered with the aerial roots of the giant banyan trees that predominated in the whole of the area. After catching her foot in one of these she decided it would be wiser to go back and proceed along the shore. But no sooner had she turned then she caught her foot again and automatically extended her hands to break her fall. The next instant she had come with a thud against a hard male body and before she could even utter her cry of protest it was effectively smothered by the bruising contact of the man's mouth on hers. She began to struggle and was told roughly to stop. Clint Fraser! He must have been strolling along a narrow path which just happened to come out at the very point where she had tripped. His name almost burst from her lips in her fury and astonishment. What a difference! The passion of his kiss brought starkly to mind what Helen had said about him.

'Let go of me!' she cried, managing to lean away from him. 'What do you think you're doing!'

'Giving you what you've asked for—' His mouth came down again, the kiss dominating and sensuous as it forced her lips apart. For long, heady moments she was compelled to endure his total domination as he held her, pressed to his iron-hard body, her arms pinned against her sides. Gasping for breath when at last he held her from him, she could scarcely speak for the white-hot fury that possessed her.

'You beast!' she hissed. 'I never asked for this!'

'Come off it,' he sneered. 'In there you offered me an invitation, and now, when I'd avoided you over there on the shore, you deliberately followed me—'

'I did *not* follow you,' she flared. 'It was just coincidence that we met here! I'd tripped over some roots!'

'What sort of a fool do you think you're trying to convince? And what's the idea anyway? You're so damned transparent—it's plain what you want—'

'Oh!' she quivered, 'you shan't say that about me, I—' The rest was lost in the blind fury of her resistance as, laughing at her protest, he crushed her body to his in a punishing embrace. She struggled desperately at the significant movement of his hand as it slid up from her waist, and at last, driven by wild uncontrollable fury, she kicked out viciously at his shins and to her satisfaction and relief his hold slackened and she was able to free herself. But she leaned, panting, against the wide trunk of the banyan tree whose roots had been the cause of all the trouble, and to her chagrin she felt the hot tears falling down her cheeks.

'You damned vixen,' he began but it was her turn to interrupt.

'And you damned brute!' she inserted before he could continue. 'If you're prone to these caveman tactics then why the devil don't you go and find someone who'll enjoy them? You ought to be among animals, not humans!' Her temper was like a searing hot furnace, but she was still weak from his treatment of her. 'I wish I were a man,' she fumed, 'I'd strangle you with my bare hands!'

'If you'd been a man,' he returned mildly, 'this situation would never have came about.'

'I'm in no mood for satire,' she flung at him. 'Keep your witticisms for those who can appreciate them!'

He said nothing, but just stood there, in the moonlight, looking at her. She wondered if he could see her tears and with a furious gesture she knuckled her eyes.

'What are you standing there for?' she demanded when at last she had all her breath back. 'Clear off! I should think you know by now that you've made a blunder!'

'I agree,' he murmured in a very soft voice. 'But, my girl, you'd have been the one to make the blunder if it had been any other man you'd been playing around with. You're damned lucky it was me. Just what was the idea?' His voice had risen slightly, and there was an imperious demand within its depths. 'Well, I'm waiting?'

She swallowed, unable to find anything to say because it was understandable that he would ask a question like that after the subtle invitation she had given him when they were dancing. And this unexpected meeting. . . . She could accept that he believed it to have been engineered by her. The implication of it all brought colour flooding to her cheeks as she realised that what had begun as mere mischief, born of pique that he had criticised her acting, had resulted in his condemning her a no-good, a girl who would deliberately throw herself at any man. Her only consolation was that he did not know who she was. 'I'm still waiting,' came the stern request again but all she did was turn away with the intention of leaving him, but she was wrong. Without warning she was seized and thoroughly shaken, then pushed against the tree again, for support.

'Watch yourself in the future!' he warned darkly. 'You might not escape so easily!' and on that he swung away, his tall figure soon melting into the darkness until all she saw was a vague form that eventually became no more than a shadow.

Karen, in her disguise, stood in the galley, over the stove, cooking eggs and bacon, her thoughts on last night and her encounter with the man to whom she was about to serve breakfast. And suddenly it was all a big joke, with only the humorous side affecting her, and she laughed softly to herself. Helen, she recalled, had seen the funny side right away, and had only refrained from laughter because Karen was so distressed, and still furious too, mainly because she was carrying bruises where Clint's fingers had eaten mercilessly into her flesh when he had shaken her.

With breakfast on the silver tray she went to the dining saloon and knocked.

'Come in.'

'Good morning, Mr. Fraser,' she said in her "mature" voice as she placed the tray on the sideboard. 'Did you have a pleasant evening?'

'So-so,' he replied noncommittally, and sat down, ready to be waited upon.

Karen put a glass of fruit juice in front of him, then the heated plate on which was a small amount of bacon and an egg.

'You don't eat enough,' she murmured. 'It's not enough for a man.'

'I appreciate your motherly concern, Miss Waring, but what I eat is my own affair. I assure you that if I wanted more I should not hesitate to ask for it.'

Karen had already turned away, her lips quivering at his reference to her "motherly concern".

'Do you want sandwiches today for lunch or a meat salad?' she asked as she placed the toast rack down on the table.

'I shall probably be going out to lunch, but I'm not sure.'

'Oh. . . . And dinner?'

'Again, I can't say.' He paused and a frown knit his brow. 'I'll let you know about both meals before you go off. What time will you be leaving the boat?'

'In about two hours,' she answered, trying to think if there were any other chores besides a small amount of washing and the tidying up of the galley afterward.

'Very well. I shall know in less than two hours whether or not I'll be having my meals here.'

She looked at him a moment, then ventured to ask if there were any special reason for his not knowing if he wanted his snack lunch prepared and his dinner later.

'My work's not progressing as it should. My heroine's unsatisfactory,' he admitted and Karen stared in amazement that he would unbend sufficiently to confide in her.

'Unsatisfactory, Mr. Fraser,' she echoed, encouraged by his manner. 'In what way?'

'I want her to be unusual, unpredictable and intriguing.' He paused in thought, frowning. 'No,' he murmured almost to himself, 'she isn't at all what I want.' He looked at Karen. 'It sometimes happens and there's only one remedy. I take time off for recreation. If my writing goes well in the next hour or so it'll go well all day, but if not—then, I shall be having my meals at an hotel.' His eyes flickered over her indifferently, taking in the drab dress beneath the white apron, the graying hair, the pale insipid lips. Something stirred within Karen—no more than the fluttering of a pulse, perhaps, so intangible as not to be disturbing.

He picked up the glass of fruit juice and, taking the action as a silent dismissal, she turned and left the saloon.

Within a couple of hours she had done all her chores and was on her way to the Vervain Hotel and the pretty little bungalow on the grounds. She had a key and let herself in, as Helen would already have left for the beach.

Twenty minutes later her disguise was gone.

'This is little less than one long holiday for you,' commented Helen enviously when, having joined her on the beach, Karen discarded her wrap and settled down to soak up the sun and increase her tan.

'I admit it. And what do you think? I've the whole day off. Mr. Fraser doesn't want either lunch or dinner. He said early this morning that as the play's not going as he wants it to, he might leave it and give himself a little recreation. It's his heroine; she isn't doing what he wants her to. She—' Karen stopped. 'Is something wrong, Helen?'

'You're off this evening?'

'Yes, that's right.'

'I've made a date with Bill. I didn't think you'd be off—'

'It's all right,' Karen interrupted swiftly. 'I'll find something to do.'

Helen frowned, absently picking up a bottle of suntan lotion and unscrewing the top.

'I don't care for your being on your own,' she began, when Karen interrupted her again to assure her that she would be quite all right.

'I shall do some extra chores on the boat,' she added. 'Then I'll be able to have my days off with you without feeling I've neglected anything. The windows need cleaning for one thing.'

'You're sure?' Helen was still doubtful. 'I wish I'd known.'

'I'm quite sure,' returned Karen and changed the subject, asking her friend if she liked her new bikini.

'Yes, very much—at least, what there is of it,' laughed Helen. 'I wonder what the great Mr. Clint

Fraser would say if he saw his middle-aged house-keeper now?'

'I don't know. . . .' Karen stretched out her long slender legs. 'I really don't know. . . .'

After spending the rest of the morning sunbathing, with the occasional swim in between, the girls donned their beach wraps and went into the hotel for a buffet lunch. And no sooner were they being shown to a table than Karen's eyes met those of her employer. She coloured hotly under his narrowed stare, and turned away, wishing she could escape, go some-where else for her lunch but already Helen was on her way to the buffet table and Karen had no alternative than to follow.

Clint was joined by the girl he was with last night and they began to chat as they proceeded along the heavily laden table. Karen could not take her eyes off Clint, whose height seemed to dominate the whole room. He was smiling and his face was transformed.

He was charm itself.

Suddenly aware of Karen's concentrated interest he flashed her an unfathomable glance, and a satirical smile touched his lips seconds later, when her colour rose again.

'What's up?' asked Helen when they were seated on the terrace, with the yellow birds flitting around, cheekily waiting to swoop and steal a beakful of sugar from the basin on the table. 'You look all hot and bothered.'

'It's Clint Fraser,' snapped Karen, taking a breath. 'He's here! When he said he'd be having his meals at an hotel I naturally expected it would be the Smuggler's Cove because that's the nearest one to where the boat's moored. But instead, he has to come here!'

'Well, there's no reason why he shouldn't,' rejoined Helen reasonably. 'Have you been talking to him?'

'No—we just looked at one another!'

Helen burst out laughing, and at that moment Clint happened to reach their table on his way to one in the far corner to join the girl already sitting there. He glanced down, eyes glinting, and yet there was a dash of amusement in them too as he looked at Karen.

'Oh, lord!' exclaimed Karen, faintly distressed. 'I wonder what he thinks. He's sure to conclude we were making fun of him.'

'So what? Karen, pet, you are forgetting that you have *two* roles, not one. To him, you're an unknown. His colourless little housekeeper has nothing at all to do with you.'

Karen had to laugh.

'Do you know, Helen, it's becoming exceedingly difficult to separate myself—I mean, to disassociate my real self totally from the person I've assumed. Do you know what I mean?'

'Perfectly.' Helen picked up her fork and studied what was on her plate for a moment, obviously interested in the delicious variety of foods she had chosen. 'Isn't that what I've just said?' she went on belatedly, still absorbed in the delicacies before her. 'You're not remembering you're *two*. And it's essential that you do, because if you happen to give the game away then you're sacked! I can't see that man making any excuses for the kind of deceit which you are practising. It wouldn't surprise me if he lost his temper and gave you a slap.'

'He wouldn't dare!' protested Karen wrathfully. 'I'd scratch his eyes out!'

'If you got the chance.' Helen at last chose a piece of lobster and popped it into her mouth. 'Hmm. . . . I shall never get back to the beans on toast I usually have for my lunch at the office. This is scrumptious!'

Karen's eyes were on Clint Fraser's glamorous companion. She was in bright yellow shorts and a scanty sun-top. Her tan was glorious, her pale gold hair a halo for a beautiful face. Clint was talking to her, while she was fluttering her lashes, and at times making play with her hands in that sort of way which reminded Karen of a model or a ballet dancer. For sure that girl knew how to make a man notice her!

When the lunch was finished, Helen went off to the bathroom and Karen got up and walked to the wrought iron rail that ornamented the edge of the terrace. Within a few seconds she was hearing a familiar voice say,

'So we meet again.' He came to her from behind and let his eyes rove over her slender figure. Her beach coat was open to reveal the delectable curves of a seductive, suntanned body. 'You've gotten over last night, it seems?'

'Except for the bruises!' she snapped, then coloured painfully, astonished that she could make an admission which seemed to savour of the intimate.

'You deserved more than bruises, my girl! You invited me to take you outside and kiss you—which surely meant more?' he added as a question but Karen was too embarrassed to offer any reply even if she had been able to think of one. 'But when it came to the crunch you didn't want to know,' he continued and there was no mistaking either the interest in his voice or the puzzlement. 'It wasn't natural, and I'd like to know just what your idea was?'

'It's difficult to explain,' she returned awkwardly.

'Difficult?' His gaze was fixed and studied. 'That in itself sounds as if there's a hint of mystery about the whole business.'

'Mystery?' she repeated, nerves taut. 'What kind of mystery could there be?'

'Don't adopt an air of innocence,' he rebuked. 'For the success of my particular work I have to be something of a psychologist; I have to study personalities. Yours puzzles me. You'll admit, I hope, that your behaviour last night was so contradictory that you must be a most unusual young woman?' She merely shook her head, unable to find anything to say.

For how could she admit that she had tempted him out of devilment, just to see how he would react? She looked up at him, generously making excuses for his conduct, because what was merely fun to her had appeared as sheer promiscuity to him, and who could blame him? Her quiet reasoning brought forth the conclusion that his reaction was natural; he had not considered it necessary to afford her any respect. It was unfortunate that they had collided on the hotel grounds, and of course he had now accepted that it was not engineered by her after all.

'Aren't you going to give me some sort of an explanation?' he asked, his words cutting into her reverie.

'I can't explain.' There was a hint of distress in her voice, an apologetic expression in the wide stare she

gave him. 'It's impossible,' she added finally, turning
away, to look for Helen.

'Impossible, eh?' He drew a breath of impatience
but he was interested in her, and that interest seemed
out of all proportion even before he said, 'What a
strange one you are. You're a most unusual and
intriguing type—unpredictable, interesting. I'd like to
know more about you. Will you dine with me tonight?'

Her eyes widened disbelievingly.

'Are you serious?' she asked.

'I have never been more serious. Perhaps,' he
suggested thoughtfully, 'you'd dine with me on my
boat? It's moored near here—at the very end of the
headland.'

'On your boat?' she repeated and he gave a light
laugh.

'Don't worry. I've a housekeeper on board, so you'll
be quite safe.

'A housekeeper?' Karen's nerves caught. He had
sounded genuine, until the mention of the housekeeper, whose presence would ensure her safety. He knew
very well that he had given his housekeeper the day
off, and the evening. 'She'll be there this evening?'

'Of course. She'll cook our dinner for us. I shall
have to tell her I'm having a guest.' He stopped, his
eyes flickering oddly. 'Is anything the matter?' he said
puzzled.

'I have my doubts about this housekeeper,' she said
lowering her lashes to conceal her expression.

'You don't believe . . . ?' His voice trailed and Karen
glanced up to see an expression of amusement on his
face. 'Good lord,' he exclaimed. 'I'd forgotten. I've

given her the evening off!' He looked ruefully at Karen and a smile broke, causing her to catch her breath at the attractiveness of him. 'What a wolf I'd have appeared if I'd gotten you on my boat and then had to confess that my housekeeper wasn't there after all.'

She laughed then, feeling as if a weight had been lifted from her at the idea that he was genuine, after all.

'This housekeeper,' she was urged to say, 'is she a sort of Girl Friday? That's what they're called, isn't it, when they work on boats?'

'No, this one could not be described as a girl,' he answered in some amusement.

'No?'

'Definitely not.'

'How old is she then?'

He looked at her oddly.

'Is it important?'

'Not really,' she shrugged. 'It was just a matter of interest that made me ask the question, that's all.'

'She says she's forty-five but I'd say she's nearer fifty-five.'

'Fifty-five!' repeated Karen, wide-eyed. 'What makes you say that?'

'The amount of makeup she wears. Trying to look younger than she is. Why women do it I don't know. They'd be much more attractive if they'd grow old gracefully.'

Karen had to laugh, not at what he had just said, but at the idea that he had decided his housekeeper was trying to make herself look *younger!*

'My friend's waiting,' she murmured as she saw

Helen standing some distance away, not wanting to intrude.

'What about my invitation?'

She looked searchingly at him.

'Your girl friend,' she murmured. 'Won't she mind?'

The gray eyes hardened.

'I'm not obliged to obtain anyone's approval for any action I might choose to make,' he said tautly.

'I'm sorry,' she said, feeling like a spanked child.

'You're going to accept my invitation?'

She paused. Did he like her? He had said she was unusual, intriguing, interesting. . . . It did seem that he liked her, she thought, a smile fluttering to her lips as she replied,

'Yes, I'd like to dine with you—' She stopped and he laughed.

'The name's Clint,' he said and that was all.

'Mine's Karen.'

'Karen—what?'

She gave a start, even though she had half expected the question.

'Boyle,' she responded, using her mother's maiden name. 'Where shall we be dining?' she asked. 'It's just that I'd like to know if it's formal?'

'The Sandy Lane—and it is formal tonight. I'll call for you in a taxi—'

'I'd rather meet you there,' she said, her glance flickering to where Helen was still waiting. 'What time? I must join my friend,' she added urgently.

'Eight o'clock, in the lobby.'

Chapter Four

She arrived a quarter of an hour late, having spent rather too long on her appearance. But the result more than pleased her; she knew that the white evening dress suited her to perfection, knew that it was modest and yet seductive, the bodice clinging to her curves as if it had been molded on to them. The silver bracelet and matching ear-drops could not have been bettered as accessories. Her small bag was embroidered with silver thread, her sandals were made of straps of silver leather.

Clint was in the lobby, tall and distinguished as he stood looking down on to the terrace below. His smile was spontaneous when, on seeing her enter, his eyes flickered in appreciation of the enchanting picture she made.

'You look charming,' he said. 'White suits your lovely hair.'

She coloured delicately, disconcerted in a way entirely foreign to her innate confidence.

'Thank you,' she murmured shyly.

'Shall we have a drink on the terrace, or would you prefer the lounge?'

'The terrace sounds nice.'

'Everything's nice about the Sandy Lane,' he assured her. 'It's probably the best hotel in the Caribbean.'

'It's sort—of homey,' Karen was saying a short while later as they had their aperitifs on the flower-bedecked terrace. 'And yet it has the sort of sophistication which people on holiday usually want.'

'I'm glad you like it.' Clint paused a moment, as if considering. 'Tell me about yourself?' he invited. 'I've said I'm intrigued by your behaviour last night. The daring of your challenge to me, a stranger, and then, when it seemed I'd oblige, you backed out—'

'Oh, don't!' she begged, her colour rising. 'Please don't remind me of it!'

'You see what I mean?' He regarded her with an inscrutable expression. 'You're totally unpredictable.'

'I can't explain,' she quivered. 'I've already said so.'

'There must have been some good reason for your behaviour—which, I very soon realised, was completely out of character. Can't you give me that reason?' He seemed inordinately interested, watching her face for any sign of a change of expression. She picked up her glass, taking refuge in silence, and telling herself that it had been a mistake to accept his invitation to dinner. 'So you're not going to talk?' His mouth hardened; he seemed more frustrated than anything else, she thought.

'I'd rather not talk about myself.' She looked apologetically at him.

'Well, don't be so unhappy about it,' he said unexpectedly. 'I've invited you out and it's up to me to see that you enjoy the evening.' He smiled, his ill humour gone. 'Drink up and we'll go and eat.'

Karen fluttered a smile in response, relieved at his change of mood.

They sat in a corner, dining in the open at a table facing the sea, the air around them heavy with the scent of exotic flowers.

They ate huge turtle steaks, juicy and tender as prime veal, and drank champagne to the strains of calypso music drifting up from below, where the steel band was playing in front of a dance area around which white tables and chairs were arranged beneath flowering tropical trees. The blooms of a hibiscus hedge glowed crimson in the reflected light from lamps hidden in the feathery foliage of casuarinas; bougainvillea climbed up a trellis, then tumbled in a riot of magenta and crimson to mingle with a bed of golden allamandas. The sea was dazzling in the moonlight, and the tall palms growing on the backshore waved their delicate spidery fronds against the deep, mysterious purple of a star-sprinkled sky.

Karen sighed, her mind drugged by the sheer magic of her surroundings. It was all so unreal—had been right from the start when she had surely been infected with madness even to think of applying for the post advertised by a man she disliked, a post which necessitated adopting a dual personality. Then there had been the meeting with Clint at Sam Lord's Castle, and her mischievous, unthinking approach which had ended in a way she could never even have visualised. And now, here she was, dining in the exotic atmosphere of this luxury hotel with the man to whom, as his middle-aged housekeeper, she would be serving breakfast at precisely eight o'clock tomorrow morning. It was not only unreal, but incredible. Yet, within seconds she was seeing the amusing side only. After all, she had entered into the masquerade partly for the fun of it, although mainly for the satisfaction, later, of proving to Clint that she really could act.

'Why the sigh?' Clint's voice came softly and she looked at him across the candlelit table.

'I'm drugged by it all,' she answered frankly. 'It's magic, isn't it?'

His dark eyes flickered; Karen had the incredible idea that he was making mental notes of all she did and said, of every gesture and glance, every expression that crossed her face.

'Is that how you regard it—as magic?'

'Yes. The atmosphere affects me profoundly.'

'Any particular reason?'

'There are many reasons.'

'Such as?'

'Well, the very situation we're in—dining here by candlelight, in the open air. And out there the dark sea, so calm, beneath a starlit sky and look at the path the moon's making on the water. It ripples like a stream of silver . . .'' Her voice trailed to an embarrassed silence.

'You're a romantic, that's for sure.' Although there was a dash of amusement in his tone his eyes were serious as they looked into hers. 'You mentioned the situation *we* are in. Has the magic anything to do with your companion?'

Karen gave him a startled glance.

'Are you looking for flattery?' she asked.

'I might be. I suppose I'm trying to understand you.'

'I intrigue you, you said?'

'More than that.' He stopped and a baffled expression crossed his face. She had the idea that he was more than a little impatient with himself. But why? And why should he be so interested in her?

She knew instinctively that he intended asking more questions and decided to forestall him.

'Tell me about yourself, Clint. You mentioned something regarding your work—saying you needed to be a psychologist. What's the nature of your work?'

'It wouldn't interest you.' Soft the voice and inflexible. This was a different side to him again, a stern, rather masterful side where the manner he adopted was meant to warn her of the futility of pursuing this particular subject.

'Then tell me about the lady who works for you on your boat?'

He hesitated and she had the firm conviction that although he had no wish to talk about his housekeeper, he at the same time did not want to snub Karen again.

'Miss Waring? There isn't anything interesting about her, I'm afraid.'

'She seems old to be a Girl Friday. Has she been with you long?'

'About six or seven weeks. She wanted a complete change from the routine of her office job and so she answered an advertisement I inserted in a newspaper.'

'She left her job?' with well-feigned surprise. 'She must be adventurous. Usually women of forty-five— Did you say she was older than that?'

'I'd say she's about fifty-five.'

'Women of that age aren't usually adventurous, are they?' Karen stared fixedly at her plate, unable to meet his gaze because of the laughter in her eyes.

'I'd never describe Miss Waring as adventurous,' returned Clint with a touch of humour. 'On the contrary, she's a staid woman, efficient but very reserved.'

'Perhaps she's conscious of her position,' suggested Karen, still avoiding his eyes.

'I don't think so. There's no sense of inferiority with employees these days, and a good thing too.'

Karen did glance up then, rather surprised by what he had said. She had branded him arrogant, full of his own importance, conscious of the place he held in the literary world. . . . Was she mistaken? Her feelings were most illogically mixed, she realised, for while on the one hand she did not want to be mistaken, on the other she was glad that he did not consider as inferior those people who worked for him.

'Is she a good cook?' she was impelled to ask, watching him with a curious expression.

'Quite good, yes. I'm not a fanatic about food anyway. And when I'm working I'm satisfied with plain meals.' He paused a moment, 'Why don't you come on board—perhaps tomorrow evening—and meet her?'

Karen, in the act of putting a piece of turtle steak

into her mouth, almost choked, but managed a swift recovery to say, 'I think she sounds shy, and wouldn't be happy for me to go aboard.'

'I don't suppose she'll take exception to any visitor I might decide to entertain,' he rejoined.

Karen made no answer and for a while they ate in silence, Clint breaking it only to thank the waiter who came unobtrusively to refill their wineglasses.

'Will you let me take you on board, Karen?' Clint broke the silence at last, his voice and manner persuasive.

She shook her head determinedly.

'No—I don't think so. Perhaps some other time,' she added vaguely on seeing him frown.

'You're a strange girl,' he said with a touch of asperity. 'An enigma.'

'Your psychology isn't working,' she said, laughing softly.

'You are quite right,' crisply and with a narrowed look, 'it isn't!'

'You sound angry.' She was enjoying herself but she endeavoured not to let it show. 'What have I done to upset you?'

'The innocent again,' he murmured. 'I wish I knew just what your little game is?'

She shot him a startled glance.

'My little game? That's a strange thing to say!'

'You were up to something last night, and now— well, you are acting damned strange!'

'Just because I won't go on to your boat? It so happens that I don't want to go on to it, and I'm sure I can please myself!'

'It's nothing to do with the boat!'

'What is it then?'

'Your refusal to talk about yourself.' Imperious the tone; Karen felt he would have ordered her to talk about herself if he'd had the power to do so. 'It angers me—' He pulled himself up, frowning darkly as if he realised he had gone too far.

'You are equally reticent,' Karen reminded him quietly. 'We're strangers and in consequence neither has any wish to confide in the other.'

He drew a breath but said, rather to her surprise, 'That's fair enough. I'm sorry if I appeared unfriendly. As I don't want to talk about myself I shouldn't expect you to do so either.'

'Why are you so interested in me?' she queried, eyeing him with an odd expression.

'It doesn't matter,' was his immediate and noncommittal rejoinder.

'It's a case of ships that pass in the night,' she murmured, her ears attuned to the haunting strains of *Yellow Bird* being played by the steel band.

'Ships that pass in the night. . . .' He looked absently at her, then nodded his head. 'Yes, I suppose so.'

He smiled then, his ill humour gone. Karen responded and for the rest of the meal they chatted, mainly about inconsequential things. When it was over, they left the table but stood for a while on the romantically lit terrace. The night was balmy, and through the mothy darkness there drifted the heady perfumes of roses and carnations and the night-scented stocks that abounded in the hotel gardens.

'Shall we dance?' Clint stood looking down at her from his superior height and within her something stirred, vague and too fleeting to grasp. She nodded, unable to help blushing as she recalled that first dance, when she had deliberately tried to flirt with him.

'Yes, I'd like that.'

She was swung into his arms, felt the warmth of his hands through the fine cotton material of her dress, quivered with a new emotion but reasoned logically that any woman must be affected by a man as handsome and distinguished looking as the one partnering her. She danced on air, so well did their steps match, and when presently she glanced around she saw that all the people at the tables were watching them. A few minutes before the music stopped, she and Clint were the only couple dancing and every eye was on them. When the music did stop and they walked from the floor to their table Clint's hand stayed round her waist, almost possessively.

They danced several more times and then walked along the talcum-soft sands of the beach, a starlit sky above and the moon-drenched sea stretching away to the indistinct line where it melted into the arc of the sky. Music could still be heard—soft strains and a little sad, haunting, like the whisper of a night breeze rustling pine needles on a lonely hillside. It seemed natural that Clint should lead her gently toward the trees, and when he stopped she looked up, her eyes dreamy and luminous as they watched the moon glide through a lacy film of cloud, only to reappear in all its argent glory, flaring, flooding the silent world with romance. Clint, looking down into her lovely face, seemed fascinated by its perfection, and a long, profound moment passed before he drew her slender

body to him. There was bliss in the touch of his hands
and heaven in his kiss; it was a heady draught
dissolving all inhibitions, all restraint. Karen had no
power of resistance. Her strong and eager arms slid
around him, and with a little exclamation that could
have been surprise he swept her into an embrace that
was almost as savage as that first one, but now there
was respect, and the pain inflicted by his iron-hard
body was unintentional. The blood surged in Karen's
veins, rushing to her heart in a wild, overflowing
sensation that was heightened by the magical setting
of moon-pale sands and silvered sea, by the intoxicating fragrance of flowers carried on the zephyr of a
breeze making music in the waving palms above their
heads.

'You're . . . beautiful. . . .' Clint's voice was a
throaty bass tone, his lips probingly insistent as they
forced hers apart, his arms almost cruel in their
strength as they caused her body to arch so that she
was masterfully compelled to experience the sensual
throbbing of his iron-hard muscles, the insistent
virility of his loins. She tried to resist his demanding
mouth when it sought the rounded firmness of her
breast but sanity seemed to be fast deserting her.
Ecstasy vibrated through her body as Clint awakened
emotions she had never before experienced. She had
the hazy recollection of saying, only a couple of hours
ago, that Clint and she were strangers. . . . And now
they were on the very brink of intimacy; she was
forced to submission when his hard possessive mouth
insisted that she offer him the sweet moisture of hers,
she was compelled to respond to his body's erotic

rhythm, know the pleasure-pain of roving hands that were as ruthless as they were gentle. The breath in her throat seemed almost to solidify, choking her.

It was only when his hand slid from her waist and then lower that some modicum of sanity returned and, taking him by surprise, she wrested her body from his crushing embrace, to stand, gasping for air, her breasts rising and falling as her heightened emotions still held her in their grip.

Karen had no idea what she expected as a result of her urgent need to escape, but Clint just stood there, regarding her in the moonlight, and he might almost have been mentally recording every sign of emotion—the breathless movements of her body, the clenched fist at her sides, the anxious question in her eyes, asking what he thought of her loss of restraint after her violent repulsion of him only twenty-four hours earlier. She saw his jaw flex, his eyes narrow as a frown knit his brow. He seemed strangely at a loss and she would have given much to know what his thoughts were. One thing was for sure: his ardour had cooled and she knew she had nothing to fear regarding a renewal of his advances. She released a long breath, alive to the fact that although relief was her chief emotion, there was a sense of loss within her, a yearning that most certainly should not have been there.

'Shall we go back, Karen?' His words came like an icy shower, so cold and unemotional was the tone in which they were spoken. She could have burst into tears of mortification, so ashamed did she feel. The incident meant nothing to him; she was a stranger still. And yet, what else could she be? She pulled

herself together, casting off her humiliation and
attempted to act with the same coolness as he. To her
surprise she succeeded, but felt that he must now be
condemning her as a no-good, while at the same time
still puzzled by her furious response to his advances
last night.

He wanted to take her home but she said she would
get a taxi, at which he shrugged carelessly and, going
to the desk, asked the hall porter to get one for her.

'Good night,' she said, a quiver in her voice despite
her previous success at hiding her feelings.

'Good night, Karen. Sleep well.'

Good night . . . and goodbye. . . . That was what he
was really saying. . . .

How could she have acted with what could only be
described as promiscuity? What must he think of her?
Yet, did it matter? She had slipped, but she was
philosophical enough to accept that it would have
happened one day. The awakening was inevitable and
if it had not been Clint who had been responsible it
would have been some other man. She now knew the
passions, the desires of her body and it was up to her
to be guarded in the future. No more risks of that
kind—at least, not until she met the man she wanted
to marry. It would be very different then.

Chapter Five

Three days had gone by since the evening Clint had taken Karen to the Sandy Lane, and only now was she fully recovered from the experience of his lovemaking. As she had said to Helen, she was beginning to find difficulty in alienating her real self from the character she had assumed. And after that experience she had found it even more difficult, although she had at last succeeded.

It had seemed so simple at the time she had embarked upon the escapade; all she had considered was her expertise in the art of disguise. In no way had she envisaged a situation where she would meet Clint Fraser as anyone other than the middle-aged housekeeper she was supposed to be. Well, it had turned out very differently, and all because of her impulsive action in going up to him and making him dance with her at Sam Lord's Castle, an action done with the anticipation of adding to his chagrin when eventually the unmasking took place.

However, by the time three days had gone by Karen had for the most part managed to forget her real self when on the boat, and to her relief any slight awkwardness she had felt on the morning following the incident had escaped her employer's notice. She felt sure he believed her to be slightly eccentric anyway, so even if she did stammer or appear awkward he would not attach any importance to it.

On the fourth morning, having cooked Clint's breakfast, Karen carried it into the dining saloon where he was waiting, as usual. He had become rather more affable toward her recently, the brief greetings morning and evening having developed to small conversations, and so she had no hesitation about saying,

'You've been working very hard these past three days, Mr. Fraser, so obviously your play's coming along well. You got over your difficulty, apparently?'

'I did get over it, yes, and as you say, I've been able to do a great deal of work during the past three days, but—' He shook his head, a frown on his brow. 'I'm afraid I'm at a standstill again,' he admitted.

'That's a shame,' she commiserated. 'Is it your heroine again?'

He nodded immediately and his frown deepened.

'I've never tried to create a heroine quite like this one—' He stopped, a slow smile dawning. 'I mustn't bore you, Miss Waring. You can't be interested in the problems of a playwright.'

'I am interested,' she assured him. 'I—er—used to know someone who was an actress.'

'You did? Who was she?'

'Oh, no one you'd know,' she said airily. 'She was only an amateur.'

'Amateurs can sometimes be good,' he said, and Karen lowered her head to hide the smile that came to her lips. Yes, amateurs could sometimes be good . . . and one day, Mr. Clint Fraser, you will know just how good!

'We were talking about your play,' she reminded him presently, 'and you were saying your heroine was giving you trouble again?'

'I seem to have run out of ideas regarding her; she wasn't giving me trouble until yesterday afternoon, when I suddenly realised that I could not envisage the way she would react to a certain situation.'

Karen looked sympathetic.

'Perhaps I can help?' she offered. 'What is the situation?'

Clint looked at her thoughtfully and said nothing for a space; Karen had the impression that he was seriously considering her suggestion. His next words confirmed this.

'She's a lot younger than you, Miss Waring.'

Karen's lashes came down, hiding her expression.

'I expected she would be,' she returned at length. 'However, I do happen to have been young once, Mr. Fraser,' she added nostalgically. 'I believe I still know what the feelings of a young woman are.'

'Of course,' he agreed kindly, but went on to add that he didn't think she would have ever been anything like his heroine.

'No?' Karen was looking down at the toe of her serviceable black shoe, scarcely able to suppress laughter. 'Is she so different, then?'

'Yes, she is, but I *wanted* her to be different. The modern girl today follows a pattern and when you've met one you've met the lot—'

'Oh, I can't agree—!' Karen stopped, aghast that in her indignation she had dropped her assumed voice, although only for a fleeting second.

'You don't agree?' He was looking oddly at her, but to her intense relief he seemed not to have noticed her slip, which was, after all, only a minor one. 'Perhaps not in your day, Miss Waring, but today—' He shook his head. 'I find the average young woman affected, arch, and more often than not, boring. Hence my desire to create a female who is different, one who is—exciting, interesting. I want the hero to be intrigued by her, unable to know what she is likely to do next.'

'I see. . . .' Karen gave a small sigh. 'I don't think I can help you, then,' she said apologetically.

He smiled at her and said soothingly, 'Don't look so forlorn about it, Miss Waring. I shall overcome my difficulty; I had to do it before.'

'Well, I wish you luck,' she smiled and left him to his breakfast.

Helen had not left the bungalow when she arrived there.

'I thought I'd do my washing,' she said, grimacing at Karen's drab appearance. 'I want to take a snapshot of you in that getup,' she decided. 'We can then have a good laugh in the years to come!'

'I don't think·I'd want to look at this again!' Karen was in front of a long mirror in the living room of the bungalow. 'To tell you the truth, Helen, I wish it was all over and I could look around for another post.'

'You're intending to stay here?' Helen was listening for the washing machine to stop.

'Yes; at least for as long as Jean stays. It seems all wrong that there should be thousands of miles distance between us.'

'I agree—but we shall all miss you. What will you do with your flat? It's your own property, isn't it?'

'Well, it's mortgaged. I might keep it on or I might sell it. I haven't made up my mind.' She paused, then said she would go and get rid of her disguise.

'I'll have some coffee ready when you've finished.'

They sat on the patio drinking it, watching the para-gliders with their brightly coloured parachutes, having fun in the smooth, aquamarine water. The sun was high, spangling the sea with diamonds; children were playing beach ball with their parents; others were flying gaily coloured kites. Elderly men and women were taking life easy beneath the protection of gaudy beach umbrellas. It was a gay scene but an uncrowded one, with tall coconut palms against the sky, and the delicate foliage of casuarinas waving gently, allowing golden shafts of sunshine to create a tapestry of light and shade on the pearl-white sands of the beach. Several red-sailed yachts glided along languidly just offshore, and through it all there was laughter and chatter, and the lilting melody of *This is my Island in the Sun* being played by a strolling minstrel with a guitar.

'I've some shopping to do for Mr. Fraser,' Karen said when Helen, having finished her washing and hung it out on the patio, was ready for the beach. 'Perhaps we'll go into Bridgetown after lunch?'

'Yes, I'd like that. I've been wanting to buy some souvenirs. If I get them today they'll be done with.' She paused a moment. 'Are you off this evening?'

'No, I've to be back on the boat by half-past seven.'

'I've made another date with Bill. It's their last day today; they fly home tomorrow.' A small sigh and then, 'I've had over a week already. Why does the time go so quickly?'

'Don't think about it,' pleaded Karen. 'You've almost two weeks yet. I don't know what I shall do when you've gone. As you know, Jean won't be back for at least another two months.'

'Does your boss know that his housekeeper's sister's away?' inquired Helen with interest.

'Yes.'

'Does he know where she lives?'

'Yes. He did ask me that, so I told him.'

Helen said nothing, merely picking up her beach bag, and a new bottle of suntan lotion that stood on the table.

The capital was a charming, bustling city where could be seen the spectacle of West Indian life in all its varied aspects. The two girls made for Broad Street, and the modern department stores where Helen bought French perfume and some embroidered cloth and several lengths of batik.

'I want the chemists,' Karen said when they came out. 'It's on the corner of Swan Street.'

'Won't any chemist do?'

'I suppose so, but Mr. Fraser told me to go to that one, so I had better do so.'

Karen wanted a certain brand of after-shave lotion, a tube of toothpaste, toilet soap and a nail brush. The shop was small but well-stocked, and Karen was soon served and coming away, having chatted for a few moments with the English proprietor.

They then took a taxi along Highway Three to spend a pleasant afternoon at Andromeda Gardens, one of the loveliest places in the whole of the island, where a stream cascaded over the massive limestone boulders which, rising to many and varied levels, formed the most unusual and fantastic setting for exotic flowers like heliconiums and oleanders, bougainvillea and hibiscus, ferns and palms and a myriad other subtropical and sweet smelling flowers. They were fortunate because the owner, the lady who started it all with the intention of giving it to the nation, just happened to be wandering around and they chatted with her for most of the afternoon.

'You exhibit at Chelsea, don't you?' said Karen, delighting the owner with her knowledge. 'I saw your stand this year, when I was there. Were you there?'

'No, unfortunately I couldn't go, but I'm delighted that our exhibits gave you so much pleasure.'

Karen and Helen came away feeling well satisfied with their afternoon out, and they put a nice finish to it by having tea on the shady patio of the bungalow, enjoying the now familiar spectacle of the glorious beach and the tranquil sapphire sea where the most interesting sight of the moment was that of the surf riders.

'Well, I must be getting ready to go,' sighed Karen. 'All good things come to an end. Have a nice evening with Bill.'

'We're going to the Pepper-pot to see the Merry-men.'

'What about Derek? Has he got himself a girl friend?'

Helen nodded.

'Yes, but she's not what I'd call the sociable type. Bill and I wanted them to make a foursome, but she seems to want to be alone with Derek.'

Karen shrugged but made no comment.

Helen came to the bedroom door when she was changing.

'Can I come in?'

'Of course.' Having taken off her sundress, Karen was in her bra and panties, her beautiful tan lending even more allure to a figure that was as near perfect as any figure could be.

She had the gray dress in her hand and a laugh escaped Helen as she said, 'You wear those—beneath that drab getup?'

'Well, you needn't look so surprised,' laughed Karen. 'There's no reason in the world why I should have to wear a chemise and bloomers, is there?'

'No, I suppose not . . . but they're so incongruous, those dainty bits of lace beneath that dress you're putting on.'

Karen slipped it over her head; its folds fell down to about six inches above her ankles. Her stockings were black, her shoes highly polished. She grimaced and said she was not sure that she hadn't overdone it.

'Mr. Fraser thinks I look fifty-five.'

Helen's eyes widened.

'He actually told you that?'

'I asked him about his housekeeper—'

'You did?' incredulously. 'Really, Karen, you were taking a risk, surely! How could you keep a straight face when he was talking about you—her—oh, lord, you know what I mean!'

Karen's eyes were glistening with humour.

'It was fun. He said she was trying to make herself look younger by the use of cosmetics, and he wondered why women could not grow old gracefully.'

Helen subsided into laughter.

'How the devil did you keep a straight face?' she asked when she had recovered.

'It was difficult,' answered Karen reflectively. 'It needed all my experience of acting, I can tell you.'

'I'll bet it did!' Helen paused, looking her over. The makeup was complete and Karen was pushing her lovely dark hair beneath the dry grayness of the wig. The glasses completed the transformation and Helen gave a low whistle.

'I know I've said it before—every time you do it, in fact—but I'm saying it again. You're an expert, Karen, and if ever you become a fugitive from justice they'll never catch you.'

Karen merely smiled, and with one last look in the mirror she said she must be on her way.

Helen accompanied her to the front door and just as she opened it an elderly gentleman happened to be passing and for no apparent reason he stopped dead on seeing Karen. Then, looking rather sheepish, he walked on, a gray-haired man of medium height and build, and a slight droop to his shoulders. He was a

few yards in front of her as she followed the path
leading from the Vervain Hotel to a place where she
could enter the grounds of the Smuggler's Cove Hotel.
And it was just at that point that he happened to turn,
and again stopped.

Frowning, Karen carried on, increasing her pace,
but as she came abreast of him he said, 'Excuse me
speaking to you, but I've seen you several times, and I
thought I would like to introduce myself. I'm George
Lawson, a widower.' He smiled benignly at her and
waited for her response.

'Oh—er—well, I'm pleased to make your acquaint-
ance, Mr. Lawson,' she said nonplused.

'I'm here for two months,' he offered eagerly. 'I've
been ill and as I'd saved a bit I thought I'd recuperate
here, in the sun. Gertrude, my married daughter, was
here with her husband last year and they recommend-
ed it. But it's lonely. . . .' His voice trailed shyly. 'You
seem to be on your own too, and I thought—well—
that you and I, that we— Are you on holiday as well?'
he asked, dragging out a handkerchief to mop his
brow. 'I'd like to keep company with you.'

Karen, laughter bubbling up inside her, had to turn
away because she had the utmost difficulty suppressing it. However, quite unable to be unkind to the man,
she said gently, 'I'm sorry, but I'm not on holiday. I
have work to do. But in any case I wouldn't want to
keep company with you.'

'Work?' he slanted her a surprised glance. 'I've seen
you about often—'

'I'm sorry,' she repeated, then stopped, becoming
conscious of a firm and insistent step behind her and
she automatically moved to one side.

'Thank you, Miss Waring,' said her employer politely. And his eyes, faintly satirical, moved from her face to that of the man who had also stepped aside.

Although colouring beneath her makeup, aware as she was that Clint Fraser had overheard much of what George Lawson was saying, she nevertheless felt the whole situation was fast becoming hilarious. Laughter bubbled up inside her again to reach aching proportions in her efforts to suppress it.

'Will you think about it?' asked the old man persuasively. 'I'm not short of money, so I could take you about a bit.'

'No thank you,' she said firmly. 'I have no wish to go out with anyone.'

'But you're on your own,' he persisted. 'I . . . like you.' He looked sheepishly at her. 'We could do very nicely together.'

'I'm sure you'll find a suitable companion, Mr. Lawson.' Karen increased her pace, hoping he would not attempt to keep up with her but she was disappointed. He accompanied her right to the boat, so she had to stop and say, 'Look, I work on this boat. The gentleman who spoke to me owns it and I'm his housekeeper. My time's occupied. Good afternoon, Mr. Lawson,' she added and, in her hurry to get away, forgot her role and ran swiftly up the gangway only to collide with her employer who happened to appear from nowhere as she reached the top.

He had caught her by the arms to steady her, staring in surprise at the speed with which she had been running. His eyes strayed to the man looking up at them; and his fine lips quivered with amusement.

'You appear to have found yourself a gentleman

friend, Miss Waring,' he commented dryly. 'Why do you run from him? He seems very inoffensive to me.'

'Mr. Fraser,' she quivered, 'I do not want to have anything whatsoever to do with him!'

'Fair enough. I shall endeavour to get rid of him for you, once and for all.' Releasing her, he turned, beckoning. 'Come here, my man,' he ordered, and without hesitation he obeyed. 'Now, might I ask what you mean by molesting my housekeeper?'

'Well, sir—I sort of—like her, if you know what I mean?'

By this time Karen, her little spurt of anger dissolved by her mirth, had turned away, her shoulders heaving, to escape to her cabin, tears of laughter rolling down her face.

'What the deuce of a pickle!' she laughed. 'Wait until I tell Helen tomorrow. Her sides'll ache with laughing!'

'I believe I've managed to put your amorous suitor off,' Clint assured her a little later. 'But it's obvious that he's fallen in love with you—'

'Rubbish, Mr. Fraser. Please say no more about it!' She was acting the outraged spinster, indignantly refusing to listen. 'I'm not interested in men!'

As it was a little too early to begin preparing the dinner Karen decided to wash her underwear. She had just finished and was shaking them out ready to hang in her bathroom, when suddenly the door to the galley opened and her employer stood there, his gray eyes widening as they moved from the lacy scrap she held in her hand to the matching bra lying by the sink. Never had Karen been more thankful for the greasepaint covering that effectively hid her blushes.

Clint appeared to make a swift recovery from his surprise, but there was certainly an odd expression on his face as he looked at her, while she was so disconcerted that she found herself speaking first, stammering out words that would have been better left unsaid.

'Oh—Mr. Fraser! You've—never come in—here before at this time! I—I—never expected you. . . .

The gray eyes wandered back to the garment in her hand; she screwed it up into a tiny ball, belatedly trying to hide it from his view. She saw his glance rove over her and, as once before, she had the sensation of being stripped. Her figure in the unshapely, loose fitting dress seemed far larger than the sort of figure for which the bra and panties were designed.

'I came merely to tell you I'd not be having dinner this evening. I should have told you this morning but I didn't know then that I wouldn't be able to work.'

'It's still not going right?' Karen said, making a tremendous effort to regain her composure even while knowing it was quite impossible with that bit of lace lying there, and the other screwed up in her hand, its dainty trimming visible in spite of her efforts to conceal it.

'No, Miss Waring, it isn't going right. I shall get myself some recreation by dining out this evening.' He looked oddly at her before turning away. She watched the door close, then her innate sense of humour prevailed and she shook with silent laughter.

What should she do with herself? Neither the thought of spending the evening alone on the boat nor in the bungalow appealed, and she suddenly remembered Bill and Derek highly recommending the Tamarind Cove Hotel for dinner and she decided to try it, remembering too that there was a very special entertainment this evening which had been advertised in the Vervain Hotel. It was late to try and book a table but she might just be lucky.

She rang from the Vervain before going to the bungalow to change and to her intense satisfaction was able to reserve a table for one.

Helen had not yet left the bungalow when Karen arrived, and as there were a few minutes to spare. Karen—after telling her that she had the evening off—related the story about the old man, and for a few uncontrollable seconds Helen was speechless with laughter. Her eyes were actually moist when at last she was able to say, 'This gets more and more entertaining every minute! And your boss had to get rid of him, you say?'

'Yes, that's right. He was obviously highly amused, and said he thought the man had fallen in love with me.'

Helen went into another peal of laughter and Karen scarcely let her recover when she related the incident of the underwear.

'I didn't know where to put myself,' she added. 'I searched for something to say—for some explanation but it was impossible. . . .' Her voice trailed as Helen's laughter rang out through the room again, her whole body affected by mirth.

'Did he say anything?' she wanted to know when eventually she had regained her calm.

'Naturally he didn't. What could he say? He looked me over,' went on Karen before Helen could speak, 'as if he were trying to see exactly what I had on beneath my dress.'

'Oh Karen,' cried Helen collapsing into a chair, 'you're going into this deeper and deeper!'

'Why am I?' casually and with a shrug of her shoulders. 'I was disconcerted at first, and I suppose I shall feel strange tomorrow morning when I serve his breakfast, but as he can't very well introduce the subject of his housekeeper's underwear I've really nothing to worry about.'

'Until the end . . . and the showdown,' Helen reminded her darkly.

Karen laughed, eyes sparkling. But she said nothing, wanting only to get rid of her disguise. Helen was concerned about her spending the evening on her own but Karen reassured her by the information that she had managed to book a table at the Tamarind Cove Hotel where a special entertainment was to be put on this evening.

'There's a famous steel band and calypso singers, and also two very famous limbo dancers. I'm really looking forward to it, Helen, so please don't worry about me.'

'Well . . . if it's what you want. But you could join Bill and me if you'd like to?'

'And play gooseberry?' with a lift of her brows. 'No; but thank you all the same.'

After discarding the wig and cleaning the grease-paint off, Karen had a bath and put on an ankle length dress of coral-coloured chiffon, which she had been tempted to buy in the shop at the Smuggler's Cove Hotel. Full-skirted and nipped in at the waist, it had a high, mandarin collar and long, very full sleeves gathered in to a tight cuff. The bodice at the back was slit from neck to waist. Her hair, newly washed that morning, gleamed when she brushed it, highlighted with tawny-gold, forming an enchanting halo for a face of exquisite beauty. A quarter of an hour later she was in a taxi on her way to the hotel.

Chapter Six

The setting for the evening's special entertainment was the long broad terrace, the tables being placed around the area where the floor show was to take place. On each table a candle flickered from its crimson jar, spreading a romantic, subdued light on to the cloth and the gleaming silver and glass. Surrounding the terrace tall lamps with naked flares set an added scene for an evening of dining and dancing and typical West Indian entertainment. The whole atmosphere was gay, with chatter and laughter and with the steel band playing for those people who had already begun to dine. Karen had been shown to her table, which to her delight was right at the front, opposite the band, when another waiter approached and a whispered conversation went on between him and the waiter who had shown Karen to her table. She caught the words, '. . . but it was booked this afternoon—'

'This lady has the table,' from the waiter, almost angrily.

At last they both turned, their expressions troubled and apologetic.

'There has been some mistake,' the first waiter said. 'This table was booked by a gentleman this afternoon.'

'Oh. . . .' Karen rose to her feet, embarrassed by the stares of people at nearby tables. 'I booked it later, so. . . .' She spread her hands and lifted her evening bag from the back of the chair where she had hung it. 'You have another table?' She was disappointed because she felt she would not be given a table so near to the front as this one was.

'That's the trouble,' apologised the waiter, 'we're fully booked because this is a special night, with famous people entertaining. It's not often that we make a mistake and I can only say I am very sorry. The other waiter did ask the gentleman to share his table with you but he refused.'

She smiled reassuringly at him, noting how impressive he looked in the immaculate white linen that contrasted so attractively with his shining mahogany skin.

'It isn't your fault, so please don't look so worried about it. I'll go somewhere else.' She had turned to make her way back to the steps leading to the exit when she saw the second waiter coming toward her, followed by the man who had booked the table. Karen gave a gasp as she saw who it was. The waiter turned.

'Karen!' There was no mistaking the pleasure on Clint's face, and swiftly she recalled his coldness as he left her on that previous occasion. Why, then, was he so glad to see her now? 'But this is wonderful! You're dining here this evening?'

'This is the lady, sir, who was occupying your table.'

'This—? We shall share it,' he said decisively without asking her. 'I had no idea this was the lady who had my table or I'd have told you I didn't mind sharing.'

Both waiters, all smiles now, inclined their heads and the first, after seeing them seated, went off to collect what was necessary for laying the second cover.

'Thank you,' said Karen demurely. She had coloured delicately, her eyes lowered, for she was recalling vividly the last time they had been together. 'It was kind of you to offer to share your table with me. I was quite disappointed at the thought of not seeing the show.'

'It'll be very good.' His gray eyes were focused on her face and she felt as if she were being compelled to look up and meet his scrutiny. What a strange coincidence that they should meet again. There were so many luxury hotels where he could have dined but she supposed that he, like she, had chosen the Tamarind Cove because of the special entertainment.

'I'm glad we met again,' said Clint when the waiter, having laid the cover and left the menu, went away again. 'I've been thinking a lot about you since we were last together.'

She frowned and shook her head, silently begging him not to remind her of it, but his reassuring smile appeared instantly, as if he were anxious to save her embarrassment.

'It's a coincidence that we're both here,' she mur-mured, more for something to say than anything else. And then she just had to ask, 'How do you come to be alone, though? Your girl friend . . . it's serious?'

'It could be. Neither of us is in a hurry though.'

A slight heaviness seemed to descend upon Karen's spirits.

'Does she live here?'

'No, on Grenada. She and some friends of hers happen to be holidaying here.' That was all; obviously he had no intention of talking about his girl friend.

But Karen, compelled by some force out of her control, persisted, 'Why aren't you with her this evening?'

'She's with her friends and I had no wish to join them.' Rigid the voice suddenly, inexorable; Karen saw a matching inflexibility in his eyes and knew that if she were to avoid a snub she must refrain from questioning him further.

She asked instead, 'Why have you been thinking about me since we last met?' He had not wanted to make another date, she recalled, but of course that was understandable, his having a girl friend with whom he appeared to be going steady.

'Because you puzzle me,' he began, when she interrupted him.

'You've said that before. I'm a very ordinary person, really—when you get to know me.' Her eyes looked beyond him to the cascading showers of a bougainvil-lea vine on a trellis to one side of which the steel band was playing.

'Ordinary?' with a lift of his brows. 'No such thing!

You're a most *extraordinary* young lady.' He paused as if taking special care about framing his next words. 'I must know, Karen, why, after repulsing me one evening, you were willing the next?'

She coloured, and shot him a resentful glance.

'Please. . . . It isn't gentlemanly to remind me of it!'

'I'm not intentionally being anything other than a gentleman,' he denied. 'I've absolutely nothing against you for your delightful reciprocation. It was a revelation to me.'

She stared, as if expecting him to expand on that but he, too, was waiting and after only the slightest hesitation she said, frankly, 'On the second occasion there were romantic preliminaries—the hotel, which you yourself declared to be something quite exceptional—the dining by candlelight, tbe dancing to the steel band . . . oh, and so much else besides!'

Clint's gray eyes had become dark and keen with interest. He seemed avid for more as he said, 'So that was the difference—and the result?'

'Yes, it was.'

'You've had the same experience before obviously, you're too beautiful not to have had—'

'No, I've never had that kind of experience before.'

Silence—the silence of disbelief. Clint's eyes widened, then narrowed inscrutably.

'You don't believe me?' A spark of hostility lit Karen's eyes, the result of an upsurge of anger at his manner. 'I don't care whether you do or not!'

His expression changed on the instant.

'I do believe you,' he assured her quietly. 'Yes, Karen, I couldn't do otherwise with that kind of indignation in your eyes.'

Somewhat mollified, she managed to respond to the persuasive smile he gave her.

'Let's see what we shall order,' he suggested, and for the next few minutes they pored over the menu, both choosing the same in the end—a starter of cold soup flavoured with garlic and peppers, then a seafood collection including lobster and scallops served in a delicious brandy, sherry and cheese sauce.

'And wine?' Clint smiled at her across the candlelit table. 'Shall we have champagne?'

'Yes, please. It's my favourite drink.' She was thinking that she had come here alone expecting to pay for herself. She would still like to do just that but was very much afraid Clint would resent even the merest suggestion that she pay for her own dinner.

'Oh, but this is marvelous!' the exclamation leaped to Karen's lips after the limbo dancers had performed their incredible act. 'How do they do it?'

Clint, watching her every change of expression, gave no immediate reply and, as once before, Karen had the idea that he was making mental notes.

'You mean, you haven't seen limbo dancers before?' he inquired strangely.

'Not as good as these,' she answered guardedly.

The gray eyes flickered. There was no doubt in her mind that he was exceedingly curious about her but, as he was disinclined to talk about his affairs she was safe; he would not expect her to do what he himself was unwilling to do. And yet, what an unusual situation they were in! Not that it mattered, for they might never meet again after tonight.

During the intervals in the floor show Karen and Clint chatted, and she could not help but be conscious of the admiration in his gaze, which seemed to be taking in every single thing about her face—and often it would become fixed on some feature—her eyes, her mouth or, as now, on the faint thread of blue transparency at her temple. A smile broke from her lips, to be mirrored in her eyes. He leaned báck in his chair as if being forced to relax, in order to fully appreciate what he was seeing. He appeared to be satisfied about something and she was puzzled. But the moment passed and the calypso singers came on. After the performance there was another interval and Clint asked Karen to dance. She trod on air, floating on a magic carpet to a realm called Paradise.

Her happiness showed, as it was bound to do. She shone up at him and heard him catch his breath. Was he beginning to like her . . . in *that* way? Impossible. Besides, there was his girl friend. But he had not been very enthusiastic when he had spoken about her, Karen reflected.

She was still thinking about the girl when he led her back to the table but she soon thrust the unwanted picture from her mind, pretending the girl did not even exist.

'I'm feeling rather guilty,' she heard her companion say and glanced up to look interrogatingly at him.

'Why?'

'It's Miss Waring, my Girl Friday as you call her. I forgot to tell her I wouldn't be in for dinner and she came back to get it ready.'

'Came back from where?' Karen could not resist asking.

'She spends a good deal of her time at her sister's bungalow.'

'Her sister lives here, on the island?'

'Yes; she works at the Vervain Hotel and lives in one of the bungalows. But she's away at present and Miss Waring must be lonely, on her own in the bungalow all day.'

'You don't need her during the day?'

'No, there isn't much for her to do at all.' His voice had changed to abruptness and it was plain that he was regretting having mentioned his house-keeper.

But Karen was tempted again and she said, her eyes moving away from his, 'What does she do with her time, then?'

'She says she reads. It's a dull life for her, I'm thinking, but it's partly her own fault, since she's obviously never been interested in marriage.' He paused, his lips quivering with sudden mirth. 'She could have had a beau today. An elderly gentleman wanted to take her out.'

Karen's eyes widened in simulated interest.

'You saw him?'

'Yes. As a matter of fact I had to get rid of him for her. I'd like you to meet Miss Waring, Karen, and give me your opinion of her.'

She flashed him a startled glance.

'Why—er—any particular reason?'

He hesitated, frowning in thought.

'She's beginning to puzzle me—' He stopped abruptly and Karen had the greatest difficulty in hiding her amusement. For it was plain that the thought now in his mind was of those dainty undies his housekeeper was washing.

'In what way?' she persisted, wondering if he would

reveal what was in his mind. But he was already shaking his head.

'It doesn't matter,' he returned casually, and changed the subject.

Karen looked at him, and although admiring him for his reticence, she could not help but be a little disappointed, feeling that if he had talked she would have had something exceedingly amusing to relate to her friend when she saw her the following day.

'You look very happy,' Clint was saying when at last the floor show was over. 'You've enjoyed the evening apparently?'

'Very much—and thank you for everything.'

'Don't thank me, Karen,' he protested gently. 'I've had a most enjoyable evening.'

She fluttered him a lovely smile, convinced that she would never be quite the same after tonight. The romance of the setting and the Caribbean entertainment; and for her partner a man so handsome and distinguished looking that women of all ages were surreptitiously casting glances toward the table at which he sat. Typically feminine, Karen naturally felt proud to be his chosen companion, and the envy of her sex.

'Are you ready to go?' Clint's voice cut into her train of thought and she gave a little sigh.

People around them were moving; tables were being cleared, candles blown out.

'I feel so sad now, Clint.' The words came from nowhere. Karen had had no intention of saying anything like that.

'Because a lovely evening's coming to an end?'

Clint's voice was gentle to her ears, his smile almost tender. The nerves around her heart fluttered, then stilled, only to begin all over again when she saw the expression in his eyes.

'Because a lovely evening *is* at an end,' she corrected, with another little sigh.

'It needn't be,' he said softly. 'Come for a walk along the beach with me.' He was at her side; she caught the tempting male smell of him, felt the touch of his hand beneath her elbow, and it needed no added persuasion to bring her to her feet and come up beside him. But yet she hesitated.

'I. . . .' She glanced at him appealingly. 'Perhaps I'd better be—be going. . . .'

A low laugh escaped him, and she thought how very different he was from that aloof and distant playwright who had disparaged her acting.

'It's early yet,' Clint slid an arm about her waist and she let him take her out into the scintillating, starlit night, where her mind lost itself in a delightful mist of reverie as she relived the pleasures of the past couple of hours. Clint led her through gardens where the air was balmy with the fragrance of magnolias drifting on the northeast trade wind breeze, and then beyond the grounds to the moon-spangled beach. Not another person to be seen, not a murmur other than the sound of the breeze in the foliage on the towering dome palms fringing the shore. Clint urged her toward the shelter of some casuarina trees and took her in his arms. It was so natural that she should be there, so right that he should be looking at her in that masterful way, one hand caressing her cheek and her throat before his fingers explored the nape of her neck and slid into the silken halo of her hair. A thrill shot through her and an ache of sheer pleasure caught her throat. Nerve fibers quivered, tiny vibrations shooting through her body, tingles of rapturous expectation. Clint's eyes lit with a sort of tender amusement just seconds before he bent his head to kiss her. There was rapture in his embrace, the thrill of ecstasy in the male moisture of his lips sliding over hers—a stimulating prelude to a kiss that was as savage as it was tender. Already drugged by the romance of the evening, and this moon-pale setting, Karen knew the vital force of idealistic desire—nothing sensual, yet with heaven no more than a breath away.

She quickened to the caress of his tongue probing the depths of her mouth, thrilled to the questing warmth of his palm as it slid into the opening at the back of her dress to explore the soft flesh over her ribs and seek the rounded firmness of her breast.

'You're so different,' he whispered, and Karen was reminded of what he had said to his housekeeper about all modern girls being alike. But *she* was different in his eyes. . . .

He held her from him; the moon sailing through a lacy gauze of cirrus clouds cast shadows on his lean, angular features, hardening them, but the floating silver disc was full again in all its glorious light and the impression was gone as swiftly as it came. The moon seemed low and close, while the stars, like powdered diamonds, receded. The overhanging branches of the trees were painted silver, beautiful and bizarre.

'Tell me, Karen, what are you thinking?' Clint's

whispered words were music in her ears, his breath
against her cheek the pure caress of a breeze at dawn.

'It's . . . romantic,' she answered, peace flowing
over her so that she relaxed within the haven of his
arms.

'Romantic. . . . Tell me, what is your definition of
romance?'

'Stardust and dreams—' The words slipped out,
from somewhere in her subconscious; she was as
surprised as he when they were uttered.

'Stardust and dreams. . . .' His murmuring repetition seemed to be made so that he would retain the
words. 'Not reality, then?' Karen could find no answer
simply because she did not know to what it related.
His next words enlightened her. 'What about sex? Is
that not reality? You believe that sex is in the mind
first and then in the body?'

'I believe that true love is spiritual first, and that the
fulfillment is physical.' She looked at him in the
moonlight, a smile stealing hesitantly to her lips. 'You
think I'm silly, don't you?'

He shook his head.

'On the contrary. I'm of the opinion that you're a
most extraordinary girl. Haven't I said so?' He smiled
down at her and everything about him was tender
until she put her arms around his neck, her fingers
relishing the impression of strength at the nape. She
heard Clint's swift intake of breath, and every nerve in
her body responded when he swept her into his arms,
crushing her to him, kissing her passionately on the
mouth, the throat, the vulnerable places behind her
ear. His fingers teased until her nipples hardened to
desire, and in a great upsurge of longing she arched

her body to the coiled-spring inflexibility of his. Little moans of ecstasy escaped her as she strove to come even closer to the taut muscles of his loins. One of Clint's hands moved with slow intimacy to her lower body, pressing her to him as if he too, could not get close enough. How she wanted him! If only she and he were alone in that primordial isolation of a world just born, free of inhibitions and the reins of society.

Words rose to her lips, as eloquent as they were simple, and whispered silently, 'I love you, Clint.'

He did not hear but he drew away, to see the glancing tenderness in her eyes; that, and the glow of lips moist from his kisses seemed to drive him to madness and she was crushed again into the punishing strength of his arms, the male hardness of his virility stimulating every nerve fiber in her body until there was only the chaos of burning need of fulfillment, a need that was a wild, unbridled desire for the feel of his naked flesh against hers, his possessive hands seeking and taking, their pleasure her bliss; rapture and desire fulfilled.

But he drew away and as she looked into his eyes she saw all that her heart desired. He cared! Her body settled, but she was transported by her discovery to the heights of heaven, with earth a million light years away. The expression in his eyes was fulfillment as high and wide as eternity, setting her soul on fire.

She had been right when she said that true love was spiritual first, and physical next. She closed her eyes and lay contentedly against his chest.

'Stardust and dreams. . . .' Clint was murmuring. She felt the tenderness of his lips against her cheek, the reverent caress of his hand on her breast as if he were touching some precious object, almost sacred. 'Stardust and dreams, and true love is spiritual. . . .' He spoke to himself and she started up, feeling that in spirit he had left her.

'Clint. . . .' she whispered, bewilderment in her lovely eyes. 'You . . . ?' What was she trying to ask him? But he knew, surely. Suddenly she was afraid, and she whispered to herself, 'I need him! Oh, God, don't let him desert me!'

Suddenly his smile came, and he bent his head to kiss her tenderly on the mouth. All her world was rosy again, her fear dissolving like frost in the April sun. He cared; she had not been mistaken, and naturally her mind leaped to the deception she was practising but she saw no real problems. When the time came his "motherly" housekeeper would leave, having properly given in her notice, and would never be seen again. Or, should Clint want to be married soon, then Miss Waring would give in her notice earlier. It was simplicity itself.

'My dear, Karen,' Clint was saying softly. 'It's time I took you home.'

Home! The one small word brought her instantly back to reality, and to the fact that her position was now awkward, to say the least. When she had embarked upon this escapade the possibility of her falling in love with him had never entered her head. She had disliked Clint Fraser to the point of actual hatred, because of her resenting his unfair criticism of her acting.

'I want to—to get a taxi,' she murmured, drawing away from him and shaking her head. 'Please—'

'Nonsense, darling! Everything's changed. I must see you home.'

The dryness in her throat actually hurt as she tried to swallow. What could she do to extricate herself from this tangle? Clint's next words only made things worse, much worse. 'We've now to tell each other all about ourselves. I'll start first. I'm a playwright. And I'm on the boat because I wanted complete quiet, away from everyone—servants, friends and anyone else who might become a nuisance to me. That's why I advertised for Miss Waring, and why she has to leave the boat every day. Fortunately she had a sister here and that was an important factor when I was engaging her. It made things so much easier all round.' He stopped and because she was staring down at her feet he tilted her face with the masterful touch of a hand beneath her chin. 'And now, love, you can tell me about yourself. What are you doing here and where do you live? That will do for a start.'

She drew a deep breath, seeing her dreams come crashing about her ears. Should she confess all, throw herself on his mercy? He loved her and although he would undoubtedly be furious, he'd forgive her . . . or would he? She slanted him a glance in the moonlight, saw the inflexibility of his jaw, the firm chin and mouth, the unfathomable gray eyes that were now fixed upon her with fine-drawn intentness. No, she dared not make a confession! All would be lost if she did. Play for time, that was the thing to do, but how? Never in her life had she been in such a plight as she was at this moment. And then, out of the blue, an idea came which, although it might not work, was at least worth a try.

'It's so very late, Clint, and your housekeeper's on her own on the boat. I'd not like it if it were me. Women get nervous, you know.'

'But—'

'Men don't understand a woman's nervousness, Clint. Take me home another evening, when it's not so late, but for tonight—well, it's far more sensible for me to get a taxi.'

He was still frowning but as she watched the frown began to fade.

'Very well, but tomorrow, I want to know where you live and all about you. Understand?' Imperious were the words and the manner of their delivery.

Fairly sagging with relief, Karen offered the meek response, 'Yes, Clint, of course I understand.'

They walked hand in hand back to the hotel where Clint called two taxis and while they waited he asked her to meet him for dinner the following night.

'I shall be working hard all day,' he said with very noticeable satisfaction. 'I've been having trouble with the play I'm writing but I shall be able to carry on now—for a while at any rate. And by the way,' he added, smiling, 'I haven't told you my name. It's Fraser.'

'Fraser?' Karen looked suitably impressed, her eyes widening and a little exclamation escaping her. '*The* Clint Fraser, but it must be! There's only one.'

'Yes, dear,' he replied and as one of the taxis arrived at that moment he handed her into it and stood for a moment, tall and straight, incredibly attractive.

'Good night, until tomorrow,' she said, shining up at

him from her comfortable seat in the back of the car.

'Good night, dear—' He stooped to kiss her lips, an impulsive action, as if it were quite impossible to resist what Karen was unconsciously offering. 'Yes, until tomorrow; eight o'clock at the Southern Palms. I'll see you in the lobby.'

Chapter Seven

As was only to be expected, sleep would elude Karen that night; in her cabin she tossed and turned, desperate to discover a way out of the mess she had gotten herself into. Deceit never did pay; she had always known it. But this masquerade had never been considered as deliberate deceit; it had been so appealing to her at the time, and never in her wildest dreams could she have foreseen herself falling in love with the man she had so much disliked as to desire to be revenged on him. She had even given him a false name, and at the recollection she found herself weeping, as despair and hopelessness flooded over her. There was no way out; she would have to disappear—yes, Karen Boyle would have to disappear but not Miss Waring, for if his housekeeper disappeared Clint would immediately feel it his duty to go to the police. Yet how could she stay on as his housekeeper, loving him as she did?

A great shuddering sigh escaped her and she got up at last, switching on the light. A quarter past one and she had not yet slept a wink. She put on a thick velour dressing gown, wrapping it around her because she suddenly felt chilled to the bone. She would make a cup of tea she decided, and went silently to the galley. She had just brewed it and was about to pick it up from the table when to her horror she heard her employer moving about in the narrow space outside the door, which was, fortunately, closed.

'Miss Waring, are you all right?' The handle of the door was turning. There was a second's inaction as fear froze her limbs, then she was precipitated into motion, springing to the door and slamming it shut, even as he began to open it.

'Yes,' she cried breathlessly. 'Of—of c-course I'm all right.'

'I've been working and went on deck for a breath of fresh air. I saw the light and naturally wondered what was the matter. Are you sure you're all right?'

'Yes—yes! I've said so!' Thank God she'd remembered to use her assumed voice!

'Then why can't I come in?'

Wildly she glanced around, as if seeking inspiration from the stove or the sink or the cupboard where all the food was stored. And then, like a miracle, an idea came to her.

'I'm—er—in my night clothes, Mr. Fraser. . . .'

'Oh—sorry,' abruptly, and she sagged with relief as she heard his quiet measured tread as he walked along the passage.

Her heart was beating rapidly, pounding wildly

against her ribs. She looked at the tea, a restorative. Drawing her dressing gown more snugly around her she sat down at the table, too scared to make a move yet to go back to her cabin.

What must she do? Karen could not have counted the number of times this question had come to her since the moment Clint had said that they must now learn about one another. And the only answer was that she would have to make a full confession. Yet immediately upon this came the certainty that Clint would not understand her original motive and, therefore, he would be quite unable to forgive her.

If they had known each other a little longer, and their love had strengthened. . . .

Play for time. . . . This was the first idea that had come to her and she found herself dwelling on the possibility of doing just that. But how could she play for time? In, say, another few weeks, he would be so madly in love with her that, although he might be furious and deeply humiliated, she was sure he would never allow his pride to spoil both their lives. No, he could not—she was so convinced of it that she continued to dwell on the possibility of playing for time, and although no immediate way presented itself she felt much more relaxed and was able to sleep when presently she went cautiously from the galley to her cabin.

Clint was as usual in the dining saloon when she took in his breakfast the following morning. He looked at her but she pretended not to notice as she put down his glass of grapefruit juice and then the heated plate on which was the usual bacon and one egg.

He came forward unhurriedly and sat down at the table.

Karen was at the door when he said quietly, 'Miss Waring, whom did you send to do my shopping yesterday?'

'Who . . . ?' uncomprehendingly. 'I did it myself—' She stopped, her nerves springing to the alert.

'A lie is not necessary, Miss Waring,' he broke in censoriously. 'It doesn't matter to me who did the shopping so long as it was done. I was interested to know who it was, that was all. The chemist's a friend of mine and I happened to meet him before I dined last evening. I mentioned that I'd sent my housekeeper in yesterday for the items I required and he rather enviously asked me how I'd come to find such an exceptionally young and beautiful lady to be a housekeeper for me.'

Karen was trembling under his curious regard, but managed to pull herself together, her brain working furiously—and with success, much to her own surprise.

'Oh, it was the young lady who's staying in my sister's bungalow,' she returned, feeling sure her voice was hollow, and not at all like the one to which he was used. Unconsciously she was twisting her fingers; she saw him looking at them and her acting ability was brought into service. 'I'm very sorry, Mr. Fraser. I feel guilty at not doing it myself. After all, my duties are very light. But Helen was going into Bridgetown and she offered, so—' She broke off, shrugging apologetically, her heart as heavy as lead because of all the deceit she was having to practise. She felt weighed down with the ineffable burden of it and for one impulsive moment she could have thrown off her wig and spectacles, and revealed who she was.

But the impulse was controlled, and in any case, he was speaking again, 'So you're not on your own all day as I surmised? I've been a little troubled about you since your sister went away. Is this young lady staying long?'

'She came for three weeks; she still has a fortnight to go.'

'She's here on her own?' He seemed puzzled and Karen explained that the arrangements were made for the holiday before her sister went away.

'I see,' he toyed with the stem of his glass, a thoughtful expression on his face. 'She must have been disappointed.' Karen said nothing and after a pause Clint asked unexpectedly, 'Would you like to sleep at the bungalow, Miss Waring?'

'Sleep?'

'I feel I might be dining out rather more often in the future, at least for a while. And it will leave you free in the evenings. So you could stay with your sister's friend. It would be nicer for you both, wouldn't it?'

'Yes, it certainly would.'

'That's what I thought. It isn't very nice for you to be coming here in the dark anyway, nor is it necessary. So you can stay at the bungalow by all means. As long as you serve my breakfast at eight in the morning, and do your other jobs, then you can take the rest of the days and evenings off.'

'It's very good of you,' she murmured. 'Helen will be very happy to have me sleeping at the bungalow at night.'

'Yes, I'm sure she will.' He picked up his glass of fruit juice. 'So that's settled, then.'

After rushing round Clint's suite and then making his sandwiches, Karen was quite naturally unable to settle to any of the normal chores, so she merely cleared away Clint's breakfast dishes and was soon leaving the boat. She hurried along the beach to where she could enter the grounds of the Smuggler's Cove Hotel and from there to her sister's bungalow.

'You're early!' exclaimed Helen, who was tidying up the living room. 'You make me more envious every day.'

Karen sat down, something she never did until she had rid herself of her disguise.

'Well, you'll not be envious of me in a few minutes.' She looked at Helen through shadowed eyes. 'I'm in a terrible mess.'

Helen whistled, expelling a breath.

'He's guessed and you've gotten the sack. . . .' Her voice trailed to silence as Karen shook her head.

'No, he hasn't guessed. My job's safe enough. It isn't that at all.' Her lip trembled but she pulled herself together. It was all her own fault and self-pity was not only out of place but futile.

'What is it, then?'

Karen hesitated, then said she would get out of her disguise and tell her all about it.

Automatically Helen followed her to the bedroom, to stand at the door, watching her almost tear off the dress, and apply pads of makeup remover to her face.

'You've not fallen in love with the man?' she queried narrowly.

'Yes,' choked Karen, 'I have.'

'Lord—what a fine kettle of fish, and no mistake! I ought to find it amusing and yet—'

'Please don't laugh,' begged Karen, going over to the washbasin and turning on the tap. 'I couldn't bear it.'

'I'll make some coffee,' was Helen's practical decision and she disappeared, a troubled expression on her face.

A quarter of an hour later, having gone out into the sunlight of the patio to drink their coffee, Karen was pouring out the whole wretched story, omitting only the scene enacted on the beach.

'My only hope is to play for time,' she ended, looking at her friend for inspiration.

'What a mess! Who'd have thought that a situation like this could possibly have occurred? It seemed such an exciting, enviable adventure when you told me about it that night at the hotel. I don't know what to advise. . . .' She tailed off thoughtfully. 'You really want to play for time? You wouldn't chance telling him everything?'

'Would you, if you were in my position?'

'No,' replied Helen instantly, 'I would not. As you've said, he hasn't known you long enough.' She stopped, pursing her lips. 'It's remarkable that he's fallen for you. It's different with you; you know who he is, and all about him. You know he's an honourable man—

well, he's looked up to and well-known. But he knows absolutely nothing about you—not even your age, your occupation or where you live—nothing! It's incredible that a man like that would fall in love under such circumstances, and so quickly. I should have thought he'd have been more cautious.' Helen's glance was troubled, her forehead creased in a frown. 'Are you quite sure that he's in love with you?'

Karen swallowed convulsively.

'Quite sure, Helen,' she nodded. 'He's not the kind of man to pretend. I just know instinctively that he isn't pretending. Besides, what good would it do for him to pretend?'

'None that I can see,' conceded Helen, but a small sigh escaped her. However, after a while she said more briskly, 'Well, Karen, if you're determined to have him, and as you can't afford to take any chances, let us get our heads together and try to sort it out. You've mentioned that he's willing for you to stay here every night after you've served him his dinner, and that certainly makes things easier because you haven't to go back to the boat. But the difficult thing is that you can't let him take you home—'

'And he wants to take me home *tonight*,' interrupted Karen almost in tears. 'I can't let him—and yet if I don't he's bound to be suspicious. I can't keep on putting him off, not now that we're in love—' Her voice cut abruptly as Helen suddenly snapped her fingers, her blue eyes lighting up.

'I have it,' Helen cried triumphantly. 'And it not only solves one problem but two at least! The apartment— it's standing empty. You're on holiday, staying there for three weeks— Well, for another fortnight. How's that? It takes care of where you're staying, and the reason for your being on the island.' She looked at Karen who was too dumbfounded to speak. 'Well, is it a good idea or isn't it?' demanded Helen, a trifle deflated by her friend's silence.

'It's a marvelous idea!' agreed Karen. 'Helen, you're a genius! Why on earth didn't I think of that? I couldn't sleep last night and had to get up and make a cup of tea.' She thought of telling Helen about the incident of Clint's coming to the galley but changed her mind, there being more pressing matters to discuss at the moment. 'A fortnight,' she murmured. 'That'll not be long enough.'

'It gives you breathing space.'

'Yes, indeed.' Karen became thoughtful, her spirits having lifted so that clear thinking was again possible. 'I could probably rent the apartment for a longer period, seeing that it's the off-season here at present.'

'But if you're on holiday,' began Helen, when Karen interrupted her.

'I'm going to tell Clint I've thrown up my job, and tell him why.'

'That'll give you a good reason for prolonging your stay—which Clint will want you to do, of course. How long do you think he'll be before he proposes?'

'I don't know. It's all happened so suddenly.'

'Too suddenly for my liking,' Helen felt impelled to say. 'Are you quite sure he's genuine? You've mentioned this other girl—and admit he said it could be serious. Is he intending to throw her over?'

Karen frowned, thinking of that fleeting moment last night when Clint had seemed so far away, bringing an access of fear to her heart.

'Don't make me doubt him, Helen,' she pleaded.

Helen's lashes flickered down, hiding her expression. Yet she just had to say, 'You're not quite sure, are you, Karen—? No, don't interrupt because what I'm going to say is logical. If you *were* sure—a hundred percent sure—then you'd not hesitate to go to him and open up.'

Karen's lips were suddenly dry, because what Helen said was true.

She thrust her doubts away; they were too unbearable to harbor, for if she lost Clint now she felt she would never get over it.

'He *will* propose,' she stated emphatically, 'I know it! But although we'll be engaged, I feel he'll not want to be married until his play's finished. Marriage would be too much of an upheaval.'

'And in the meantime Miss Waring is to continue in her post of housekeeper?'

'Of course. There's no reason for her—me—to leave. Clint would be in a mess without someone to get his breakfast and do the chores.'

'You'll be seeing him regularly?'

'Yes. He told me this morning that he wouldn't want me to cook his main meals as often as in the past—at least for a while, so he's obviously intending to see me every night.'

'For a while?' repeated Helen, suddenly suspicious. 'Why the qualification?'

'I can't say. It isn't important.'

'You're sure?'

'Helen, please believe that he's genuine. I know he is!'

'All right, forget it. He'll be seeing you home every

time you go out, so you and I had better go along to the apartment today and take a few things that'll make it look lived in. There are only the bare bones there at present as you know. You mustn't forget the key, either, when you go out. I've put it in the top drawer in Jean's dressing table.' She paused but Karen made no comment. 'You'll come back here every night, after he's left you?'

'Yes, I shall have to because of my disguise. It takes some time as you know, and I've got to be on the boat by seven at the latest. I'll have to be up at half-past six. I hope I shan't disturb you.'

'Not at all; I'm up at that time. The sun's pouring into my window so it would be impossible to sleep even if I wanted to, which I don't. The early mornings here are too wonderful.' Helen was silent for a while and then, 'You're seeing him tonight?'

'I hoped you wouldn't mind?'

'Not in the least. As a matter of fact, I can go dancing with a bloke from the hotel here. I met him yesterday morning just before you arrived. He's on his own and gave me his room number, telling me to phone him if I cared to go dancing with him.'

Clint was already at the hotel when Karen arrived by taxi, looking adorably young and unsophisticated in an ankle length dress of cornflower blue whose perfect cut accentuated her delicate curves and the boyish slimness of her waist. Her hair, cloud-like about her shoulders, the play of light on her tanned skin, the liquid beauty of her eyes . . . all these were taken in by the man who, tall, assured, and with a sort of dynamic grace in his movements, was coming toward her, a smile softening the stern reserve of his features. Envious eyes were turned upon Karen from every woman in the lobby; a tentative rapture stole through her nerves and her heart was light with joy. Clint's polished manners were portrayed in the slight inclination of his head in greeting, and in the way he put his hand beneath her elbow, a gesture of gallantry, and a winning smile was his instant reward. He ushered her away toward a winding staircase leading to a balcony overlooking the gardens and the drowsy Caribbean. As always it was a magical scene, with a million stars in the dark sapphire sky and the moon filtering wraith-like clouds to embroider the landscape with fragile patterns of delicate fretwork. Karen, a sigh of contentment on her lips, leaned back in the chair which Clint had drawn out for her. He studied her from his place opposite, seeming to be taking in every change in her features resulting from the gentle play of light created by the movement of foliage against the lamps which had been placed within it. Only one other couple was on the balcony, seated right at the far end, and it seemed to Karen, glancing over gardens drenched in moonlight to the palm-fringed shore beyond, that she and Clint had the entire world to themselves. She was on air, so happy that she was frightened.

'What are you thinking?' Clint teetered back in his chair as if wishing to view the lovely picture from a greater distance. But his manner faintly disconcerted her, and she now realised that even as she had entered the lobby she had sensed there was something different about him. 'Your face tells me you're happy and yet I sense anxiety. You can confide, you know, dear. I shall be more than interested to listen.'

Her eyes flew to his, nerves springing to the alert at his keen perception.

'Why should I be anxious?' she asked, unable to find anything else to say.

'There could be many reasons,' was his cryptic reply and now her eyes fell before the keen examination of his. 'However, tell me about yourself. Where do you live on this island and why are you here?' he went on when she did not speak.

She told him she was on holiday, and that she was in an apartment on the grounds of the Coral Court Hotel.

'On holiday? On your own?'

'Yes.'

'You had no friend who would come with you?' That disconcerting quality in his manner was still there and a prickling sensation ran the length of Karen's spine. Some sixth sense warned her that this ought to be the moment of truth, and for one impulsive second she toyed with the idea of speaking out, of ending the anxiety he had spoken of. Anxiety? It was so much more than that! But she cast the idea aside. What was between her and Clint was too slender a foundation to support the truth at this stage. No, she must wait . . . and hope.

'I wanted to come alone,' she replied eventually. 'One does need to be alone at times.'

He nodded in agreement, bringing his chair back to the table as the waiter appeared, ready to take the order for their drinks. Karen watched him give the order, noting the chiseled leanness of his bronzed face, his air of culture and good taste, the aura of male confidence about him, accentuated by the languid tone he used. And yet he was gracious as he smilingly requested the waiter to bring two menus with the drinks.

'How long are you here for?' he asked when the waiter had gone.

'Three weeks, initially, but I've already had one.' She had seen about retaining the apartment earlier in the day and had been told that she could have it indefinitely.

'Initially?'

'I can stay longer if I wish.'

'You have employment in—' he stopped as if he had made a slip '—at home?'

'I gave up my job just before I came here. I worked in an office and when my boss retired I was to be transferred to a man I detested. So I decided to leave, intending to get another post on my return.' That at least was the truth, even if it was subtly manipulated, thought Karen, but she did wonder how many more lies would be told before the final confession was made.

'That was rather drastic, wasn't it?' He was frowning, as if he considered her to have been recklessly unwise.

So he was not contemplating marriage yet. It was as she had surmised: he intended finishing his play first.

'I didn't think so at the time. I could never have worked for the other man.'

'Where is your home?' The question came after a slight hesitation, and Clint was staring beyond her as he spoke.

'London. I have a flat there.'

'You live alone?'

She nodded; her hair swayed, catching the light which brought out the enchanting tints of tawny-gold.

'Yes, I live alone.'

'You've no parents?'

'They were killed in a train accident four years ago.'

Clint's face softened to compassion.

'That must have been terrible for you. How old were you at the time?'

'Eighteen.'

'So you're twenty-two now.' He paused a moment, becoming thoughtful. 'Have you other relatives?'

'I've a sister.' Now, she thought somberly, was when the lies would have to begin.

Clint was looking puzzled.

'If you've only one relative—this sister—why don't you live together—' He broke off, smiling ruefully. 'It's not your sister I want to learn about, but you. Just sit there Karen and talk about yourself.' His voice seemed to have undergone a slight change—nothing tangible and yet a strange uneasiness assailed her. For a while she was relieved that he did not want her to talk about her sister—since to do so would mean she would have to lie—at the same time Karen considered it very strange indeed that he should be so casual about the girl who would eventually become his sister-in-law. Clint was speaking again, and there was an unfathomable expression in his eyes as he added, 'What do you do with your leisure time? Tell me about your hobbies.'

Her long dark lashes fluttered down. Now was the time for subtleties, for avoidance, where possible, of deliberate lies. He had asked about her hobbies and obviously the information to leave out was that she belonged to an amateur dramatic society.

She began to talk—about her childhood which was happy, about the time when at eighteen, she and her sister, younger by two years, had been left to fend for themselves.

'The house was ours, of course,' she went on, 'but there was not very much money. And so we both left school and found work. Later, when my sister obtained a post abroad we decided to sell the house and share the money. I put the deposit down on a flat and that took most of my money because flats in London are so expensive, and the house we sold was neither large nor in a very good state of repair.' She had been looking at him, but now her eyes wandered, thrusts of scarlet hibiscus and purple bougainvillea catching her immediate attention as floodlights were switched on to illuminate the terrace down below where the steel band was assembling at one end.

During the whole of her narrative Clint had been listening with unmoving countenance, as if he were waiting for one particular piece of information. And when finally she said, 'And that's all. Mine hasn't been a very exciting life,' there was an impenetrable expression on his face and an odd inflection in his voice as he said, 'Your hobbies—' Clint's eyes were sharp, uncomfortably searching. 'You haven't mentioned them.'

'My hobbies?' she repeated, having difficulty in keeping her voice steady, for she had caught the measured significance in the content of his words. 'I love reading—biographies and poetry mainly—' She paused, the sensation of impalpable feathers touching her spine. 'I swim and play tennis, and recently I've tried my hand at painting.'

Silence. Etched into the now austere male features was an expression of deep censure.

'Karen,' he murmured very softly at last, 'I did say, a few minutes ago, that you could confide—that I would listen with interest.'

He knew of her deception! For a paralysed second it seemed that her heart had stopped beating. Yes, he knew . . . but where was the fury she had expected. True, he was regarding her sternly, and by some trick of the light his face was more formidable than ever before. But no sign of anger was portrayed. If he *had* learned of the masquerade surely she would not be here now, drinking cocktails on this flower-bedecked balcony with the moon-flushed gardens below and the soft West Indian music drifting up to them!

Still fearful, her limpid eyes bewilderedly enlarged, she asked in a low tone, 'Clint . . . why are you—you talking t-to me like this?'

'I believe you know,' he replied and although the sternness came through, not a trace of anger affected the even tenor of his voice.

Karen could only stare, the hand holding her glass shaking slightly, because of the wild beating of her heart.

'You've somehow learned of the deception?' Even as the words were out she regretted them. He could *not* know! For the strength of anger resulting from the knowledge that he'd been duped, made a complete fool of, could never be repressed to this extent.

'Your chief hobby's acting. You belong to the Parkside Amateur Dramatic Society. You were in my play, *One Stolen Hour*—'

'Oh, Clint!' she cried, unable to keep from breaking in. 'Why aren't you angry? How can you be so calm about a deception of such magnitude?' Her eyes were moist, her face as white as the coat of the waiter who had come to take their order for dinner. 'Why . . . ?' Her tremulous voice faded to a questioning silence as she saw the perplexity in his eyes.

'Good heavens, Karen,' he said reassuringly, 'it isn't all that serious. Magnitude?' He smiled indulgently. 'It's only a minor deception which hasn't done any harm at all.'

'No . . . harm?' She blinked at him dazedly. 'No harm to—to us? To your opinion of me? But it must have!' she cried without giving him the opportunity to answer. 'For me to adopt the disguise of—'

'Disguise?' he echoed, looking at her as if she were a little unhinged. 'Karen, my silly child, I'm staggered that you could consider you'd committed a crime. I can fully understand why you didn't enlighten me that you were Gloria Standish in my play, because I seem to remember that I wasn't particularly nice to you on the occasion we have in mind. And afterwards, on the hotel grounds, I fear you might have heard my totally unwarranted remark about your acting ability. It was unforgivable of me and I now revise my opinion. I have to,' he continued wryly, 'because about a quarter of an hour before you arrived I was on the terrace and a man came up to me. He'd recognised me as Clint Fraser, and said he wanted me to know just how well the Parkside Amateur Dramatic Society had performed my play, *One Stolen Hour*. He and his wife are regular supporters of the company. They had seen the play and considered the acting excellent. He saw me with you last evening but did not want to intrude. If I was seeing the young lady again would I convey the message that she was superb in her role of Gloria Standish and he and his wife hoped to see her again when the next season begins. Don't look so tragic,' he teased. 'There's no harm done.'

She managed a smile, but her heart was still heavy. He knew only a minor part. That was the reason for his lack of anger; and it was no wonder he considered her to be attaching too much importance to the matter.

'I'm sorry about what I said regarding your acting, Karen,' he said contritely. 'I realised afterward that I was wrong and in fact I came to find you and apologise, and to take it all back but you'd gone home.' He smiled and, leaning forward, he covered her hand with his. 'It's understandable that you'd be reluctant to tell me you were the bitch in my play whose acting I'd criticised. I don't blame you, but tonight, I wanted you to confess, and that's why I asked you to talk about your hobbies.' His fingers tightened around her hand. She thrilled to the warmth and tenderness of his touch but a weight still lay on her spirits. If only he had guessed *all* and taken it so calmly. . . . But of course that was impossible. If he *had* guessed all he could never have remained so calm about it. However, there was only one deception now—the major one, but at least he now knew who she was, the girl in the play.

'I suppose I ought to have told you,' she admitted.

'It was natural that you'd not want me to know—' He broke off, eyeing her quizzically. 'I'd have had to know sometime, darling,' he told her and those words wiped away all her dejection and a lovely smile lit her face.

'Thank you for not being angry with me, Clint,' she murmured, but he interrupted her to say, 'Am I forgiven?'

She choked on the words as she said,

'*I* have nothing to forgive, Clint—oh, nothing at all!'

The taxi drew away and Karen inserted the key in the door of the apartment where she was supposed to be living. Her heart was beating rapidly because Clint had insisted that he come inside to say goodnight, and she knew a delicate and exciting access of expectancy as she turned to him after he had closed the door behind her.

'This is the living room,' she flicked a hand expressively.

'Very comfortable. Almost as good as my boat.'

'Oh, not as good as your boat—' she began, then stopped, nerves quivering at the slip. 'I mean—well, they were talking about your boat at the party, and I gathered it was something rather special.'

He nodded his head.

'*I* think it is. You must come over soon and I'll show it to you.' He had come close, a towering giant whose features were carved in masculine perfection. With a little cry of pleasure she went gladly into his inviting arms, feeling small and helpless, utterly compliant beneath his strong male dominance.

After-shave still lingered—the scent of pines and heather moors and the freshness of dawn all mingling

to drug her senses to a profound awareness of the
male appeal of him. The vital force of sexual desire
controlled her mind; rapture caught her throat at the
closeness of his virile body as his arms brought her
possessively against him. His kiss sent blood pulsing
through her veins, driven by the rising turbulence of
her emotions. Her lips parted to his masterful command and his tongue explored the sweetness of her
mouth. She was so close that she could feel the
sinewed hardness of thighs, the muscular strength of
his loins as he thrust them against her slender frame.
A sigh that was a whisper of sheer ecstasy escaped
before her lips were crushed again as his moistly
sensuous mouth enclosed hers, the roughness of his
tongue sending fire through her veins. Her whole
body quivered within his embrace as she soared to
ecstatic heights of bliss when his hand strayed
possessively to the tender curve of a breast and the
rising nipple hardened to the pleasure-pain of his
insistent fingers. Her body was no longer her own for
the natural instinct of male dominance was strong
within her, and surrender to this dominance was her
own fulfillment. Yet in her surrender there was no
subservience. Subconsciously she conveyed this to
him. Her capitulation was honourable, of his persuasion but *her* choosing. Her own power was equal to
his, though not manifest; her gifts were bestowed
freely—not the spoil of a conqueror flaunting his
power. Her love was a tender, sacred offering and she
gladly gave when he wanted to take, arching her
seductive frame in response to the stormy torment of
the possessive hand that crept to the lower part of her
body, sensuously caressing her soft flesh while at the

same time compelling her to come closer to the thrusting male hardness of his loins.

'You intoxicate me.' His voice was frayed by passion, his breath hot against her face, his hands warm and strong as he lifted her. Carrying her to the divan he laid her down, a smile of tenderness curving his mouth as he stood for a long moment, his eyes devouring the beauty of her body, the alluring rise and fall of her breasts, the tempting feminine contours which the dress outlined in tantalising allure. He lay down beside her, a hand cupping her small firm breast within its lean brown strength. Ecstasy vibrated through her limbs; her arms came about him and she turned her body into his, her hand gently tugging at his shirt, bringing it out so that she could feel the leanness of the flesh covering his ribs.

'Karen . . . my own darling! I can't wait for you! You'll come to me?' He held her from him, his eyes dark with latent passion and virility, and in hers the dreamy cloud of longing. 'I want you now—this moment.'

The merest hesitation, and then, 'Yes, darling. . . .' Her voice was a warm temptation, and for long, long moments his passion flared and Karen was swept headlong into its turbulence as his body heaved above her, thrusting its hardness against her loins. 'Let me take your dress off. . . .' His hands manipulated the fastener, sliding it down.

Karen never afterward knew just how and when she changed her mind. It seemed all wrong, some-how, to make love like this, sullying what ought to be pure and sweet and undefiled. She whispered, holding his hand against her cheek, 'I don't want it to be this way, Clint.' It was a cry from the depths of a body chaste and clean. 'Please let us wait.'

For an instant it seemed that he had traveled too far along the path of desire to draw back, but the expression in her eyes, the plea in a voice that trembled childishly, were too much for his honour and he came away.

'How right you are, my love. . . .' With gentle fingers he zipped up her dress again, then drew her to him, to kiss her tenderly on the lips. 'I'm so very glad you changed your mind. It was important that you should.'

'Important?' She looked at him, her eyes still dark and drowsy from his lovemaking. 'Important,' she repeated, her heart skipping a beat for what appeared to be no reason at all.

'Yes, but I can't explain.' Releasing her, he moved away and tucked his shirt back into his slacks. He brought out a comb, pushing it through his thick shining hair, and as she watched he seemed, as on several previous occasions, to be making mental notes. The wraith of an idea filtered into her consciousness only to be instantly thrust away.

He was *not* using her as "copy" for his play! He wouldn't do a thing like that to her!

Chapter Eight

They stood outside the door of the apartment, holding hands, trying to say good night but the minutes stretched and still Clint made no move to go.

The gardens around them were illuminated by lights in the trees and bushes; the moon, argent and cold, sailed along between cloud banks, lending a strange aura of mystery to the scene. The trade wind blew gently, swaying the trees to create shadows that were pitched, swooping like night birds seeking prey. The sea, drowsy and smooth, spread away to be lost in a mist of opal light.

'Well, Karen, I really must make a move. It's past midnight and you ought to be in bed.' Taking her in his arms Clint bent his head and kissed her softly parted lips. 'I shan't—' He hesitated as if reluctant to voice what was in his mind. And it was with mixed feelings that Karen heard him say, 'As I want the play finished in as little time as possible I shan't be seeing you for a few days, but I'll be thinking about you.'

So he wanted it finished as soon as possible! Her heart leaped with joy.

The sacrifice was worth it because the sooner he finished the play the sooner they would be married.

'I understand,' she smiled.

'I know now where you are so I can easily get in touch.'

'I'm out for most of the time,' she returned, once again aware of some slight misgiving. Why wasn't he making a definite date?

'I'll leave a note—or, better still, I can phone the hotel. They'll give you the message. Good night, Karen. Sleep well.'

She stood watching his long strides taking him toward the hotel, where he would be able to get a taxi. Only when he was lost to view in the mothy darkness of the shrubbery did she turn and enter the apartment. She felt flat, drained in a way that frightened her. Helen had been very skeptical about Clint's sincerity, and Helen had always been very astute. . . .

The idea that he was using her persisted, strengthened by certain things recalled, unbidden, by her mind. Clint had said his heroine was unsatisfactory as he had had her; he wanted her to be both unusual and unpredictable . . . and that was how he had described *her*—right at the very beginning. He had wanted to know more about her, he said. Another point was that after he had been out with her he was able to tell his housekeeper that his heroine was now satisfactory. This had happened twice . . . and each time it was after he had been with her, dining and dancing . . . and making love.

'He *can't* have been using me! Oh, I just *know* he's

genuine!' But the wish was father to the thought; she had to admit it because of the unsettling qualms which she was unable to shake off.

She went to the hotel and got a taxi; ten minutes later she was entering the bungalow to find that Helen had just a moment ago come in.

'Hello! And how is the romance progressing? I think I'm in the same boat—I rather like my new boy friend. . . .' Helen's voice faded on a note of anxiety as she saw Karen's expression. 'It's finished?'

'No—well, I can't say.' Karen was close to tears but determinedly she held them back. 'He's using me—' Breaking off she shook her head. 'I can't believe he'd be so hateful, so specious!' She looked at Helen through stricken eyes. 'He just isn't that kind of man.'

'What kind of man?' inquired Helen patiently.

'I had an idea—it came to me when we were in the apartment.' She stopped, still reluctant to say what was on her mind.

'Yes? You had an idea?'

Karen moistened her lips.

'Helen, do you think he could be using me as copy for his play?'

'Using you?' Helen's blue eyes widened. 'No—I mean, the thought never occurred to me. What was the reason it occurred to you?'

Karen gave her a full explanation and when she had finished Helen's eyes were deeply troubled.

'I hate to say it, Karen, but it certainly does seem that your idea was correct.'

'What a fool I am,' quivered Karen bitterly. 'It's Clint who's been doing the acting. I think I hate him.'

'I'm very sure you do not,' declared Helen. 'However, that's unimportant. What is important is that although things look black against him, we ought not to jump to conclusions at this stage.'

'How am I to find out, one way or another?'

'It's simplicity itself. You have access to his study. All you must do is take a look at some of the pages of his manuscript.'

'Of course! I've never looked yet; I felt it would be wrong—prying, sort of.'

'Well, you'll have to take a look now, just to put your mind at rest.'

At rest. . . . If she discovered he'd been deceiving her she felt that her mind would never be at rest again.

As soon as she had taken in Clint's breakfast the following morning Karen went along to his study as usual but this time her first act was to go over to a table and look at some of the papers lying there. They gave her no clue but as there was little time she decided to look at the manuscript itself, which was always on the desk; Karen had watched it grow, marveling at Clint's ability to write so much in a day. It was upside down; she turned it over to look at the beginning and saw the title at the top of the page! *Stardust and Dreams*. And it had been typed in at a different time from the first page, as the letters were less black.

With pulsating nerves she turned the manuscript over again to leaf through some of the last pages, and it needed only a brief examination to confirm her suspicions; Clint *had* been using her, acting a part so that he could discover her reaction, which was the copy he required. She stood for a moment, her eyes dark with pain for, strangely it wasn't a shock, but a drained, sickening feeling in the pit of her stomach. She put the papers back, unwilling to search for those parts that might refer to the intimate side of their association—although she had the strong conviction that he would not put anything like that in the play, simply because he had never done so before, at least, not to her knowledge. She had seen two of his plays on television and one in a London theatre and in none had there been any intimate scenes such as had been enacted between Clint and herself.

Quickly she began to vacuum the carpet, but she had not finished when Clint entered, to stand for a moment in surprise.

'It's taken you a little longer this morning?'

'Yes—sorry.' Forcing a smile as a barrier to the almost irrepressible urge to tell him who she was and that she knew of his deceit, she added, 'I shan't be more than five minutes, but if you'd prefer that I leave it—?'

'No; carry on. I can wait. Oh, and by the way, I've had a change of plans. I'll be dining on the boat for the next few evenings.' He went off and had not returned when Karen went back to the dining saloon to clear away his breakfast dishes. Her mind was working to full capacity, with revenge rising above her heartache. She was level headed enough to realise that a man like that was not worth having and, therefore, she had lost nothing. She was determined to view her situation objectively, remembering that she was not the first girl to suffer disillusionment at the hands of a man.

But she had no intention of letting him get away with it; she would give him copy—of a kind he would certainly be happy to have!

Helen was very quiet after having been told that Clint definitely had been using Karen for his own ends, making up to her, pretending to be in love with her just to collect copy for his play.

'It's a wonder you didn't grasp the fact that he wasn't genuine,' said Helen frowningly at last.

'I agree, especially as he never actually said he loved me.'

Helen's eyes opened wide.

'He didn't?'

Karen shook her head.

'No, but he acted as if he did and I just took it for granted. I expect it's inexperience—but it'll never happen again!'

'Pity you had to learn the hard way,' said Helen sympathetically.

'I'm glad you were here, Helen. I'd feel even more unhappy if I'd been on my own.' It struck her that Helen had come for a holiday, and she made a firm resolve not to dwell on her own misfortune but to try to put on a false front, just for her friend's sake. And so she said casually, 'I'm not going to fret over it. I'm not the first girl who's been duped—' She stopped, colour fluctuating in her cheeks. 'I suppose you could say I've only got my deserts—for the deception *I* have been practising.'

'No, it's not the same at all; there was no real malice in what you were doing, no intent to hurt.' She paused, then asked the obvious question. 'What about Miss Waring?'

'I've decided to give him a week's notice and leave.'

'Good for you! It'll do him good to have to cook his own meals!'

'It's only his breakfast and dinner—and not always his dinner as you know. I expect he'll get someone else anyway.'

'You'll give in your notice tomorrow?'

Karen nodded.

'Yes, first thing,' she replied tightly, the pain in her heart excruciating in spite of her resolve, and the fact that she had sensibly accepted that Clint was not worth having anyway.

'You could settle for the showdown,' suggested Helen. 'At least it would give you the satisfaction of confounding him.'

'I've thought of it but I want to meet him again. He says he might phone the Coral Court Hotel or slip a note under the door of the apartment.'

'You want to see him?' Helen looked at her, puzzled.

'Yes. If it's copy he's after then he'll get it—but not the kind he wants!'

Helen's eyes flickered perceptively.

'I don't know quite how you're going to go about it but I'm glad you're fighting back.'

'What about you?' queried Karen, as the thought suddenly struck her. 'Last night you were saying something about your new boy friend.'

'Roger—yes.' Helen's blue eyes were alight. 'We got on like a house on fire. Kindred spirits—you know, the kind you just sense is your sort of person.'

'Yes . . . I know.' Karen successfully hid her own

fierce, jarring pain as she said, 'How long is he here for?'

'He works at the hotel; he's in the office. That's why he has the evenings off.' She paused, biting her lip. 'I've said I'll see him every night, but I don't like leaving you—'

'I'll be all right,' interrupted Karen reassuringly. And then she added, 'If it develops what will you do? He's English, I suppose?'

'Yes, from Brighton originally, but like Jean he wanted to get a job abroad. He came here on holiday but with the intention of trying for a job in one of the hotels, and he was lucky, getting in the office rather than being a waiter or barman, because then he'd have had to work in the evenings. You asked what I'll do if it develops. Well, I'd like to get a job here too, but, meanwhile, I shall have to go home as planned, then come back later.'

'I'll be coming home with you,' Karen said. 'But I too might come back and try for a job. I'd like to be closer to Jean, but I'll not come back until Clint's gone.'

Helen made no comment on this, but suggested they go into Bridgetown and look around the shops. Karen agreed and it was when they were in a restaurant having lunch that, through an arch which led to another large dining room, Karen espied Clint . . . and his companion was the girl he had been with at Sam Lord's Castle. So he wasn't working after all. He was out enjoying himself with the girl he would probably marry.

'Anything wrong?' from Helen on noticing the sudden pallor of her friend's face.

Karen shook her head instantly. She was not going

to spoil Helen's lunch by telling her that Clint was in there with another girl.

'Nothing. This lobster's delicious, isn't it?'

'Lovely. As I've said more than once, I shan't get used to my beans on toast in a hurry.'

Karen smiled but made no comment. It was only natural that despite her resolve she should keep thinking of Clint, especially when he was so close, lunching with another girl. She glimpsed him now and then but he was far too engrossed with his companion even to glance up. Well, the idea of giving him her notice was at least satisfying, and she was very glad, the following morning, to see the consternation on his face when she told him she would be leaving his employ.

'You're giving me a week's notice?' Clint stared at her disbelievingly. 'But you knew, Miss Waring, when you accepted the post, that it was for six months.'

She nodded, swallowing the hurtful little lump in her throat. How she loved him! It was so hard to leave him, knowing he needed her, and yet she was determined to harden her heart, to keep in her mind what he had done to her. He was not deserving of the least consideration, and she was firmly resolved that he would not get it.

'I didn't know just what it would be like, Mr. Fraser. I'm not cut out for life on a boat.'

'Your life isn't spent on the boat,' he reminded her sharply.

'It isn't the sort of post I expected,' she returned, adopting a stubborn attitude. 'I'm leaving, Mr. Fraser; I've made up my mind so there isn't anything you can say that would make me change it.'

'Not if I offer you more money?'

'I'm overpaid as it is.'

'This is very sudden, Miss Waring?' His gray eyes were narrowed and searching.

'I agree—but I want to leave.'

'You do realise that you are letting me down badly?'

'I have to think of myself,' she said shortly.

'You've another post in view? Is that it?'

Karen shook her head.

'Your breakfast's getting cold.' Her eyes slid to the heated plate on the table. 'I shall be leaving a week from today.'

'Just a moment—don't go, Miss Waring. You haven't offered me any kind of explanation, so I'm at a complete loss as to why you've suddenly sprung this on me. I consider you have no justification for your attitude in refusing to give me an explanation.'

She was hot beneath her greasepaint but she managed to sound cool and casual as she said, sidestepping the comments he had just made, 'There's no argument, Mr. Fraser, so please don't let's waste words. I'm determined to leave next Monday. That gives you time to get someone else.'

His scrutiny was keen, interrogating; naturally he was nonplused, because for one thing she had never spoken to him so sharply; her voice had always been edged with respect.

'So you're not willing to give me the explanation which I'm entitled to?' Anger was linked to the perplexity in his voice. 'Well, if that's what you want—' A flip of his hand denoted his disgust, and his unwillingness to carry the conversation further. 'You may go, Miss Waring.' He reached for his grapefruit, his manner one of icy impassivity. She stumbled blindly from the saloon, tears ruining the heavy makeup on her face. She removed it in her cabin and then, stealthily, left the boat and made her way to the bungalow.

Karen went to the apartment each day, in case there was a note under the door, or any messages for her at the hotel. It was not until the third day after she had given in her notice that she found a note had been slipped beneath the door. With trembling hands she slit the envelope.

'Will you dine with me tonight? I'll call for you at half-past seven. Love, Clint.'

Love. . . . Karen set her teeth as anger flowed through her, fiery in its intensity. It was obvious that he was running short of copy and so he was dating her in order to collect more. She glanced to the top of the page to see the date. Yes, she would dine with him tonight. And yes, she would give him the opportunity of collecting copy!

She was waiting when he arrived, and in spite of herself she was still seeing in him all that was perfect—the even white teeth when he smiled, the firm yet sensuous mouth, the long lithe body giving the impression of latent virility.

'Well, my love, I see you're ready.' He made to take her in his arms but she dodged away, saying,

'Not now, Clint. You'll spoil my lip rouge.'

'You can repair it,' he laughed, advancing towards her, grace and confidence in every step he took. He was in white slacks and a pale blue jacket, fashioned in the draped line, popular in warm countries for casual elegance and comfort. He took her hand, pulling her to him. 'What's wrong with you?' he asked, sudden anxiety in his voice. 'Aren't you feeling good?'

How well he did it she thought, pretending to be concerned when all he wanted was to use her, because he had come to a standstill again.

She let him kiss her, resolutely holding her emotions in check.

'You don't need to repair anything,' he said on releasing her. 'Come on, dear, I've a taxi outside. We're going to the Sugar Cane Club. There's a good show on tonight.'

The hotel was packed but Clint had booked a table with a good view of the small stage where the steel band was playing. In the taxi he had told her that his housekeeper was leaving but there was a lack of real concern in his manner. Obviously he had gotten used to the idea. In fact, he was in high spirits and Karen was impelled to say, as they sat at their table drinking cocktails before dinner, 'Is the play going well, Clint?'

'Exceptionally well! I'm a bit stuck at the moment and so I thought we might as well have an evening out.' His smile was meant to be infectious but she ignored it.

'How long will it be before it's finished?' Her voice was cool, and she lifted a hand languorously to smother a yawn.

'I can't say, but certainly it will take less time than I estimated at first.'

'And what shall you do then?' she queried indifferently.

He frowned at her without answering.

'You're not the same, Karen,' he accused, his eyes stony and searching. 'Is something wrong?'

'I suppose I'm a little tired. I was out late last night, dancing.'

'Dancing? Who with?'

'Oh, a bloke I met in the hotel. Can I have another drink, Clint?'

'Yes. . . .' His mouth was taut, his jaw flexed. He beckoned to a passing waiter and ordered her drink.

'This man you were dancing with,' he began. 'You say you were out late?'

Karen lifted her brows in a little arrogant gesture.

'Yes, I was out late? Are there any more questions?'

'Karen,' he exploded. 'What the devil's gotten into you?'

I'm providing you with copy, she said, but silently. I'm ruining all your concepts about your heroine—and I hope I ruin the whole play while I'm about it!

Aloud she said, 'Take no notice, Clint, as I've said, I'm tired.'

'I can't help but take notice,' he returned with increasing impatience. 'It's not you—something's happened and I demand to know what it is.'

Was she going too fast? It would seem so. If she went on like this he was apt to get up and walk out on her, despite his desire to get copy.

'I'm sorry, Clint.' She gave him a winning smile. 'Forgive me. I didn't mean to be pettish.'

During dinner her manner alternated between

charm and boredom. She criticised the band, the limbo dancers and even the table service. Clint, his expression betraying his exasperation, now and then gave her the kind of look that plainly said he would like to shake her. She not only had him completely baffled, but to her intense gratification she had him gradually losing faith in her, which meant that his play would suffer.

'Shall we go?' he said tautly as soon as the meal was over.

'Go?' she pouted. 'Aren't you taking me dancing?'

'No, Karen,' he replied. 'I am not!'

She shrugged indifferently.

'You're in a strange mood tonight,' she complained.

'*I'm* in a strange mood!' he ejaculated, the cold glitter of anger in his eyes.

'Yes, just look how you are with me at this moment. We're still almost strangers, remember, so please don't begin quarreling with me as if we'd been married for years!' A hard, unmusical tone had entered her voice, not the result of anger or indignation, but caused by the pain in her heart that a situation like this had come about between Clint and herself.

'Strangers, are we?' grittingly and with dark fury creasing his brow. 'So that's how you regard us?'

'Ships that pass in the night, remember?' She smiled sweetly at him. 'You agreed with me.'

'I believe I did.' His whole manner had changed and it was pride that edged his voice. Apparently he had taken enough. He had tried hard though, having been quietly patient for most of the time, attempting to soothe away her fractiousness. And once he even asked if she were feeling off-colour, though the anxiety in his voice was obviously assumed; Karen had no doubts at all about that.

The journey back to the apartment was a silent one for the most part, both Karen and Clint being deep in thought. She felt drained because the evening had been an exhausting experience, because her acting this time affected her personally. Her heart seemed to wrench from its moorings every time Clint had looked sharply at her, and yet doggedly she had continued, to the end of the act. No, it was not quite the end. That would be when they parted at the door of the apartment. A shudder ripped through her as if an icy wind had touched her naked body. To say goodbye like this. . . . And tomorrow . . . how was she to go into that saloon on the boat and give him his breakfast without betraying any sign of emotion?

She would be glad when she had finished with him altogether, and now wished she had not bothered to give him any notice at all but had said she was leaving and just walked out on him. A man as heartless as he deserved no better treatment.

The taxi took them to the front of the hotel, where they alighted and she said he need not trouble to come to the apartment with her.

'I'll see you to your door,' he said curtly, and in silence they went through the lovely gardens toward the apartment.

'Good night,' began Karen as she put the key into the door.

He waited until the door was open and she had turned to face him, having snapped on the light, so that it lit up the room behind her.

'I intend to find out what's happened to bring about this change in you.' His voice, imperious and arrogant, had the immediate effect of making her bristle. So he was still trying, was he?—trying to get the copy that would enable him to have a few more highly successful days on the play!

'I'm far too tired to talk, Clint.'

'Tired or not, you'll talk,' he said deliberately.

Her eyes blazed.

'Who do you think you are, speaking to me like this! I haven't the slightest intention of talking. There isn't anything for us to talk about.'

'There's plenty,' he insisted steadily. 'Up till now you've been so very different from any other girl I've known, but tonight—'

'I'm not in any way different,' she broke in to deny. 'All modern girls are the same—when you've seen one you've seen the lot.'

Silence, electric and profound. Karen knew she had taken a daring chance in repeating words that had come from his own lips, spoken to his housekeeper, but she could not resist it.

'What,' he demanded tightly, 'made you say a thing like that?'

'It's true,' she replied, lifting a hand to stifle a yawn. 'I really must ask you to go, Clint. As I told you, I was out very late last night—'

'Yes,' he gritted, 'you've told me!'

She gave a deep sigh.

'You know, Clint,' she frowned, 'you accuse me of being unpredictable, but you're equally unpredictable. I should hate to be married to anyone like you. Good night,' she said again, 'I'll see you sometime—'

'By God, you won't shut me out!' His foot was in the door; it was pushed inward, forcing Karen back. She saw and heard the door slam shut, held her breath as Clint moved purposefully toward her. 'Now,' he snapped, his inclement gaze holding her eyes. 'I'll have an explanation!'

'I don't care for your manner, Clint,' she said, adopting an air of injured innocence. 'Please go—'

'What's caused this damned change?' he thundered. 'There must be some reason for it!'

'You're having a bad time, aren't you, Clint? What with your Girl Friday leaving you, and now your being repulsed by me.' She gave a light laugh. She was acting a part, one that she had acted about a month before in the production of *One Stolen Hour*.

'Repulsed, eh?' He stared at her calculatingly and then there was a sudden dramatic change as all his anger evaporated and he stood looking down at her, a reproachful expression on his lean dark face. 'Karen, what *is* the matter with you? You've changed—you're not the same girl I took out last Saturday.'

'Will you please go?' She toyed with the sequins on her evening bag, appearing to be bored and therefore finding something to do with her fingers.

Clint's teeth gritted together at the action.

'I know I said you were unpredictable, but I never expected you to be this unpredictable!' he snapped.

No . . . his heroine was letting him down badly. He would not be enjoying his writing, that was for sure. And on recalling his words about scrapping a play if he wasn't enjoying it, she was vindictive enough to hope that *Stardust and Dreams* would be scrapped.

'Are you angry because I won't let you demonstrate

your particular kind of love making?' she inquired,
inserting a sneer into her voice.

'I don't care for your turn of phrase,' he objected. 'I
thought we were different!' The reproach in his voice
arrested her attention and she stared, half believing
he was genuine after all. There was certainly a dull,
hopeless sort of expression in his eyes. But the next
moment they had hardened and the impression
passed, and with it her doubts. He *was* acting—and
making an excellent business of it, as he had done
from the first.

'From what?' archly as she moved away, toward the
window at the far side of the room from where he was
standing. 'Why should we be different? I said we're as
ships that pass in the night. We had a flirtation and it
was nice while it lasted but it's over—'

'Stop it!' he thundered, advancing toward her.
'What the devil are you up to?'

She laughed, a harshness in her voice resulting
from the effort she was making to hold back the cloud
of bitter tears that had gathered behind her eyes.

'It's the truth. I mean—no one bothers about love
these days, do they? Life's for living, and tomorrow
you'll probably have someone else and so will I.'

'So that's it. . . . My God,' he spat out contemptuously, 'you were right! You're no different from the
rest!' He stood looking at her, and suddenly she had
the incredible impression that, mingling with the
shades of harshness in his eyes there was a sort of
vacant glaze of bitterness and disillusionment which
caused her heart to contract. Was it possible that she
had made a mistake? Did he love .her? With a little
intake of breath she was about to speak, to ask him

outright if he cared, but the impulse was stemmed almost immediately by a logical recognition of fact as her eyes focused the picture she had seen through that archway in the restaurant in Bridgetown—Clint and his girl friend. Having told Karen he could not see her for a few days as he would be working hard on his play, he yet had the time to take another girl out to lunch.

Determinedly Karen hardened her heart, producing a laugh as she said archly, 'I must say, Clint, that *you* are a little different from the rest in that you've a certain finesse which I've never come across before. I did enjoy our little—er—affair, even though it's finished now.'

'Finished, is it?' The vibration in his voice was like the guttural warning of a jungle cat about to attack. She saw his fine nostrils quiver as crimson threads of fury crept up the sides of his mouth, discolouring the dark tan of his skin, and a tremor of uneasiness went through her. Apprehensively she wondered if she had carried the farce beyond the limit of what he could take. He looked ready to murder her, she thought, his vicious fury filling the very air around them. 'Be careful,' he snarled. 'You know very little about me. I can punish, so don't flaunt your promiscuity in my face. As for its being finished—that'll be when *I* say so!'

She was really frightened now, her voice quivering and frayed as she asked him to leave.

'I shall leave when I'm ready.' So soft the tone, like the whispered threat of a predator about to take its prey. Without being conscious of what she was doing Karen dropped her evening bag on to a chair and backed away, a trembling sensation in her knees. Endless moments dragged by before he said, in the same dangerously quiet tone of voice, 'Come here.' He was pointing arrogantly to a spot on the floor right in front of him. Instead of obeying Karen moved further from him, as far as she could before she felt the window sill touch her back. Her heartbeats became erratic, painful against her ribs, her nerves were knotted by fear. Why had she goaded him this far?—to the actual point of physical attack?

'Please go—please don't hurt me—' A harsh and ruthless laugh slashed through her faltering plea and a shattering weakness began to spread through her body when he repeated his command for her to come to him.

'No! I—you're trespassing! You haven't any right to be here—' She got no further, every vestige of colour draining from her as, with the spring of a tiger on the attack he covered the distance between them, and before she had time to move, her wrist was caught in a vice-like grip and her protesting body jerked ruthlessly to the whipcord hardness of his. An arrogant hand beneath her chin brought her head up so that his sensuous mouth could crush hers in brutal, dominating savagery. Desperately she struggled, terror lending her strength to kick out at his shins as she had done once before but this time she was mercilessly shaken, a cry of protest escaping her as her tongue was caught between her teeth.

'Let me go, you fiend!' she cried. 'I'll have the police on you if—' The rest was smothered by his kiss but once more she began to struggle, managing to drag her mouth from his. He caught a handful of hair, jerking her head right back, and another cry issued from her lips as the pain in her neck seemed to shoot right down into her chest.

'So it's finished, is it?' he snarled, holding on to her hair, compelling her to look up into his eyes. White to the lips, she was drowned in a deluge of terror that threatened to deprive her of her senses as she saw the smouldering embers of primitive need in his expression. She was lost, she thought, her heart pounding so madly that she felt physically sick. The agony was still in her neck and she dared not move; she closed her eyes to the approach of his mouth, giving a stifled moan as it cruelly bruised her lips. His tongue with thrusting arrogance touched the roughness of hers. She was a captive in his arms, utterly helpless against his strength and, to her shame, vulnerable to his masculine enticement. For even his cruelty drew her, his magnetism far too strong for her feeble efforts at resistance. Rapture flooded her whole being even though she winced at the steel of his hand when it found its way inside her bodice and the lean brown fingers took masterful possession of her breasts. And when his other hand forced her slender frame against the throbbing hardness of his loins she found herself swept irresistibly into the maelstrom of an all-consuming passion equal to his own, and for long moments she swayed dizzily to a tempestuous rhythm that spread rapture into every nerve and cell in her body.

At last, breathing heavily, he held her from him, a sneering lift of triumph to his mouth as he saw the dark and dreamy glaze that covered her eyes. His gaze settled on her heaving breasts for a moment, before

seeming to become fascinated by the rhythmic rise
and fall of her stomach.

'Well, Karen,' he said in some amusement, 'it wasn't
finished, was it? But it is now, because *I* say so. You're
free of me from this moment on.' And without another
word he swung away from her and left the room,
closing the door quietly behind him.

Chapter Nine

Helen was still out when Karen returned to the bungalow, and a feeling of immeasurable relief swept over her. Helen knew of the date with Clint and would naturally want to know all about it but Karen was in no mood for answering questions that could only be an embarrassment, revealing in all its stark truth the merciless retaliation of the man she still loved. With shadowed eyes still swollen by tears she glanced down at the angry bruise on her wrist. That one was visible but she wondered how many others he had inflicted on her body. Never in her wildest dreams could she have visualised the sheer unbridled savagery to which Clint had subjected her. Listlessly she went to the tiny room in which there was a bed, wardrobe, small dressing table and a chair. Helen was occupying the airy, well-furnished room that was Jean's and although when Karen informed her she would be sleeping at the bungalow Helen had naturally offered her the better room, Karen would not hear of her relinquishing it.

She sank down on the bed, fully expecting sleep to elude her, and wishing with all her heart that she didn't have to go to the boat tomorrow and face the man who had treated her so ruthlessly.

What a revelation his behaviour had been! And yet, it was reminiscent of that first encounter on the grounds of Sam Lord's Castle. But, strangely, through it all Karen had been aware of a nebulous sense of perplexity which she found it impossible to grasp.

The silence of the tiny room was heavy and depressing after she had gotten into bed, to lie awake, staring into the dimness, seeing nothing.

She still loved Clint with passionate intensity, so how was she to get over it? She was philosophical enough to accept that the pain would fade with time, but in no way could she visualise having anyone else. Clint was her ideal, a god in her eyes, and no other man could ever come anywhere near his perfection.

She would never be able to settle for second best.

The following morning she rose very early, with the deliberate intention of delaying her meeting with Helen, and by half-past five Karen was in her disguise and on her way to the boat. She would spend the extra hours in polishing the furniture and cleaning the windows. And she might as well do some packing and bring away most of what few things were still on the boat, consisting mainly of her housekeeper's clothes.

To her surprise and dismay Clint was already up, and his eyes widened on seeing her arrive so early.

'Do you usually come at this time?' he asked.

'No, but I want to clean the windows, and do some polishing. It'll then last for a while—until you get someone else to take my place.'

He was on deck, his face drawn, his eyes faintly protuberant as if he had been staring through them for unrelieved hours of concentration. Pain touched Karen's heart even while she admonished herself for feeling any sort of sympathy for him. It was all so very plain as to the reason for his haggard appearance. His play had gone wrong because of the unexpected behaviour of his heroine, and so he hadn't slept. Well, that was what she had wanted—for him to ruin it, and vindictively she hoped that he would scrap it in the end. Stardust and dreams. . . . That had been her definition of romance when asked for it, and that was exactly what her brief romance with Clint had been. Stardust and dreams . . . abstract, fading with the dawning enlightenment that he had ruthlessly used her for his own ends—for his own glory and financial gain, in fact. Playing with her, pretending to love her . . . making love to her. Well, his triumph, like her happiness, had been short-lived. The play could never be what he had planned, and she was very sure that the famous Clint Fraser would never produce anything mediocre, for if he did then his reputation would suffer.

'You needn't trouble,' he said broodingly. 'I shall not be staying here after tomorrow. I'm returning to my home, so you must have all your belongings off the boat sometime today.'

'Your play, Mr. Fraser,' she began, marveling at the steadiness of her voice, 'is it not going well? Is that why you're leaving?'

'It's not going well,' he answered tautly, looking through her rather than at her. 'In fact, I shall never finish it now.'

'Not finish it?' with well-assumed concern. 'But surely, after all the work—'

'The work's unimportant,' he broke in irritably. 'Perfection was my aim, and this play can never be perfect now.'

'But what will you do with it?' she asked, because she really wanted to be sure that he meant to scrap it.

'Throw it away.' The bitterness in his voice brought a quality of harshness with it and Karen, swallowing hard, was on the verge of feeling sorry for him when a sharp stab of recollection brought back the picture of him and his girl friend lunching in the restaurant in Bridgetown.

'I'm sorry to hear that,' she said speciously. 'You've been several weeks on it and it seems such a waste.'

'You'll pack your things this morning?' he asked, ignoring her sympathetic comment. 'You can go when you like.'

'But your dinner tonight?' It was ridiculous, but now that the actual parting from him was at hand, she wanted to stay, to look after him. 'I can come back to do that, surely?'

He was already shaking his head, and there was a sort of dejected tiredness about him as he said, 'I don't need you to do that. I'm dining out this evening.'

Dining out . . . with his girl friend? Yes, Karen was sure of it and the knowledge was a knife turning in her heart.

A few minutes later he came to her, an envelope in his hand.

'Here's your money,' he said. 'I'm paying you to the end of the month.' Karen opened her mouth to object but he gave her no time as he went on, 'It so happens that you gave me your notice,' he said, 'but as things have turned out I'd have been asking you to go anyway, in which case J'd have been obliged to pay you the full six months' money—'

'No, you wouldn't,' she broke in, then stopped as his mouth compressed in anger.

'Take this!' The envelope was thrust at her so that she had no alternative than to take it. 'I probably shan't see you again as I've work to do in my study and I shall be there for a couple of hours or so. There's money for your fare back to England—no,' he said sternly, 'don't interrupt. I brought you here and it's incumbent on me to pay your fare back.'

Karen had finished packing and was ready to leave but she stayed in her cabin, undecided about saying goodbye to Clint, who had been closeted in his study since breakfast time, not making a sound. And without the familiar rhythmic sound of the typewriter the boat seemed dead. Gloomily Karen looked at the suitcase that lay on the bed—the other having been taken to Jean's bungalow weeks ago with Karen's "younger" clothes—and a shuddering sigh that was almost a sob escaped her. This really was the momentous and heartbreaking end to an escapade that should never have taken place. Clint had lost his play and she her heart.

Her ears suddenly became alert as she realised that Clint had come from his study.

Karen emerged from the cabin, her suitcase in her hand.

'I'll say goodbye, Mr. Fraser.' Her eyes fell to the large, polyethylene bag he carried. It was full of clean papers . . . the manuscript. Where was he taking it? She wondered.

'Goodbye, Miss Waring. Have a safe flight home.' Swinging on his heel, he left her there, the lone occupant of the boat. Tears rose easily but she dared not let them fall, not with all this paint on her face. Slowly she followed as soon as he was down the gangplank. She kept him in sight as he strode away toward the Smuggler's Cove Hotel, her brows creasing in a frown as her curiosity increased. He was walking quickly; she hurried to keep him in view, and just as she reached the place where she could enter the grounds of the Vervain Hotel she realized with a little thumping sensation in her heart that Clint was on his way to the back of the Smuggler's Cove Hotel where the refuse was put in readiness to be collected. She stopped in the shelter of some bushes, waiting for him to come back, which he did—without the bag.

Something within her seemed to snap; she knew it wasn't logical—indeed it was highly illogical—but the thought of the manuscript being carried away with the hotel refuse was so painful that she wanted to cry. And yet she had worked and schemed for just this!

'I'm glad it's gone!' she whispered fiercely . . . but knew she was not glad at all.

Helen had told Karen yesterday that as it was Roger's afternoon off today she and he were taking a trip to Welshman's Gully, and so Karen had the bungalow to herself as she thankfully got rid of her disguise and began to unpack her suitcase. But insistently the nagging picture of the manuscript being destroyed was on her mind. The tremendous effort Clint had put into the play, the eagerness with which he had spoken about it, the very likely possibility that one day in the future he might be able to finish it . . . all these conjoined to spur Karen's thoughts to an action, the result of which she could not at the moment visualise. She had no idea what she would do with the manuscript, but the urgent matter of the moment was to rescue it before the collection truck arrived, which it did every day about this time, and without any more time being lost in reasoning she dashed out, hurrying across the wide lawns and gardens of the Vervain Hotel and onto the grounds of the Smuggler's Cove where she made for the back of the low, spreading building. It seemed an eternity before she got there, and when she did, she stopped, breathless, to stare in dismay at the activity going on.

The rubbish was all contained in huge bins placed against one wall, and it was plain that most of them had already had their contents emptied into the truck, whose churning mechanism was effectively reducing them to pulp.

'Wait!' cried Karen on seeing two men lift what appeared to be the last of the bins, as all the others were back in their neat positions against the wall. 'I've lost something!' She ran on, waving a hand and to her relief the men stopped to stare at her. 'Something was thrown away by mistake,' she gasped on reaching them. 'May I look inside the bin before you empty it?'

'You can, miss,' agreed one of the men who belonged to the hotel staff, 'but was it in this one? All the others have been emptied.'

'It might be in that one,' she began, then stopped. There were eight large bins in all so the chances of it being in the last one seemed very remote indeed. However, she asked the man to remove the lid . . . and she couldn't believe her eyes when she saw, lying on top of a pile of clean newspapers, the polyethylene bag containing Clint's manuscript.

'That's it!' Thankfully she accepted it from the man when he lifted it out for her.

'It looks important,' he remarked, obviously wondering how anything of that size had been put accidentally into the bin.

'It is important. Thank you very much for your help.'

'That's okay, miss. I'm glad you got it.' He was still looking puzzled but Karen just smiled at him and moved away.

But now that the manuscript that had caused her such heartache was safely in her hands she wondered what she would do with it ultimately. Perhaps, she thought, she would one day post it to Clint, anonymously. Of course he would know that the rescuer could be none other than Miss Waring, but that was all. His curiosity as to her reason would never be satisfied.

Her action had at the time seemed to have been purely instinctive, inspired by her love for Clint and nothing more. But now she knew there had been some other spur as well, knew without any doubt at all that if she had left the manuscript there she would never have been able to get it out of her mind. Perhaps it was the fact that she had always deplored waste of any kind, and to have allowed the destruction of a manuscript that was almost finished would have been a waste both of Clint's time and his inspiration.

Yes, she was glad she had rescued it, she decided, and after putting it away in one of the drawers in her bedroom she settled down with a magazine. But the effort to concentrate was too much and she decided to wash her hair. The shampoo she used was expensive but it always left her hair gleaming and scented with the fragrance clinging for a full day even if she got her hair wet again when it had dried. After toweling it vigourously she went out to the patio to let it dry in the fresh air of the hotel gardens. She sat in a lounge contemplating the immediate scene of exotic flowers flaunting perfume and colour, of bikini-clad figures on the nearby beach and of surf riders on the shimmering, aquamarine sea. Along one side of the extensive grounds, and at right angles to the silver shore, magnificent dome palms speared the metallic blue of the Caribbean sky. Insects murmuring in the hibiscus bushes, humming birds in the poinciana trees; a pink and green lizard rigidly still against the amphora-shaped earthenware vase where flourished a bougainvillea vine that had spread right up the wall of the bungalow and across the top of the living room window . . . all this would have been magic to Karen a few days ago.

Naturally as she sat there her thoughts were on the manuscript she had rescued, and gradually it was borne on her that she had no right to have it in her possession. It was not her property and, in effect, she had taken it unlawfully. Her nerves jerked when she thought of what Clint might say if he knew what she had done, and that the work he definitely meant to be destroyed had been rescued and was in someone else's possession. The more she dwelt on it the more doubtful she became as to the wisdom of her action, one that was as impulsive as that which had precipitated her into the vast web of deceit from which she had escaped only at a cost so dear that it would be years before she recovered.

Serious qualms assailed her, causing her heartbeats to quicken. Perhaps it was her general state of mind that made it appear almost a felony for her to have Clint's manuscript in her possession. She'd no right to it, and as the disturbing moments passed she felt she would have to get rid of it, to take it back—But, no! It was unthinkable that she should put it into one of those bins, to be taken away tomorrow. Another, more acceptable idea flashed into her mind and, rising, she went inside to assume the disguise which she had believed she would never use again.

She would have liked to run to the boat right away with the manuscript but although she suspected that Clint would not be on it she could not be absolutely sure, so it was far too risky to go as she was, for the last thing she wanted now was to let him know of the masquerade! He would murder her, she thought, recalling with a convulsive shudder what she had already suffered at his hands.

With the greasepaint applied, she donned the same dress she had worn that morning and then, after hastily crushing her newly washed hair beneath the wig, she put the polyethylene bag containing the manuscript into a canvas shopping bag and hurried from the bungalow, not bothering to lock the door. She had gone through the grounds of both hotels when she turned, heart leaping, as she heard footsteps behind her. Mr. Lawson! Anger lit her eyes even before he said,

'Can I walk with you? I'll carry your bag if you like—?'

'No, you can't. I'm sorry—and I'm in a hurry!' In order to get away from him she forgot all about her disguise and started to run, and only when she had left him well behind did she resume the sedate pace she always used when approaching the boat, just in case Clint should be some place where he could see her. She hurried through the path to find that the old man was nowhere in sight.

If Clint should be on the boat she had an excuse ready: she had forgotten something. But as she saw no movement, no figure on that part of the deck which was visible to her, she walked resolutely up the gangplank and sped along to the cabin she had used. Kneeling down, she lifted the lid of a low bunk and dropped the manuscript inside, wincing as, closing the lid, its corner scraped her head. One day the manuscript would be found, and Clint might just finish it—Her thoughts were cut as she heard a step on the deck. So Clint was still on board. Her heart began to beat rapidly at the prospect of having to face him again, so she waited, hoping he might just be leaving the boat, but he seemed to be pacing about so she decided to get it over and done with and, opening the door of the cabin, she stepped out into the narrow corridor, and walked along it to the deck.

'Miss Waring . . . I saw you running. Is anything wrong?'

'You—s-saw m-me running?' she repeated tremulously.

'Yes, and very spritely you were too.'

'It was that old man,' she offered, 'he was making a nuisance of himself again.'

'I see. Why have you come back?'

'I left something behind—my brooch.'

'And you have it now?'

'Yes—thank you.' He was looking oddly at her, the concentrated intentness of his gaze alerting her to the fact that something had captured his eyes. Automatically she fluttered a hand to the place focused, and to her horror touched the silken softness of her own dark hair! When the lid of the bunk scraped her head her wig must have moved slightly. Paralysed for a micron of time, during which there was the fear of brutal treatment, she turned, fleeing to the gangplank. But the deck was slightly wet from the few drops of rain that had fallen while she was in the cabin and her legs shot out from under her. She knew a fierce, blinding stab of agony before she fell into the water.

She awoke to the instant knowledge of what had happened, and to the physical sensations of dizziness and nausea, with the awareness of a dull ache at her temple. But soon the dizziness and nausea passed and she sat up. She was in her cabin, lying on the bunk bed with a cool white sheet covering her nakedness.

Burning colour stole into her cheeks as her brain registered the fact that Clint must have stripped her of her wet clothing.

Clint knew everything now and fear rose to vanquish her embarrassment as she wondered what sort of punishment he would inflict on her this time. Everything had gone wrong! She could have wept, but instead she sat up, thankful to know that apart from the ache in her temple she appeared to be none the worse for her experience. She slid from the bed, wrapping the sheet tightly around her. No sound. But she could not get off the boat without her clothes.

Well, this was the showdown—and how very different from what she had planned! Hers was to have been the laugh while Clint was to eat his words of criticism of her acting.

Her eyes dilated as the door opened quietly and Clint stood there, stern and frighteningly dark. She swallowed, trying to remove the constriction in her throat. Was she to receive similar treatment to that which she had already tasted? There would be little hope of escape dressed as she was in nothing but a sheet which she must assuredly lose if it became necessary to struggle with him again. What a mess to be in!—at the mercy of the man who, judging by his expression, was having the greatest difficulty in repressing his anger.

Endless moments passed before he spoke and when he did it was to ask prosaically, 'How do you feel? Is your head aching?'

'Just a little,' she answered in a low tone of voice.

'Any other aches or pains?' He came into the cabin

as he spoke, closing the door behind him—an ominous move it seemed to Karen whose fretted nerve-
ends were playing up.

'No—I haven't anything else wrong with me. Thank
you for bringing me out of the water.' She stared at
him and it did seem that the fury in his eyes
evaporated somewhat on seeing that she was practically none the worse for her experience.

'Well, Karen,' he said, tautly. 'Perhaps you will tell
me what this is all about?'

She nodded immediately, deciding that the best
policy under the circumstances was to make a full
confession, leaving nothing out, humiliating though it
would be to her to admit that she loved him. Rather
that, though, than come in for another of his brutal
attacks during which her scanty covering would
undoubtedly come away.

'I did it to be revenged on you, Clint,' she faltered,
sitting down on her bed and drawing the sheet more
tightly around her. 'As you thought, I did hear your
disparaging comments on my acting, and I was
piqued. At that time my boss had left and I wanted a
job. I knew the advertisement was yours; the prospect
of getting the job was attractive in that I'd make you
eat your words about my acting, and also it enabled
me to be near my sister.' She stopped, staring wanly at
him. 'I didn't realise what would be the outcome of it
all. It was a mischievous act,' she quivered, tears on
her lashes, 'but certainly not a wicked one. However,
it—it served me right that I—I f-fell in love with
you—'

'You—' he broke off and it seemed for a moment as if

nothing would have given him greater satisfaction than to strangle her. 'There's more, obviously,' he rasped. 'Carry on! It's an interesting story. I want to hear the rest of it!'

'I believed, like a fool,' she added bitterly, 'that you returned my love but I soon realised what your little game was, and that you were putting on an act, only pretending to love me so that you could use me for your own ends.'

Clint seemed to be practising infinite restraint.

'And what,' he demanded through his teeth, 'was my little game, as you term it?'

'You were merely using me for copy—Oh, yes, you were,' she went on hurriedly when it seemed he would open his mouth. 'Don't forget that I saw two sides of you. You told your housekeeper that your heroine wasn't satisfactory, that you wanted her to be unusual, unpredictable. Well, that was how you described me, Karen, but I didn't catch on at first. I was unpredictable in your eyes because of what had happened that first night at Sam Lord's Castle. Well, I flirted with you just for a joke, because I knew who you were, remember; I had the advantage of you. And it was because you'd said such horrid things about my acting that I tried to flirt with you—just to be able to remind you, later, when the job on the boat folded up, that I *could* act.' She paused, mainly for breath because her words had been heated and spoken swiftly and for the most part with indignation.

'Do continue,' Clint encouraged steadily, and he stepped back to lean against one corner of the wardrobe, his hands folded across his chest. 'I rather think,' he added sarcastically, 'that *you* ought to be writing plays.'

Her eyes flew to his, for something about his manner brought feathery tingles of doubt—and apprehension—to her spine. However, she carried on, 'As your housekeeper I several times asked you about the play, and learned that it went right only after you'd seen me—not your housekeeper—after you'd been out with Karen. . . .' She trailed off, her colour rising at the hint of amusement that had entered his eyes. But it had no softening effect; they were still as hard as granite.

'Do tell me more,' he invited patiently, and made himself more comfortable as if expecting the story to be a long one.

Falteringly she said, 'I don't understand your attitude, Clint?'

'You will,' grittingly, 'in just a few moments.'

Startled, she grasped the sheet more firmly around her, wondering if she imagined it or if there really was a threat in his tone.

'Well, as I couldn't very well condemn you out of hand—'

'You couldn't? That was generous.'

Karen averted her head at his cold sarcasm and tried to keep her voice steady as she continued, 'And so I decided to take a look at your manuscript, which I had never done before, and the first thing I noticed was the title. It was right at the top of the page.'

'It usually is,' with the same icy sarcasm, and her colour deepened. She was feeling decidedly uncomfortable and if it weren't that she was so scared she could have told him to go to the devil; she wasn't telling him any more. But she *was* scared—very, alone with him in this tiny cabin and clad only in a sheet which, if he should choose, could be whipped off her with one swift movement of those lean brown fingers.

'*Stardust and Dreams*. . . .' Her lips began to quiver so she spoke swiftly, hoping he had not noticed. 'You stole my title—'

'*Your* title?' with a lift of an eyebrow. 'Why, are you writing something?'

At that her eyes did sparkle and, forgetting her fear for an instant she said recklessly, 'Don't be so damned sarcastic with me! I'm telling you what you want to know but if you go on like this I shan't speak at all!'

His response was a significant raking of her body and a very quiet warning for her to take care as she was in a most vulnerable situation.

'Carry on,' he ordered in the same soft voice, 'I'm determined to hear the whole idiotic story.'

'Idiotic?'

'Carry on,' he prompted. 'My manner's deceptive. My patience is almost exhausted. The way I feel at present I could strip that thing from your back and give you something that would make you smart for a month.'

Vivid colour stained her cheeks and instinctively she clutched the sheet between tightly closed fists.

'I was saying that, as Miss Waring, I could look at the manuscript and I very soon discovered that my suspicions were correct. You *had* been using me, and so I decided to give you copy all right—the kind that would ruin your play altogether. Your heroine was more unpredictable than you could ever have visualised, wasn't she?' For some reason she could not explain, Karen was gathering courage, and she added triumphantly, 'I was cleverer than you, Clint! Your acting isn't half as good as mine! In fact, you weren't very clever at all, really, because I saw through you!'

'So I wasn't very clever, eh? But you were?'

'Yes, I was! I saw through your falseness!'

At that his eyebrows lifted a fraction.

'You?—daring to mention falseness?' he said, for the moment diverted.

She had the grace to blush but her chin lifted all the same.

'My deceit was done for a joke more than anything else; yours was sheer rottenness!'

The gray eyes glinted dangerously but Karen failed to notice as, the sheet having slipped a little, she was busy bringing it up to her chin again.

'How much of the manuscript did you read?' asked Clint curiously.

'Not much, but enough. The last few pages you'd written told me all I needed to know. . . .' Her voice trailed as he took a step that brought him closer to her. Involuntarily she got off the bed and stepped back, her heart fluttering uncomfortably, as if she had something alive inside her.

'And from those few passages you gained all the proof you needed to make you put on that act?'

'Yes. I gave you plenty of copy—and I ruined the play, didn't I?'

'Oh, yes, you made an excellent job of that.' He was

coming closer but Karen was unable to retreat any further because the backs of her legs were touching the bed. 'It's finished—scrapped!' He was towering over her now, a menacing figure, big and powerful and very frightening.

The colour drained from Karen's face and her voice was strained to huskiness as she quavered, 'Don't you dare touch me. I'll scream—' She cut her words raggedly as Clint, his fury breaking the bonds that had been controlling it, grabbed her roughly, jerking her toward him.

'You'd scream, would you?' he gritted. 'Then let me give you something to scream for!' His fingers were steel as they fastened on her shoulders, and he shook her until he himself was breathless.

'Do you know what you've done?' he thundered, his face twisted with fury. 'You're so clever, did you say? My God, girl, I ought to beat you for your cleverness!' Wrathfully he flung her from him but made sure she fell on to the bed. The sheet came open and she clutched it to her again, every nerve in her body rioting.

'I hate you,' she seethed.

'Then that makes two of us! You've made me act like a brute!' Although there was wrath in his voice, Karen somehow gained the impression that he was not now quite as angry as before, and the tautness of her nerves slackened a little.

'Can I help if it you've a violent nature?'

'I haven't a violent nature!' he denied explosively, and in the next breath he was adding, 'I could strangle you, slowly, for what you've done!'

'And you say you haven't a violent nature?'

He gritted his teeth and cast her a smouldering glance.

'All that work—for nothing. The best thing I've ever written! Gone—destroyed!'

'The best thing?' she repeated slowly, her eyes searching his face. 'How can it be, when you haven't got the right ending?'

'But I have! Although *you* don't know it!'

'You have?' Bewilderedly she felt that his words ought to have conveyed something of vital importance to her but her mind was dazed, her nerves chaotic, and so clear thinking was difficult. 'I don't understand, Clint,' she added in a tremulous little voice.

'You will—one day!' he rasped. 'If I don't kill you beforehand!'

Now, she thought, was the time to tell him the play was safe, but instead, she started to cry, the result of overwrought nerves and the sick feeling within her because of the shaking she'd received.

'What the devil's wrong with you now?' he demanded heartlessly.

'I w-want my—my clothes—'

'They're wet!'

'I expect they are,' she gulped. 'How—c-can I get some more?'

'I suppose I shall have to get them for you, from the bungalow.'

'I'd be grateful. Helen's out but the door isn't locked. My room's the one at the back, the tiny one—' She broke off, colouring. 'If you'd please bring my beach shorts and top—they're drying on the patio—'

'Don't put on another act with me,' he advised. 'I couldn't stand it! The modest miss, eh? I've just stripped you, remember?'

'No, I don't remember, because I was unconscious!'

Clint drew an exasperated breath and let it out slowly, as if the exercise would give him some sort of control.

She looked up into his face, and in one fleeting second of time his expression changed and she just happened to catch it. A great surge of emotion rose up from somewhere near her heart, settling in her chest to make breathing difficult. A trembling hand stole to her cheek.

'I think—think I've m-made a m-mistake. . . .'

'A mistake?' he barked. 'You've made half a dozen! This disgusting and deceitful masquerade, for one thing—'

'You'd never have written your play if I hadn't come to you as Miss Waring, because you'd never have met me—Karen—the girl you wanted to use!'

'The play *would* have been written,' he corrected, 'but differently! I came here specifically to write the play!'

'Well, that might be so, but later you changed it, because you didn't know how to handle your heroine.'

'Didn't I?' Soft the voice and dangerous. 'Well, I know how to handle her now!' and before Karen could grasp his meaning he had taken her in his arms and for several excruciating moments she knew once again the savagery of his hard demanding mouth.

He released her at last and stood looking down into her face.

'Clint,' she faltered, lifting a hand as if in entreaty,

'you mentioned your—your heroine—and then you kissed m-me. And just now you said you had the right ending—'

'The right ending,' he broke in and now his words were bitter, 'but no play!'

'Clint—I—the play is—'

'If you'd read a bit more, your malicious misinterpretations of my motives would never have occurred!'

'Wh-what part, Clint?' The tears were sparkling on her lashes again but in her heart there was joy, for in spite of the dark anger and bitterness on Clint's face she knew without any doubt at all that he loved her. 'You see—'

'Pages one hundred and ten and one hundred and thirty-six!—but it's too late now!' He strode to the door. 'I'll get your clothes,' he said and was gone.

Pages one hundred and ten and one hundred and thirty-six. . . . No sooner had the door slammed, its vibration shaking the cabin, than Karen was down on her knees, opening the bunk and lifting out the manuscript. With feverish haste she found page one hundred and ten. Written lightly in pencil on the wide margin were the words, 'It was at this point that I realised that although I was getting copy from Karen, I had fallen in love with her.' For a long while Karen could only stare, her mind a tangle of unconnected thoughts. If only she had gone back a little instead of reading the last part. Swallowing convulsively she flicked over the next pages to read one hundred and thirty-six. Another handwritten note was in the wide margin. 'It was hard not to make a date but I must get this finished with all possible speed. We can then be married and have a prolonged honeymoon cruising the Caribbean.'

It seemed an eternity before she heard Clint coming along the passage and stopping outside the door. Her heart was full, her eyes shining with happiness. What a wonderful surprise he was going to get! Every nerve tingled in anticipation of her reward—his arms about her in a loving caress, his lips, tender and gentle, claiming hers.

The door swung inward; she saw the small leather case he carried, saw his eyes widen in disbelief on seeing the manuscript there, in the prominent position where she had put it, so that he would notice it immediately when he came in.

'What—?' Dropping the case on to the floor he took a couple of strides and picked up the manuscript. 'Where the devil did this come from?' He swung round to stare interrogatingly at her.

'I rescued it,' she told him happily, then went on to explain how she came to know it was with the refuse. 'But then I didn't know what to do with it, Clint, so I decided to bring it over and leave it in the bunk here, for you to find sometime in the future. I've just read the notes you'd written. But I knew you loved me before then. And,' she added simply, 'I love you. I've already told you—' She stopped, staggered by his thunderous expression. 'Aren't you glad—?'

'So it was in there all the time we were talking? Then why the hell didn't you say so! I've been nearly out of my mind for the past hour, cursing myself for acting so foolishly, and all the time it was in there?

I've had about as much as I can take from you!' He advanced purposefully toward her. 'You're going to get—'

'Don't you dare touch me!' she cried, tears of disappointment in her eyes. 'I thought you loved me and would be glad because you—you s-said you'd gotten the—the ending—h-happy ending I th-thought—' Her words broke on a choking little sob. Clint's eyes softened miraculously but she failed to notice, '—but you don't love me and I don't love you—Oh, please go away! I want to get dressed. The sooner I'm out of here the better!'

It was less than half an hour later that Karen and Clint were standing close together on the sunlit deck of the *Fair Mermaid*, the last of the misunderstandings having been straightened out. Karen had learned that although Clint's original intention was to use her for copy—because she seemed to be the perfect example of the heroine he intended to create—he had realised, after that night at the Southern Palms Hotel, that his bachelor days were nearing their end.

'You captivated me, darling, and after we had made love so wonderfully I knew without any doubt at all that you were the girl for me.' His voice was filled with tender emotion, his eyes dark with love as, bending his head, he took her eager lips in a long, passionate .iss that instantly stimulated her emotions, quickening the blood in her veins, creating an intoxicating lightness in her body.

After a while he held her from him, tender amusement in his gaze as he saw the dreamy expression in her eyes.

'Any more questions, sweet?' he asked after a space. 'Or have we cleared everything up?'

She hesitated, and then told him she had seen him lunching with his girl friend, when he was supposed to be working hard on the play.

'I did take her to lunch, yes—' He stopped, frowning at the idea that Karen had seen him.

She smiled a little wanly and said, 'It strengthened my suspicions that I'd made a mistake in thinking you loved me.'

'It must have done. It was unfortunate that you saw us together. I decided to take her out as a final gesture and to tell her I'd met the girl I was going to marry. She took it very well,' he added. 'But it had never reached the serious stage. We got along well together and enjoyed each other's company—and the day might have come when it developed into something deeper. But after I met you. . . .' His tender gaze was fixed on Karen's lovely face, and with a little exclamation he bent his head and kissed her quivering lips. It was a gentle kiss at first, and indeed he never meant it to be anything other than gentle, but at the cloudy desire in her eyes, the tempting mouth, honey-rose and faintly moist, his ardour flared and she was swept into the vortex of his lovemaking, crushed against his virile body, her mouth possessed in a way that left her in no doubt that Clint would always be her master.

She was breathless when eventually he released her.

'Clint,' she gasped, impishly teasing, 'You're cruel! I

don't think I ought to marry you—' The rest was
halted by his expression and the faint lift of an
eyebrow.

'I wasn't aware that I had asked you to marry me,'
he reminded her with well-feigned arrogance.

She coloured, lowering her lashes. But a moment
later she tilted her chin and said,

'Well, since there's Women's Lib and all that—*I*
shall propose to *you*. Will you—?' Again she was
stopped, this time by a slap that was meant to
hurt—and it did.

'You, my girl, can forget Women's Lib! I'm the
master and I'm also old-fashioned enough to feel it's
the man's prerogative to do the proposing.' He paused
a moment, his eyes challengingly severe. 'If you feel
you can't live with my cruelty then you only have to
refuse. Will you marry me, my dearest love?' The
change in his tone was dramatic, and the look in his
eyes was now one of tenderness and deepest love.

Karen snuggled against the hardness of his breast,
murmuring softly, 'Yes, dearest Clint, I will marry
you.'

'I adore you,' he whispered close to her hair. 'I don't
think I can wait until the play's finished,' he added
decisively, and Karen leaned away to ask, 'Will it take
long, Clint, now that you have the ending you want?'

'About a month.' The gray eyes were satirically
mocking. 'Are *you* willing to wait that long, my love?'
And without giving her time to answer he added,
sternly, 'No putting on an act, my girl! I've had about
as much of that as I can take. Your acting days are
over, understand?'

She pouted.

'It's fun, Clint—a great hobby, and as I do it so well—' She broke off as he gave her a little shake.

'That's the trouble; you do it too well!—Miss Waring!'

Mischief brought a sparkle to Karen's eyes.

'Aren't you glad she decided on the masquerade?' she asked, peeping up at him from under her lashes.

Ignoring that Clint said, 'You weren't perfect in that particular role, you know. For one thing, your hands interested me. They were young hands. Then there were those absurd scraps of lace you were washing—' He broke off, amusement in his gaze.

'Helen and I had a good laugh over that,' admitted Karen, catching his humour.

'And over a good many more things, I expect?'

She nodded her head, thinking of Helen and wondering what she would have to say about all this. And Karen wondered too if Helen would eventually marry her new boy friend and come to live on Barbados. She rather thought she would.

'I asked you if you could wait a month?' Clint's voice, interrupting Karen's train of thought, was strong yet tender, and faintly masterful. Holding her from him, he looked deeply into her eyes, saw the dreamy cloud of longing and added on that same note of mocking satire, 'No, apparently you can't. We shall be married within a week.'

As Karen had no objection to this she remained contentedly silent, and after a long interlude of kissing and caressing Clint said, a laugh in his voice, 'Darling, could I ask a favour of you? I have a hunch that my housekeeper won't show up any more—that she's walked out on me, and as I'm still in a hurry to finish the play—which has a stupendous finale, as you know—would you come over each morning and "do" for me?'

A ripple of laughter escaped Karen as she replied, 'I'd love to do for you, Clint. I'm so glad Miss Waring's walked out on you.'

'And I, my dearest,' he said when he had kissed her, 'have to admit that although she caused me a great deal of trouble, I'm so very glad that she walked in on me in the first place.'

SHADOW AND SUN

"Are you afraid I'll compromise you if you stay a moment longer under my roof?"

"There's not the slightest chance of that," she snapped.

"No?" He stood so near she caught the male scent of him and felt her knees go weak.

"Then perhaps it's this you're afraid of."

His head came down. His mouth found hers. She struggled fiercely, but only for a moment. The searching warmth of his lips, the insistent manner in which his embrace moulded her to him set fire to her passions. Her need for him betrayed her, and she discovered herself clinging to him with an ardour that appalled her, but which at the same time she could not control. She lost herself in the taste of his lips, in the hard pressure of his body against hers. . . .

MARY CARROLL

is an internationally known American writer who has published here and abroad. She brings to her romantic fiction a varied background of teaching and travelling that gives her a unique insight into the world of romance.

MARY CARROLL
Shadow and Sun

Chapter 1

Britt Ryan lay back in the sweet smelling grass and gazed with a mixture of awe and irritation at the Chateau de Laon topping the crest of a nearby hill. Quartz-flecked, the great edifice cast a sentinel effect over the countryside, its sparkling battlements and turreted towers standing as stolidly inaccessible against the blue sky as a sugar castle in a fairy tale. The chief difference being, Britt thought, that the lord of the manor was an ogre and not a prince.

If Philippe Dolman were a man of his word, she might at this moment be snapping photographs behind those impressive stone walls, not sharing a meadow with three white cows two kilometers away. Her budget allowed for only one week in this Mediterranean area of France near the Spanish border, and three days of that were already gone.

Dolman, sunning himself in Majorca, would return when he chose and not a moment sooner, according to the gatekeeper who was not at all impressed that Monsieur Dolman had already missed by two days keeping his appointment with Sydney Fernham.

True, Britt Ryan was not Sydney Fernham, but the gatekeeper didn't have to know that. The given name was as proper a one for a girl as for a man, and until she was allowed to meet Philippe Dolman face to face, she had no intention of explaining why she was here representing herself as a male photographer of the Paris magazine *La Revue,* or how she happened to have in the pocket of her jacket his letter of introduction.

To say nothing of his camera, she thought with a wry smile. Poor Sydney. He would claw down every rope and pulley holding him in traction at Sisters of Mercy Hospital if he knew she'd taken not a single photograph for his deadline in a few weeks.

But what could she do?

Until Dolman returned, she couldn't set foot on the chateau grounds. The two Doberman pinschers leashed to the arm of the surly gateman had made that plain enough.

Sighing, she stood and dusted her tan riding pants. Too bad she didn't have a horse to go with them! Her daily treks on foot from the hotel in Perpignan through the autumn countryside were pleasant enough in the crisp morning air, but she was glad today she had thought to bring along a lunch of cheese and bread to break the return trip under a warmer sun. At least now in the early afternoon a few clouds were coming up.

Shading her eyes, she lifted them toward the sky—then caught her breath. What had momentarily blotted out the sun was not a cloud at all, but an enormous balloon, striped red and white and floating lightly as a butterfly directly toward her. Dangling beneath it in a golden gondola, a dark-haired man—one arm about the shoulders of a blond girl beside him—caught sight of Britt and leaned out, calling, "Bon jour, mademoiselle!"

Britt caught a glimpse of a wide, sensuous mouth turned up in a tantalizing grin, a strong chin set with a cleft, and searching eyes beneath dark brows. For an instant she could imagine herself extending her hand

and being drawn up beside him. Tingling excitement danced on her spine. How fabulous to drift through space in that exotic contraption—and with such a partner!

"Bon jour!" she called. But she was too late, she realized, for the intriguing balloonist to hear.

Quickly she snatched up the camera from the grass, and just as the balloon floated into line with two turrets of the chateau, she clicked the shutter.

"Oh, Sydney!" she breathed. "Just wait until you see that!"

"Perrier, please." Britt gave the waiter a smile and settled herself in a wire chair on the terrace of the hotel. Beyond her the River Tet twinkled with hundreds of tiny lights and the sweet smell of flowers sharpened by the twilight mingled with what she imagined was the salt air of the sea.

She said as much to the waiter when he returned, but before he could answer, a broad-shouldered man sitting at the next table turned to comment. "It *is* the sea you smell, though it's seven miles away. The wind is right this evening."

Britt stared in stunned delight. "Why, you're the balloon man!"

The tantalizing smile that had stirred her in the meadow appeared on his lips. "I recognized you at once when you crossed the terrace," he said.

And no wonder! Britt's hand flew to tuck in the black ringlets that had worked their way from beneath the beret she wore jauntily cocked over one eye. She was still attired in the same tan riding pants, rumpled plain shirt and worn suede jacket in which she had tramped across the countryside.

During the hours since her return she had been too busy exploring the shops and gardens of the quaint little town to bother changing her clothes, and when she decided to dine in a kitchen cafe she had discovered on a side street, there seemed no need to.

But here on the hotel terrace among other guests dressed for the evening, she must look like a tramp! A blush the shade of a wild rose flooded her creamy cheeks. But the balloonist, who without invitation had swung around to join her at her table, seemed intent only upon making himself comfortable.

"I've never seen anything quite so thrilling," she stammered, "as your balloon in that blue sky this afternoon."

His dark-eyed gaze shifted slowly to take in the high color of her cheeks. "Really? You're not accustomed to balloons?"

All at once she felt like a child. "I've seen a few, but not at such close range."

His glance moved from the hollow of her throat to the top button of her shirt. "I could have plucked off your beret."

"I know." Darn her heart for pounding so! He was rude, this arrogant stranger. In a moment she would say good night and leave him sitting alone.

He leaned back and regarded her coolly. "What were you doing out there? Having a picnic all by yourself?"

The sarcasm underlying his words ruffled her further. "Not exactly," she answered stiffly. "I'm here on assignment, but thanks to a rather thoughtless gentleman, I've been unable to get my work done."

"So you're lolling about the fields instead?"

"I was having lunch before walking back to town!"

"Ah, I see." He looked about restlessly. "Let's have some wine, shall we?"

"No, thank you."

But he was already motioning to the waiter. "Cotes-du-Rhone," he commanded. "And I drink it cold."

Britt rose. Frowning up at her he said, "You're not going?"

"I'm afraid I must."

"But I've ordered wine." He stood and reaching behind her, pulled her chair nearer to his. "Sit down. I want to hear more about this unreasonable oaf who's left you at loose ends in our charming countryside."

With a firm hand on her shoulder, he pressed her down into the chair. "You aren't French, are you?"

"I'm English," she replied, furious at herself for giving in to his insistence. "But I'm working in Paris."

The wine came. He tasted it and filled her glass. "What kind of work do you do?"

"I'm—a photographer."

"Oh." He grimaced. "One of those."

The nerve! She ought to slap his face, Britt thought. "You have something against photographers?"

He gave her a bored look. "Only one in particular who's made a nuisance of himself trying to interview me."

Who was this man sitting much too close? Britt thought in sudden panic. Someone she should know? A famous balloonist perhaps?

"I finally agreed to see him," the man went on. "But now I wish I hadn't."

Britt went on staring at him. If he'd had the courtesy to introduce himself, she might have recognized the name. "Perhaps the interview won't be too bad."

A slow smile erased his displeasure. "Perhaps he won't show up." He lifted his wine glass. She saw how even his white teeth were, the way his dark hair fell over his brow and curved onto his cheek in thick sideburns that lent a contoured look to his face and set off heavy brows above a straight, aristocratic nose.

How annoying that he made her feel like a knock-kneed schoolgirl when he was so attractive! Probably he amused himself in his spare time by bowling over lady tourists.

She drew herself up. "I'm Britt Ryan. I don't believe I caught your name."

He ignored the comment. "Ryan? You said you were English."

"My father was Irish."

"Then you ought to say so and not leave a fellow puzzling over where you got those remarkable green eyes." He gave her another disarming smile. "Though I should have guessed they came from the Emerald Isle."

"They came from Land's End," she replied curtly. "I was born there."

"Oh?" He twirled his wine glass lazily. "Let me guess. Your father was a herdsman."

"A seaman," she answered and could have bitten her tongue off. What business was it of his?

But he seemed genuinely interested. "Where did he sail from?"

"Mostly out of Plymouth. I lived with an aunt."

"Not your mother?" he said softly.

"My mother died when I was ten." Maybe he was a psychiatrist, she thought fleetingly. He was so skilled at drawing out information!

"I was fourteen when I lost mine." He scowled suddenly. "She ran away with an Italian count."

"Oh. I'm sorry."

He fixed a solemn stare on her. "You sound as though you mean it."

She blushed. "It couldn't have been pleasant for you."

"Oh, it wasn't so bad. I never cared for her actually."

"Never cared for your mother!" Britt's green eyes widened. "I never heard of such a thing."

He gave a little laugh. "Then that's two new experiences you've had today. Almost having your hat lifted by a passing balloonist, and sharing a drink with a man who disliked his mother." He lifted his glass. "I think you'll find when you grow up there are more of the latter around than you ever imagined."

Britt pushed her chair back abruptly. "Thank you for the wine."

His arm shot out to detain her. "You haven't even tasted it."

"Then save it. Perhaps someone more mature will come along whom you can force it on."

He grinned, and rising, caught her elbow. "I see I'm guilty of a double sin." Her heart thudded crazily under his dark-eyed scrutiny. "Underestimating your age and forcing a drink on you. Will you forgive me?"

"Neither matters."

"Both do," he replied, and to her amazement she found herself seated again. "I've been exposed to the graces on one or two occasions," he said with a twinkle "Please give me a chance to prove it."

"I really must go."

"Why?"

She caught her breath. "And you claim to have manners!"

He threw back his head and laughed. "You couldn't have come from Land's End. You're prickly as a desert cactus!"

"And you're the rudest man I've ever met!"

He sobered instantly. "I'll wager I am." His tanned hand came out and covered hers on the table. Immediately she tried to withdraw it, but he held on firmly, slipping his other palm beneath it. "Britt Ryan," he said softly, "I think you've led a sheltered life."

Her face grew crimson. "I have not! I worked in a tea shop from the time I was ten. I've known all types."

"And served them clotted cream?" He spoke in the same soft tone, never taking his eyes from hers.

"It wasn't that kind of tea shop. We sold it by bulk.. And coffee too. I ran the grinder."

He put his head to one side. "Did you now?" A strong thumb massaged the bottom joint of her index finger. "I love the smell of fresh coffee."

"One grows tired of it," she replied before she could stop herself.

"You see," he said quietly, "what a civilized conversation we're having?"

She released an exasperated sigh. "*Why* are we having it?"

"Why?" He lifted his thick brows. "Because when I leaned from my gondola this afternoon and looked down at your pixie face in the meadow, I made up my mind I wanted to know you."

"I don't believe that." But it might be rather nice if she could!

He bit back a smile. "Then what's your explanation?"

"I think you were bored out here with no one to talk to. When you saw me crossing the terrace, you thought you'd have a little fun."

The smile played about his lips. "I am having fun."

"Which proves my point," she answered huffily.

"Do you think—" He turned her small hand over in his larger one and studied her palm. "That I couldn't find someone else with whom to amuse myself if I chose?"

She snatched her hand away and laid it quickly in her lap. "I haven't noticed anyone hovering about."

"Then take a look behind you." He leaned back to watch her head swing around.

Crossing toward them was a tall slender girl dressed

in a clinging white dress. Her silky blond hair brushed her shoulders, and she moved with the graceful ease of a jungle cat.

"Margo," the man said in response to Britt's puzzled look as she returned her gaze to him. "Don't you recognize her?"

"Why should I?"

"She was with me this afternoon."

In the gondola! With a shock Britt realized that though she had been aware of the presence of a woman, she'd had eyes only for the man.

The balloonist smiled knowingly. "She won't take it kindly that she failed to make an impression."

"Then don't tell her," snapped Britt.

The man rose as the beautifully dressed girl approached, and Britt wished with all her heart she could dissolve under the table.

"Margo St. Croix," he said smoothly, "meet the maid from the meadow." With an amused glance at Britt he pulled out a chair for the girl on his other side. "Her name is Britt Ryan."

Tawny eyes flecked with gold took Britt's measure. "You look as though you've just come in."

"From the meadow?" Britt's face went hot. "As a matter of fact, I have. I like to take my time when I walk." She pushed her chair back and stood. "I only stopped to refresh myself with a glass of Perrier before going up to my room." She forced a smile. "Nice meeting you. Have a pleasant evening."

"Do get some rest." The man's dark eyes twinkled. "After that strenuous journey, you must be exhausted."

Who *was* that rich boor who amused himself at the expense of others? Britt fumed—as she'd been doing for hours. Pity the poor photographer he'd maligned. And that girl! Ten to one she had retractable claws. What kind of copy would a couple of arrogant snobs like those two make? Who'd want to read it?

But still she couldn't get the balloonist out of her mind—and worse, she admitted finally, she didn't want to.

Retracing her steps to the window, she stood glaring defiantly down at the river lighted like a fairyland. But the scent of hothouse lilies of the valley floating from a bouquet on the dresser assailed her, and she collapsed suddenly on the window seat, dismayed at the ache within her.

What was she doing here alone in this hotel room with only a few francs left in her purse and her only hope for tomorrow a harebrained scheme that wasn't materializing? She didn't care about a career. All she truly wanted was someone to love and to love her, someone who'd wake up beside her in the morning and look at her as if she were the treasure of his life.

She wasn't a beauty, of course, like that willowy Margo. She was too short, too rosy-cheeked in times of crisis, too—how had he said it?—pixie-faced. But she had looks enough so no man need be ashamed of her. Unless she were wearing a dirty pair of riding breeches and a wrinkled shirt! The contrast between herself and Margo must have been shocking. No wonder the balloonist had thought her a joke.

A tremor rippled through her. Now *there* was a pair of eyes to wake up to. Liquid, glowing. And his hands. How strong and protective they were. How tenderly he had held hers. Her heart began a slow pounding. She leaned against the window ledge and closed her eyes.

Imagine floating over the countryside in the company of a man like that. Only he'd have to be gentle, not caustic as he'd been when he spoke of his mother. And he would have to be gallant, not rude. She could almost feel his lips against her ear, covering her mouth. Soft, warm persuasive lips . . . exploring lips . . .

The telephone jangled.

Britt shot up from the window seat. Sydney? But it was nearly midnight. Surely in a hospital—

It rang again. She crossed quickly and lifted the receiver.

"Britt?" The voice was crisp, authoritative.

"Who is this?"

"I can scale tall buildings in a single leap. I'm swifter than a zephyr—"

The balloonist! "Are you drunk?"

A hearty laugh came over the wire. "Of course I'm not drunk. Are you still awake?"

"You might have wondered that *before* you rang," she replied sharply.

The line exploded in a sigh. "You're the touchiest creature. Don't you ever laugh at anything?"

"I have a wonderful sense of humor!"

"I'm delighted to hear it."

"What do you want anyway?" she said crossly.

"I called to find out what you're doing tomorrow."

"What difference does it make?"

He sighed again. "Just answer my question."

"I wasn't aware you'd asked one."

There was too long a pause. Her pulse leaped. He hadn't hung up, had he?

"Miss Ryan."

She breathed a sigh of her own. "Yes?"

"Let's drive to Marseilles tomorrow."

"Marseilles! Are you insane?"

"My dear girl, people go there every day. They've even built roads for that purpose."

She laughed in spite of herself. Instantly he voiced his approval. "There! Doesn't that make you feel better?"

She ignored the jibe. "I can't go running all over the country. I'm a working girl."

"But you're not working now. You told me that yourself."

"I wasn't working today, but tomorrow I'd better be, or I'll have to wait on tables or something."

His voice sobered. "That bad? Anything I can do to help?"

He almost sounded as if he meant it. "Thanks," she said in a warmer tone, "but I'll manage somehow."

"Who is this rogue who keeps evading you? I'll go and punch him in the nose."

She laughed again. "He'd be certain then to welcome me with open arms, wouldn't he!"

"He'd better, or I'd know the reason why."

"I'd almost be willing to let you have at him, if I could only get hold of him."

"There, you see." His tone was low, persuasive. "He isn't available, so you can't work. There's no alternative but for you to go to Marseilles with me."

"In the balloon?" she said, only half teasing.

He laughed. "Don't I wish! But I'm afraid we hung her up on an apple tree after we left you."

"You didn't!"

"The nylon has a three-foot rip to prove it."

Britt saw again the dazzling splendor of the balloon as it passed over the valley. "But that's terrible!"

"Isn't it? The midday wind was too high. But never mind. In a few days I'll have her patched up. In the meantime, there's always the automobile. Mundane, but useful."

"I'm sorry I can't go with you." With a little shock she realized how much she meant it. "Early in the morning I have to strike out again and see if I can track down my man.''

"What a terrible conscience you have. Why not be more like me? I have an appointment too, but I'd never let a little detail like that interfere with something I'd rather do.''

"Bully for you." She hoped he caught her sarcasm. "Too bad we can't all be that carefree.''

She heard his exasperated sigh. "Well, if you're absolutely set on going, I'll drive you.''

"What? You'd be bored to death!''

"Try me and see." The warmth in his voice enabled her to see his eyes again.

"Well—''

"Judging from the time it took you today, it must be a terribly long walk." His tone grew teasing. "Ride with me; you may even make it back to the hotel before nightfall.''

She gave up, laughing. "Oh, all right, if you insist.''

"What time shall I pick you up?''

"How about nine?" A thought struck her. "I don't even know your name.''

"Don't worry. I know yours. It's Irish. Your father was a seaman and a violator of child labor laws.''

"Will you be serious!" Then a new thought popped into her mind. "Will your friend be coming too?''

She heard his low laugh. "Margo? Hardly. Anyway, she's in Nice by now, or at least I hope so. One crash per day is enough.''

"Do you mean she flew there tonight?''

"That's where I've been. Seeing her to the airport. She took enough luggage for a month's stay. Listen, you'd better ring off and get some sleep, or you'll be all bleary-eyed for your ogre tomorrow." She heard him take a long, slow breath and let it go. "Pleasant dreams.''

Replacing the receiver, she was aware that the husky voice persisted in her ear. What was it about him that was so compelling? she wondered. What caused her to feel weak simply thinking about driving through the countryside with him tomorrow? He was arrogant and caustic. Rude.

She took a breath to slow her pounding heart. But he was also charming, she admitted, and even a little sweet. Which was his true nature?

Perhaps he didn't have one. A warning note struck in her brain.

Chapter 2

"Will you please slow down!" With one hand Britt hung on to her beret and with the other, gripped the door of the smart little Ferrari.

White teeth gleamed in her companion's tanned face. "Am I frightening you?"

"You're scaring the stuffing out of me!" At the hotel the staccato beat of her heart had been easily attributable to the sight of the balloonist's lean, muscular form displayed to best advantage in tan chinos and an open-necked shirt and to the way his dark eyes carefully appraised her, but now it hammered from sheer terror that at any moment they would both be thrown out into the roadway.

She raised her voice over the roar of the motor. "There's not the least hurry, you know. He probably won't even be there, and even if he is, I can't very well talk to him if I'm lying in the ditch with a fractured skull!"

The man at the wheel laughed, but he took his foot off the accelerator and allowed the car to coast down into the misty valley. At the bottom he turned to her with a wide grin. "How's that?" he said.

She put her hand on her heart. "Better—though it may take me a while to recover."

"Then we'll rest." He whipped the automobile off into the shade of a small clump of lemon trees and stopped the motor.

Mixed feelings of annoyance and anticipation collided headlong in Britt's brain. "We haven't time to stop."

He lifted a dark eyebrow. "You've just assured me there's no hurry."

She colored. "But we don't have all *that* much time."

Watching her edge toward the door, he said, vastly amused, "I think you're more afraid of me than of my driving."

"I certainly am not!"

"Perhaps it's yourself you fear then."

"What a ridiculous idea." But she hoped her shirt collar hid the pulse going wild in her throat. He was quite possibly the most desirable man she'd ever met and quite the most cocksure as well. It would never do for him to know the unsettling effect his smoldering gaze had upon her. "It's just that you don't seem to realize how important it is for me to get there."

He shrugged, eyes glinting with mischief. "Get where? That's the only reason I've stopped. There's a fork in the road ahead. How can I know which direction to take unless you at least tell me where we're going?"

"The Chateau de Laon," she replied promptly.

The balloonist opened his mouth as if to speak, but no sound came.

"Do you know it?" said Britt.

"I've heard of it."

"But do you know how to get there?" she insisted. "I don't. Back down the road a way you turned left when I would have turned right, but you were going too fast for me to try to stop you. Now I'm completely lost."

Some of his color had come back. "I think I can find it."

"Fine, then." She folded her arms beneath her high young breasts. "Shall we go?"

But he had settled back into his seat, making no attempt to start the motor. "First I think you should explain what you want to do when you get there."

Britt frowned. "I've told you. Three days ago I had an appointment with Philippe Dolman to take some photographs of the chateau."

"You said you were on assignment and some fellow had been giving you the run-around. You didn't mention the chateau. You didn't mention Philippe Dolman."

Britt blinked. "Do you know him?"

A momentary flicker appeared in his dark eyes. "Why do you ask?"

"Something in the way you said his name."

"It's rather well-known," he answered brusquely.

Britt turned down the corners of her mouth. "And don't think he doesn't take advantage of that! The way he throws his weight around makes me sick."

He stiffened. "What do you mean?"

"It's perfectly obvious, isn't it? We peasants depend

upon people like him to make our living, and he doesn't even bother to show up for his appointments. He could care less what's happening to us."

"How do you know what's detained him?"

Her green eyes sparked fire. "Are you defending him?"

"Somebody should," he answered a bit lamely. "Anything could have happened to the poor fellow."

"I'll believe that when I hear it," she sniffed. "He's having too good a time in Majorca, that's all. And there's poor Sydney wired to his toenails at Sisters of Mercy, thinking all the while I have everything well in hand here."

"Sydney." Her companion said the name as if it were the missing piece of a jigsaw puzzle he'd just uncovered from beneath a corner of the carpet.

"Sydney Fernham." Britt had the grace to blush. "You see, it's something of a swindle actually. Sydney is the one who has the appointment, but he's broken both legs, and the copy for the article and the photographs have to be on the editor's desk the middle of next month."

"Wait." He fixed bright eyes upon her. "Start at the beginning. What happened to Sydney?"

"He had a skiing accident." She squirmed uncomfortably. "Well, not quite. He fell out of the chair lift on the way up the slope."

A reluctant smile curved the sensuous lips. "Go on."

"Look, we don't have all morning. It's already nine-thirty and—"

But he held her with his unrelenting gaze. "We have time for this."

"Well." She hesitated. "I suppose it's only fair to give you some kind of explanation since you've gone to all the trouble to drive me out here. I can at least fill you in on the main facts."

"An excellent idea," he murmured.

She sighed. "Here they are then. I work for a business service which supplies temporary secretarial assistance for Paris offices, and—"

"You said you were a photographer!"

"I am, but photography is only a hobby—so far. But if I can land this job—"

"Sydney's job?" he said in an acid tone.

She shot him a puzzled glance. "How can I explain if you keep interrupting?"

"A thousand pardons," he answered drily.

Her frown softened. If only his knee weren't touching hers, this would be all so much easier. "Sydney Fernham is on the staff at *La Revue*. He lives in the flat above me. Sometimes we have supper together."

"You see each other."

"No, we do not *see* each other!" she answered crossly. It was true that Sydney had lately made some rather pronounced romantic overtures, but the last thing she wanted was for this attractive man to think she was romantically involved with someone else. At least not until she was certain how she felt about him. "Sydney and I are friends."

He made no comment.

"He got me interested in taking pictures," she went on. "In the park, you know. By the river. That kind of thing. And I'm good at it. Really good!"

She moved away from him a bit and felt a stab of disappointment that he seemed not to notice. "I have an eye for composition, Sydney says, and he should know. He's tops. Then about two months ago—" She hesitated, possessed suddenly with the uncomfortable feeling that the man staring so fixedly was no longer interested in her, but only in what she was saying.

"Two months ago," he prompted.

"My office sent me to help out at *La Revue,* and that's when I discovered what a fabulous place it is."

"You decided you wanted to work there permanently."

She nodded. "But not as a flunky. On the staff, taking pictures. And if Philippe Dolman would only cooperate, I might have a chance."

"And if he doesn't cooperate?"

"I may murder him!"

A glint came into the dark eyes. "He might wish to do the same if he could hear you now."

Britt grinned impishly. "I wouldn't blame him actually. It's no good to be hoodwinked." Then her tone changed. "But he won't be sorry if he lets me have my way. I'll do a good job. Besides—" She lifted her chin saucily. "He owes it to the French people."

"What do you mean?" said her startled companion.

"Philippe Dolman owns the most gorgeous chateau in the whole of France and not half a dozen people out of his own tight little circle have ever even seen it."

A softer note came into his voice. "You consider it beautiful, do you?"

"I should say!" Her eyes grew starry. "The architecture, the paintings—"

"How do you know?"

"I saw it." She made a face. "Well, not really. Just half a dozen photographs. You see, one of my first tasks at *La Revue* was to research some back copies, and in one of them was an article about a diplomatic dinner held at the chateau—let's see. When was it?"

"April, a year ago."

Britt blinked.

"It was in all the papers," he said quickly.

"Was it? I didn't notice. I wasn't interested then."

"Why are you now?"

She frowned. "I've told you. Way back last spring Sydney got this assignment to do an in-depth feature of any chateau he chose." She shook her head despairingly. "And what did he pick? Chenonceaux. *Everyone* has seen Chenonceaux. No imagination whatsoever. What he needed was a spectacular subject."

The man across from her eyed her with reluctant admiration. "So after you saw the photographs of the Chateau de Laon, you gave it to him?"

She laughed gleefully. "I did! But he had a terrible time setting up the interview. Dolman was the most obstinate creature you can imagine."

A grim smile creased the tanned cheeks. "Maybe Monsieur Dolman enjoys his privacy."

"Oh, he definitely does. And he isn't entitled to it. Not so much of it anyway." She settled back down in the seat and said smugly, "If you want to know what I think, I think the Chateau de Laon ought to be taken away from him and given to the French government so all the people could enjoy it, not just one stuffed shirt."

"In much the same way some castles in your country belong to the National Trust?" he asked indifferently.

"Yes," Britt replied, "and those that are privately owned are shared with the general public. Visitors from all over the world come to admire and learn about their history." There was no response from the stern profile beside her, but she could not resist talking to such a captive audience about her favorite project. "If I can pull off this assignment, Sydney is going to do what he can to see that I'm taken on at *La Revue.*" She warmed to her topic. "It's a very influential magazine, you know. I may just have to put a bug in his ear."

"Do you mean you'd try to stir up public opinion and force Dolman to give up the chateau?"

Her eyes sparkled. "Why not?"

He sat staring at her for a moment. Then abruptly he

turned the key and floorboarded the accelerator. Britt felt herself thrown back against the leather upholstery as the car shot out into the road. Fields and fences rushed past.

Britt was speechless. Then as they took a turn on two wheels, she shrieked, "What in the world is the matter with you? Do you want to kill us?"

"I want to be absolutely certain you keep your appointment," he shouted back.

"I hope to heaven I have a chance!" Three white chickens missed death by an inch and flew squawking into a meadow. "I'll tell you one thing, you madman," she screamed. "If you know what's good for you, you'll slow down before you get to the chateau or that gatekeeper will probably shoot you!"

A muscle rippled in his jaw. "Do you really think so?"

"Yes, I do! Watch out! We're coming to it." Her voice rose hysterically. "There's the gate!"

"And there's the gatekeeper."

Britt saw a man and two Doberman pinschers flash by in a blur orchestrated by the deafening blast of a horn. The gates slid open. The Ferrari sailed through.

"You murderer!" Britt raged as they came to a halt in a spray of gravel before the imposing chateau she was too stunned even to notice. "You could have killed us both!"

He shut off the motor and turned a contemptuous look on her. "We weren't for a moment in danger."

"Then you're blind—as well as stupid! We could have crashed right through the iron grillwork. I don't know why we didn't."

"We didn't because my horn activates the mechanism that opens it," he said coldly.

Britt's mouth fell open. "Why—you're—" She sucked in her breath. "You're Philippe Dolman!"

"How astute of you to guess." He opened the door on his side and got out. Over his shoulder he said, "If you're still interested in keeping your friend's appointment, I'd hurry if I were you. You're three days late already."

Chapter 3

"I think it was horrid of you not to tell me!"

Britt and Philippe Dolman were seated in a sunny garden room. Tea had been brought, and crisp pastry, but Britt had touched nothing. Acute embarrassment, anger and badly damaged pride had all but paralyzed her. To make matters worse, it was obvious that Philippe was enjoying her discomfort.

She glared across at him. How could she ever have thought that stony face attractive? And just last night she had called those obsidian eyes liquid and glowing. Philippe Dolman was a monster!

He spoke. "I suppose it hasn't occurred to you that it's I who should be offended?"

Did he think she was utterly stupid? Of course it had occurred to her! Why else would she be in such agony? She'd never get the interview and photographs now, and it was too late to make arrangements with another chateau. Sydney might even lose his job. "You brought it on yourself," she snapped.

He eyed her coldly. "That's to be your defense, is it?"

"It's the truth. You deliberately led me on just to hear what I'd say. It's not my fault your trick backfired."

He got up suddenly and set his cup on a marble tabletop. "You tricked *me*."

"I didn't trick anyone!"

"No? Two days in a row you introduced yourself as Sydney Fernham to my gateman. That's not a trick? And you told me yourself your coming here was a swindle."

"*Something* of a swindle, I said. What you haven't given me the opportunity to explain is that the minute I came face to face with you, I intended to be frank about everything."

"Why should I believe anything you say? You lied once."

"Only to get past the gatekeeper!" If she could make him understand that much at least, then maybe something could be salvaged from the horrible mess she'd made of things. "Can you see that man out there paying the slightest attention to my story about Sydney falling out of the chair lift?"

Dolman's mouth twitched at one corner, but Britt saw only his stern frown and went on at a furious rate. "Once past him and those wretched dogs, I would have openly declared myself. I don't need to masquerade as Sydney. I have my own portfolio of significant work."

In a lofty tone he mimicked her words from the car. "Photographs of the park? The river? That sort of thing?"

Her green eyes iced over. "Among others. You

would have had complete assurance I could do competent work before I started."

He looked about innocently. "Where is it?"

"Where is what?"

"The portfolio."

She flushed. "At the hotel, of course. Surely not even you would expect me to burden myself with a briefcase while I walked from Perpignan."

"Today you rode."

Her color deepened. "I forgot it."

"You forgot it." He lifted skeptical eyebrows. "This was to be your big morning, I understood. Do-or-die day."

She jumped up, almost overturning the tea tray. "You don't want to listen to me! You don't care in the least about being fair."

"Fair!" The word seemed to sting him as nothing else had. "Give me one good reason why I should treat you fairly."

He advanced menacingly. She backed away, dismayed that as angry as she was, the scent of his skin, mingled with a crisp, woodsy fragrance of shaving lotion, still had the power to stir her.

He enumerated her sins on his fingertips. "You persuaded your friend Sydney to harass me until I finally set up an appointment with him. You came here under a false pretext. You labeled me an obstinate stuffed shirt who isn't entitled to his privacy *or* to the chateau which has been in his family for six centuries, and, if that isn't enough, if you had succeeded in your loathsome scheme you would have done all in your power to launch a vicious campaign in your magazine to discredit me. And you expect me to be fair!"

Britt fell back a pace, stunned by his vehemence and by her own culpability. "I wouldn't really have launched a campaign against you. Until the moment I said that, I'd never thought of such a thing."

"But you found it a delicious idea! It held enormous appeal for you."

"I was joking! Couldn't you see that? And you accused *me* of not having a sense of humor."

Her reference to the bantering tone of their conversation the evening before momentarily silenced them both.

Britt spoke first. "I wish we *had* gone to Marseilles," she said quietly. "I'd have learned your name. All this unpleasantness could have been avoided."

"And your little scheme would have succeeded," he said ironically.

She bridled. "How would it have succeeded? Would you have excused me from palming myself off as Sydney Fernham? If you'd have done that *after* Marseilles, why can't you do it now?"

"I know too much about you now."

His smugness infuriated her. "You don't know anything about me! You think I'm a liar and a cheat, and I'm neither."

"I think you've done a fairly good job of convincing me that you're both."

"You *want* to be convinced. You want Chateau de Laon all to yourself. You can't stand the thought of anyone out of your social stratum catching a glimpse of that magnificent carved stairway or the *Cordelova* on your walls."

She flung her arm out in a wide arc that took in the whole of the room. "All this fetching plasterwork, these ornamental cornices might be cheapened if some poor little girl from the provinces got a peek at them."

He was looking at her with a peculiar intensity. "How do you know about *Cordelova?*"

"Even at Land's End children are taught to read," she said haughtily.

"Children read fairy stories. They don't trouble themselves finding out how wallpaper is embossed to simulate leather."

"I didn't say I know how it's done," she shot back, but most of the fire had gone out of her, and she turned her back on him to gaze out on a garden ablaze with late autumn color. She wished at this moment she were back at Land's End, that she might hear the comforting sound of the coffee grinder instead of the cold voice of Philippe Dolman.

"Most of this conversation has centered on you," she heard him saying. "Suppose I tell you how it happens *I'm* here today."

"You came in a balloon," she answered dully, not bothering to turn around.

"Yes, I did!" She heard the sharpness of his tone and was aware that he had crossed to stand behind her. "At risk of life and limb, I might add."

"You could have caught a boat." She swung around to face him. "As you so glibly told me, 'people do that sort of thing every day.'"

Before the last word was out he had her by the shoulders, his voice cutting fiercely through her sarcasm. "I'm going to explain this, and damn it, you're going to listen!"

Her heart came up in her throat. She had never seen anyone quite so angry.

"A hot air balloon is not a plaything. It can't be bundled up like an extra pair of socks and crammed into a suitcase. And it can't be launched just any day some featherbrained adventurer decides to take a ride. There has to be a sustaining wind of a proper velocity."

With every word, his anger seemed to increase.

"Three days ago," he went on grimly, "neither condition prevailed. Nor the next day either." He narrowed his eyes threateningly. "Nor the next. But because I had made an appointment with some fool from Paris, and I don't take my obligations lightly, I decided to return whatever the risk."

She wanted to remind him he hadn't been at all concerned about keeping his appointment when he proposed going to Marseilles today, but she didn't dare.

"Margo and I are damned lucky we only snagged in an apple tree," he concluded. "We could have gone down in the sea."

His tirade, overly dramatized or not, had visibly shaken Britt, but she made an attempt at recovery. "And that would have been my fault, I suppose?"

He jerked her to him. "No," he answered in a tight voice. "It would have been *my* fault for placing unnecessary importance on a trivial scheme designed to make your fortune."

She twisted free of his grasp, her creamy cheeks afire.

"I'm sorry you and *Margo,*" she spit out the name, "imperiled yourselves for my sake. I'm sorry you ripped your balloon and cut short your capers on Majorca. But I'm not in the least sorry the interview is off."

She crossed the room quickly and snatched her jacket from the chair. "I wouldn't spend the next three days in your company if they *gave* me *La Revue.*"

But before she reached the door, he caught her arm and swung her about. "Wait just one minute."

"What for?" she taunted. "So you can further play on my sympathies?"

He ignored the slur. "We are now past the point of

discussing how and why either of us happens to be here. We are now going to sit down, if you can control your abominable temper—"

Her mouth flew open, but he left no entry for her objections. "—and talk about the feasibility of your project."

"There *is* no project!"

"There damned well better be," he answered and dragged her unceremoniously back to her chair.

When he'd made certain she would stay where he had placed her, he poured himself a fresh cup of tea and sat down opposite her. "Well. What do you propose to do?"

She stared, incredulous. "You don't honestly think there's the slightest possibility we could work together after all that's been said here this morning?"

A glimmer flickered in his dark eyes. "We've cleared the air at least."

"Are you saying you want to be interviewed, that you want me to photograph the chateau?"

He set down his cup. "I'm saying I intend to fulfill the agreement I made with Sydney Fernham, and I expect you, as his surrogate, to go through with his end of the bargain."

Britt was stunned into silence.

Finally she said, "I'm not sure I have time now to do it properly."

"You have until the middle of next month, you said."

She surveyed him coldly. "You can't get through your head, can you, that I have to make a living? I could afford to spend a week here, no more, and half of that's gone."

"My fault." He spoke crisply. "I'll reimburse you for any expenses you will have after the time you originally set aside."

Britt blinked.

"Furthermore," he went on in a brisk tone, "I expect both the article and the photographs to be superior, so you will please take as much time as necessary to see that the highest standards of excellence are met."

All was not lost for Sydney after all! Maybe not even for herself if she handled with kid gloves this mercurial man who quite obviously believed himself to be a god. "I can guarantee quality," she said numbly.

"Good. That much is settled then. Will you start this morning?"

"I— Yes." Was this really happening? Five minutes ago he seemed on the verge of choking her, and now he was commanding her to begin work. "But I refuse to take any photographs until I've explored the place thoroughly," she added in an attempt to restore some part of her eroding authority.

"Very well." He got up. "I'll see that the staff is informed."

"You're being very decent about this," she began hesitantly.

His gaze settled on her, and she was aware once again of the devastating effect his concentrated attention had upon her.

She wet her lips. "I hope you'll forgive my— rudeness."

For a moment she was afraid he might counter her apology with sarcasm, but his penetrating gaze faltered, and he said quietly, "I was discourteous to you as well. Shall we forget it?"

"Yes! I'd like that very much."

She waited, believing in a moment his tantalizing smile would reappear and they would once again be on the same footing as when the morning had begun.

But instead, he walked away toward a desk in the

corner and began to flip through an accumulation of mail. When he became aware that she was still standing there, he turned and said with cold formality, "Was there something else?"

She felt her face go hot. "I— No. Except that I was wondering if there might be a particular part of the chateau you'd prefer I saw first."

A look of annoyance crossed his face. "It's your project. Suit yourself." And he returned his attention to his mail.

Chapter 4

The rest of the morning Britt wandered aimlessly through the long corridors of the chateau, scarcely noticing as she poked her head into one palatial apartment after another the grandeur that surrounded her.

All she could think of was the total disinterest with which Philippe Dolman had dismissed her. She might have been a speck of dust! Was that why he was allowing her to go ahead with her plans? So that at every turn he could humiliate her? Was ignoring her to be his way of getting back at her for that silly speech she'd made in the car?

She sat down on a brocade love seat at the head of the oak staircase and stared disconsolately at the intricate carvings which decorated it. He needn't bother to humiliate her. She'd done that herself. What a pompous little fool she must have appeared, ranting about how she would like to take away his chateau and give it to the French government, calling him a stuffed shirt and declaring herself to be as fine a photographer as Sydney.

She cast a dejected glance at the camera in her lap. An artist was the master of his craft's tools, and all she knew how to do was put the film in and click the shutter. If Sydney hadn't discovered her naturally keen eye for composition, she wouldn't be in this mess now.

Or if those first few photographs she'd shot at the Tuileries hadn't turned out so beautifully, she'd never have dreamed up this crazy scheme in the first place. Even if she had, Sydney would have laughed at her.

Her gaze moved up to an imposing portrait of a marquis on the opposite wall, and she thought dismally, *I don't deserve to be here. I ought to be typing letters in some dark cubbyhole on the Rue D'etretat. How I wish I were!*

A shuddering sigh escaped her.

"Tired already?"

Startled, she swung about to find Philippe Dolman studying her from the open doorway of the second floor library. His unexpected appearance sent a swift shock of admiration coursing through her. His strongly muscled frame was clothed in closefitting riding pants and his knit shirt opened at the throat to reveal a thick mat of the same dark hair which capped his head.

"I'm a little tired," she confessed weakly. "But mostly I'm overwhelmed." She hoped he couldn't guess by what!

He came toward her easily, and a surge of excitement

seized her. *He* certainly belonged here. In another age he might have been a king.

"Everything is even more wonderful than I imagined," she heard herself gushing, and despised the nervousness which inspired it. No man had ever had such a disquieting effect on her.

From beneath a furrowed brow he surveyed her. "Have you decided what to photograph first?"

Her thoughts scrambled about like startled mice. Snatching at one, she blurted, "The tower dungeon."

"What?"

She started up. "But if that displeases you, I can easily switch to something else."

His frown deepened. "Not at all. I think it's a first-rate idea. After all, if it hadn't been for the dungeon keeping 'safe' our enemies, there'd probably be no chateau at all." He put his head to one side and gave her a penetrating stare. "Perhaps that was your idea?"

It *had* been, when she'd first seen the dungeon, but she wasn't about to risk antagonizing him again. "Such a thought never occurred to me."

She saw at once her answer had annoyed him anyway. She quailed. The last thing she wanted was another scene.

But when he spoke, his voice held no anger, only resignation. "When we first met on the hotel terrace, you impressed me as a saucy, fiery little Irish girl who didn't give two pins for anyone's opinion."

Her heart sank. Saucy, he had said. Fiery.

"You verified that opinion when we spoke on the telephone and in the car this morning—and even for a while in the garden room."

His eyes bored into hers.

"But then you began displaying another side of

yourself—as you're doing now." His look pinned her like an insect to the love seat. "An obsequious side, a side in which humility almost borders on fawning." He stared coldly. "It's a side I'd rather not have seen."

Abruptly he turned and went toward the staircase. As he descended, he called back carelessly, "Luncheon is served in half an hour on the back terrace. You're expected."

When Britt had partially recovered from the stinging reproach Philippe Dolman had delivered with such nonchalance, she could scarcely contain her fury.

"Why that arrogant, aristocratic snob!" she stormed, pacing the wide hallway and brandishing her camera as if it were a sword. "The nerve of him, calling me obsequious!" That meant degradingly submissive, didn't it? Submissive—in a pig's eye!

She banged the camera into the palm of her other hand, but the blow served only to further incense her. Who did he think he was, she raged, that he could brazenly stomp on her sensibilities as if she were mere dirt beneath his Gucci boots!

Well, he'd asked for it, and he was certainly going to get it. She'd show him just how obnoxious she could be. Before she was through, he'd *beg* her to be humble! He hadn't the manners of a stable boy—nor the common sense either—or he'd have recognized the difference between sincere regret and fawning. He'd know the strength of character required to admit one's own error in front of an enemy. He was a clod! A nincompoop.

But gradually rage subsided into the simple ache of badly wounded feelings, and once more she sank onto the love seat, this time perilously close to tears. His treatment of her wouldn't matter half so much if she hadn't been so attracted to him or her imagination so

drawn to the sight of him in that dratted balloon . . .
She pressed her fingers tightly against her eyelids.
Wasn't it just like her to fall in love with a brute?

She sat up straight. Fall in love! The stone walls of
the chateau seemed to waver like a mirage. She
couldn't be in love. She hated the man!

Oh, did she? another part of her taunted. Why, then,
was she so upset? Ordinarily, as Philippe had guessed,
she cared little what other people thought of her, and
yet this man's opinion had wounded her to the quick.

Her throat closed around a sob. What was she to do?
Run as fast as she could? Take the first train back to
Paris? What about Sydney? He was counting on her.
What about her hopes for a job at *La Revue?*

The devil could take the job! she thought angrily.
She didn't want it anyway. She wanted a husband. She
wanted a home and children. But short of resigning
herself to Sydney, whom she thought of as a somewhat
bumbling younger brother, or placing an ad in "Situations Wanted," it looked as if she'd have to spend the
rest of her life alone. Philippe Dolman wasn't falling in
love with *her,* that was plain enough! Worse, she
obviously repulsed him now, and in the face of that,
how could she stay on here feeling as she did?

But how *did* she feel? she argued miserably. A part
of her loathed him, or at least loathed his insensitivity.
A part of her hated his brashness and arrogance.

Yet . . . whenever she remembered the way he had
held her hand on the hotel terrace . . . the way her skin
burned at the pressure of his knee. . . .

Something inside her gave way, as it did each time his
cool-eyed gaze touched any part of her. She couldn't
handle this! Not only was he physically magnetic, she
admitted hopelessly, but his whole personality drew her
to him. Every fiber of her being urged her to make

herself important to this man, to make herself so vital and indispensable that even in the briefest separation he would feel as if breath itself were taken from him.

But this was madness! Sheer nonsense. The romantic setting of the chateau was inspiring such fantasies. She'd known Philippe Dolman less than twenty-four hours. She'd never believed in love at first sight.

But neither had she ever felt as she did now. Be it love, simple physical attraction or a combination of the two, it had aroused feelings she'd never known could exist. With a sinking heart she realized as vulnerable as she felt now she'd never be able to withstand another attack of the sort Philippe had just delivered. The sensible course was to put as much distance between him and herself as she could.

But even as the thought formed, she recognized sadly that she had no intention of acting upon it.

How then was she to survive?

She sat on for a time, dully regarding the mosaic pattern of the tile beneath her feet. She was hopelessly trapped.

But slowly it came to her that Philippe himself had provided the key for survival. Coolness, aloofness. Her flagging spirits lifted with the glimmer of hope the thought provided.

If she could maintain the strictest privacy in the chamber of her heart— If she could manage not to give herself away by look or deed or word, then perhaps she had a chance to leave here with some portion of her pride intact.

After all, how long could this assignment last? Another week? Ten days at the most. In the presence of Philippe Dolman she would appear the model of efficiency and decorum—the same attitude she presented in the Paris offices where she went to type letters and take dictation. If Philippe were as middle-aged and paunchy as her usual employer she'd have no trouble, would she? Anyone could pretend for a fortnight!

Besides, she'd have periods of respite at the end of each day. She could return to the hotel in Perpignan and fall apart there if necessary without anyone being the wiser.

She stood up. A renewed confidence took hold of her. She could manage it!

Thank heavens for this luncheon too, she thought, hurrying down the stairs. It would provide just the opportunity she needed to impress Philippe with her new image before the old one imprinted itself indelibly on his mind. Pinning a tight little smile on her lips, she took a deep breath and opened the terrace door, feeling almost eager for the challenge.

A fresh breeze had sprung up from the west, and autumn sunlight filled the valley. To her right under a gay parasol she could see a table laid for the meal, and far away to her left through a golden haze, a rider on horseback taking a low fence with practiced ease.

Crossing to the edge of the terrace, she shaded her eyes with one hand. It shouldn't be—but it was. Philippe. She swung around and discovered the table was set only for one.

Her brave new resolves wilted. So he wasn't dining with her after all. She should have known the lord of the manor wouldn't sit down with the help.

Too bad such niceties hadn't mattered on the hotel terrace, she thought bitterly, taking her place at the table. He could have saved them both a lot of trouble. But he was slumming then, she supposed. A lump came up in her throat. And anyway, he hadn't known then what he knew now about her, as he had so plainly pointed out.

Her gaze went back to the valley. Horse and rider

were preparing to take the fence again. Automatically her hand went out and brought the camera to her eye. Remembering how she had swung it about in the upper hall, she wondered vaguely if it would operate at all. It might be a blessing if it wouldn't. She'd have no recourse then, but to return to Paris and forget she'd ever heard of the Chateau de Laon or its intriguing owner.

But the reassuring click came.

With a sigh she set the camera aside and cupping her chin in her hands, watched wistfully as Philippe Dolman atop his mount cleared the fence and cantered away.

Chapter 5

A Louis XII clock was striking five when Britt descended into the wide entry hall. The major part of the afternoon she had spent in the upper regions of the chateau, photographing first the dungeon tower and then a series of small apartments replete with hidden staircases, trapdoors and odd little nooks in which she decided political prisoners must at one time have taken refuge.

She was exhausted, but her sparkling eyes and rosy

cheeks belied her weariness. Her activities had transported her into another period of history, and when she saw Philippe Dolman standing, hands on his narrow hips, watching her descend the stairs, she realized with a start she hadn't given him a thought in hours. Perhaps working here at the chateau would not be such an impossible task after all.

"Finished for the day?" A leather riding jacket of burnt orange covered his open-necked shirt now and by his flushed face and the sharp scent of the outdoors which assailed her nostrils as she approached him, she concluded that he too had spent an exhilarating afternoon.

"I think I got some excellent shots," she answered.

"Of the tower?"

"And of the apartments adjoining it." Abiding by her noontime resolutions would be much easier, she thought with dismay, if he were not looking at her with such frank approval. Evidently Philippe Dolman's moods changed with the hour. "The apartments are cunningly designed."

He nodded. "Men of the cloth hid in them during times of persecution, I'm told. And at other periods, political dignitaries used them for hideouts whenever they needed to beat a quick retreat."

"I thought so!"

With a glance he took in her high color and sparkling eyes. "Come into the study. We'll have a sherry, and you can tell me what else you've discovered."

She was on the point of refusing, but he moved briskly ahead, leaving her no alternative but to follow. Swinging open a door, he led her into a cozy paneled room where a small fire burned in the grate. A decanter of wine and two glasses stood on a low table before it.

Her heart knocked. Had he been waiting for her?

"Sit down." He motioned toward the chair nearest the fire and took up the wine. For a moment a smile played on his lips. "I'm not forcing this on you, am I?"

It seemed a hundred years ago that she had accused him of that instead of just last night! "I'll enjoy it, thank you."

How difficult it was not to respond to his good humor with a smile of her own, but if she let down her guard, even for a moment, who knew what might happen?

He handed her the brimming glass. "Perhaps this will perk up your appetite. Cook tells me you only nibbled at your lunch."

Her face went hot, but he spared her the embarrassment of an answer. "I'm probably to blame. I came down rather hard on you, I'm afraid."

Quick tears stung behind her eyelids. Anger, she found, was a far easier emotion to bear than pity.

"I'm rather inept at dealing with the feminine mind," he went on in a softened tone. "I sometimes have difficulty remembering how sensitive a woman can be."

"It doesn't matter," she said quickly and took a sip of the wine. When she could trust her voice again she said, "Did you enjoy your ride?"

He appeared mildly surprised.

"I saw you from the terrace." She returned his look squarely. "In fact, I snapped your picture. *La Revue*'s readers are sure to want to see the owner of the chateau taking his leisure."

He chuckled. "Developing my equestrian skills is something more than a leisure time activity I'm afraid. Through the years the Chateau de Laon has been noted for its horses and its riders, and I'm bound to hold up the tradition though I much prefer taking to the air in a balloon than from the back of a horse."

"You compete then?"

He nodded. "But only in the meet held in autumn in Limoges. We always go up for that because in conjunction with it we can spend some time at my farm which is nearby. I have twelve acres of walnuts dropping from the trees in this season."

We, he had said. Who did that mean? Margo? "I've never been to Limoges."

"The city is lovely, but it's the countryside that appeals most to me." He stretched his long legs toward the fire and sighed contentedly. "I love the crisp autumn mornings, heat in midday, and then the cooling off at night that demands a fire." He stared in silence at the flames.

In a moment he spoke again. "The fall rains begin about the same time as the meet, however, and generally we end up rushing out between showers, grabbing a hatful of nuts and rushing in again."

Britt blinked. "You pick them up yourself?"

He laughed. "Of course. It's fun."

"I'm sure it is." Her face colored. "I only thought—"

His disquieting gaze settled on her. "What did you think?"

"I hadn't imagined you'd consider nut gathering worthy of your time."

"It might be interesting to know what else you imagine about me," he replied coldly.

She set down her glass and got up. "One thing I imagine is that you have far more important things to do than to sit here chatting with me."

"If I did—" His tone was even. "I'd be doing them."

Their glances locked, and Britt felt an icy finger of excitement against her spine.

"I invited you in for a drink because I want to know you better. But that won't be possible unless you sit down again and make yourself comfortable until dinnertime."

"It's getting late," she heard herself say, though a part of her longingly pictured the two of them cozily ensconced before the fire while darkness gathered. "I've quite a long walk ahead of me."

He laughed. "What an absurd thing to say."

Her nostrils flared. "I don't see why."

"Because you're not going anywhere for one thing. And even if you were, I certainly wouldn't allow you to strike out alone this late in the day."

She felt a smothering sensation in her chest. "What do you mean, I'm 'not going anywhere'?"

"Just that. I had my man Rene go over to Perpignan with one of the maids and gather up your things at the hotel."

Her lips parted, but he went on before she could speak. "You said you were pressed for time. I thought I'd save you some."

She had all she could do to control her anger. The gall of the man, sending a couple of strangers to pack up her things!

"Well," she said, "if I'm no longer staying at the hotel, where *am* I staying?"

"In Margo's apartment for the next few days," he answered casually. "It's just beyond the library on the second floor. There are rooms I much prefer, but they're in the south wing." His eyes moved over her. "I thought you might be too lonely all by yourself out there."

Britt flushed. Obviously Margo was his mistress. But if he had any thoughts about Britt Ryan filling in for her on a temporary basis—or any other basis, for that matter—he had another think coming! "I doubt if Margo would appreciate my intrusion," she said coldly.

"Margo won't know. She'll be away for at least a week, and by that time the housekeeper assures me some redecorating I'm having done will be finished, and you can move into one of those rooms."

Britt drew herself up. "In a week I'll be gone."

He eyed her lazily. "I doubt that. We agreed, don't forget, that whatever you submit to your magazine has to be top-notch."

"I never intended otherwise," she said haughtily. "I want that job, remember?"

His jaw tightened. "You made that rather plain on the drive out this morning."

She felt her color rising. "I don't think it's at all necessary for me to stay here."

"Do you *mind* staying here?"

"I see no reason to."

"Then I'll give you one." He poured himself another glass of sherry and stood looking at her as if she were a schoolchild in need of stern discipline. "I have an erratic schedule. I never know from one hour to the next where I'll be."

"I'm quite aware of that," she answered drily.

"Then you won't find it difficult to understand that we'll have to work together at my convenience. When I have time for your questions, that's when I'll answer them."

What stunning arrogance! "Maybe I won't have any questions."

He smiled tolerantly. "That's hardly likely, is it?" Then he went on in the same authoritative tone with which he had begun. "I'm busy most days. Probably the only time I'll have free for you will be the evening. I'll want you here, not down the road in Perpignan."

She flushed. Certainly one could read more than one meaning into that!

"And another thing," he went on. "I'll want to go over your work very carefully. I shall be interested in the most minute details you submit to your magazine."

This last drew her up short. "You intend to censor what I write?"

"That's rather a harsh way of describing supervision, isn't it?"

"That depends upon what you mean by supervision."

He set down his glass with a sigh. "You enjoy being difficult, don't you?"

Britt's Irish temper flared. "Really, Monsieur Dolman! There's no pleasing you, is there? One moment I'm fawning and obsequious; the next, I'm difficult!"

He shot her a cool glance. "Perhaps soon you'll be able to strike a happy medium."

I'd much rather strike you! she thought angrily, but managed to control herself enough to say, "I'm sure if we tried, we could work out a time agreeable to us both, and one that would still allow me to go on staying at the hotel."

He gave an exasperated sigh. "What is it about the hotel that you find so attractive? This is the Chateau de Laon." His waving arm encompassed the room. "France's most beautiful, according to you. You have an opportunity to stay in it, Miss Ryan. Why don't you want to?"

"Because," came her haughty reply, "your living arrangements don't fit my style!"

For a moment he appeared stunned. Then a slow smile curved his sensuous lips. "Ah. I see."

"Fine! Then I'll gather my things and head back to Perpignan."

He advanced, dark eyes blazing. "Perhaps you are afraid I'll compromise you if you stay a moment longer under my roof?"

What a devil he was! "There's not the slightest chance of that," she snapped.

"No?" He stood so near she caught the male scent of

him and felt her knees go weak. "Then perhaps it's this you're afraid of."

Before she knew what was happening, he had his arms about her. His head came down. His mouth found hers.

She struggled fiercely, but only for a moment. The searching warmth of his lips, the insistent manner in which his embrace molded her to him set fire to her passions. Independent of logic or prudence, her need for him betrayed her, and she discovered herself returning his kiss, clinging to him with an ardor that appalled her, but which at the same time she hadn't the least inclination to control. The room receded. She lost herself in the taste of his lips, in the hard pressure of his body against her.

Finally they drew apart, staring at one another numbly.

Britt was the first to find her voice, though it came out only a whisper. "That wasn't very professional of me."

He pulled her to him, his strong hand firm at the nape of her neck. "Nor very bright of me," he said thickly. His hot breath curled in her ear, and longing raced again within her.

"You'll probably run like hell now," he murmured hoarsely. His lips moved to her temple, then back to her expectant mouth. "Probably we should both run— but in opposite directions."

The phone jangled loudly on the desk. They sprang apart. It rang again, and Philippe crossed swiftly to answer it.

Britt, still under the spell of his kiss, watched his dark brows come together in a sudden frown, heard his voice sharp with annoyance.

"Margo? Where are you?"

Britt's heart turned over.

Philippe's frown deepened. "But I wasn't expecting you before the middle of next week."

Dazed, Britt put together the rest of the conversation. Margo was coming back to the chateau though Philippe objected. Her arrival, he told her irritably, would interfere with a project he'd just begun.

Me, thought Britt with sickening insight. I'm the project, and naturally it would never do for his mistress to appear just as he was getting it underway! She felt her face catch fire. All she wanted now was to escape . . . to run like hell, as Philippe had said. Oh, if only she had!

She heard him hang up and turned to face him with a nonchalance she was far from feeling. "Is Margo returning?"

He nodded. "Though I don't know why." He was lost in thought for a moment. Then he said vaguely, "You'd better move your things."

It wasn't my idea to put them in her apartment, Britt felt like screaming. Instead she heard herself say mildly, "I hope my room is still available at the hotel."

He gave her an absent-minded look. "I'm sure it is, but we've already settled that question. You're staying here. You can choose whichever apartment in the south wing pleases you."

How handy! she thought bitterly. *Stashed away there, I'll be far enough removed from Margo so that if you're clever enough you can keep both pots boiling at once. It might be worth staying around just to watch you try!*

"I'll make the change after dinner," she said curtly.

"I think you'd better take care of it at once," he replied. "Margo was calling from Perpignan. She's on her way."

Chapter 6

In little more than a quarter of an hour Britt had transferred her meager possessions from Margo's suite of rooms to an elaborate apartment in the isolated south wing and was back again in the study, sitting stiffly in front of the fire with Philippe, awaiting the arrival of Margo.

Philippe glanced at his watch for the third time in as many minutes. "She ought to be here by now."

A cold knot settled in the pit of Britt's stomach. Since Margo's call, he had indicated in no way that he even remembered what the ring of the telephone had interrupted. She cast a sidelong glance at his chiseled profile, recreating in her mind a picture of the two of them in each other's arms. How tender he had been, how right she had felt enclosed in his embrace. And how suddenly it had all ended.

She swallowed. "Does Margo have her own car?"

"What?" Philippe stared at her as if for a moment he had forgotten she was there. "A car? No, not in Perpignan. Velosue, a local taximan, is driving her."

"She'll be along soon then," said Britt, wishing her words could magically produce the opposite effect and spirit Margo back to Nice.

Uneasily she remembered the catlike grace of the blonde, the tawny slanting eyes which had surveyed her coldly on the hotel terrace. There was sure to be a dreadful scene when she discovered the "maid from the meadow" had somehow, in a day's time, entrenched herself in the chateau, and Britt had had enough of scenes for one day.

Was it only this morning, she wondered dizzily, that Philippe had roared with blaring horn through the gates of the chateau, revealing himself as its owner? In the scope of a single day he had wounded her to the quick and sent her passions soaring to the sky.

His voice broke through the silence. "You're certainly solemn."

Why wouldn't I be? she longed to fling back. *I've fallen in love with you, and since Margo's call, you're hardly aware I exist.* Instead she said quietly, "I'm tired. It's been a long day."

"And it isn't over yet."

The bleakness in his tone stirred her numbed hopes. Was it possible he was no more eager for this encounter than she? Possible that what appeared to be impatience to see his mistress was actually dread?

"I've an idea," she said, starting up. "I'm really not hungry. What if I skip dinner and go on up to bed before Margo arrives? That would leave you free to explain in your own time what I'm doing here." She waited a moment. "Wouldn't that be better?"

He hesitated only an instant. "Perhaps it might."

It was the right answer and one she expected, but at the same time she felt as if a door had been shut in her face. "I'll hurry on then."

"Britt—" He got up and came toward her. "It must appear to you that I'm not handling this well."

A coldness squeezed her heart. "You needn't explain. I understand everything."

"How can you when I don't?" He laid his hand on her arm, and she felt an electric thrill sweep through her. "I ought never to have allowed what happened a while ago without first making clear what Margo means to me."

But Britt was sure she already knew what Margo meant to him. "It was only a kiss!" she said harshly. "It's already forgotten."

The effect of her words changed his expression like a whiplash. The softness around his mouth disappeared, and a hard glint came into his eyes. "I see. My mistake."

The coldness of his tone broke through her anger. She was on the point of retracting her words, but suddenly the furnishings of the room sprang out of the shadows. The door from the hallway swung open and light flooded the room. Margo, a willowy column in softest blue cashmere, stood on the other side.

"Well, hello!" Her tawny eyes swept the two of them still standing together. "Am I interrupting something?"

"Certainly not," said Philippe smoothly, moving toward her as she lifted her face for a kiss. "We were just about to give up on you and go in to dinner. What kept you?"

Margo's eyes lingered on his lips. "Velosue's rickety taxi. What else?"

Britt flushed, feeling as if she were part of an audience in a darkened theater waiting for the lovers on the stage to embrace.

But all at once Margo turned to her with a dazzling smile. "Whom have we here, darling?"

"Why, Britt Ryan," said Philippe. "I introduced you last night. On the hotel terrace."

Britt flinched. He might as well have said, she's the girl I picked up, remember?

"Oh, of course." Margo put out a slender hand and smiled. "How are you?"

Then, brushing past, she flung her leather gloves onto the sofa. "I hope Philippe has been showing you the chateau. He's much too selfish with it, you know." Looking from one to the other of them, she seemed completely at ease, not at all the angry feline Britt had expected.

Margo smiled bewitchingly. "The chateau is a treasure house of wonderful things, but Philippe is such an old hermit he likes to keep them all for himself."

Philippe frowned. "You know that's not true."

Margo laughed and turned conspiratorially to Britt. "He despises being told that, so I tell him as often as I can, just to rile him."

Britt managed a weak smile. Margo's words had almost echoed her own smug statement in the car, and she wondered if it were her conscience or Philippe's eyes—which she dared not meet—that seemed to be boring into her.

"Shall we go into dinner?" he said gruffly.

Margo hooked her arm in his and planted a kiss on his cheek. "Oh dear, now I've gone too far, haven't I? Shame on me." She halted and swung back toward Britt.

"But look at us, Philippe. Rushing in ahead of our guest as if she didn't exist." She linked her other arm in Britt's. "Do forgive us. When we're apart, even for a day, it seems like centuries, and once we're together again, I'm afraid we're not aware of anyone except each other."

"I can see that," said Britt stiffly.

"It's so unusual for us to have company," Margo chattered gaily. "Especially female company." She smiled up at Philippe. "It's quite delightful, isn't it, darling?"

Philippe's answer was an unintelligible mumble, and he passed ahead of them into the dining room, pulling out Margo's chair first, then Britt's.

She felt the pressure of his fingertips on her arms as he slid the chair beneath her and despised her faithless heart for pounding so. If, as she had suggested, she had gone up to bed without dinner, would Philippe have thought to remove this third place from the table? And if he hadn't, how would he have explained it to Margo?

Then, listening as he glibly launched into the story of Sydney Fernham and the chair lift, Britt acknowledged bitterly to herself that he would have had no more trouble explaining the extra place than he had had convincing her with only one kiss that he cared for her and no one else.

In her bedroom at last, Britt reflected that the meal she had just endured and the quarter hour's conversation afterward in the study was the longest, most painful ordeal of her life. Not even the endless weeks during which, as a child, she had waited out her father's voyages, had seemed so torturous.

But at least now, she thought, settling between the smooth linen sheets, she had been through the fire. The rest of the week while she finished the assignment should be child's play compared to it. Margo would occupy Philippe, and she could get on with her work, needing only to recall what she had learned at the dinner table in order to banish any wayward longings.

Margo and Philippe were engaged to be married.

She had heard the announcement from Margo's own

lips, and not a word of denial had come from Philippe. True, he had not exhibited a great deal of enthusiasm, but doubtless, Britt thought, her own prejudice had colored her appraisal.

The engagement would be announced publicly the weekend after the equestrian meet at Limoges, and it would be announced in grand style at a costume ball patterned after the account of another held in the chateau during an earlier century.

Margo had uncovered the old manuscript herself in which the details were given, and for months she had been at work consulting with costumers in Paris, artists from the Barbizon area, and musicians from St. Tropez.

Margo had embarked then on the guest list which, it seemed to Britt, would include half the titles of Europe. While his fiancée had elaborated, Philippe had said little, occupying himself with his food and glancing only occasionally from Margo's animated face to Britt's frozen one, fixed in a polite little smile.

She was lucky she supposed, tossing about in the canopied bed, not to have made a bigger fool of herself than she had already done. What if Margo hadn't come back tonight?

Immediately a parade of fantasies began behind her eyelids: Philippe embracing her in the tower, pulling her up behind him on his horse, leaning from the staircase to kiss her.

Stop it! she commanded herself and sat up in bed, grateful for the moonlight which illuminated every feature of the elegant room and brought reality sharply into focus.

She must concentrate on what truth she could find in this situation, not on how badly it hurt.

Philippe, not unlike most of his countrymen—and

men the world over, she supposed—responded positively to an attractive female; and obviously he had found her attractive to some extent or he would not have bothered to phone her in the middle of the night and invite her to drive to Marseilles.

But that action and the resultant scene in the study this afternoon were separate and apart from the mainstream of his life: his plans with Margo.

I was to be only an interim distraction, she thought, swallowing back her tears. Plainly Philippe had decided during Margo's absence to entertain himself with the naive little innocent he'd caught sight of leaning from his balloon and had wasted no time in moving her from her hotel into his lair.

But there her sense of fairness halted her musings. When they had started out this morning for the chateau, Philippe had not even known where they were headed. It was Sydney Fernham he planned eventually to meet at the chateau, not Britt Ryan.

But—she quickly countered—it must have occurred to him while they were quarreling in the morning room that Lady Luck had played directly into his hands; thus his insistence that Britt stay and fulfill Sydney's commitment. He'd have his little fling, and then by the time Margo returned Britt would be gone, and no one would be the wiser except the servants.

Probably everything would have gone like clockwork, too, Britt feared, shame burning her cheeks as she recalled the abandon with which she had kissed him. By the time she returned to Paris she would have been hopelessly under the spell of his charms and spending her time anguishing over why Philippe hadn't called, why he didn't get in touch with her. Finally she would have seen on the society pages the account of the masquerade ball and the subsequent announcement of the forthcoming marriage. Probably then she'd have jumped from the Eiffel Tower!

But Margo had saved the day.

According to what she had disclosed at dinner, the friends she had hoped to meet in Nice had gone on to Rome.

"The place was deadly dull," Margo had announced languidly over dessert. And anyway, why should she stay there when she could be here at the chateau with "her darling Philippe"?

Britt lay down and pulled the sheet to her chin.

Darling Philippe.

How stupid of her to have hoped, even for a moment, that the Fates might have had in store for her a god. With clay feet, she reminded herself, but a god nevertheless. She recalled how Philippe had looked when he approached her in the hall this afternoon, how his lips had seared hers in the study, the way his arms had molded her to his body. . . .

She pushed her wet face down into the pillow. It was business as usual tomorrow, and for a few days longer. Then home to Sydney—as ordinary a person as herself and the only likely candidate for the man in her life if she but had the courage to accept the truth. The career she planned at *La Revue* had no real substance. She recognized it now only as a ploy to tide her over until she was ready to face up to the fact that her life would never be a romantic, love-filled adventure, the beginning of which she had been expecting since she was no more than seventeen and still minding Aunt Tillie's shop.

The facts were that life in the golden autumn of Southern France sparkled with the colors of the rainbow. For Philippe and Margo and others like them, she reflected wistfully, it held all the gloss and glitter of kings and queens.

But for Britt Ryan of 12 Rue de Mont it would always print out on sleazy paper and only in plain black and white.

Chapter 7

Britt rose early the next morning, and after break-fasting alone in a sunny little room filled with potted marguerites and trailing ivy, she went directly to the large reception room beyond the entry hall to begin photographing an impressive collection of Breton antiques.

Her last resolve before falling asleep after hours of tossing had been to stop feeling sorry for herself. Life gave of itself to those who gave of themselves, and withheld from those who grumbled and growled about their lot. She was done with that sort of behavior, she decided. The thing to do was to get her work done here as quickly as possible, arrange an interview or two with Philippe when she was sure Margo would be present as well, and then return to Paris.

At breakfast she had formed a plan for the article she must write to accompany her photographs and had settled on which rooms and objects would best illustrate the grandeur of the chateau.

Now following her planned course, she leaned closer

to a carved curio cabinet and fixed her camera's sights on a delicate porcelain pitcher on a shelf inside. But just as she was ready to snap the shutter, a shadow fell over the pitcher and spoiled the shot.

Whirling in disgust, she found herself face to face with Philippe. His appearance indicated he had slept as poorly as she. Not even his tan could conceal the pallor of his drawn face.

"I have to see you," he said through tight lips.

She lifted her chin saucily. "Well, here I am. Have a look."

He grabbed her arm roughly. "Not here. Come into the study."

She dug her heels into the thick pile of the carpet. "I've seen the study, thank you. There's nothing there I care to photograph."

"We can't talk here."

"That's quite all right. I've nothing to say anyway."

His jaw muscles leaped to ridge his cheeks. "Then you can damn well listen to me." With superior force he pulled her stumbling toward the study and shut the door behind her.

"Sit down."

Her green eyes glared icily. "My, my, another display of your lovely manners."

He took a seat on the sofa and jerked her down beside him. "The first thing I have to know is whether you meant it when you shrugged off as meaningless what happened in this room yesterday."

"You mean Margo's call?" she said with manufactured innocence.

"I mean our kiss!"

"You have your nerve asking me that after all I heard at the dinner table."

His dark eyes sparked with a primitive fire. "You do care. It meant as much to you as it did to me."

Her lip curled. "In other words, nothing."

He jerked her to him. "I want you to promise me something. Promise that you won't close your mind·to anything, not *anything* for the next couple of days."

His nearness made breathing difficult. "What do you mean?"

"I mean that I have to work things out." He took her hands in his. "I can't just throw over everything all at once, but I promise you, if you'll just be patient—"

What was he saying? That there was hope for the two of them after all? Britt's heart began a slow thudding.

"You see," she heard him saying, "Margo didn't come back from Nice because no one was there to entertain her. She came back because she found out you were here."

Britt blinked. "How could she have done that?"

He gave a harsh laugh. "She has her methods, and I'm just beginning to discover the extent to which she'll go to have her way."

"Are you saying the things she said last night aren't true?"

He put his arms about her and spoke against her cheek. "I'm saying they aren't final." His hands moved down to her hips and she subdued a wild urge to lift her lips to his.

"What if Margo should come in now?" she whispered.

"She won't," he murmured hoarsely. "She always sleeps until noon."

A surge of rage swept over Britt. She shoved him back and came off the couch. "You're really too much, do you know that? Playing both ends against the middle and brazen enough to think you'll win!"

He leaped up. "Why are you so angry?"

"Why wouldn't I be? Do you think I'm a complete idiot? How neatly you've worked things out! Day or night one or the other of us—Margo or I—will always be on tap!"

"It isn't like that at all!"

"Margo lives here, doesn't she?"

"Yes, but—"

"You're engaged to her, aren't you?"

"Don't get hung up on that! There's so much more you don't understand."

Britt glared. "Are you engaged to her or not?"

He released a sigh. "Yes. I am."

Britt all but reeled from the simple admission. For a few brief moments when he had had his arms about her, she'd almost believed that Margo had lied and the answer to the question she had finally made herself ask would be no. Her legs threatened to give way, and she caught hold of a high-backed chair to steady herself.

"I think you're despicable." Her voice as well as her legs was trembling, but she went on relentlessly. "You're the worst kind of bounder—using your looks and your money." Her eyes swept over the room. "Using this house to feed your pleasures. I'd pity Margo for the life you'll lead her except that she's asked for it, moving in here with you, and for all her fine ways, living more commonly than any back street girl in Paris."

White-lipped, he regarded her. Finally he said in the same caustic tone he had used to refer to his mother, "And I pity you for your self-righteous bigotry, Britt Ryan. I hoped when I kissed you—" He lifted dark brows. "When *you* kissed *me*—that at least a little of my wickedness rubbed off."

In two strides he crossed the room, and when after a minute she moved unsteadily into the entry hall, he seemed to have vanished into thin air.

Determinedly Britt went back to photographing the

porcelain pitcher, noting the fine edge anger put to the work. Each time the brooding face of Philippe Dolman interposed itself, she clamped her jaws together more firmly and gave her whole attention to making that particular shot the best so far. When this article ran in *La Revue,* she vowed grimly, it had to be the most stunning pictorial essay ever produced. Nothing short of that would satisfy her rage.

But toward noon, her spirits flagged and when she stopped to change film, she set her camera down and leaned wearily against a marble column. Anger was the most exhausting of emotions, she thought dejectedly. Joy put wings on one's feet; love could lift one to the heavens, but fury— She sighed. Fury only made one ill.

Suddenly a cheery voice brought her to attention.

"Ah, there you are. Miss Ryan, isn't it?"

A squat little lady of seventy or so was approaching from the study. "I was assured you were somewhere on the ground floor." She extended her hand. "I'm Martinique LaSalle. I'm sorry I wasn't about to greet you last night." She smiled warmly. "That's one of my duties, you know, but I was away on a short vacation." She drew in the corners of her mouth, changing her smile to a wry grin. "Quite short, in fact."

Britt took the pudgy little hand. "How do you do?"

"Have you had your lunch?" Bright blue eyes snapped. "I suspect not, nor morning coffee either."

Britt laughed. "Do I look so dreadful?"

"Not at all. Only thoroughly exhausted. Photography must be quite a tedious task." She made a clucking sound. "You career girls. I don't know how you do it."

"Neither do I." Britt felt herself relaxing in the company of this sympathetic lady whom she took to be the housekeeper. "I'm not a career girl actually."

"Oh? My error. I understood you came in Mr. Fernham's place for *La Revue.*"

"That's true, but I'm only filling in for my friend. This is not my regular job."

"I see." The round little eyes disappeared into soft folds of flesh. "Then come and rest awhile. We'll lunch together, and you can tell me what you think of the chateau."

Over *coq au vin* and a plate of delectable fruits, Britt spoke of her morning's discoveries and received from Martinique LaSalle some helpful suggestions for focusing the article around the period pieces collected by the Dolman family through the centuries.

"That's a marvelous idea," said Britt, immediately discarding her own plan for the superior one of Madame LaSalle. "You're so familiar with every aspect of the chateau, you must have been with Monseiur Dolman for quite a long time."

The round little face crinkled with delight. "I put on his first diapers. I'm his aunt, dear child. Didn't you know that?"

Britt blinked. "Why, no."

"I suppose I assumed Philippe had spoken of me, or—" Her smiled dimmed, "that Margo had. You did meet Margo?"

Britt nodded.

"Lovely girl," said Madame LaSalle without enthusiasm. "Though somewhat unpredictable."

Britt agreed silently and sipped her wine. The less said about Margo St. Croix the better, she thought. Once away from this place she hoped never to think of her again. "Do you live nearby?" she asked, setting aside her glass.

The woman laughed. "On the second floor, my apartment adjoins Margo's. But the chateau is not my home, actually, Just before his death, my husband and I bought a cottage near the Spanish border, but I'm able only to vacation there from time to time, though I hope one day not too far hence—" She let the words trail away, then picked them up at another point. "I was at the cottage last night, as a matter of fact. I had intended to stay another fortnight, but when Philippe called to say that Margo was returning, of course I had to come back at once."

"I'm afraid I don't understand," said Britt, though with a sinking heart, she was beginning to.

"As I said Margo lives here too, in the apartment adjoining mine. She has ever since she left school. Because we're distantly related and because during Philippe's boyhood I made the chateau my home, I was the natural choice to serve as chaperone."

Britt's lips parted. "You're related to Margo? Then Philippe and Margo are kin."

Martinique laughed. "By no more than half a dozen drops of blood. They're something like sixth cousins, but their fathers were quite close as boys and continued that relationship through their business and social dealings for the remainder of their lives. They died together actually, in an automobile accident near Monte Carlo. Margo was fifteen, in school in Switzerland.

"Her mother had died years before and Henri—Philippe's father—was to be her guardian in the event anything happened to her own father before she came of age. The responsibility fell of course to Philippe."

Britt was aware of making an appropriate remark, but she was too stunned by what Martinique LaSalle had said to know what it was. She could only hear with ringing clarity her own dreadful accusations of the early morning, none of which it appeared now had the slightest basis in truth.

"Naturally it would have been unsuitable for Philippe and Margo to live alone in the chateau, so I was summoned, and I've been here ever since, though I will say—thanks to Margo's penchant for the jet set, as she calls it—she's often away for weeks at a time, and I'm free to go home then. I can't understand why she decided so suddenly to come back last night. Nice is her favorite spot this time of year.

"Of course," the woman babbled on, "since she and Philippe are to be married—" A plump hand came out and covered her mouth. "Oh dear, now I've said more than I've a right to."

"Don't worry," said Britt woodenly. "Margo told me of their engagement herself."

Relief cleared Madame's troubled brow. "Then you know about the ball too?" She sighed contentedly. "It's to be a sumptuous affair. I'm really quite surprised Philippe agreed to it at all."

"What do you mean?"

"He's such a private person, my nephew. Though he values the chateau and everything in it, he considers the place his home, not a showcase." The bright eyes fixed themselves upon Britt. "I'm a little surprised that he's allowed even your article. Or was that Margo's idea too?"

"I hardly think so," said Britt drily.

"Well, I suppose now that he's to be married, it's just as well he's had a change of heart. Margo will never be content unless she's constantly entertaining." The sun left her smile. "Poor Philippe," she murmured. "I wonder if he knows what he's letting himself in for."

Poor Philippe indeed! Britt hid the turmoil of her emotions behind a mask of calm. He could have told her Martinique LaSalle lived here! For the second time he had led her into a trap and let her snare herself with her own words. She had half a mind to pack up her things this moment and get away as fast as she could. It seemed the longer she stayed, the bigger fool she made of herself, though how she could top her angry words to Philippe this morning, she had no idea.

"Margo's coming home so suddenly," Britt heard Madame LaSalle saying, "has spoiled Philippe's surprise for her too."

"Oh?" Britt wished she could terminate this luncheon before she was provided another disturbing insight into Philippe Dolman's life. "What kind of surprise?"

"He's having the apartments in the east wing completely redecorated. He's always preferred the south wing himself, but Margo was so opposed to living there after the wedding—it's so removed from everything, you know—that he finally gave in to her. But she wasn't supposed to know that he had done so until just before the ball. That's why he accompanied her to Majorca for a month before she left for Nice. He thought the two journeys combined would allow ample time to complete the work, but she's such a little snoop—" Madam broke off and smiled apologetically. "I daresay she's on to the entire scheme by now."

So the redecorating was the project he had spoken of, not herself at all. And if he had been in Majorca for so many weeks, it was little wonder Sydney had had difficulty contacting him. She had been mistaken about so many things concerning Philippe that he must think her a terrible fool. "Perhaps Margo hasn't awakened," she said lamely. "I understand she sleeps until noon."

"Ordinarily. But she was up before nine this morning."

Then she could have come into the study, Britt realized with a tremor. How would Philippe have handled that?

"She's out riding with her groom-to-be," said Martinique with a touch of irony.

Britt had a quick picture of Philippe reaching out to

Margo instead of herself, lifting Margo onto his horse. So much for fantasies! And for love at first sight and all the other stupidities in which she had indulged the last few days. A little shudder seized her, and she pushed back from the table. "The lunch was lovely, but I ought to get back to work."

Martinique LaSalle put out a warm hand. "You were wonderful company. It's so refreshing to have a willing ear to chat into. Men are so impatient with women's trivial talk, and Margo—" Madame LaSalle drew herself up resolutely. "Never mind. I've said quite enough about Margo for one day. I'm sure you're already thinking I'm overcritical of my charge."

"Not at all," answered Britt, feeling a bit sorry for the dumpy little woman and for Margo too. Obviously they had quite different views of life and must chafe each other badly. "It won't be long before you'll be relieved of your responsibility and can go back to enjoying your view of the Pyrenees."

The other woman gave her a wistful smile. "I won't deny I'm dreaming of the day."

Chapter 8

Much to her relief, Britt was able for several days to avoid all but mealtime contact with Philippe and Margo. On the day following her luncheon with Martinique LaSalle, the costumers arrived from Paris with finery for the ball. Fittings occupied Margo, and Philippe took advantage of her preoccupation by overseeing the decorators.

The next day the two of them spent both morning and afternoon preparing for the Limoges meet, and on the third day Britt herself found occasion to be absent from the chateau.

She was in need of delivering some of her film to the photographer in Perpignan who had agreed to process it, and when she learned that Martinique was driving into town, asked if she might accompany her.

Martinique was glad to have company and throughout the drive chattered almost constantly on a variety of topics. Britt had already discovered Philippe's aunt to be an invaluable source of information concerning the furnishings of the chateau as well as its history, and she was eager to hear anything which would cut short the inevitable interviews she must conduct with Philippe before the assignment was complete.

But at least he had made no further reference to the daily inquisition he had first planned to submit her to Probably because such meetings were no longer appropriate. Margo had returned, and whatever amorous adventures Philippe had been considering, he had now abandoned.

While Madame LaSalle chattered on, Britt let her own thoughts dwell briefly on Margo. Despite an inclination to dislike the girl, Britt had to admit that Margo seemed to be exerting every effort to be pleasant. Whenever they met, Margo had a ready smile, and though once or twice Britt had wondered at its sincerity, still there was no denying the girl's graciousness.

Why, Britt wondered, did Philippe question her excuse for cutting short her visit in Nice? And what had he meant when he said she had her methods for finding out what went on at the chateau in her absence? Did one of the servants do spy duty? But that was out of the dark ages! Britt glanced across at the woman behind the wheel. Certainly the informant could not be Martinique who seemed barely able to conceal her distaste for her charge.

But if Philippe's suspicions were true and Margo had returned because of Britt's presence, then that fact cast an entirely different light on Margo's motives as well as her behavior. It would appear either that she was skating on thin ice with Philippe and recognized the necessity of constant vigilance, or that she was simply a jealous-natured person. Or— Britt sighed. Perhaps the truth lay somewhere between the two.

"Tired?" said Martinique with a sympathetic smile. "I shouldn't blame you, you've been working so steadily the past few days."

"I want to get finished," said Britt.

"Well, I'm glad you've decided to take this day off at least. Will you be able to find enough to occupy your time until four?"

"Oh yes. Perpignan's a fascinating place. If I run out of things to do, I can always sit by the river."

Martinique pulled up at a corner on the main thoroughfare. "Shall I drop you off here then?"

Britt got out. "Where shall we meet?"

"This same spot?"

Britt nodded in agreement and waved her off.

The photographer, whom Britt sought out first, promised to have her work completed shortly after three, so with nothing special to do until that time, she found herself assuming the relaxed pace of the citizenry and wandering happily through the little shops lining the streets.

In one she purchased a card to send to Sydney, and in another some small native crafts for other friends in Paris. An autumn haze cast a golden glow over everything it touched, and for the first time in days a sense of peace stole over her.

By lunchtime the walk had stimulated an appetite, and Britt stopped at a sidewalk cafe for an omelette and fruit. Then for an hour she was content simply to sit and watch the passing crowds.

Gradually, however, thoughts of Philippe intruded on her tranquil mood. How nice it would be, she reflected wistfully, if she could turn back time to the morning the two of them had started out for the chateau. If only she had behaved differently on that ride!

Yet what real change would it have made if she had? Philippe would still be engaged to Margo. That—not a few careless words in a lemon grove—was the true stumbling block in their relationship.

But what good did it do to look back? There was no way she could alter anything that had happened to her since she came here, and even if she could, did she really want to? Philippe was still as arrogant and rude and caustic at times as he had been the first evening they met. Not at all the kind of person she could envision herself spending a lifetime with.

But on the other hand, she could not deny there was that about him which held an almost overpowering appeal for her. His unexpected moments of gentleness . . . an undercurrent of strength which he kept on a tight leash . . . and—most disturbing of all—the naked yearning he displayed for her whenever they were alone.

Now in the sunlight of the sidewalk, her imagination conjured up again the warm male scent of his skin when he had held her in the study. She felt again the tanned smoothness of his cheek against hers—his hands moving over her body.

She stood up suddenly. What kind of fool was she, to go on reliving a dead dream? The moment she heard of his engagement, she should have put all thoughts of Philippe Dolman out of her mind.

Now she would, she decided with determination.

She would walk over to the hotel terrace, order an ice, and concentrate on the beauty of the afternoon. Soon enough she'd be back in the hustle and bustle of Paris, and she'd be grateful enough then for a lovely memory of this drowsy afternoon in Perpignan. Why mar it with frustration and sad thoughts?

Striding along purposefully, she soon reached the hotel, and settling herself at one of the little tables, set aside her purchases and placed her order with a smiling waiter.

But she had barely begun on her ice when, looking up, she saw to her dismay, a familiar figure approaching the table. *Philippe!*

Her heart came up in her throat. "What are you doing here?"

Without greeting, he pulled out a chair and sat down, eyeing the dish in front of her. "I was famished for a strawberry *granite* the same as you." He flashed a smile at the waiter. "And a glass of Perrier, please. Perrier, Britt?"

"No, thank you," she answered stiffly.

When the waiter had gone, Philippe cleared his throat. "Where have you been?"

"I had some business to attend to. Then I went shopping."

His glance moved over her packages. "I can see that. But I'm more interested in where you've been for the past several days."

"At the chateau, of course. You've seen me."

"Only at mealtimes."

So he'd noticed! "I've been busy. So have you, I believe."

Taking his cue from her, he spoke in a detached manner. "Is your work going well?"

"I should be finished by the middle of next week if the shots I'm having printed today turn out as I hope."

His tanned fingers toyed with a folded napkin. "You sound eager to leave."

"I am rather."

A silence fell over them. The waiter brought Philippe's ice, and they ate to the accompaniment of small metal spoons clinking against the sides of their dishes.

Finally Britt said carefully, "I'd like to apologize to you. I misjudged your relationship with Margo. I spoke rashly and what I said was in poor taste. I hope you'll forgive me."

He leaned back and looked at her. "A proper little speech," he murmured. "Quite properly delivered."

Her cheeks burned. "You're infuriating," she said from between clenched teeth. "Do you know that?"

His gaze held steady. "Yes, I know that."

"You work at it, don't you!"

His smile was caustic. "I don't have to, unfortunately. It's almost a reflex."

"Why did you sit down here? Just to spoil my afternoon?"

"I wanted to see you, and there never seems to be an appropriate time to meet at the chateau."

His voice had lost its bantering note, and for the first time Britt noticed how lustreless his gaze was.

"I'm generally about," she said in a less hostile tone. "You should have mentioned at dinner last night that you wanted a meeting."

He moved his glass of Perrier in a slow circle on the tablecloth. "The kind of meeting I hoped for," he said softly, "I wouldn't care to mention in front of others."

She shoved her dish away. "Really, Philippe!"

At the use of his Christian name, his head came up. In a low, carefully controlled voice he said, "I want to hold you in my arms again. I want to kiss you."

"You're engaged to Margo!"

"Do you think I don't know that?"

"Then what you're saying is indecent!"

"Wanting you the way I do is indecent."

Britt's lungs squeezed shut, and she started up from the table. "I won't sit here and listen to this."

His hand came out and caught her arm, his eyes voicing their own command. "Let me stay this close to you. For a little while at least."

Trembling, she sank back into her chair. "There isn't rhyme or reason for your behavior. In less than a month you're announcing your engagement. If you're not in love with the girl, why are you marrying her?"

"I never considered love when I asked her."

Britt stared. "You can't mean that!"

His strong chin jutted stubbornly. "But I do mean it." His eyes moved over her face. "I'm not even certain I love you."

His bluntness struck her like a blow. She stood up, her chair tumbling backward. "Well, there's certainly no question in *my* mind! I'm quite sure you don't!"

Again he caught her arm, his smoldering gaze still fixed upon her. "But if I don't, then why am I constantly thinking of you?"

"Let go of me, please!"

"Britt—" He got to his feet. "I have to know how you feel about me."

"Why?" she answered in a strangled voice. "Is that part of the challenge?"

His iron grip closed around her wrist. "I don't know what it is. That's what I'm trying to discover before it's too late."

"Before you're married, you mean?" she said bitterly. "Perhaps if you're that much in doubt you'd better call the whole thing off."

"I've considered doing that—and I will if I can be sure what I'm feeling for you has substance, that it's more than some stupid game my ego is playing with yours."

She struggled to free herself. "I haven't any idea what you mean by that."

His grip tightened. "When you kissed me—was that a game? Were you only playing at passion?" Now his eyes were unnaturally bright. "You admire the chateau, I know. And you can't be all that fond of Paris life—"

She broke free with the sheer force of fury. "You think I'd try to win your affections so I could be lady of the manor? So I could move up the social ladder? If so, you're right to worry about ego! Yours is all-consuming, Monsieur Dolman!"

"How can we solve anything, Britt, if you always blow up?"

She glared, white-lipped. "I don't have to solve anything! It's you who are in a quandary."

"I have to know if you care for me."

She gasped. "Do you know what you're saying? You're asking me to tell you that I love you so it'll be worth your time to go off in some corner and try to make up your mind whether you love me! Well, that problem I *can* solve. I don't love you. I don't even *like* you!"

Whirling, she ran blindly down the steps leading to the street. She heard him call her name, aware that the only other couple on the terrace was staring, but she ran on heedless of where her steps were carrying her. Only one thing was important: to get as far away from Philippe Dolman as she possibly could—and as quickly.

Chapter 9

The minute Britt and Martinique arrived back at the chateau, Britt pleaded a headache. Martinique offered an old family remedy, but Britt declined it with a wan smile and begged her friend to make her excuses at dinner. Then she fled to her room.

Flinging herself on the bed, she thought gratefully that at least there was one thing good about being the only occupant of an entire wing. No one could hear her sobs.

All the pent-up anguish of the afternoon spilled onto the down pillows until at last, worn out and hiccoughing, she sat up again. Her dull gaze traveled over the room and fell finally on the packet of photographic prints she had tossed aside without even bothering to look at them.

No matter. Whatever their quality, they would have to do. She was getting out of this place tomorrow, pictorial essay or no. Sydney would simply have to put together what she gave him or toss it into the waste bin, whichever suited him best. She had made a terrible mistake coming here, and every minute she remained served only to compound her misery. If only she could leave tonight! But where could she go? Even Paris was not far enough removed.

She wiped her eyes and hiccoughed again. Why not go to Land's End then? Aunt Tillie was always begging her to come. Wasn't this the perfect time? She'd spend a fortnight or two there and then go up to London to find a job. Certainly she'd had enough of France. The French were too volatile, too unstable.

Philippe was volatile and unstable.

A fresh burst of tears choked her. What was all that nonsense he had spouted this afternoon about calling off the wedding? He hadn't the slightest intention of doing that.

But he had looked so weary, so genuinely baffled. How could a man as certain of himself as Philippe be so indecisive when it came to matters of the heart?

Nevertheless, there had been nothing uncertain about him the first time he had gathered her into his arms. He had known then exactly what he wanted. And yet—

Her breath caught. Hadn't he said—just before Margo rang—that perhaps they both ought to run. *In opposite directions!* So he'd been in doubt even then. He had tried to buy time with her, she remembered slowly. The next morning in the study he had wanted her to promise she would keep an open mind. What was it he had said? *There was nothing final about his plans with Margo.* In essence the same thing he had said this afternoon. He couldn't turn everything over all at once, he had told her, and asked her to be patient.

A bewildering array of sensations swept over her. She'd done nothing he'd asked her to do. Her mind had been closed from the start. She'd been anything but patient!

What if— Her heart began a slow pounding. What if he really were in love with her? But then he would know it, wouldn't he? She knew she was in love with him.

The admission rocked her. After all that had happened, surely her feelings had changed. But gradually she forced herself to acknowledge that they had not. She was still in love with him. Probably she always would be.

Then why hadn't she said so when he asked her this afternoon? What kind of foolish pride was it that always made her say the opposite of what she really felt? Perhaps that was Philippe's affliction too. Neither of them trusted the other enough to expose his own vulnerability.

She lay back on the bed. If only he were here now, she mused, she'd send all his doubts packing quickly enough. Her arms ached to hold him. Desire glowed hotly at her center. But she'd had her chance this afternoon, and she'd turned her back on it. There was little reason to hope she'd ever have another.

Evening fell slowly over the valley. From her window, Britt, freshly showered and wrapped in a thin dressing gown, watched the shadows of the chateau fill up the dales and hollows. She heard the faint call of a loon and the laughter of the servants floating up from the dining room as they cleared away the dishes.

Behind her on the writing desk lay the stack of photographs she had picked up in Perpignan that afternoon. After her bath she had studied them carefully, a warm glow of satisfaction growing in her as she examined each one. They were all excellent. The details of the Breton antiques stood out with superb clarity; the triple archway she had photographed at sunrise yesterday was even more impressive than she'd hoped.

But dearest to her heart were the first two shots she

had taken: the striped balloon suspended delicately before the turrets of the chateau with the blue sky as its background; and—even dearer—the photograph of Philippe on his horse.

Quickly she crossed to the desk. How sharply Sydney's fine lens had lifted Philippe from the distant meadow and captured him floating, like the balloon, over the fence. She brought the picture to her lips. This one she would not share with *La Revue*'s readers, she vowed. It belonged to her alone. No matter how far from this place she wandered in her lifetime, it would always have the power to call her back, even if only in memory.

A soft sound at the door brought her up sharply. A knock? Or was it her imagination?

The sound came again. Probably the maid with a tray of dinner Martinique had offered to send up.

But when the door opened, Philippe stood on the other side.

Catching sight of him, Britt felt her body respond as if he had touched her. She wore nothing beneath the flimsy dressing gown that covered her and was acutely aware that the last of the evening's light was outlining her every curve, but she had no power to move. None even to speak.

He stepped into the room and shut the door. "Your packages," he said quietly and tossed them on the bed. "You left them on the terrace."

She watched him cross toward her as if they were both participants in a dream. Some part of her sang, *he's come! he's here!*, but the rest of her was paralyzed.

Then she heard her name break hoarsely from his throat and found herself in his arms.

He covered her face with kisses, his hands moving over the diaphanous material of her robe, their heat penetrating the filmy barrier, his fingertips curving over the swell of her breasts. His muscled chest pressed hard against her, the taut lines of his body molded hers.

"Philippe," she moaned. "Oh, my darling, darling Philippe."

His embrace tightened, his mouth came down on hers. They swayed together, each discovering in the other's movement fresh starts of passion, new fires that blazed at every nerve's end.

At last, limp and trembling, they pulled apart and sank beside each other on the window seat. He brought her hands to his lips.

"I thought I'd never be finished with that interminable dinner so I could come and find you."

Britt fought her way back to reality. "After this afternoon, I wonder that you wanted to."

He groaned and pulled her to him again. "I had to hold you." His lips moved in her hair. "I had to hear you call me darling."

His skin against her face warmed her like fine wine. "You didn't know I would."

"I did." He gave a low laugh. "No matter what you said when you ran away."

Uneasiness stirred within her. "Perhaps it would have been best if you'd listened."

"I knew you didn't mean it, not when I looked at your face." He traced her cheekbone with a gentle finger. "That high color, those wonderful eyes—seas I've waited all my life to drown in."

"I was furious with you," she murmured.

"But now you're not." He kissed her again. The minutes ticked by on the ormolu clock on the dresser. Finally he released her, his face flushed, his eyes heavy-lidded. "I'd better leave, or I never will." But even as he spoke, he reached for her again.

She pulled away. "There's so much we need to sort out, Philippe." She swallowed. "There's Margo."

"Margo," he muttered. "I'd all but forgotten her."

"You're going to be married to her. You can't have forgotten that."

His eyes glowed darkly. "For the moment I had. You make me forget everything except how much I want you." He started to take her in his arms again, but she evaded him.

"I feel guilty meeting behind Margo's back. She's been friendly to me."

He laughed harshly. "You need to know her better."

She turned a puzzled gaze on him. "You never speak of her with tenderness," she said quietly.

"I never feel any."

"Then how can you plan to spend your life with her?"

A flush rose from his throat. "It's past time for me to marry. I thought she'd make a suitable wife."

Britt recoiled. "And now that you've changed your mind, you'll simply toss her aside?"

His lip curled. "No one ever tosses Margo aside. Tenacity is her strong suit, and once she has her claws in you—" He broke off. "I'll think of some reason to break it off with her. Some arrangement more advantageous to her than marriage to me."

Britt felt as if the blood in her veins had turned to ice. "What would that be?"

He shrugged. "Money—if the amount is large enough. A chateau of her own in a more desirable location." He brought Britt to him. "Don't worry. I can easily handle it though you'll have to be patient. It's bound to take time." His lips found hers, and he murmured against them. "But let's not think of that now. We've managed to steal a time for ourselves. Let's make the most of it."

Britt saw herself yielding to the pressure of his hard body against her own, welcoming his quick fingers loosening her gown—but simultaneously she was aware of another self pulling away, resisting.

"Don't," she said sharply. "We mustn't."

Frowning, Philippe lifted his head. "What's to stop us?"

Her heart hammered. "For one thing, you don't love me."

His sensuous mouth curved upward in a lazy, tantalizing way. "You're thinking of what I said this afternoon."

"Of course I am."

"Don't. Not now." His fingers caressed the back of her neck in a slow, hypnotic fashion. "Love," he murmured. "What is it? Is it the need I have for you, Britt? Is it the yearning that won't let me sleep?" His breath warmed her cheek. "Is it love that drove me here this evening, sick with wanting my arms around you? If that's love," he muttered hoarsely, "I've plenty of it, my darling—and more."

She stiffened in his arms. "It's none of those things."

His embrace tightened. "Then it's not important."

"I think it is."

"If we want each other—and you can't deny we do—" He kissed the hollow of her throat, the valley that divided her breasts. "That's all that matters."

"Not to me." She felt drugged, her legs had turned to water, her loins ached. But she went on resolutely. "I won't settle for less than love."

He seemed to find her remark amusing. "You can't even define it."

His words broke the spell. She pulled away. "It doesn't need defining. Love has a life of its own apart from flesh, apart from all the vagaries of the senses. It's guided by its own light, warmed from its own fires—"

"I'm fire enough for you," he said hoarsely and reached for her.

When she backed away, he flushed angrily. "I can't believe you'd throw away our chance to be together for some foolish emotion that exists only for romantics, for dreamers."

"It exists for me. And persists." Her eyes were bright with unshed tears. "Even while you stand before me and admit it's unreturned."

His brow furrowed. "Britt—"

He took a step toward her, but she whirled away and clutched the edge of the writing desk, her blurred gaze fixed desperately upon his photograph. "I wish you'd go now," she whispered.

"Britt, listen to me."

"Please!"

She stood stiffly, forcing herself to go on staring at the print while every fiber of her being strained after his receding footsteps. When at last she allowed herself to turn, the room had grown dark—and empty.

Chapter 10

Britt rose at daybreak after a sleepless night, dressed quickly and stole down for a last look at the garden's dewy freshness and at the valley below, dappled by the early sun.

What a beautiful place this was! No wonder Philippe had been appalled at her frivolous suggestion that it ought to be taken away from him and given to the French people. Knowing him as she did now, she felt if he were capable of love at all, it was the chateau and everything it stood for to which his heart belonged.

Not that she could blame him entirely, she thought casting a longing look at the craggy walls upon which wisteria almost as old as the stone itself clung tenaciously. There was a strength in this venerable building, an enduring quality which if it ever became a part of one's life would no doubt be as impossible to separate from oneself as breath or blood.

She shivered a little in the fresh morning air. It was good she was leaving. Another day or two and she would have fallen irreversibly under the spell of the place, a circumstance she could ill afford since after today she would share no part of the Chateau de Laon—nor any part of the life of its principal occupant.

With a sigh she turned her thoughts to matters over which she had a little control at least. There were still several areas of the chateau she wanted to photograph—an hour's work at the most. Then she planned to bid goodbye to Martinique and perhaps to Margo too, and be on her way. Just how she would manage to get into the village with her luggage was a problem she had yet to solve, but surely between now and noon someone would be going who would give her a ride.

A cool greeting came suddenly from the direction of the garden room, and turning, Britt saw Margo framed in the doorway. She wore a pale satin robe which clung seductively to her slim lines. Her hair was sleep tossed, her expression sullen.

"You startled me," said Britt with a smile. "I wasn't aware anyone else was up. It's very early for you, isn't it?"

"When one can't sleep," Margo replied curtly, "what point is there in lying in bed? Unless, of course, one isn't alone."

What was *that* supposed to mean? Britt wondered uneasily. And what had come over Margo? Was she always this ill-humored upon arising? "I'm sorry you had a restless night." She almost added that she'd had one as well, but under the other girl's scrutiny, she fell silent.

"Come inside," Margo commanded. "I want to talk to you."

Britt's heart stopped. Of course. This had to concern Philippe. But she had no desire to tangle with Margo over a matter that was already closed. In a few hours she would be gone from here. There was no need for a scene.

"I'm afraid I haven't time," she answered Margo as smoothly as she could. "I've some work to do before the sun gets any higher."

Margo turned on the path. "Damn your work," she said from between clenched teeth. "It doesn't mean a row of pins to me—nor to you either, I suspect—and I'm through with playing cat and mouse."

Britt spoke in a clear voice. "I don't know what you mean. I wasn't aware we'd been playing games."

"Oh, *really!*" Margo sneered.

Britt held on to her composure. "I thought your graciousness was quite sincere."

"I was willing for you to think that when it served my purpose. It no longer does."

"And what is your purpose, if I may ask?"

"I'm sure you don't need to, but if you're bent on carrying on with your naive pose, I'll be pleased to explain it to you."

With the feline quickness that characterized her every move, Margo flung open the door of the garden room and stalked inside.

Britt followed at a careful pace, her mind leaping ahead to anticipate Margo's accusations. Obviously she knew about last night. No doubt that was what had set her off this morning. But what else did she know?

Margo enthroned herself in a high-backed chair before the tea table and plunged immediately into the matter at hand. "Just what is it you have up your sleeve? You can't be silly enough to hope for marriage. Philippe would never demean himself to that extent." Her eyes narrowed. "Is it money? Is he paying you?"

The remark was so unexpected—and so farfetched! Britt almost laughed despite her shock. "You were going to do the explaining, I believe."

"In my own time I will. But first I mean for you to tell me how long you intend to stay here."

Britt caught herself on the point of revealing her plans, but the fat was in the fire now. If she could see how it burned without committing herself, what was the harm? "That depends," she answered mildly. "Why do you ask?"

Margo said without hesitation: "Because now *I'm* making the rules. Point one, for however long you stay you are not to be alone with Philippe. Not at all. Not for any reason.

"Point two," she went on. "Don't think you can meet secretly again. I know he was in your room last night. I know you've met privately with him in the study. And even before I left Nice, I knew you were planning to sleep here."

Britt had had enough. "Hold on! I came here to do an assignment for a magazine. That's *all* I'm here for."

"That might have been your original intention," Margo purred, pleased to have riled her adversary. "But you made the mistake of falling in love with your subject, didn't you?"

Britt flushed. "Are you telling or asking?"

"I don't have to ask!" Margo shot back. "It's written all over your silly face every time you look at Philippe."

Britt's cheeks flamed. "It occurs to me," she countered, "that if you have to spy on your fiancé, your position is terribly insecure."

The remark hit home, but Margo was quick to score a comeback. "Philippe's no saint. Like any other man, he'll take what he can get. It's my business to see it's not offered."

Britt yielded to an irresistible urge to puncture her conceit. "How do you know it hasn't already been?"

Margo bared white teeth. "Because I know Philippe.

When he's on the prowl, he's restless as a tiger, wretched, edgy. He was beside himself when he came down last night." Her hollow laughter filled the little room. "Don't worry. If it had happened, I'd know."

Britt was appalled at herself for allowing Margo to believe she would encourage a sexual conquest, but she had gone too far to back out now. "Knowing is one thing," she taunted. "Doing something about the next time is quite another."

Margo responded like a steel trap set to spring. "You let it happen, and I promise you I'll bring this chateau crashing around Philippe's ears. He'll never recover from the damage I'll do. Make no mistake about that."

Britt felt her blood run cold, but she managed a jaunty reply. "You haven't that kind of power."

"Oh, haven't I?" Margo spat back. "Try me and see."

Shaken, Britt stood up. "You don't frighten me, and I'm sure if Philippe heard you, he'd only laugh, but it doesn't matter anyway. I've finished my work. I'm leaving before noon." She paused, savoring her moment of triumph. "So you see, Margo, you've revealed yourself in all your ugliness without cause. In another few hours I would have gone away from here remembering you as the gracious, lovely mistress-to-be of the Chateau de Laon—not as the cat you really are."

But instead of the spiteful response Britt expected, Margo leaned back with a relaxed, somewhat thoughtful smile. "What a surprise," she said in a buttery tone. "You're so much smarter than I gave you credit for being."

Miffed, Britt could only respond: "I suspect you underestimate most people."

Ignoring the remark, Margo held on to her pleased expression. "I was almost certain you'd stupidly bow your neck and sputter about for a while longer. But for you to capitulate immediately—that's quite amazing. I congratulate you."

Britt caught her breath. "I am not capitulating! My decision to leave was made yesterday afternoon. It has nothing to do with what you've said."

Margo smiled lazily. "Have it your way. You're going. That's all I care about."

Britt had half a mind to change her plans, but even if she bested Margo, there would still be her feelings for Philippe to subdue and that task she had neither the heart nor the strength for.

Holding her tongue, she drew herself up and without a glance at her antagonist, marched from the room, feeling very much the loser in a battle in which the forces against her had been overpowering from the start.

After her haughty exit, Britt found herself too badly shaken to photograph anything and decided instead to pack first and try later for the remaining shots.

But it took less than half an hour to gather her few possessions and make ready for her departure—far too short a time for her to have regained her composure. With a sigh, she set her bags outside the door in the hallway and rang for the houseboy to take them below.

At least one good thing had resulted in her flight from Margo. She had run headlong into the gardener loading his truck with flowers from the chateau gardens. At the sight of the masses of blossoms, Britt remembered that it was Philippe's practice to keep the cathedral in Perpignan supplied with fresh bouquets. She had made arrangements to leave when the truck did at mid-morning.

Consulting her watch, she saw she still had an hour and a half. If she omitted photographing the moat, which really wasn't particularly appealing, she'd have a little time to rest and say her goodbyes to Martinique and still be on hand when the gardener was ready to leave.

She turned toward the window, then halted, astonished by the scene it framed.

Across the way on a knoll, Philippe and a group of estate workers were inflating the red and white balloon.

For a moment the sheer delight of seeing the splendid contraption mended and being made ready to take to the air shut out all other thoughts. Then almost at once she realized that Philippe and Margo—whom she now saw crossing the grass toward him dressed fashionably in a tan and white blazer and pale pleated skirt—were about to set forth on a journey.

Her heart turned over at the sight of them together. Even from this distance, they made a striking pair. With their height and aristocratic bearing they were a regal couple. But it was all a sham. Neither really cared for the other.

Britt turned away, sickened.

But seeing them together had set going the recorder in her brain. Margo's vicious comments replayed themselves. In accompaniment, the tawny eyes, sharp as a leopard's, gleamed with malicious pleasure at the idea of having driven Britt away from the chateau. That was the bitterest medicine of all, particularly since it wasn't true. But if she had gone on trying to convince Margo of that, she'd have come away looking more like a fool than ever.

Still it was some consolation—though a tardy one—to realize that although Margo had pretended to be certain no intimacy had occurred between Britt and Philippe, she was not certain at all. She had given herself away at the very beginning by asking if Philippe were paying her. If she knew so much, she would not have needed to ask what Britt had had up her sleeve.

Despite the rawness left by Margo's insults, Britt found herself smiling. Margo was definitely running scared. And yet—

Britt's heart stood still.

There was something so terrifyingly calculated in the way Margo had said she would bring down the chateau around Philippe unless Britt desisted at once from seeing him. It was Margo herself who had a trick up her sleeve, Britt decided uneasily. But what was it? What could she possibly do that could harm Philippe? With his six-hundred-year-old name, he could hardly be more solidly established if he were the president of France! Probably this was only another bluff. Yes . . . surely it was. . . .

But still the cold thought persisted. What if it weren't?

Then she remembered with a start that none of this was any of her affair. *You're leaving, remember,* she chided herself.

By tomorrow at this time she'd be back in her flat on the Rue de Mont; by next week, on her way to England. Any part she had played in Philippe's life or in Margo's dramatics was over.

It was a little sad though, she thought, stealing another glance at the magnificent balloon bobbing in the morning light, that Philippe was to have no happiness in his marriage. Margo was a despicable witch. He'd never have a moment's true joy with her.

But perhaps Margo was to be pitied too, she countered stubbornly. What kind of husband would Philippe make if he were marrying her only because it was the right time in his life for him to take a wife? He'd admitted he felt nothing for Margo, and even a cat deserved to be stroked now and then!

Britt got up, concluding her ruminations by concocting a panacea: perhaps the truth of the matter was they both deserved each other! Let them fight it out for the rest of their lives if they chose. It didn't matter in the least to her.

Still— She paused on the threshold to look back at the elegant suite she was seeing for the last time. If, as she assured herself, she didn't care what happened to Philippe, why was her heart aching so?

Was she a fool for running away instead of staying and fighting for the only man she'd ever loved? Suppressed desire cracked the protective barrier of her hard won resolutions and flooded her suddenly with an intensity that shook her.

She wanted Philippe body and soul—and she wanted love too. Because it was all or nothing with her, she was settling for nothing. Walking away from the Chateau de Laon with only memories of a few stolen kisses when she might have had so much more if she'd been less proud.

She was denying some of her most basic human needs because of rigidly old-fashioned ideas that had been hammered into her as a girl and because of a foolish romantic notion that love was the only lasting foundation in a relationship between a man and a woman.

But at least one of them was in love. If Philippe were not, did it really matter so much? In the long run what difference would it make if it were only for a little while that the two of them were able to find joy, fulfillment and sexual satisfaction with each other? She was a grown woman now. Aunt Tillie wouldn't be scolding over her shoulder.

She sank weakly in an armchair, her head spinning. Thank God she was leaving. It wasn't only the chateau which had gotten into her bloodstream, but Philippe himself. He had the power, if he were to come through the door at this moment, to take her without a whimper. One kiss and her principles would topple like a row of dominos. Her cheeks burned with shame, but her titillated senses would not allow her to deny that now where Philippe was concerned, she was totally defenseless.

Chapter 11

When Britt entered the garden room where she had been told by a maid she would find Madame LaSalle at coffee, she was surprised to see Margo there as well.

The two of them exchanged brief glances, Margo accompanying hers with a smile. Evidently, Britt thought searingly, Margo had decided to resume her masquerade of friendship, at least in the presence of Martinique.

"Ah, here's Britt now," Margo said gaily to Martinique. "And just in time."

For what, wondered Britt. The chance to see Margo and Philippe, arm in arm ascending in the balloon?

Martinique set down her coffee cup with a clatter, her eyes round as marbles in her pudgy face. "You can't be serious about leaving today, Britt. Why, Philippe told me himself he hoped you could be persuaded to stay on for the ball."

A scowl replaced Margo's smile. "Oh, you know Philippe," she said crossly. "He bends over backward to be hospitable." Then remembering her role, added, "He doesn't understand that Britt's a career woman. She has to be about her work."

"Which is now finished," said Britt, turning to Madame LaSalle. "I thank you for having made my stay so pleasant."

"Oh, my dear, we've all grown so fond of you."

"Yes, indeed," purred Margo. "Quite fond."

Martinique started up suddenly from her chair. "Does Philippe know you're leaving? I think not. I'm quite sure if he did, he'd have mentioned it at breakfast. I'll just send one of the girls—"

"Please don't do that!" Britt said sharply, aware that she was pleasing Margo, but quite unable to do otherwise since just the thought of having to face Philippe had set her heart pounding.

"Perhaps Miss Ryan and Philippe have already said their farewells," said Margo softly.

Britt shot her a level look. "We haven't, but I'm sure you won't mind doing it for me."

"Not at all," Margo replied airily. "If it can wait until I return."

"Margo is on her way to Tours for a week," said Martinique. "And Philippe is off this morning for Lyon in his balloon." She fixed a sad-eyed gaze on Britt. "I'd hoped to enjoy your company in their absence. Now I suppose I might as well go on up to the cottage." She turned to Margo. "Though I hadn't thought of going until you and Philippe and the Rimbauds went to Limoges for the equestrian meet."

Margo spoke irritably. "It doesn't matter to me what

you do. We certainly don't need you at Limoges. As a matter of fact, if anything diverting is going on in Tours I may skip the meet altogether."

Britt, still recovering from her surprise that Margo and Philippe were setting out in different directions, took in this latest bit of information with a startled look which she tried to hide by bending over the coffee pot.

"You're not going?" said Martinique, as baffled as Britt. "But isn't Philippe counting on you for the team events?"

"He'll manage well enough. Or he can drop out of the competition if he can't. He doesn't care a flip for it anyway, and it's all deadly boring, if you ask me. Particularly the days afterward that we always have to spend on that wretched farm."

"Why, I love the farm!" cried Martinique.

"Then you go," said Margo curtly. "And speaking of going—" She turned to Britt. "You may ride with me as far as Tours. Rene is driving."

"No, thank you."

"Oh, but I insist."

Martinique frowned. "If she doesn't choose to, Margo—"

"I have transportation to Perpignan," said Britt.

"With whom?" snapped Margo.

Britt allowed herself a little smile. "The gardener. So you needn't worry."

Margo lifted her chin. "I won't. As long as you're properly taken care of." She paused in the doorway. "It was an interesting experience knowing you. I'll look forward to your article." Her lips curved scornfully. "If it comes out."

"Well!" Martinique stared at Margo's retreating back. "What a strange thing to say. What did she mean, Britt?"

But Britt was unaware that Martinique had even spoken, for just as Margo exited, the door to the garden opened, admitting Philippe.

He wore light tan trousers and a silk shirt that revealed temptingly his heavily muscled torso. In his hand he carried an unopened bottle of champagne, which he lifted now in a mock salute. "Anyone care to wish me a safe landing?" he said lightly, but his dark eyes were solemn as they rested on Britt's flushed face.

"I'm afraid you've missed Margo," said Martinique. "But Britt and I will wish you well, of course." She held up her cheek for a kiss. "Are you leaving soon?"

"I'm waiting on the wind," he replied, "but I suspect I can be off within a quarter of an hour." He turned to Britt, eyeing her neat twill suit and high heels. "Not your usual picture-taking garb, is it?"

"Britt's leaving us," said Martinique. "I wanted to send for you, but—"

"But I knew you were busy," Britt broke in crisply. "I saw the balloon from the window. I'm glad to see it's back in working order."

"So am I." He regarded her calmly, as if, thought Britt, what had passed between them last night was an illusion. "You've never had a close look at the balloon, have you? Why not come now, and I'll show you the gondola."

Blood poured into her cheeks. "Thank you, but I haven't time. I'm just going."

"With the gardener, I believe you said? Then you'll have plenty of time." Philippe took her arm and propelled her to the door. "He's still cutting chrysanthemums."

But I didn't say how I was going, Britt thought numbly. Had the gardener told him? "I wouldn't want to keep him waiting."

"Oh, go along," said Martinique. "You'll enjoy seeing the balloon, my dear. It's quite a spectacle."

As the door closed behind them, Philippe said sternly, "Thought you'd sneak away, did you?"

"I wasn't sneaking!"

"It's customary for guests to say goodbye to the host," he chided, though if Britt had had the courage to look at him, she'd have seen laughter lurking at the corners of his mouth.

"We said everything we needed to last night."

He had no reply for that, and they moved in silence toward the balloon, dancing now against its tethers in the rising wind.

"Come," said Philippe when they had circled the craft. "We've just enough time before the men are ready to release the ropes for you to see the interior. The view from the ground is only one aspect of ballooning. You have to get up into the gondola to get the real feel of the sport."

Britt hesitated. "I'm sure that's true, but—"

Philippe put out his hands to pull her up. "What you will see will make an interesting side note for your article," he insisted.

Despite her distress at being near Philippe again, Britt did very much want to stand in the golden basket. Something childlike within her had responded to the striped balloon dancing on the ends of its ropes, and finally she gave way to her fascination by grasping Philippe's hands and allowing him to haul her up.

It *was* thrilling!

Standing at the basket's rim and looking across at the chateau, she felt excitement explode within her chest, and laughed aloud in sheer delight.

Philippe beside her grinned widely and circled her waist with his arm. She seemed not even to notice so absorbed was she in this new adventure. "This is like something from another age!" she exclaimed.

"It is. Ballooning started here in France in 1783."

Britt clasped her hands together. "It's so thrilling simply to be standing here, I can't imagine how you bear it when you're actually afloat."

"Look behind you here." He turned her gently toward the center of the gondola. "You'll get an idea of what equipment is needed. Better still—" He cleared a spot on a bit of canvas covering the floor. "Sit down a moment and have a look up toward the balloon. That perspective will give you a clearer picture of its size."

She did as he suggested and then watched with interest as first he increased the heat in a hissing little furnace and then tossed a bulky canvas packet over the rim of the gondola.

"What are you doing?"

"We don't need that," he said. "Nor this one either, I think." A second packet followed the first.

"What is that you're tossing out?"

"Ballast," he said cheerfully. "Its absence will make the craft lighter. It's usually jettisoned during ascent."

Britt watched as three more bulky packets went over the side. "Are you overloaded?" she said, puzzled at his actions. "Is that why you're getting rid of some of them?"

"That's it exactly." His eyes sparkled, but Britt was too intent on studying the furnishings of the gondola to notice. "What is that little stove for?"

"It produces the hot air we need."

"Oh, of course. Well, everything seems ready for your take-off." She got to her feet. "If I'm not to be a stowaway I'd better—"

A sharp intake of breath cut off her words. To the left of her astonished gaze the chateau's south turret glided by. On the right the road to Perpignan wound beneath them like a ribbon through the valley. "We're afloat!" she gasped.

Philippe came up beside her. "My! How did that happen?"

"How will we get down?" she cried.

"Oh, don't worry. There's nothing to it really." He gave her a reassuring smile. "But since we're adrift, shouldn't we enjoy the ride?"

She tore her gaze from the fascinating panorama below her. "The gardener's waiting for me," she said distractedly.

"I daresay he's given up on you by now," Philippe murmured. "Look. There are some hikers waving."

Britt leaned over the side of the gondola to wave back. The countryside passing slowly beneath them cast its spell. She was totally enraptured.

Philippe's dark eyes rested tenderly on her flushed face. "Marvelous, isn't it?" he said after a moment.

Britt could only nod. Below them tile roofed houses drifted past. Sheep, like carved figures from a crèche, fed in the meadows. "Everything seems to be moving except us," she breathed, spellbound. "And the silence! It's not at all like being in a plane."

"The wind is our motor. We're moving at the same speed it is so there isn't any sensation of motion."

She turned starry eyes upon him. "Is this the way birds feel?"

He laughed. "I'll ask the next one that goes by."

Abruptly she moved to the other side of the gondola. "Oh, come and look! All the apple trees are upside down!"

Minutes later they floated over a town. Children on their way to school waved their book bags and shrieked joyously.

Britt waved back. "What place is that?"

"Mazamet, perhaps. Yes. There's the cathedral."

His arm came around her as he pointed. Their eyes met. The muscled portion of his upper arm fell solidly against her shoulder. Her heart pumped furiously.

"Shouldn't we be getting back?" she said in a small voice.

His gaze held her. "Do you really want to?"

Dry-mouthed, she nodded.

"But all you've done so far is look at the countryside. You don't even know how the balloon operates. What will you say in your article?"

She moved away from him. "It doesn't have to be a technical account." She could hardly speak her pulse was racing so. "*La Revue*'s readers don't look for scientific explanations."

"For your own information then," he scolded lightly. "Aren't you even curious?"

"Of course. But I already know about the ballast." She glanced around the gondola. "I was wondering, however, why you're not steering."

His white teeth gleamed. "Because I can't," he said disarmingly. "Except for climbing up or floating down, there's little I can do to maneuver the craft."

An incredulous look came over Britt's face. "Are you saying we can't turn around and go back?"

He laughed. "Not exactly."

"What does *that* mean?"

"It means if we really had to go back, I could make the balloon rise by turning up this propane burner which would add hot air to the balloon; or I could release some hot air and we would descend."

"But I don't want to go up or down!" Britt cried. "I want to go backward!"

"In order to do that," he went on patiently, "we would have to find air currents, either above or below us, that happen to be going in that direction."

"Then you'd better get started looking!" she said sharply.

"Must you really go back to Paris today?"

"My work at the chateau is finished."

She saw the slow rise of his chest. "You didn't answer my question."

"Yes! I have to go back to Paris today." If only he wouldn't look at her that way. If only the sky weren't so blue, and Philippe so near—

"Why?"

"You know why." Her eyes glittered with gathering tears. "Do you have to humiliate me every time we're together?"

In a swift movement he had her in his arms. "Humiliate you?" His lips moved against her face. "That's the last thing I want."

"Then don't touch me," she said brokenly. "Don't tease me when I've already told you how I feel."

He lifted her chin, and she saw his eyes filled with the naked longing that was always her undoing. "But I'm not sure how *I* feel," he answered hoarsely. "Shouldn't I have a chance to find out?"

She pulled herself free and fixed her gaze on a winding stream below. Beside it white cows grazed and tiny purple flowers dotted the grass. Floating along in the sky with Philippe beside her was like a dream. They would never be more alone—or further apart.

"Even if I wanted to stay," she said woodenly, "I couldn't. It's dangerous, Philippe."

He caught her to him again, his voice intense. "Dangerous? How could it be?"

"Margo threatened me. Or rather it was you she threatened through me."

"How? When?"

In a carefully controlled voice Britt repeated her

morning's encounter in the garden, omitting only the impression she had left with Margo of intimacy between herself and Philippe.

"She said unless I stopped seeing you, she'd bring the chateau down around your ears."

"There's nothing she can do to harm either of us," scoffed Philippe. "Or the chateau either, unless she's a mind to blow it up with dynamite, and I can't see that, can you?"

"She meant it, Philippe. If you could have heard her—"

"I've listened to her often enough to imagine what a show she put on. I've always excused her spiteful little ways as those of a spoiled child. They never amount to much more than temper tantrums."

"I think you underestimate her. She has someone spying on us."

"Not up here." He pulled her to the rim of the basket and pointed out over the valley where the balloon's shadow skipped along a sandy road. "Up here we're the spies. Look." He laid his cheek against hers. "If we had a pair of binoculars we could even see what that farmer's wife is cooking for lunch."

Britt laughed in spite of her anxiety. "If only all of life were this kind of voyage." She sighed and turned up her face to his. "No tumult, no noise. Just this silent drifting."

His mouth came down on hers, hungry, searching. His arms tightened about her. Her better judgment which demanded that she resist him slipped from her as earth's fetters had done, and she answered his need with her own, pressing her body to him, her heart leaping as she felt the pressure returned. If only they could go on together for the rest of time, she thought dizzily. Weightless, with no responsibilities except to each other, no destination except each other's arms.

Reluctantly Philippe released her. "I do have to get busy now," he murmured with a hoarse note of regret. "Look below."

She leaned out. "The river you mean? Which is it?"

"The Dordogne. That means we're nearly there."

Britt blinked. "Where?"

With a formidable hiss, hot air began escaping from the balloon. "The farm." He worked steadily, in a deft, skilled way. "Follow the river to your left. In a moment you should be able to see the walnut orchard. Then the house beyond it."

"Oh, yes! I see it. And dozens of people crowded in the meadow. They almost look like a welcoming committee."

"In a sense they are. They're the retrieval crew."

Britt turned to stare at him. "But Martinique said you were going to Lyon. Why aren't they waiting there to haul you in instead of here?"

He flashed a smile. "I don't always tell Martinique everything. Besides, what does it matter to her where I go?" He laid his arm across her shoulder. "Or whom I'm with?"

Britt felt a shiver of apprehension. "It matters to Margo."

"Forget Margo, will you?" He gave her a quick kiss. "I want you to enjoy the descent."

As lightly as a butterfly settling on a daisy they floated down into the meadow; whereupon the cheering crowd of men who had followed on the ground the aerial tracks of the balloon fell upon the gondola like a swarm of ants, and before Philippe had popped open the first bottle of champagne and handed Britt an overflowing glass, they had the ropes secure.

Philippe's smoldering gaze found her eyes above the wine glass. "We've landed in our own world now, darling. There are no Margos here, and for a week, no one has to know that we're here either." He lifted his glass. "To our happiness."

A dozen objections crowded Britt's lips, but bringing her glass to his in response, she denied them voice. A week, he had said. All to themselves.

Fate had given her a second chance to be all Philippe desired. What did it matter if afterward she found she'd made a mistake? She had the rest of her life for regrets, but only seven days to share with Philippe.

Chapter 12

Philippe's farmhouse on the banks of the Dordogne was the most charming Britt had ever seen. There was none of the austerity of the chateau, but still its thick plank walls exuded a sense of history and permanence. Topped with apricot tiles—the typical roof of this area of the Dordogne—it clung snugly to the sunny side of a hill. Surrounding it were fields of maize, carefully tended vineyards sloping down to the river and acres of venerable walnut trees.

Within, the main section of the house consisted of a combination hall and sitting room which Philippe referred to as the *séjour;* a small, but pleasant dining area overlooking a meadow speckled with white cows;

and a rambling old farm kitchen Britt fell in love with the moment she saw it. Up the wooden staircase leading from the *séjour* was a cozy bedroom with its own little fireplace, a bath and a tiny sitting room.

The remainder of the dwelling was made up of two angling wings, one containing several bedrooms and baths; the other, a study and game room replete with darts and billiards and on the walls a gleaming array of harness buckles which Philippe announced had been collected by his great-grandfather.

"Oh, it's wonderfully warm and welcoming," said Britt with a deep sigh of satisfaction as they concluded their tour. "But my favorite room is the kitchen." She returned to it and ran her hand lovingly along the gleaming wooden drainboard, polished by countless years of use.

Philippe came up behind her and lifting her hair, kissed the nape of her neck. "I'm glad you like it because you're going to have to do the cooking, I'm afraid."

"Really?" She turned and teasingly traced the cleft in his chin with the tip of one finger. "What would you have done if I hadn't come along?"

"Madame Londine, the overseer's wife, usually provides, but we don't want a third party popping in at the wrong times, do we?" He nuzzled her neck. "I'd rather eat beans from a can and be alone with you."

A mixture of delight and anguish shot through her. She had set herself an alien course in agreeing to remain here. Could she stay true to it?

"There'll be no canned beans, thank you," she said shakily. Removing herself from his arms, she opened a cupboard door. "But the cupboard is bare. I'll have to have provisions."

"Make a list." His eyes traveled over her. "While you're changing into something more comfortable, I'll take it over to the Londines' cottage and someone can fetch what we need from the village."

For the first time, Britt remembered her luggage. "Philippe! My clothes! They're in the gardener's truck. I haven't anything except what I'm wearing."

He gave her a slow smile. "You won't need many clothes."

She felt color rising hotly from her throat. "I'll certainly need something! What am I to do?"

Laughing, he took her in his arms again. "It just so happens one of the crew took your bags out of the gardener's truck while we were with Martinique and loaded them into the gondola. That's why I had to get rid of a little ballast before we could ascend. In fact, you were leaning on the largest of them—covered with canvas, of course—when you were asking about the propane burner."

"What a rascal you are! And so sure of yourself," she pouted. "How did you know I'd agree to your little adventure?"

He chuckled. "You didn't agree, if you remember. You were kidnapped. But short of jumping out of the basket, what choice had you?"

His warm skin against her cheek gave off a tantalizing scent of maleness, and she felt as if everything substantial in her life were giving way to a consuming desire. She took a deep breath to steady herself. "It was pure chance you caught me before I left."

He shook his head. "It was in the stars. Margo made quite a point of coming out to the balloon just to tell me you were leaving. With her, she said, but I doubted that. When I came in to check, I saw your bags in the gardener's truck and sent back for one of the men to fetch them." His lips moved over hers. "After that, the balloon did the rest. I remembered the way you looked up at it from the meadow that very first day. I knew you'd never be able to resist coming aboard if you were given the chance."

"But what happens," she whispered, "when Màrgo's spy notifies her that we're here together?"

"Though Margo doesn't know it," he said, letting go of Britt, "her spy was given the sack this morning."

"What! Who was it?"

"That prissy little minx who served us tea the first morning you came. She must have gone straight away and called Margo in Nice. I'd been puzzling ever since Margo's return just why she came back so abruptly. Then last night when I was leaving you—" He paused, both of them remembering what had happened in Britt's room. "There that girl was, hovering by the door. She had a supper tray for an excuse, but everything fell in place when I thought it over, and this morning I sent her packing."

"Does Margo know?"

"She may by now. I'm sure the little snip went right to the telephone when my man delivered her in Perpignan, but Margo would have left for Tours by then, so the message is probably just catching up with her."

"She'll be furious."

Philippe shrugged. "Let her be. It's I who should be angry. The idea of using a man's own servant to spy on him, particularly if the man is one's own fiancé." Too late he realized that with his mention of Margo and marriage, he had introduced into their hideaway world an unforgivable intrusion.

Britt turned away. "I'd better make my shopping list."

With the groceries from the village, Madame Londine sent over quiche, piping hot from her own oven, and when Britt had tossed a salad from the fresh garden produce she found tucked in the basket of supplies, she was able to lay a tempting supper in the dining area of the *séjour*.

Philippe, who had changed to riding breeches and another of the soft shirts that showed off so well the solid strength of his chest and arms, had laid a fire in the cozy sitting room. When Britt brought in the tray of food, he opened a bottle of Bordeaux, and they sat down to eat.

The strain which his remark about marriage had created, had eased with their settling-in duties, and now Britt felt securely wrapped in an aura of warmth and wholeness.

My cup runs over, she thought, watching the shadows of the fire dancing on Philippe's beloved face.

Catching her eye on him, he leaned back from the table and said with a contented sigh, "Delicious!"

Britt smiled. "Thanks to Madame Londine. Tomorrow I'll cook you something delectable myself." Her green eyes sparkled. "An old Ryan recipe."

"Irish stew, I hope," he said with a twinkle.

She made a face. "How did you guess?"

"What else would one do with potatoes and carrots and celery and parsley?"

"Make chicken pie," she answered laughing. "I'll try the stew on Tuesday."

Together they washed the dishes and tidied up the kitchen. "Let's go for a walk down by the river," Philippe suggested.

Britt agreed quickly, relieved that the encounter she both dreaded and anticipated was to be delayed a while longer. When she came down from upstairs with a sweater, Philippe was standing with his back to the fire, a faraway expression clouding his chiseled features.

"A *sou* for your thoughts," Britt said lightly. "Or should I offer a franc in these days of inflation?"

He smiled a little and took her hand. "I was just thinking how swiftly this day has gone. Our week will be over before we know it."

"Oh, Philippe, don't!" she whispered.

"Never mind," he said quickly. "We'll make the most of it." He slid his arms around her and kissed the hollow of her throat. "After tonight, nothing can separate us."

Britt swallowed. "I hope the weather holds," she said irrelevantly, her pulse throbbing.

"It won't, I'm afraid." On the porch the sharp air bit into their skin and they could feel the moisture it held. "See the circle around the moon?" he said. "That means rain in three days, they say, but I doubt if it will hold off that long."

For an hour they strolled contentedly along the riverside. The valley was so still, Britt felt they were indeed in a world all their own, and her anxieties, which had been alternating with spasms of desire throughout the evening, dimmed in the night's calm silence.

She felt so right with Philippe beside her. She belonged here, and she belonged to him—or she soon would.

Her heart began a painful pounding. She imagined herself drawn close into his arms, his hands upon her body in a way she had never before been touched. Would she know how to react? Would her emotions express themselves naturally, so that Philippe would understand how dearly she loved him? Would he know that even deeper than her physical yearning there lay within her a core of caring far more enduring than passion? Was she capable of sharing that with him, or would she be so caught up in the tumult of the moment she would forget all else except the exquisite desire which racked her each time they kissed?

Philippe's touch startled her. "Ready to go in?"

She took a breath. "Yes."

Once they were in the house, however, Britt, dry-mouthed and trembling, clutched at straws. "Could we sit a while beside the fire?"

Amusement flickered briefly in Philippe's dark eyes. "Whatever you like." He took a seat on the sofa and pulled her gently down beside him. "Happy?" he said quietly when she was nestled against his chest.

She nodded, hearing his heart beating steadily beneath her ear.

"But a little frightened?"

"Not of you," she said quickly. "You mustn't think that."

He touched his lips to her temple. "There's no one here but me," he murmured.

"There's me," she said wistfully.

His low-voiced chuckle sounded in her ear. "You're always so serious," he chided.

And Philippe is not, an inner voice warned. *This is a game to him, one he's played often.* But at once she was penitent. No one could have been more thoughtful and tender than he had been this evening. Or more gentle and loving. She turned in his arms and lifted her face. "Kiss me, Philippe."

A muffled groan escaped him. He gathered her to him, his strong hands moving up her spine, into her hair, while his mouth found hers. Lying back, he pulled her across his body, his hands slipping down over her hips, returning to curl about her shoulder, to cradle her head.

Her inner tension dissolved like a wax candle under the heat of his kiss. A warm pool of passion spread in her loins.

"Britt," Philippe moaned thickly. "My darling, my sweet dear Britt."

All at once he shifted, rose, and swung her up in his arms. She clung to his neck, eyes closed tightly against pinwheels of lust whirling behind their lids. Dimly she heard the creak of the wooden stair, and felt their bodies rising even as her passion soared.

But suddenly her cheek met cool linen sheets and something snapped within her. She found herself struggling with Philippe's taut body poised beside her.

"No, Philippe! No!"

She shoved with all her might, the thrust carrying her own body back across the bed. In an instant she was up, hugging her shoulders, her eyes wide in the moonlight. "I can't. Oh, please understand, but I can't!"

Philippe, dazed, sat up. "My God. What kind of woman are you?"

She hurried around the bed and knelt, her arms clasping his knees. "Forgive me." She wept into the rough cloth of his riding breeches. "I thought only fulfillment mattered. I thought I could."

He pushed her aside. Still huddled beside the bed, she heard the sound of his boots descending the stairs, then the slamming of the front door.

She held her breath. In a moment he would come back. Take her in his arms, patiently, as if she were a child. He would tell her he understood, comfort her.

The chill of the house stole over her. The downstairs filled up with silence that moved relentlessly up the stairs. When it climbed to the bedroom under the eaves, Britt collapsed across the bed in a storm of hysterical weeping.

Chapter 13

Britt woke to the tantalizing aroma of coffee drifting up the staircase from the kitchen below. For a moment she lay still, staring up at the rough-hewn logs in the ceiling while the events of the night before slowly fell into place.

For what seemed like hours, she had lain taut, listening for Philippe's step, starting at every snap and pop of the house as it responded to the evening's lowering temperatures. But he had not returned.

At last she slept. Sometime later she had awakened, chilled, and reaching to pull the feather comforter closer around her shoulders, she thought she heard someone walking on the graveled path that led around the house. She had gotten out of bed then and padded to the window, but there was no one in sight. Thin clouds scudded over the moon, and the Dordogne lay silver in the crooked arm of the valley.

Now it was morning.

She sat up. Was Philippe making breakfast, or had he gone over and roused Madame Londine to come and do it for him? Filled with apprehension for what the day might hold, Britt was preparing to throw back the covers when she heard footsteps on the stairs. Snatching the comforter back to her bosom, she stared at the door.

In a moment she heard a gentle knock. When she called, "Come in," the door swung open and there stood Philippe with a breakfast tray.

"Good morning," he said evenly, nothing in his expression or his voice betraying the slightest emotion.

Her hand went up involuntarily to smooth her sleep-tousled hair. "Good morning."

Crossing to the bedside, he set the tray down on a table. "If you'd rather have tea—" he began.

"No, no!" She wet her lips. "This is fine. Lovely." Her eyes searched his face. "You were kind to bring it to me."

"Take your time with it," he said tonelessly. "There's no hurry to go anywhere. It's raining." He turned then and went out.

The coffee scorched Britt's throat, but she scarcely noticed. Nor was she aware enough of the flaky croissant melting on her tongue to wonder who had baked it or where it had come from.

Philippe had brought her breakfast.

He couldn't be too angry then, could he? Or was that simply the act of a civilized host, something he would have done for any guest, no matter how despicable? She nibbled listlessly at the roll. What had be been referring to when he said there was no hurry about going anywhere? Where did he think they would go? Yesterday he had made a big thing of the fact that they were alone in this isolated spot. Now he was talking about leaving.

Or was it she who was to go?

A coldness clutched her heart. That was it. The next move was up to her, and Philippe meant for it to be toward Paris.

She huddled miserably in the soft folds of the comforter. There was no way she could know the extent of the damage her abrupt refusal of him had caused last night. Certainly he had been furious enough when he left her, but now this— She glanced toward the breakfast tray she had set back on the table. Yes, it *was* a tender gesture, a reconciliatory one. He had had all night to reassess her actions, and he had forgiven her.

A slow rising joy spread in her veins. With light steps she moved across the room to the closet. Rifling through the meager assortment of garments hanging there, she chose a burgundy sweater she knew accented the green of her eyes and the creamy tones of her skin, and to go with it, a soft tweed skirt she had paid double for on Regent Street simply because she couldn't bear not to own it.

Satisfied with her appearance at last, she took the tray from the table and made her way carefully down the stairs to the kitchen.

Philippe was sitting at the round wooden table in its center staring into a cup of coffee, but at her step he looked up sharply. No smile of greeting changed his solemn expression.

Britt took a breath. "That was a smashing breakfast," she said with forced cheerfulness. "You must have risen early to make it."

"I didn't go to bed," he answered quietly.

"Oh?" She turned from the drainboard, her heart in her throat. "I'm sorry to hear that."

"Since I was up anyway, I walked to the village baker's and got there just as the croissants were coming out of the oven."

"But that's quite a long way, isn't it?" she said timidly.

"Three or four kilometers." He got up and took his coffee cup to the sink.

"Philippe— I'm sorry."

He made a sound that wasn't quite a laugh. "It doesn't matter."

"I think it does."

Suddenly his eyes blazed. "You're a bit late worrying about it."

"I didn't say I was worried." She struggled to control the quick anger his condescension had ignited. "I said I was sorry."

"Shall we go upstairs to bed then?" he said in a brittle tone.

"Certainly not! You're a beast even to suggest such a thing after what happened."

"Then why did you bring it up?"

"Oh, really! You're impossible. One can't even apologize without being the victim of your testiness."

"You've had your part in contributing to that."

"I said I was sorry!"

His sigh exploded in the quiet room. "Forget it, will you? It's wretched enough wondering how we're to get through this damned day without our raking up all of that again."

She drew herself up. "You can do as you please. I'm leaving, of course."

He regarded her with an indulgent smile. "And how do you think you're going to manage that?"

"The village is only three or four kilometers, you said. I walked further than that to get to the chateau from Perpignan."

"What do you plan to do in the village?"

"Catch a bus. I was on my way to Paris, you know," she added haughtily.

"The last time a bus came through Vincome it was

carrying Spanish refugees from the civil war. Contrary to what you must believe, in the provinces all roads *don't* lead to Paris."

Britt absorbed this morsel of information with mixed feelings. If, after all, she couldn't leave today, then she might find a way to make her peace with Philippe. Even if everything were over between them, it was important to make him understand she had not purposely teased him to the height of passion only to turn him away. But in his present mood he would listen to nothing. Perhaps then his worry that the day might be a long one was legitimate. And what about tomorrow? And tomorrow and tomorrow?

"What do you suggest I do?" she said. "Obviously I can't stay here the rest of the week. If you'd put your mind to it, I'm sure you could come up with an idea."

"If it weren't Sunday, I might," he said sullenly.

"Oh." Now she saw the problem. Tradesmen or farmers who might be going beyond the village toward Paris or toward some larger town with public transportation would not be traveling today. She looked about her with a sudden feeling of desperation.

For the next twenty-four hours they were trapped here.

"Well, since it won't be Monday for a terribly long time," she said with a briskness she was far from feeling, "I'll start helping the day pass by tidying up the kitchen." She pushed up the sleeves of her burgundy sweater. "Then afterward, I'll put on the stew, and if it's stopped raining by then, maybe we could go out and gather a few walnuts."

He looked at her with amazement.

"Well?" She glared back. "I'm certainly not going to sit around all day and watch you sulk. I'd rather scrub the floors."

Suddenly he burst out laughing.

It was Britt's turn to look amazed. "I don't see what's so funny."

"You wouldn't." He went on chuckling as he picked up a dish towel. "You never laugh at anything."

"That isn't true!"

"When have you laughed?" he challenged.

"Why—yesterday!" She gave him a triumphant look. "I distinctly remember laughing in the balloon—several times! And once or twice after that, I think." She frowned. "Let me see—"

All at once they were both laughing. With hot water to her elbows Britt washed the china cups and saucers and scalded the coffee pot. Then while Philippe watched in wide-eyed astonishment, she scoured the sink with a foul smelling powder she found beneath it, and whipped out the chopping board and set to work with a vengeance on the carrots and potatoes.

When the stew was bubbling on the stove and its mouth-watering aroma filling the downstairs rooms, she whisked upstairs and made her bed and straightened her room.

When she came down again, cheeks flushed, Philippe was reading contentedly by the fire while rain dripped steadily from the eaves.

"I thought this was chicken pie day," he said without looking up.

Her hand flew to her mouth. "The chicken! I completely forgot about it. And it won't keep." She wheeled around toward the kitchen. "I'd better set it to boil at least."

His calm voice stopped her. "I've already done it."

She whirled. "You? I didn't know you could even poach an egg."

"I'm quite a good cook," he said indignantly. "Have you already forgotten who served you breakfast?"

She crossed the room slowly and sat down in the

chair opposite him. In a soft voice she said: "You're very nice, you know."

He answered gruffly. "I'm glad you like me."

"I love you."

His startled eyes fixed luminously upon her. "Then why that god-awful fracas we had last night?" he murmured.

"Because I care too much," she said. "About everything. You, me. Tomorrow."

He leaned forward and took her hands in his as he had done on the hotel terrace the evening they met and traced her lifeline across one palm. "It says here tomorrow will take care of itself."

"But not if one spoils it with foolishness today," she whispered.

He kept his eyes on her hand. "What I wanted to share with you I wouldn't call foolishness."

"In the right context neither would I. I realize for some people last night would have been the right context. But not for me." Her voice dropped. "I didn't know that until it was almost too late."

He was quiet for a moment. "I think you did know it."

Her eyes flew to his.

"But you tried to push it out of your mind to please me. And *I* knew that." He paused. "And took advantage of it."

They stared across the space between them.

"So what shall we do now?" he challenged.

A smile began at the corners of her mouth. "Well," she answered in a small voice tinged with mischief. "We could always put on our rain slickers and gather walnuts."

Chapter 14

The morning passed so swiftly neither Britt nor Philippe would have believed it was noon when they came in from the orchard had it not been for their stomachs demanding to be fed.

The stew had simmered to a fine rich broth and the little chunks of succulent beef bobbing about in it melted in their mouths. Crusty croissants left over from breakfast and glasses of white wine, followed by a plate of black and white grapes Britt had discovered growing in a tangle at the edge of the orchard, completed the satisfying meal.

"Go and have yourself a nap, why don't you?" suggested Britt when she saw Philippe fighting back the third yawn.

It was plain the idea held enormous appeal for him, but he hesitated. "What will you do?"

"Oh, don't worry about me. I'll tidy up here." She stacked plates and bowls. "Then I'll read or take a walk if the sun comes out." She smiled. "I'll be perfectly content."

Still he hesitated. "You're certain?"

"Of course. Why wouldn't I be in such a lovely place?"

"*I* always am," he agreed, "but—"

"But Margo isn't?" she finished for him.

"She hates it here. If we aren't playing backgammon or shooting billiards-or planning for guests to come or drinking with those who are already here, she all but climbs the walls. I can't imagine her sitting down with a book or going for a stroll on her own."

Britt picked up the dishes. "We're quite different, Margo and I," she answered lightly.

"You are indeed," he murmured. He set a foot on the stairs, glanced up toward the bedroom where Britt had slept, and then turned abruptly and strode off toward the wing that contained the other bedrooms he had shown her yesterday.

She stood still, the dishes in her hands, until she heard the door of one of the rooms close. After their talk earlier, nothing further had been said about what had happened last night—nor about tonight. Philippe's choosing a separate room for himself was the first indication Britt had had that the evening to come might pass without unpleasantness. But already she had felt a new understanding growing between them as they had wandered in the orchard, filling a basket with nuts and taking shelter once in a sweet smelling hay shed when a deluge descended.

There Philippe had talked a bit about his childhood at the chateau where Martinique had assumed the maternal role after his mother's departure; and Britt told him what it was like to tend a tea shop when one could barely see over the counter.

She had found it easy to laugh in that relaxed atmosphere, and had noted what pleasure her gayer spirits seemed to bring to Philippe. It was obvious the farm meant a great deal to him and that when he was here some of the pressures of upholding family traditions at the chateau were lessened.

After the dishes had been put away, she curled up in a window seat and tried for awhile to read from an old history of the area she had discovered in one of the bookcases, but her eyes kept straying out to the cows grazing under the walnut trees and to the yellow poplars shimmering in the sun which had just come out.

Finally she laid the book aside, and emptying the walnuts from one of the baskets into a burlap bag she found in a cupboard, went outside to gather for the evening meal some of the swollen fruit from a fig tree by the kitchen door.

A pearl gray cat with half a dozen kittens trailing after it soon came to wind its tail about her legs. Setting the fruitfilled basket aside, she settled herself on the kitchen steps and watched with serene amusement the kittens pouncing on the fig leaf she dragged along through the dirt before them.

Half an hour later Philippe discovered her there.

"Did you have a pleasant sleep?" she inquired lazily, feeling herself as relaxed as the kitten stretched in her lap.

He sat down beside her. "I feel I could take on the world. What would you like to do?"

She leaned back on her elbows. "Nothing in particular. Except—" She set her head to one side. "I noticed a little punt down by the river this morning. Could we have a ride in it?"

"I'd like that. How good are you with a pole?"

She smiled up at him. "Fishing, or otherwise?"

He laughed. "Propelling the boat is what I had in mind, but since you've mentioned it, why shouldn't we try our hand at pulling a few fish out of the water? Trout amandine for dinner? How would you like that?"

"With you as the cook? I'd love it!"

In all, they hooked four fine fish, which Philippe, under the watchful eyes of the cat and her kittens, cleaned by the back door just before fresh showers began. Humming, he set about cooking them while Britt had a bath and changed into a long green dressing gown that matched her eyes and looked, she assured herself after careful scrutiny in the mirror, enough like a lounge dress to avoid suggestiveness. Not for the world would she want Philippe to think that anything about her tonight was intentionally seductive.

However, when she started down the stairs, he was emerging from the kitchen and from the sensuous manner in which his eyes moved over her, she knew despite her care, she had failed.

She halted, her hand on the railing. "I was just coming down to look for a match before I dress," she said quickly. "It's rather chilly upstairs, and I thought I'd get a fire going."

"No need to change." His gaze settled on the open collar of the gown. "We're in the country, after all and not expecting anyone. Besides, if you come along just as you are, we'll have enough time for a drink before dinner's ready."

Reluctantly she came down the rest of the way, apprehension chilling the pleasant warmth left over from the day's activities. But Philippe seemed not to notice her hesitation and when she had seated herself at one end of the sofa, instead of sitting down beside her, he took a chair at the opposite end of the fire.

"I had a lovely day," she said quietly when he had handed her a drink and settled himself with one of his own.

He stared into the flames. "I imagine," he answered in a tone matching hers, "that's your subtle way of telling me you hope the evening goes as well."

She swallowed. "I'm sure it will."

He gave her a keen-eyed glance and took a sip of his drink. "I enjoyed the day, too," he said in a lighter vein. "You're a fine companion."

Her cheeks warmed. "If a bit cruel at times," she murmured. "Am I forgiven?"

A muscle rippled across his jaw. "If I say yes, it doesn't mean I want you any less."

"I can't do anything about that."

When he said nothing, she went on. "I realize now that some of my earlier responses to you were misleading." She stared down at the glass in her hand. "I gave you the wrong impression and you decided to bring me here. Then I disappointed you. Or perhaps disgusted you is a better way of saying it. But in spite of all that, Philippe, and in spite of the clumsy way I handled things last night, you've shown me a pleasant time." She lifted eyes bright with tears. "You've shared your haunts with me and made me feel—" She shook her head helplessly. "—cherished."

"Because that's what you are." His voice throbbed with controlled emotion. "Cherished." The word on his lips took on a magical quality that set her heart racing.

"You're quite a woman," he went on in the same hoarse tone. "Not the saucy little girl I first imagined you to be."

"You were attracted to that girl," Britt said in a small voice.

"Like a moth to a flame," he agreed. "I expected to get singed." His dark eyes glowed in the firelight. "But the burn turned out to be fatal."

A smart reply that might have lightened the moment eluded Britt, and the tenderness she felt she dared not voice.

"Last night," he went on, "I thought all manner of

horrible things about you. Then this morning when I watched you setting our lives in order for the day, making do with this sullen, brutish lout you were trapped with in the country—"

"Don't, Philippe—!"

"The pieces began to fall in place," he continued, undeterred by her objection. "I began to recognize you, Britt Ryan, for the person you are." He set down his glass. "Are you ready for this?"

She stopped breathing.

"I think I'm in love with you."

Her lips parted.

"Love," he repeated softly. "That's the name of your game, isn't it?"

She found her voice. "I play for keeps," she whispered.

He gave a low laugh. "Don't I know it!"

He covered the space between them and took her in his arms. For one terrible moment she wondered at his sincerity. Was this just another ploy? If he said he loved her, did he think then she would come willingly to him?

But in another instant, all doubts vanished in recognition of the new way he held her. There was tautness still in his lean lines, and searching in the warm firmness of his lips, but the feverish urgency of last night's embrace was missing.

The man who held her now had made time in his heart for the slow ripening of love based on understanding, on caring. . . .

He cherished her.

Britt's heart sang, and she nestled joyfully into his arms.

Suddenly the door of the *séjour* burst open, admitting a blast of cold air mixed with rain and wind. A harsh voice rang out in the room. "How very cozy!"

Britt and Philippe sprang apart.

"Margo!" Philippe glared. "Didn't anyone ever mention that it's rude not to knock?"

The blond girl swept into the room, her tawny eyes ablaze. "This is the home of my fiancé. All doors should be open to me."

"And obviously you think they should stay open," he muttered, brushing past her to close out the wind and the rain.

Margo turned her blazing eyes on Britt. "What a slimy trick! Waiting until I left, then sneaking off up here with Philippe."

"No slimier," Philippe said drily, "than hiring spies. There was more than one, wasn't there?"

She flashed an angry look at him. "From appearances here, I should have hired an army." She turned again to Britt. "I warned you, you stupid fool. Too bad you didn't have the sense to listen to me as you pretended."

"I wasn't pretending. That was your idea."

"Take off your coat," Philippe commanded Margo. "There's a great deal we need to talk about."

She plopped herself by the fire and threw her damp wrap on a chair. "On that much at least we can agree."

"But any discussion will have to wait until after dinner," he said calmly. "I've trout amandine ready for the table, so dismiss your driver or whoever brought you out here and let's sit down to it."

"I drove myself," she replied haughtily.

All the better, thought Britt. The prospect of sharing dinner with Margo was dreadful enough without having to consider that she might be spending the night as well.

The meal went smoothly. Anger, it seemed, served as a stimulant to Margo's appetite. While Britt only picked at her fish, Margo had two servings and was even gracious enough to compliment the chef as they left the table.

"I shall miss those impromptu Sunday night suppers you used to fix for us on cook's night off," she said to Philippe when they had gone again to sit in the *séjour*.

Britt's heart leaped, and she cast a swift glance at Philippe who seemed as surprised as she at Margo's use of the past tense. Was she giving up then, without a fight?

"And you," said Margo leveling a hard look at Philippe, "will miss the chateau, no doubt."

He uncoiled like a spring from the sofa. "Miss it? What are you talking about?"

"Our future, Philippe." She turned a cold gaze on Britt. "Or are we to have separate futures now that she's come into the picture?"

Before he could reply, she said, "Are you going to marry me or not?"

Her bluntness threw Philippe. To Britt, time seemed to stop while he searched for an answer. "That's one of the things we must discuss," he said finally.

A smile more like a sneer lifted Margo's lips. "Then you haven't really decided, have you, whether or not your little Cornish fishergirl is worth throwing me over for?" Her scornful gaze swept Britt. "Surprised?" she said archly.

In truth, Britt *was* surprised. Shocked, actually. The moments after Philippe had declared himself to be in love with her had been too brief for any talk of marriage, but Britt realized now that subconsciously she had translated his words into a proposal. But Philippe had hesitated too long over Margo's question to have reached the same conclusion himself. The nucleus of joy that had sustained her through the strained meal hardened now into a lump of fear in the pit of her stomach. She was the outsider here, not Margo, and she wished with all her heart she were anywhere else in the world.

"What did you mean about the chateau?" Philippe persisted.

Margo found a cigarette in her expensive handbag, and waited while Philippe lifted a candle flame to its tip. Through the whirling smoke she exhaled she sent him a heavy-lidded stare. "Whether you continue to own it or not is your choice entirely."

"There's no question of that," he snapped.

Her lips curved upward. "Would you cling to it at the cost of the family name?"

"What kind of nonsense is this?" he exclaimed.

"It's a bargain, Philippe."

"Then state your terms," he said loftily, his eyes cold.

"These are your choices. Either you announce our engagement at the masquerade ball as planned and marry me in December, or you deed me the chateau."

Philippe's face relaxed. "Choices!" He laughed. "Your side is rather heavily favored, I'd say."

Her gaze hardened. "Not when you consider the other alternative."

"What might that be?" he said with a smile.

"If you refuse to marry me or to deed me the chateau, I'm prepared to go to the Paris press with a story about you that will knock their ears off."

Britt spoke for the first time. "Do you mean *La Revue?*" She almost laughed. "Do you think they'd care what you said about Philippe and me? I'm not even employed there!"

Margo's malicious laughter sounded discordant in the cozy *séjour*. "That doesn't surprise me at all. I never believed your ridiculous pretense of photographing and interviewing. You came to Chateau de Laon to snare Philippe Dolman, and when you failed there, you transferred your shabby little tryst to the countryside. But it isn't going to work here either." Her tawny eyes flicked back to Philippe. "Unless you're fool enough to want it to."

"I've never sought the social spotlight as you have, Margo." Philippe's contemptuous tone came as a shock to Britt. Even in their worst disagreements, he had never spoken in such a way to her. "The Paris column or scandal sheets, or whatever you have in mind, can say what they want of me. I couldn't care less."

Margo's eyes narrowed. "Philippe." Her voice held a deadly note. "I am not speaking of common ordinary bedroom antics. I'm talking about decadence."

He frowned. *"Decadence?"*

The blond girl crushed out her cigarette and rose. "Let me make this quite plain. I intend to live the rest of my life in the Chateau de Laon." Her gaze bored into the perplexity filling Philippe's dark eyes. "I can live there with you, Philippe. Or without you. But make no mistake about this: I have the weapon to make the chateau mine, and if you force me to, I'll use it."

Philippe recovered himself as she reached the door. "You're still the silly schoolgirl you were at fifteen," he scoffed. "The queen of the dramatics society. When you're able to carry on a mature conversation, I'll expect to hear from you."

"Oh, you'll hear." Margo's voice was low and throaty and pregnant with vague threats so ominous that a shiver of dread rippled up Britt's spine. "I'll be in Tours until the end of the week. Where I go from there depends on whether you come to fetch me home." She opened the door. "Or whether my lawyer comes to fetch you to court."

"Philippe?" Britt's voice broke the silence that had

shrouded them ever since the door closed behind Margo. "What is she going to do?"

"Nothing probably. She's bluffing. Blackmail is second nature to spoiled, selfish people like her. She's had her way about everything all her life. The possibility that we might not marry is something she can't handle any other way than with empty threats and histrionics."

Britt stared at him. The *possibility* that they might not marry. She clung to the back of a chair. "She cares a great deal for you," she heard herself say.

"She doesn't care a pin for me!" Philippe snorted. "Nor I for her. Whatever else there is between us, caring isn't part of it."

"And yet you're still considering marriage to her."

He crossed swiftly and took her in his arms. "I know this is difficult for you to understand, darling. Arranged marriages, marriages for convenience or property or to maintain bloodlines aren't a part of your background."

That brief statement delivered with such assurance did more to crystallize Britt's feeling of being an outsider than all of Margo's venomous outpourings. She stiffened. "You're quite right, of course."

Immediately he sensed her coolness. "Such things are as foreign to you as your idea of love as a foundation for marriage was to me."

He tightened his hold on her. "I never expected to care deeply for any woman, Britt. I never pictured myself as a man enslaved by any emotion and certainly not by love."

Abruptly he released her and jamming his hands into his pockets, turned toward the fire. "Above all else, I've treasured my right to come and go as I please, to set the tempo of my life as I alone saw fit."

"Do you think love will preclude those things?" she said softly.

He turned back to her. "It already has."

She stared at him. "And you don't like it?"

His chin jutted stubbornly. "No."

Now it was she who turned away. "I see." She took a wavering breath. "Then you've no problem, have you? If you go ahead with your plans to marry Margo, you won't sacrifice anything that's important to you."

"She's threatened me!" he exclaimed angrily. "I could never give in to that."

Britt felt an enormous weight pressing down upon her, compacting her into some minuscule version of herself she'd never recognize again. Philippe was rejecting her and seemed not even aware of doing so. The precious moment of confession which Margo had interrupted would never come again, and the stony truth of that was unbearable.

"I'm tired," she said without looking at him. "I'm going up to bed."

"Yes, go on," he said indifferently. "Where did I lay my slicker, do you know? I need a walk in the fresh air."

"I hung it in the cupboard by the back door," she replied.

"Good night then."

Chapter 15

When Britt came down the next morning after a long night of fitful sleep, she found the dinner dishes still on the table in the dining room, Margo's crushed out cigarette emitting a foul smell from the ashtray in the *séjour,* and Philippe sound asleep in his clothes on the sofa.

Fearful that she might wake him, she let her eyes touch only briefly the thick lashes that swept his cheek, the stubborn chin, the full, sensuous mouth, just the sight of which was enough to set her trembling.

Shutting the door softly, she went about tidying up the kitchen clutter and the dishes she had brought in with her. She had lived here almost as a wife, she reflected. Cooking, cleaning, gathering produce from the farm. A farm wife. She leaned against the wooden drainboard and closed her eyes. What if Philippe had been a farmer instead of a prominent landowner whose family dated back hundreds of years? What if instead of the chateau, he had owned only this walnut orchard, the white cows grazing in the meadow, the gray cat and her kittens?

Tears trickled down her cheeks. *I would have*

131

churned in this kitchen, she though sadly, *and fed my babies here, all of whom would have had strong chins and long black lashes that swept their cheeks when they slept.*

"Britt—"

She whirled, dabbing hastily at her damp face. "Philippe. Did I wake you?"

Still half asleep, he stared at her, his hair tousled, his eyes heavy-lidded. Longing so fierce it all but made her cry out racked her. She would never sleep beside him, never wake in the morning to kiss his mouth, curving now in a drowsy smile.

He crossed and put his arms around her, his hand pressing her head against his chest. "You're so industrious," he murmured. "Up at the crack of dawn, off to do the milking."

His lightheartedness was more painful than anger would have been, she was ashamed to realize. It meant that the yearning and anguish she had battled with through the long night were not shared by him. The sweetness that had passed between them was already forgotten.

But in a moment she knew how wrong she was.

As if he had taken her into his arms only to lead her back with him into the dream world from which he had come, he moved his lips on hers. Their searching into the warm softness of her own mouth spoke to her in a language that needed no words of reassurance. The hands that slid down her hips, then up across her back were reaffirming that she was his. They took the shape and measure of her in a way that said far more of what she meant to him than syllables and sentences ever could have done.

The embrace shook her as nothing had since she had come to love him. The passion in his kiss, so controlled, yet so promise-filled made contact with the deepest

core of her being. What they were sharing now, she
realized dizzily, made a mockery of the torrid conflicts
that had torn them apart before. This was truth. This
was love.

After a time he released her slowly and led her to a
sunny corner of the kitchen.

"I spent half the night thinking," he said when they
were seated beside each other, her hand in his, their
eyes still filled with the magic of the world that had just
opened before them. "I'm going to Tours this morning."

Britt reeled from the impact of his words.

But before she could speak, he went on. "I think you
were right to be worried about Margo's threat. Whatever she has in mind to do —providing I refuse to heel
to her—is sinister. I'm so accustomed to her dramatics I
couldn't see that last night, but you sensed it, and I
have to find out what it is."

Britt had lost her bearings completely. In his arms
she had known with complete assurance that he was
hers alone, and within a minute he had shattered her
strongest confidence. He was going to Margo. Was
there any place in the world she herself could go to
escape the desolation suffocating her now?

As if reading her mind, he said, "I want you to stay
here—if you think you can, all alone, and wait for me."

Britt tried to comprehend what he was saying. Wait
for him? "What for?" she said woodenly.

"Because you're a part of me now," he said. "Just
now—didn't you feel it? Didn't you know it?"

She caught her breath sharply. "Yes! Oh, yes—yes!"

He smiled. "Then you know nothing in the world can
separate us."

She couldn't stop herself. "Then why go to Margo?
Stay with me, Philippe! Can't we forget we ever knew
Margo?"

"She's too entangled in my life to do that," he said gently. "I'm her guardian. She's lived in my home for years, I've handled her estate, advised her financially—"

"Of course. I understand," Britt murmured. "But oh, I wish—!"

"So do I, darling." He brought her hands to his lips. "But this is a problem we have to work out. I have to find out what she plans to do and then convince her that no matter what it is, she can't win. She and I will never be married."

Britt felt as if the sun had suddenly risen inside her. "You're not going to marry her? You're certain?"

He laughed. "Of course. Didn't you know that last night?"

Britt blinked. "You thought I knew?"

He gave her a puzzled smile. "I'd already told you I loved you before Margo came. Did you think I didn't mean that?"

"But you acted so strangely after she was gone. So—indifferent to me. When I said you could go on with your plans to marry Margo, you didn't deny that you were going to. The only thing you seemed upset about was that she had threatened you."

He signed. "I did object to that. Strenuously. I still do. I can't imagine what possessed her."

Britt paled. "I gave that some thought myself after I went to bed. I think it may be my fault."

"Yours? Why do you say that?"

"I let her think— Well, she was so certain she could keep us apart that I pretended things had gone much farther between us than they actually had. When she found me here—" Britt's voice died under her embarrassment.

Philippe grinned wickedly. "Ah! So you've gotten a

little of your own back! That must have caused an uncomfortable moment or two."

"More like half the night," she murmured.

He leaned across and kissed her lightly. "Don't worry, darling. I think there's more to Margo's motives than you could have stirred up, and whatever it is I intend to get to the bottom of it today, but as far as marriage to her is concerned—" He shook his head. "Never."

Britt appeared reassured, but one uncertainty still troubled her. "There was another reason for me to think you might go ahead with your plans," she said. "You dislike the changes loving me has brought into your life." She recalled the strong jutting of his chin, the irritation in his eyes when he had stood, hands jammed into his pockets, before the fire. "You were quite plain about that."

He reddened slightly. "It's true that I sometimes feel a bit shackled." He grinned ruefully. "But if I tried to hide that, soon enough those bright eyes of yours would ferret it out, so I might as well confess it, hadn't I?"

The color drained from her face. "Then how can we be happy together?"

He leaned across and kissed her tenderly. "Because, my darling," he said in a teasing tone, "I'll grow accustomed to the leg irons and the ball and chain. After a while I'll forget entirely the joys of the unshared life. In fact, one or two aspects of prison life I'm already beginning to appreciate." With one finger, he lifted her chin. "Waking up this morning, for example, and finding you here."

He kissed her again. "I want always to find you here—or wherever I am." He traced the soft curve of her cheek. "If I chafe a bit from time to time," he murmured, "you won't mind too much, will you?"

"Not if I'm certain you're happy," she whispered.

He gathered her into his arms then, and once more she lost herself in the wonder of his closeness.

"Certain?" he said at last.

She sighed deeply. "Certain."

Chapter 16

As soon as he had disclosed to Britt his plans to go to Tours to see Margo, Philippe telephoned the chateau, and shortly after lunch one of the estate men arrived, driving the Ferrari.

"I'll drop him off in Limoges," said Philippe as he bade goodbye to Britt. "The stableboys are bringing the horses up from the chateau today in preparation for the meet, and he can keep them company. He'll be glad for a holiday," he added with a grin. "Back at the chateau he'd be cutting grain."

From the front door of the farmhouse, Britt watched the Ferrari speeding away and recalled with a pang the day Philippe had driven her so recklessly to the chateau. That seemed a million years ago, so much had happened in between.

What would happen now? she wondered, sitting down on the front steps. What would Margo tell

Philippe when he confronted her with the news that no matter what she did, they would not marry?

Clouds suddenly covered the sun and a chill breeze came up out of the east. Britt snuggled more closely into her sweater. Rain again today probably. Despite what she had told Philippe about being perfectly content to stay here alone, there was a difference, she was discovering, between enjoying a solitary walk or a book by the fire when another person was somewhere in the house, and finding contentment when no one else was there at all. Philippe had hardly been gone five minutes, and already she was feeling depressed.

Well, she wouldn't allow it!

She stood quickly. There were walnuts which needed to be spread for drying on the wire trays Philippe had showed her in one of the outbuildings, and mushrooms to gather, and more nuts, too, if the rain held off.

She could write a letter to Sydney and walk into the village to mail it. There were fruit jars in the cupboard; she could boil up a pot of figs and bottle them. The hours would pass, she assured herself, and Philippe would return.

Besides, there were dozens of happy thoughts she could occupy her mind with. Philippe loved her! That was some kind of miracle in itself and one she'd not had half enough time to consider.

Humming, she went back into the house, choosing the writing of a letter to Sydney as her first duty. The walk into the village and back occupied most of the rest of the afternoon. At five she made herself a pot of tea, stirred up the fire in the *séjour* and settled down once again with her history book.

At a quarter after the hour, she heard a car coming up the lane. Looking out the front window, she could hardly believe her eyes. The Ferrari was coming over the cattle crossing.

"What happened?" she cried when Philippe swung open the door and stepped out. "You couldn't have been to Tours and back in this short time."

"I only had to go as far as Limoges," he answered curtly, and her heart turned over at the grimness of his expression.

"Come inside then," she said as calmly as she could. "I've made a pot of tea."

But once in the *séjour* Philippe went straight to the liquor cabinet and poured himself a generous measure of Scotch.

"It's something terrible, isn't it?" said Britt when he had come to sit beside her.

"It's out of all reason," he answered numbly.

"Tell me!"

"Margo is prepared to take me into court on a morals charge."

"What?"

"She plans to claim I violated my position as her legal guardian."

Britt frowned. "I don't understand. Do you mean she thinks you've mishandled her finances?"

"She's going to claim I've mishandled *her*."

Britt's jaw dropped.

"She's going to say," he went on tonelessly, "that I went to her bedroom and attempted to seduce her."

"Philippe!"

He snorted in disgust. "Did you ever hear such trash?" Setting down his glass sharply, he strode to the fire. "And won't the scandal sheets love that! I could cheerfully wring her lily-white neck."

Britt stared, dumbfounded. "How did you learn this?"

"She was there. In Limoges. On the way back yesterday she met the Rimbauds, friends of ours. They have horses coming up for the meet too and decided to check on them, so Margo joined them instead of going on to Tours. When I stopped at the stables to let out Raoul, there they all were."

"So you had your talk in Limoges." Britt tried to sort her jumbled thoughts. "She told you there of this horrible plan?"

He nodded. "We keep rooms in Limoges during the meets. All the riders do. We went into one of those."

Britt's eyes opened wide. "This is where you are supposed to have assaulted her?"

"Oh, no, no. She figured all this out some time ago. The supposed seduction," he said with bitter sarcasm, "took place at the chateau."

"How ridiculous!" cried Britt. "Especially since you and Martinique go to such pains to see that Margo is properly chaperoned. Of course," she admitted, "if either of you had wanted to carry on an affair, you could easily have managed it, but as far as propriety is concerned, your reputation is entirely safeguarded, it seems to me, by the presence of Martinique. The court would uphold those arrangements, wouldn't it?"

"I'm sure it would." He sighed. "But there's a hitch. The night Margo came back from Nice, Martinique wasn't there. Margo was supposed to stay at least a week in Nice. Martinique was still at her cottage."

Britt's spirits sank. "Naturally that would be the night Margo would single out."

"I'm afraid so."

Suddenly Britt's eyes shone with new hope. "But I was at the chateau that night."

"Yes, but isolated in the south wing." He smiled glumly. "There's no way you could have known what went on in the other part of the house."

Britt was silent for a moment. Then she spoke in a

clear voice. "I'll say then that you spent the night with me. I'll testify that you were never out of my bedroom the entire evening."

Philippe regarded her with amazement. "You realize what that implies?"

"It's certainly a more acceptable situation, isn't it, than—" Margo's descriptive noun came to mind. "Than decadence."

"One hell of a lot more acceptable." He slumped again on the sofa. "No one would be much concerned over—what did Margo call it?—'bedroom antics'— between the two of us, but between a guardian and his ward—particularly if the ward is unwilling, as she'll of course claim—that's quite another matter."

"Then it's settled," said Britt shakily. "We needn't worry any more about it."

He eyed her keenly. "What you would claim, Britt, isn't true."

"Neither is Margo's claim!"

"Yours is just as farfetched," he answered quietly.

"No one need know that but you and I."

He looked at her for a long moment. "You'd publicly testify to have done what you never would have in order to save my name?"

She raised her green eyes. "Wouldn't you do it for me?"

Swiftly he pulled her to him and buried his face in her hair. "Is this part of love too?" he said hoarsely. "Sacrifice?"

"Every detail of our lives now is a part of love." Her muffled answer came from his chest where she had laid her head to hear his heart beat, its steady rhythm calming her agitation. "We're too strong for Margo, Philippe. There's no way she can hurt us."

But she felt his tenseness. "I'm afraid there is. She has witnesses."

Britt sprang back. "What are you saying?"

"I did go to her room that night."

Britt could scarcely breathe. "You were with her?"

"No, of course I wasn't 'with her.' At least not in the sense she's claiming, but I can't deny I was there, and her spies will testify to that."

His glance took in Britt's ashen face. "Oh, darling," he said quickly. "Don't look as if the world has come to an end. We'll figure our way out of this somehow."

Britt spoke without inflection. "What were you doing in her room?"

"Oh. That's what's worrying you, is it?" His jaw hardened. "Isn't trust one of love's virtues as well as sacrifice?"

"Don't be cruel!"

At once he was contrite and brought her to him again. "I'm sorry, darling. It's just that this is such a damnable mess. It's made me bitter."

Britt said nothing.

"But that doesn't answer your question, does it?" He sighed. "I'm hedging because the answer is so incredible. Margo's ruse to get me to her room was so obviously a setup I should have known at once she was up to something. But that it might be *this*—why, it simply never occurred to me!"

He took Britt's hand. "You see, that night after you went up to bed, Margo and I sat for awhile in the study. There were some details about the ball she wanted to discuss, and we had a nightcap. Then just as she was leaving to go to bed herself she mentioned casually that she had some suggestions for remodeling her apartment into one we could occupy after our marriage.

"As you perhaps know, the purpose of my redecorating the east wing was so that we could occupy that, but I wasn't ready to disclose that. And I especially wanted to avoid a discussion of it that particular night—" He squeezed Britt's hand. "Because by that time I was having serious second thoughts about the marriage itself. So when she insisted that I see what she had in mind, I gave in. She said to give her a few minutes while she had some furniture switched around in the apartment."

As Philippe continued to speak, Britt felt the anguish which had gripped her lessening its hold. Margo had tricked him into coming to her bedroom. He hadn't gone there voluntarily. As long as that were true, she could handle whatever else he had to tell her.

"She rang for a couple of the servants to tend to the furniture," Philippe went on, "and she said she'd send one of them to tell me when she was ready for me to come."

Britt sighed. "Oh, Philippe. And she called *me* naive."

He flushed. "I know. I tell you, it never occurred to me to be suspicious. I thought it was just another of Margo's selfish unreasonable ideas."

"She'd count on your thinking that."

"She counted on something else too. She made me wait an hour. It was late. Finally I decided she'd given the whole thing up, and I changed into my night clothes. I was half asleep when a maid came and knocked on the door."

"To tell you her mistress was ready for you." Britt shook her head sadly. "The same maid you fired, of course?"

He nodded. "And there was another one I met in the hall on my way to Margo's apartment."

"But they don't know what went on once you were inside," Britt said in a more hopeful tone. "How can they attest to that?"

"Margo screamed."

"Screamed?"

His jaw tightened. "When I came in, she was up on a little table holding up a piece of drapery. Instantly she seemed to lose her balance. I broke her fall, but not before she shrieked. She made quite a noisy thing of it."

Britt sank back on the couch. "Dear heaven."

"Incredible, isn't it. I'm amazed she had enough time to think out all the details on as short a flight as the one from Nice."

Britt looked thoughtful. "Perhaps she didn't. I'm more inclined to think she plotted all this sometime ago and was keeping it ready for a rainy day."

"What do you mean? Why would she have?"

"She was quite emphatic when she told us she planned to live the rest of her life in the chateau."

"Living there is an important element of her social prestige. It's the main reason she wanted to marry me, I'm sure."

"This scheme was her insurance then, in the event you didn't propose."

"You're saying, in other words, that she'll have the chateau at any cost."

"She said so herself."

For a while they were quiet, each one lost in his own thoughts. Finally Britt said, "What are you going to do?"

"The only thing I can. Talk her out of it."

"Do you think you'll be able to?"

"I couldn't today, but I plan to have another go at it."

"You're going to Tours after all?"

"No. She'll be in Limoges with the Rimbauds for two more days. I'll go back to see her in the morning."

Britt's heart sank. It seemed to her, looking at Philippe's weary countenance, that part of Margo's plan might be to wear him down to the point where he would finally give in. Certainly each time she could force him to come to her put him in the position of beggar and strengthened her own stand.

"What if you just ignored her threats?" Britt offered tentatively.

Philippe shot her a surprised look. "Let her take me to court, do you mean?"

"Do you really think she'll go that far?"

He flushed angrily. "Of course she will. Not five minutes ago you said as much yourself."

"No," she said slowly as if she were seeing their plight for the first time. "I was quoting Margo when I said she'd have the chateau at any cost. But now that I've had a few minutes to think about it, I doubt that she's reckoned the cost."

"You're talking nonsense."

His curtness hurt, but she tried to keep in mind how much was at stake and went on patiently. "You see, Philippe, if she does drag you into court, no matter how the case turns out she will have injured herself."

"How?"

"If you're proven guilty—" she swallowed. "You won't be, of course, but if you were, there would always be people in Margo's social set—just as there are in every stratum of society—willing to believe the worst. They'd always wonder and discuss whether or not she'd enticed you. On the other hand, if you were acquitted, then she'd certainly look like a fool."

Philippe's chin came out. "What difference would any of that make?" he said crossly. "It would all be after the fact by that time. Your argument works both ways, you know. Whether I win or lose, doubts will have been planted in the minds of those who now regard me highly."

Are you including me as one of those? Britt wondered uneasily. *Or does my opinion no longer count?*

"Please listen to me with an open mind, Philippe. What I'm saying is that Margo will never carry things that far. She's a clever girl. Let her stew in her own juice for a time, and she's bound to realize that the nastiness she's threatening you with will rub off on her if she drags it into the public eye."

Suddenly all hostility seemed to leave him. "You're a wonderful antidote for Margo's poison, do you know that? When I left Limoges I was ready to murder her." The strain eased from his face. "But she's not worth the effort, is she?"

An airiness took hold of Britt. "You'll find a way to handle her."

Coming to Britt, he lifted her chin tenderly and kissed her on the lips. "Of course I will. Don't worry."

Chapter 17

The evening passed swiftly. Britt made the chicken pie she'd promised and after dinner they took another walk by the river. The rain which had marred the earlier part of their stay was gone now, and the heavens shone with a million stars.

Gazing up at them, Britt said dreamily, "I can almost imagine the sky is the River Tet with its fairyland lights and that in a moment we'll come upon the hotel terrace in Perpignan."

Philippe brushed his lips against her cheek. "Do I sense in that remark a certain wistfulness?" he teased.

"In a way I wouldn't mind if we were back in Perpignan on the first evening we met," she admitted. "There are things I might have done differently."

"You wouldn't have fallen in love with me. Is that one?"

She nestled against him. "I'd never want to change that, no matter what happened."

"And anything could," he said with a return to his earlier grimness.

"Oh, now see what I've done. I've spoiled your mood."

But he moved on to another thought. "If we do manage somehow to come out of all this unscathed, what of your career, Britt?"

What career? she almost said. The photographs she had taken for Sydney and the material she had gathered for the article had passed so completely from her mind that she had difficulty now recognizing herself as the cocky girl who had bragged to Philippe in a grove of lemon trees that she might gain a place on the staff of *La Revue.* Now she said with complete conviction, "I never really wanted a career."

"I find that hard to believe."

"It's true nevertheless. I was only filling in my time working until—" She broke off, acutely embarrassed.

"Until Sydney asked you to marry him?" he probed gently.

"He could have asked a dozen times," she mumbled. "I'd never have answered yes."

He stopped and turned her to him. "What if I ask?" he said thickly.

Her heart came up in her throat. "Ask and see," she managed.

The moon shown on his face, the craggy wonderful face that long ago had won her heart. "When I solve my problems with Margo," he said huskily, "will you be my wife, Britt Ryan?"

"Oh, Philippe!"

He gathered her in his arms. The moonlight on the Dordogne, the stars in the sky, the luminescent moon . . . all paled beside the shining hope radiating from the two of them, assured that some day soon they would be one.

All morning Britt's heart sang. *Philippe had formally proposed. She had accepted.* There was no sweeter song than that. Even the loneliness which enveloped her as she watched the Ferrari disappear down the road to Limoges could not hold out long against the pure joy surging through her veins.

If she could have dissuaded Philippe from making the journey to Margo, she would have, but bringing it up again last night and spoiling their happiness was unthinkable, and this morning Philippe had been so optimistic, so certain he could change Margo's mind that Britt hadn't the heart to discourage him

Besides, how did she know he wasn't right in going again to talk to Margo? He knew her well—far better than Britt. His could be the right course after all.

For a time Britt walked in the orchard, gathering nuts, but mostly daydreaming. What would life be like in the Chateau de Laon? Far different, she was sure, when her role was that of mistress instead of guest. The prospect was so exciting she could scarcely calm herself enough to think sensibly about it, but of one thing she was certain. No wife who had ever occupied that magnificent dwelling had ever loved her husband more than she would love Philippe.

That was the fundamental thing. Everything else— her lack of proper training for such an awesome task as hostess of the grandest chateau in the land, her ignorance of the social world—all those details would take care of themselves somehow as long as first place in Philippe's heart belonged to her. She leaned against a thick tree trunk and closed her eyes. Dreams did come true—and on a much grander scale than one could ever imagine!

Toward noon when she was cutting a bouquet of dahlias from the front garden, singeing the woody stems as she went, she heard the familiar roar of the Ferrari, and in a moment it appeared at the end of the lane.

She was about to express her delight by shouting, "Welcome home!" but the words died in her throat when she saw Philippe's face— a carbon copy of the one with which he had returned yesterday.

"What happened?" A weird feeling of *déjà vu* took hold of her. This had all taken place before, and she hated it as much now as she had then, for it was plain all had not gone well in Limoges.

Tight-lipped, Philippe led her into the house. "She's agreed to listen at least," he said when they were seated before the cold grate.

"But that's wonderful!" Britt's eyes scanned his face. "Isn't it?"

"In one way."

"But you're not happy."

"You know Margo," he answered roughly. "She always has a price."

Something cold closed around Britt's heart. "What is it?"

"She won't discuss anything further until you've gone back to Paris."

Britt felt as if a brick had slammed into her face. Not so much because of Margo's ultimatum, but because it was so obvious Philippe had agreed to it. "Do you want me to do that?"

"You know I don't."

"But you accepted the provision nevertheless?"

The color in his cheeks deepened. "I'm negotiating with her, Britt!"

His obvious annoyance cut her, but she let the remark pass. "What did you say to her?"

"About her threat?" He seemed relieved to change the subject. "I told her I was sure she hadn't thought the matter through, that there would be repercussions I was certain she hadn't considered."

Britt waited.

"She was so agreeable it was amazing."

So graciousness was to be her tack, thought Britt, feeling all at once as if the earth were sliding from beneath her. No one could be more gracious than Margo when she put her mind to it.

Philippe went on. "She said perhaps she hadn't given the matter enough thought, and she'd be happy to hear what I had to say about it. But then when I started to tell her, she cut me off. 'Every minute Britt is at the farm,' she told me, 'complicates the case.'"

Britt forced a calmness into her voice. "I don't see how."

He frowned. "Think, Britt. If I'm forced to defend my morals, how will it appear if word gets out that I've had a girl here for a week?"

"A girl!" Her tone reflected the pain he had inflicted by his insensitive choice of words. "If that's all I am to you—some *girl*—"

He came at once and put his arms about her. "I'm only telling you how it will appear to others," he said soothingly, but his words seemed to bear an echo of Margo.

Britt's voice trembled. "Nothing we need be ashamed of has happened here, Philippe."

"We know that, but who else does?"

"I've never cared much about other people's opinions." Her green eyes shimmered. "That was one of the things you admired about me, as I remember."

His face took on a set look.

"Don't go back to see Margo," she pleaded. "Stay here. Let's be the way we are, Philippe, not the way she wants us to be."

"I can't risk that."

His words stung as nothing else had. "Not even for me?"

"Dammit, Britt! This is *all* for you."

She shook her head. "It's for the chateau."

"If I don't have the chateau," he said stonily, "I have nothing to offer."

"You have yourself!" She swallowed back her tears. "You're all I want."

He looked at her and suddenly his defensiveness melted. "I'm yours already," he muttered thickly, gathering her into his arms. "We're going to be married, remember? But first you must return to Paris. Just for a short time. I'll call you every day. Then when the whole mess is resolved, I'll come for you, and we can start our life together as we should, free of all entanglements."

He kissed her. "Can't you trust me to handle Margo, Britt? Isn't your love strong enough for that?"

Her tears spilled over. "Is yours?"

They clung to each other. His kisses covered her face, his powerful embrace closed out all but the assurance of his devotion. Finally he put her from him and said gently, "Go and pack your things now. I'll drive you to Limoges, and you can take the train from there."

Chapter 18

It was winter in Paris, if not according to the calendar, at least in Britt's heart. The gloom of the city streets contrasted dismally to the golden days along the Dordogne and even to the rainy ones, and depressed her in the same way the winter months had always done at Land's End. Ordinarily in Paris there was a gaiety which had a way of lifting her spirits at any time of the year, but in the dark days since she had ridden in on the train from Limoges, the lovely city had shown her only its coldest face.

Her rooms on the Rue de Mont had been invaded in her absence by an army of ants. Sydney's left leg had refused to mend properly, and he was back in traction. And despite Philippe's promise to call every day, a week had passed, and she had heard nothing.

She felt her deepest fears were now confirmed. She'd been right to believe that Margo would try to wear down Philippe's resistance. Perhaps by now she already had.

In a morning paper Britt had read, as best she could through her tears, the list of entrants in the equestrian meet. Both Margo and Philippe were named. Probably tonight the two of them and their friends, the Rimbauds, were enjoying dinner together. Laughing . . . talking. It was plain Philippe had forgotten her entirely. His proposal had been spawned in some vagary of his mercurial nature, and now back with his own kind, he had discarded it as easily as a ballast bag tossed from his balloon when it was no longer needed.

Sitting down at the small kitchen table in her flat, Britt stared absently at a trail of ants wending their way over the edge of a cabinet top. All her efforts to eradicate them had failed, but now she felt it no longer mattered if they took over the whole place. She had decided to move anyway, to carry out her plan to visit Aunt Tillie and then go up to London. This afternoon she had submitted to the editors of *La Revue* the photographs she had taken at the Chateau de Laon and the material she had gathered for the article. Her work in Paris was finished.

There was an irony to that too.

Since her return she had gone every day to the hospital, but this morning she had at last brought with her for Sydney's inspection the completed article and the photographs. When he had fumed previously at the delay she had begged him to be patient.

"The only way you can view them with the same perspective as the editors is by considering the photographs alongside the article. Then you'll be able to make criticisms, and I can make the necessary changes before we submit."

But according to the delighted Sydney, no changes were needed.

"My word!" he had cried. "They're super!" Twice more he ruffled through the glossy prints and referred to the paragraphs she had labored over for days. "What a gorgeous place, and you've captured it perfectly. It makes me want to get up, broken legs and all, and rush to see it. Can you imagine how the readers will react?"

"You think I can take it all over to your editor today then?" Britt's heart came up in her throat. "What will I say?"

"Make a clean breast of things," he had told her with amazing cheerfulness. "God knows how long I'll be laid up here. They're going to need somebody. It might as well be you."

"Do you really think they'll hire me?"

"Why not? You've done a smashing job." He had looked at her then with genuine concern. "It's not the job I'm worried about though. It's you. I've never seen you quite so—" He searched for the proper word. "Lifeless. I think the pace at the chateau might have been a bit rich for your blood."

She smiled wanly. "I guess it's a good thing I won't be subjected to it any further."

Dismal as her words were, they stirred hope in her. If her heart had mended enough for her to joke about her shattered plans for the future, then maybe her emotional state was not as desperate as she had feared.

That consolation, coupled with Sydney's praise had enabled her shortly after noon to present a brave face at the editor's desk where she made her explanations as succinctly as her dry mouth would allow.

"So you see," she concluded. "It was because of the stiff competition here at the magazine that Sydney preferred to keep his accident a secret and to submit my work in place of his. He felt if he couldn't come through with the chateau article he might lose his place here on staff."

The editor was highly annoyed. But not at Britt, as she had first thought. At Sydney for having concealed for so long his invalidism, a breach of friendship which the woman finally decided to forgive by ordering two dozen red roses and a five pound box of sweets to be delivered to his bedside.

Then she turned her attention back to Britt's photographs. While she perused them, Britt looked nervously about the office, a starkly modern space, too cold, in Britt's opinion, to be termed a room, but quite suitable for the brusque young woman behind the desk whom Britt could not imagine caring in the least for her photographs filled with the autumn light of coastal France and the mystery of the chateau's ancient shadows.

Finally the editor looked up and gave Britt a thorough scrutiny. "Sydney underestimates himself. There's competition at *La Revue*, yes, but when one is the best it doesn't matter." She looked over the rims of her heavy glasses. "And Sydney *is* the best." Her gaze bore into Britt. "You, however, are not far behind him. How would you like a job?"

That was the moment—the moment that had cost her so much to achieve—when Britt knew she was leaving Paris.

When the editor spoke the words she had so fervently wished to hear only a few weeks before, something in her snapped. She had come full circle, she realized numbly. When she had left Paris for Perpignan her goal had been to work on the staff at *La Revue*.

Now she had achieved it—and found it meaningless. It was time to move on.

Quickly she murmured her appreciation of the offer, collected payment for her work, and fled.

Back in her apartment she sipped absently from a cup of coffee grown cold. The sandwich she had made for her evening meal lay untouched on her plate, and she thought wryly what a feast it would be for the ants if she gave in to her strongest desire which at that moment was simply to get up and walk out of the apartment and never look back.

It would be symbolic of walking away from all that had happened to her in the days since she had come to know Philippe Dolman. He had proposed marriage, yes, but with a provision: *He had first to solve his problems with Margo.* She'd scarcely noticed his words at the time, so enthralled had she been in the wonder of his asking her to marry him. Now they haunted her. Obviously he had not been able to solve his problems with Margo. Even if he despised Margo, he would marry her before he would allow the slightest taint to his historical name or before he could face the prospect of giving up the chateau. She'd been a fool to think for even a moment that she might be more important to him than his heritage.

Still, nothing could ever make her forget the way she had felt in Philippe's arms or the way his mouth had moved on hers, speaking with a language only her heated passions could respond to. Even now just the thought of him, though he was miles away and in Margo's arms probably, made desire course through her veins like liquid fire.

Her heart twisted. If all she were to have out of life were memories, then what a fool she was not to have had the best.

She could have lain beside Philippe that night at the farm—and every night afterward. If she had done that—given in to all that was primitive and fundamental within her—he might even have resisted Margo's threats and stayed with her.

A sob escaped her throat. *To thine ownself be true.* Such a wise man, Shakespeare, but he ought to have defined what he meant by that phrase that had guided her the night she shoved Philippe away. Her baser nature was the self she should have listened to, not the puritan promptings which left her with a cold bed now and an even colder heart.

What did it matter to Philippe that she had maintained her integrity? Not enough certainly to have kept him true to her.

Loving Philippe had spoiled her for everything else too. Her life here in Paris. The job at *La Revue*. Everything that had once been bright and beautiful had lost its sparkle because of him.

Yet that wasn't quite true, was it? Or fair. Long before she had known Philippe, she had known restlessness, the longing she still had for husband, home, and children. The need to be cherished, as Philippe had vowed she was.

Oh, why must every thought bring her back to him! Was there no way she could find peace?

Suddenly she knew there was a way. She could go back to the farm. Peace was there beside the slumberous river, among the old walnut trees heavy with their bounty, in the simple hominess of the *séjour* where quiet gave way only to the ticking of an ancient clock on the mantle.

The farm was as close to home as any place Britt had ever known and with all her heart she longed to be there now. The beauty of it was there was nothing to stop her! Philippe would be in Limoges at the meet until Sunday. If she left tonight, she could have three whole days alone to say her goodbyes to everything that had won her heart by the Dordogne.

Trembling, she clasped her hands to her throat. That was most of what was wrong, wasn't it, now that she had faced the fact that Philippe was lost to her? The

pain that remained still tortured her because Philippe
had uprooted her so suddenly. She'd had no time to
wean herself gently from what she had come to trust.
She needed that time. And she would have it!

Obtaining the key to the sturdy old farmhouse was
the only part of her adventure Britt dreaded, but when
she arrived late the next afternoon in a hired car—a
luxury she still couldn't believe she had treated herself
to—Madame Londine was gathering hips and haws and
spindleberries in a thicket near the gate and seemed
overjoyed to see her.

"You've come back!" the ample lady cried. "And
just at the right time too. I've cleaned the place from
top to bottom and left it open to air. You can go right
on, and later I'll send you up a bit of supper."

True to her word, Madame's young son arrived just
before eight with a steaming pot of stewed chicken and
vegetables and a loaf of crusty bread.

"Fromage, too," said the boy, producing a cheese in
a string bag.

Britt took his offerings gratefully and gave him a bit
of money for his trouble.

The boy went off whistling up the lane, and Britt
bolted the door, carrying her delicious smelling treasure into the *séjour* where she had set up the little table
on which she and Philippe had shared their meals.

The first few moments after she had entered the
empty house, doubts had assailed her. This had been a
foolish idea, a silly impulse she should never have
responded to. Everywhere she found reminders of
Philippe. A pipe on the desk, the pair of old boots he
had worn into the orchard, their fishing poles tipped
against one corner of the kitchen.

But gradually the warmth and coziness of the cottage

overcame her feeling of aloneness and she felt strangely enfolded again in Philippe's love.

She had done well to come back, she thought now, testing the tempting stew for hotness. This was the environment in which her wounds would heal. She would shore up her memories here and make them fast for the years to come. The house would give her courage; the grounds and the river, peace of mind. After she had gathered together her things in Paris she could go back to England, if not fulfilled, at least reconciled to a degree.

She ate with a hearty appetite and listened without alarm to the gradually rising wind which rattled the shutters and whistled about the chimney.

Chapter 19

Sometime toward midnight Britt woke to the increased howling of the wind and a heavy driving rain which struck the windowpanes of her attic room like a barrage of stones. Nestling further into the warmth of her bed she thought with gratitude of the barn safely sheltering the hired car. Thank goodness she had had the presence of mind before she came up to bed to go out and latch the door. Assured that everything, including herself, was safe and secure, she drifted peacefully back to sleep.

In the morning she woke to find the storm still raging, though with lessened intensity. Through the rain splattered window of the kitchen, she could see one big tree down in the orchard and the veritable rivers the garden paths had become.

Humming, she set about making her breakfast. The weather had cooperated perfectly with her plans to absorb all she could of the warm strength the house exuded. She could spend today curled up in the *séjour* reading and thinking and sorting out the pieces of her life which were still intact—much as one might if she were recuperating from a severe illness, she thought ruefully. In a storm like this she need fear no intrusions from the outside world. By tomorrow the disturbance would have all blown over and she could have her walk along the river and through the orchard.

The first part of the morning passed much as she had hoped. Madame Londine trudged over during a break in the rain, bringing a dozen eggs and a pail of fresh milk, but other than that interruption, Britt spent the hours in contented solitude.

She had just entered the kitchen to set about stirring up an omelette for lunch when over the sound of the dying wind she heard a familiar roar.

The Ferrari? Her heart stopped. It couldn't be!

Racing to the window, she took the corner of her apron and smeared steam from the pane. *It was!* And the little car had already passed over the cattle crossing.

She wheeled back toward the kitchen, panic-stricken. Philippe mustn't find her here. For a wild moment she thought of crawling into a cupboard. He was supposed to be in Limoges. Why wasn't he? Had something happened? Had he been injured at the meet?

Every other thought except his safety left her mind.

She rushed back to the window. There a totally unexpected sight greeted her.

Philippe was not alone.

Margo, dressed in a close-fitting riding habit, was emerging from the front seat of the car and just behind her, unfolding from the back, came a middle-aged couple who were strangers to Britt.

Paralyzed, she watched while Philippe paused near the bonnet of the car and pointed back toward the orchard. Margo said something, and the man and woman laughed. Then all four turned toward the house.

One thought blazed across Britt's mind. Escape! She lunged toward the stair, but her foot had barely touched the second step when Philippe's puzzled voice came from the other side of the door.

"Why, it's not even locked."

Britt froze. The door swung open. Philippe's shocked gaze met her own.

"Britt? What on earth—!"

Faces crowding the doorway behind him blurred. She tried to speak and failed.

Philippe stepped forward, a stunned look on his face. "What are you doing here?"

"As if you didn't know!" Margo disengaged herself from the mass of accusing eyes trained on Britt and flung herself at Philippe. "What a lowdown, scheming, nasty trick."

"Certainly you don't think I knew she was here!" said the incredulous Philippe.

"Certainly I *do!*" Scarlet with rage, Margo faced Britt. "What happened?" she spat out. "Did you get your signals crossed and come creeping out of your hidey hole before you were supposed to?"

The bewildered couple in the doorway melted out

into the yard to the obvious relief of Philippe, who shut the door almost in their faces and then turned white-lipped to Britt.

"Explain yourself at once," he commanded.

His tone had the effect of a bucket of cold water thrown over her head. Britt's voice erupted harshly from her throat. "How decent of you to offer me the opportunity!"

"The charade is over." Margo glared at them both. "It's too late for explanations." Her lip curled. "Though I'm sure they'd be fascinating."

Philippe directed his anger at Margo. "Be quiet. Let's hear what she has to say."

Fury so intense it was suffocating swept over Britt. He could at least have granted her the dignity of her name! Planting her hands firmly on her slender hips, she spoke in a hostile tone that rang menacingly across the *séjour*. "I arrived last night. I was trapped by the storm. And I am now leaving."

As swiftly as a cat, Margo blocked her way. "Surely you can come up with a better story than that."

Philippe crowded up behind her. "Why did you return at all?"

The question knifed into Britt. "I left my camera here," she lied.

"Oh, *really*," said Margo.

Britt felt her face catch fire. "You can believe it or not. I couldn't care less."

Margo's eyes blazed. "I suppose next you'll say you flew out from Paris on a broomstick."

"I came in a hired car," said Britt through clenched teeth.

"Where is it?" demanded Philippe.

"In the barn." Tears stung Britt's eyelids. He had turned his back on her completely. "Madame Londine can easily verify the time of my arrival if the truth matters to anyone." Her voice broke. "Let me pass, please."

Margo remained where she was. "No suitcase?" she said coldly.

Britt caught her breath. The suitcase! And all her things strung about in the room upstairs as if she'd been here all the time. For an instant she thought she might faint, but one look at Philippe's closed face drove a fresh spurt of adrenalin through her bloodstream.

"I'll be back for it," she said coolly. "But first I'm going to invite your friends in. Since my presence here has caused a scene and embarrassed them, the least I can do is offer them a cup of coffee."

Her aplomb had a disquieting effect on Margo and on Philippe as well, and both stepped aside to let Britt pass. When she returned in a moment with the hesitant couple, Philippe had recovered himself enough to introduce them.

"Britt Ryan, may I present Elaine and Edouard Rimbaud. Miss Ryan has been at the chateau—" He cleared his throat. "And here at the farm photographing for her magazine, *La Revue.*"

He went on in the face of Margo's saccharine smile. "I was under the impression she'd already left for Paris, so it was rather a surprise to find she'd not."

"We're quite pleased to meet you," Elaine Rimbaud said. It was clear from her expression she found Philippe's explanation a thin one, but she smiled graciously. *"La Revue* is a favorite publication of mine. Are you new on the staff? I don't seem to recall—"

"Quite new," Margo supplied in a dry tone. "There might even be one or two editors not yet aware she's been employed."

"Have a seat, Elaine," Philippe intervened quickly.

"You too, Edouard. I'll just step out in the kitchen and help Britt fetch the coffee—"

"I don't need any help," said Britt with unmistakable firmness. "I'll just be a moment."

But in the kitchen, she collapsed on a stool, trembling violently. Margo was despicable, but Philippe was worse! How could a man who had once professed love—proposed marriage even!—behave as he had done? Every word he had spoken was directed toward pushing her out of the house, she thought furiously, and how Margo was enjoying that!

Suddenly out of the blue a wild, crazy, wonderful idea popped into her mind. She got up swiftly and set the coffee pot on the stove. While it heated, she scurried about the kitchen like a madwoman, cracking eggs into a bowl . . . setting a tray with plates and silverware. . . .

When she finally sailed into the *séjour* with the coffee, her cheeks were rosy and her green eyes sparkled brightly. "Here we are. Wait until you hear what a smashing idea I've just had."

The Rimbauds looked up with anticipatory smiles, but Margo glared, and Philippe glowered darkly.

Britt gave one and all a dazzling smile. "We have just enough time for lunch together before I go."

"Lunch!" cried Margo.

Philippe came out of his chair. "Don't be absurd!" Then remembering his role: "What I mean is, the weather is so unstable. You mustn't delay getting on the road."

"I agree," said Margo barely disguising her anger. "Don't let us keep you."

"An hour more won't make any difference," said Britt airily. "I'm sure you're starving after your drive." She set the coffee tray down. "By the way, how is it that you've left the meet before its finish?"

"The weather, my dear," said Edouard Rimbaud, taking the cup she handed him. "The course is a muddy mess. In fact, the whole thing was canceled at dawn. It was still pouring when we left."

Britt made a clucking sound. "What a shame! But what a lucky break for me." She turned a brilliant smile on Margo. "It gives me a chance to have a nice visit with you. Now, if you'll excuse me, I'll just dash out and put the finishing touches on our lunch."

Philippe's voice knifed coldly across the room. "Don't bother, please. We had a late breakfast."

She shot him her sauciest smile. "No bother at all. The eggs are all ready for the omelette. The cheese is grated. The only problem is we haven't any fruit, but perhaps it won't matter if we have a sweet wine instead."

In less than a minute Philippe had followed her into the kitchen. "Just what is this all about?" he hissed. "Aren't things difficult enough without prolonging them?"

Britt pushed past him with her bowl of eggs. "Better not let dear Margo catch you fraternizing with the kitchen help."

He grabbed at her arm, but she eluded his reach. "You'll cause a spill!" she snapped. "Get out, please, and leave me alone."

He blocked her way to the stove. "Have you lost your mind? Jeopardizing everything that's important to us by antagonizing Margo?"

"Nothing that concerns you—or Margo—is important to me."

He paled. "Darling! You don't mean that."

"Darling! How dare you call me that?"

He caught her shoulders. "I love you, remember?"

"A fine way you have of showing it!"

"Things are very precarious, Britt!"

"Then don't make them more so. Wouldn't Margo
love to walk in and find you touching me?"

His hands fell to his sides. "You're right, of course,
but my God, I've missed you."

"Is that why you called every day?" she scoffed
bitterly.

"I thought you'd understand. I don't know who she
has spying on me. I couldn't risk it. But if I'd known
you were here—"

"You'd have run a hundred miles in the other
direction." Deftly she slid the eggs into the pan, anger
sharpening her movements. "Fetch the wine, please,"
she said briskly just as Margo, hawk-eyed, appeared in
the doorway with the coffee tray.

The lunch was a triumph for Britt, who, finding
revenge a sweet appetizer, finished her portion of the
omelette with glowing satisfaction. The Rimbauds, too,
ate heartily, obviously convinced that the scene which
had greeted them on their arrival concerned only some
minor indiscretion and was of little significance.

But as Britt had hoped, Philippe and Margo were
miserable. Margo's tawny eyes blazed as she picked at
her food, unwilling as yet to reveal her hand in front of
the Rimbauds, yet raging inwardly because Britt had
outmaneuvered her.

Philippe chewed mechanically as he tried without
success to keep up with Britt's bright chatter.

Finally, however, their ordeal was over. With the
same sparkling smile Britt had worn throughout the
meal, she pushed back her chair. "Now I really *must*
run. I hope you'll forgive me, Margo, for leaving you
with all the tidying up. I'm afraid the kitchen's a
frightful mess, but as you suggested earlier, I really
should be on my way."

In less time than it took the outraged Margo to carry

a plate to the kitchen, Britt was down again with her suitcase, saying her farewells.

"I'll carry your case to the car," said Philippe.

"I can manage nicely," Britt said, but Philippe ignored her.

When they rounded the corner of the house, he turned on her furiously. "You win the prize, do you know that? Subjecting us all to that grotesque meal."

"I thought it was rather tasty," she answered smugly. "Margo seemed to love it."

"You could wreck everything!"

Britt glared up at him. "I couldn't care less."

"If you don't care, then what are you doing back here?" he challenged.

She felt her face go hot and moved quickly ahead of him on the path. "I told you. I left my camera."

"I won't buy that," he said after her. "The last thing I handed up to you when I helped you on the train was your camera. *Sydney's* camera."

"Then I must have left it on the train," she mumbled.

He caught up with her at the barn door and turned her with a swift thrust of his hand. "Tell me the truth. Why did you come back?"

"I came to rob you!" she flung at him. "Be sure you check my suitcase before you put it in the car."

They glared at one another. All at once Philippe swept her to him. "What's happening to us?" he muttered thickly. "We have a precious five minutes alone, and we're wasting it quarreling."

Britt caught the scent of his skin, felt the warmth of it upon her face. Every instinct bade her yield to him, urged her to confess the love consuming her. For a moment she wavered. Then she pulled away. He was still playing the ends against the middle, and she'd had enough of that to last a lifetime.

In a toneless voice she said: "Are you going to open the barn door, or shall I do it myself?"

He stared at her. "Where are you going from here?"

"Does it matter?"

"Dammit, of course it does! Where can I reach you?"

"Why should you want to?"

He ignored that. "Back in Paris? Is the address the same?"

"No, it isn't, so don't waste your time. You won't be able to find me." She choked. "Not that you'd ever try."

He gripped her arms again. "Darling, I promise you it won't be long now. Have faith in me. Wait!"

"If there was ever anything to wait for, it doesn't matter now," she answered in a dead voice. "It's over, Philippe."

"Are you going back to Sydney? Is that it?"

A terrible weariness came over her. "What if I am? It's no business of yours." She lifted a blank face to his. "I don't want to hear your name or think of this place or the chateau ever again. Get out of my way, please."

She saw the pain spring into his dark eyes, and for an instant she came perilously close to relenting. How welcome had been the shelter of his arms . . . his face close against her own. . . . Then suddenly she remembered his accusing attitude and the way he had sided with Margo, bending over backward to assure her that he hadn't known that she, Britt, was at the farm.

Sickened, Britt turned away. Philippe hesitated only a moment longer. Then without a word, he swung open the barn door, and before she had turned the car around, he had vanished into the orchard.

Chapter 20

Britt spent the next four days after leaving the farm packing and preparing to leave Paris. A listlessness far worse than any she had experienced on her first return to the city possessed her. The slightest effort seemed to require all of her energy, and at the end of a day she felt as if she had spent its hours trudging through hip deep mud or pulling an ox cart.

Finally on the morning of the fifth day, she sent her bags ahead to the railroad station and stopped by the hospital to say goodbye to Sydney.

She found him in the midst of a frantic telephone conversation which he terminated immediately when he saw her in the doorway.

"Britt! Thank God! I thought I'd missed you."

She set down her train case. "I told you I wouldn't leave without stopping by. What's wrong?"

"Everything! The magazine called half a dozen times."

"*La Revue?* What does that have to do with me?"

"Everything," he said again as if it were the only word he knew. "You have to go back to the chateau."

168

"Chateau de Laon?" She gave a bitter laugh. "I wouldn't go there again for any reason ever."

"You must," he said decisively. "Today. They're flying you down."

"I'm on my way to Calais," she protested. "My ferry leaves at six this evening."

"At six this evening you'll be dressing for a costume ball." He picked up the telephone again. "Wait a second while I let my editor know I've found you at last."

Britt crossed quickly to his side. "Sydney! What is this all about?"

"I'll explain in a moment. The magazine is waiting to call Dolman."

"They mustn't do that!"

"Britt, my editor is beside herself."

"That has nothing to do with me."

"It has everything to do with you," he answered grimly. "Now sit down in that chair until I'm done with this," he commanded, "or I'll break your beautiful neck."

"You'll have to catch me first!" she answered indignantly.

"You walk out of here, and you'll take my job with you!"

Seeing the usually calm, affable Sydney in such a rage cowed Britt into doing as he ordered, and she listened numbly as he confirmed with his editor that Britt Ryan would be at the airport ready to go in an hour's time.

"There!" He replaced the receiver. "Thank God. If you hadn't shown up here, I don't know what I would have done."

"Well the first thing you have to do now is explain yourself," said Britt coldly, "and I'm *not* going to the Chateau de Laon no matter who thinks I am."

He stared solemnly at her. "You forgot the release, Britt."

She stared back blankly. "What release?"

"No publication can print an article or photographs of the type you submitted without the subject signing a release." His voice was fraught with strained patience. "I warned you about that, Britt. I even gave you the printed release form. Why didn't you follow through?"

Britt paled. "The release! I never once thought of it after—" She swallowed. "Philippe Dolman never mentioned it."

"He didn't have to. It was your responsibility. Worse than that," he went on, "Dolman claims he never saw the text of your article, never even saw the pictures. Good Lord, Britt! What were you thinking of down there? What were you doing?"

A wave of dizziness washing over her made the room spin. "He was so insistent at first," she began feebly. "He said he would want to check every word, supervise everything."

"He had a right to. It's his chateau. Naturally he'd want to know how it was to be presented."

"But then he forgot about it," Britt protested. "He didn't care about the article or the photographs. He never asked to see them."

Sydney gave her an incredulous look. "What in heaven's name did he think you were doing there then?"

"He— We— Oh, it's all too hopelessly complicated. Don't ask me to explain, please."

"The *magazine* is asking you, Britt! You have to produce some answers." Sydney sighed explosively. "Oh, hell. Let it go. Right now the issue is the masquerade ball. Get down there, do a bang-up job, and maybe they'll forget to draw and quarter you."

"What does the ball have to do with this?"

Sydney gave her a pitying look. "I don't know what's happened to you. You must have been hit by a bus or dropped on your head. Can't you see? The man wants retribution! He's got *La Revue* by the throat. He could sue the pants off us. But there's something big going on at the chateau tonight. This cockeyed ball. According to my editor, Dolman says it marks the most important occasion of his life, and he wants pictures, a story, the works."

Britt stared dumbly. *The most important occasion of Philippe's life: the announcement of his engagement to Margo. And he's seeing to it that I'm there to witness it.*

"I can't go, Sydney. They'll have to find someone else."

"He won't *accept* anyone else!" Sydney was all but shouting. "Aren't you listening to me? You're the one who bungled the original article. Now if this ball, the *finale,* isn't tacked onto it, *by you,* heaven knows what will happen. He's a powerful man. He could ruin the magazine."

Sydney lay back on the pillow and closed his eyes. "Why I ever let you talk me into this damned mess to begin with, I'll never know."

"You were happy enough when I showed you the photographs," said Britt, regaining a bit of her spirit.

"That was before I knew the sky was falling," moaned Sydney. He opened his eyes. "Britt, if you've a drop of compassion in your veins, get on that airplane. Get the pictures. If *La Revue* blackballs me, I'll never get another job anywhere."

Britt stared bleakly at him. "It's that important?"

"I can't *tell* you how important it is! Britt, please!"

The plane set down in the same meadow from which Philippe had launched the balloon the day he had taken Britt to the farm, except now instead of soft green, the grass was brown and frostbitten. Inside the chateau's formerly peaceful walls there was unbelievable activity.

The wide halls were filled with chattering guests and scurrying seamstresses darting in and out of apartments making last minute alterations of medieval costumes. The scents of expensive perfumes weighted the air, and everywhere a feverish excitement could be felt.

Britt, camera in hand, made her way slowly to the end of the south wing where the social secretary in the entry hall had directed her. She passed the elegant apartment she had formerly occupied and found, without surprise, that the room earmarked for her tonight was hardly larger than one of the closets in the other suite.

At the sounds of laughter mingled with conversation, she set the camera on a table and went to the window. Below, she saw Philippe was entertaining in the garden with a champagne party, and her heart thudded painfully as she watched him move with ease among his guests.

How traitorous the heart was, she thought. Here was a man who was vengeful and cruel, who had forced her to come here for the most painful ordeal of her life: witnessing his engagement to another woman. A man who had once professed to love her and whom—in spite of all this—she still loved.

How was that possible?

Yet, watching him, hearing his laughter floating up, she could not deny that this was so. Would she always love him? Years from now would the mere mention of his name strike a blow to her sensibilities? Would her pulse always race when she remembered the touch of his lips, his hands moving over her body?

She turned away from the window. How would she get through this night? How could she bear the sight of Margo, radiant in her victory?

A knock sounded at the door. Opening it, Britt met the smile of an excited maid. "Your costume, mademoiselle."

Britt stood aside as the girl entered, bearing a sleek velvet gown, the color of the sea. *The color of my eyes,* thought Britt, startled. "I'm sure there's a mistake," she said quickly. "I've brought my own costume."

Sydney had instructed her that a milkmaid's attire had been set aside for her at a costumery on her way to the airport, and it lay now in its box on the table beside her train case.

"You're Mademoiselle Ryan?" said the girl.

Britt nodded.

"This is correct then." The girl hung the dress, then laid a white velvet box on the table. "Your jewels. Shall I send for the fitter now, or would mademoiselle have her bath first?"

"I—" Britt shrugged helplessly. "The fitter first, please."

When the girl had gone, Britt took up the velvet case and opened it. Inside lay an emerald necklace so startlingly beautiful against the white cloth, that she gasped. Paste, of course, and imitation diamonds in the clasp, but how skillfully made! How dazzlingly magnificent.

With trembling fingers she lifted the necklace from the box and laid it against her creamy throat. The green stones picked up the color of her eyes at once and set a sparkle in them that hadn't been present since the day Philippe had put her on the train in Limoges.

Who had supplied such splendor, she wondered, turning again to gaze admiringly at the dress, its deep rich pile of velvet all but glowing? Surely not Margo! This room she could credit to her, thought Britt, with a grim little smile, but not velvet and emeralds.

Martinique, then. She was the one, of course. How

dear of her! Philippe's aunt must have guessed how sorely in need her reporter friend would be of some little bit of glamor on this most bitter of nights. Margo had said Britt's feelings for Philippe were written all over her face. Martinique must have read them there and taken pity on her.

Whatever the reason, she thought, gratefully bringing one soft sleeve to her cheek, the assurance that she would appear at the ball as elegantly attired as the wealthiest guest bolstered her faltering spirits, and by the time the fitter arrived, Britt found she was able to greet her with a smile and to lend a willing ear to the seamstress's gossipy chatter concerning the ball.

Britt discovered, however, that making her entrance into the empty ballroom a few minutes before the guests were due to assemble was quite a different matter from turning slowly in her velvet dress before the approving eyes of a dressmaker.

The ballroom was immense, the decorations overpowering in the medieval grandeur they reproduced. The hushed expectancy that held the room gripped Britt as well, and she stood trembling in the doorway, aware that she should be shooting her photographs before the hordes of guests in their billowing costumes blotted out the setting. But still she stood transfixed.

Margo had outdone herself. If this was any indication of the kind of hostess she would make for the Chateau de Laon, then no doubt Philippe was proud of her. Every detail was perfect.

"Ah. Here you are."

Britt turned. Philippe! He had come soundlessly into the room, dressed for the ball, the "very perfect, gentle Knight" of Chaucer's tale, slim, broad-shouldered and dark, his sensuous mouth curved in a half-smile, his voice low and disturbingly resonant. "I've been looking for you."

When Britt could trust her own voice, she replied coldly, "Did you think I'd dare disobey your command to appear?"

A subtle change occurred in his eyes. "Would you have come if I hadn't commanded?"

"Certainly not!"

His shoulders lifted slightly. "I thought as much."

"Why should I?" she retorted. "I've no business here."

"It seems you have." His gaze went to the camera in her hand. "I'm glad to see you've recovered the tool of your trade."

Blood raced to her cheeks.

She was dressed in the same finery as his guests, but she was not a guest. The camera marked her. All evening, according to his plan for humiliating her, she would have to carry it, shattering the soft glow of torches with garish bursts from her flashbulbs. She was to be the incongruous element, the out-of-place twentieth century element in this ancient setting, as out-of-place as she had always been in the life of Philippe Dolman. This was what he had fetched her here to tell her in the cruelest way he could.

Her voice came out a whisper in the silent ballroom. "I despise you."

He regarded her solemnly. "You think I've betrayed you."

"You've done worse than that. You've forced me into the dust, and now you're grinding your heel on me. Does it make you happy?" Her eyes glittered with unshed tears. "Does it give you pleasure?"

"To see you here?" His glance moved over her. "The greatest pleasure imaginable."

"You've chosen your bride well," she choked. "You deserve each other."

"I hope so," he answered quietly. "I expect to be supremely happy with her, and it's my fondest hope that she will be happy with me as well."

"She will, I'm sure, with the chateau as her home," Britt flung at him.

"And the farm."

Britt flinched. The farm, the dearest place in all the world to her. He was even more cruel than she had imagined! Her heart ached so she could scarcely breathe. "If you'll excuse me, I have work to do."

"Not now," he answered, and before she was aware of what he was doing, he had taken the camera from her.

"But it has to be now! In a few minutes the room will be so crowded I won't be able to get a clear shot of the decorations."

"It doesn't matter."

Britt's eyes blazed. "I see! You've forced me down here, but you won't let me do my job now that I'm here. That's your scheme, is it? You want me to go back to Paris empty-handed so you can ruin the magazine." She had gone the color of chalk. "Oh, you do a thing up to perfection once you set your teeth to it, don't you, Monsieur Dolman!"

"Not always." A muscle rippled in his cheek. "But this time—" His nostrils flared. "This time nothing less than perfection will do."

"Britt, my dear!" Martinique, a well-rounded cream puff in gold satin, descended upon them. "How beautiful you look!" She planted a kiss on Britt's pale cheek. "I'm so glad to see you. And the color of your gown, my dear. It couldn't be more perfect."

"Thanks to you," said Britt stiffly. "Now if I can have my camera, please—"

"Camera?" Martinique frowned. "Oh no, my dear. Not tonight. Philippe?" She turned to verify her objections with her nephew, but Philippe, camera in hand, was halfway across the ballroom.

Chapter 21

Britt stood seething in the shadows of the ballroom entrance while the guests in their magnificent costumes arranged themselves for the Grand March which would officially begin the ball.

Without her camera, she was not a photographer hired for the occasion, and without an escort, she was not a member of the bejeweled body of revelers surrounding her. She had no role at all. Philippe was a monster!

Trembling with rage, she watched as he made his way through the crowd and took his place beside Margo at its head. The orchestra struck the first note of the march, and the dazzling spectacle began.

Margo, her golden tresses arranged in a towering coil, was radiant in miles of white satin and lace. What would she choose for her wedding gown? Britt wondered. Anything less elegant than her present attire would be an anticlimax, and anything more elegant

would tax the imagination of even the most skilled
designer. How ironic, Britt thought with a stab of
malicious satisfaction, if the bride upstaged herself at
her own engagement party!

But Britt's brief indulgence in vindictiveness was
short-lived. Even she had to admit that the dark-haired
Philippe in burnished waistcoat and close-fitting trousers cut to follow the lean tautness of his thighs and
muscled calves made the perfect counterpart for
Margo's glowing blondeness. They were a strikingly
handsome couple, and the waves of admiration that
rippled over the crowded ballroom as they made their
way across it, attested to the fact that everyone there
regarded them as a storybook couple.

Had Britt been alone, she would have turned and
fled. But just as the music had begun, she had felt a soft
hand upon her arm and turning, discovered she had
been joined by Martinique. Now the older woman
clung to her, starry-eyed, while the intricate pattern of
the march evolved.

"Isn't it magnificent?" Martinique breathed.

"Stunning," Britt managed. Just what *La Revue* had
sent her here to photograph, she thought bitterly. Now
what would happen to Sydney's job? How could she
ever explain Philippe's ruthless behavior?

Once more Philippe and Margo, who had circled the
entire room, appeared almost within touching distance.
Philippe's dark eyes sought out Britt's brimming ones,
and she looked quickly away. This was beyond endur-
ance!

"You must excuse me," she murmured, pulling away
from Martinique, but the older woman only gripped
her arm more firmly.

"The most beautiful part is about to begin. You
mustn't miss it."

"Let me go, please!"

But Martinique seemed completely oblivious to Britt's agony. "Look! Philippe is giving the signal for the music to stop. He's going to make the announcement."

When the orchestra stopped playing, the great hall became still at once. Philippe mounted a turreted cupola affixed to a center supporting column and began to speak.

"Ladies and gentlemen, honored guests. Ordinarily on occasions of this sort if there are announcements to be made, they come at the stroke of midnight. They are the high point of the evening toward which all the rest is directed."

He paused a moment and leveled a gaze on Margo. "But it is my desire tonight that you should all be aware from the start of the joyous circumstances which inspired this ball so that we might celebrate together throughout the evening."

Not a whisper broke the hush of the hall. Britt wondered if even Martinique would notice if she crumpled in a faint. *Philippe and Margo*. Days ago she had faced the truth of their forthcoming marriage, but now that the moment for the announcement of it had arrived, she could not bear the pain of it. Philippe lost forever. What point was there in living?

Philippe's voice rang out again. "In addition, let it be known that our joy here tonight is two-fold." He took Margo's hand in his and lifted it.

"First," he said, "may I present to you Margo of the house of St. Croix. The much beloved ward of my late father, and since his death, my ward."

Through tear-blurred eyes, Britt saw Margo step forward and bow in a low-sweeping curtsy. She saw the dazzling smile that brought gasps of admiration from the thrilled onlookers. There was no mistaking that Margo was beauteous almost beyond belief—and equally as cruel and selfish. She would destroy Philippe.

Suddenly to Britt this was the most difficult part of all to bear. Was there nothing she could do to stop their marriage? Could she cry out now? Make a devastating scene? Create havoc on the night of Margo's triumph? What would Philippe do? Would he marry her anyway?

Philippe spoke again. "You are present here tonight as witnesses to the coming of age of Mademoiselle St. Croix, who after this evening will assume her new role as mistress of her family's ancestral estate on the island of St. Croix in the Carribean Sea."

"And who invites each of you," Margo took up in a clear voice, "to come and visit there whenever you can."

Cheers filled the ballroom. Britt's dazed stare fixed itself on Margo's radiant smile as she received the congratulations of her friends. At Britt's elbow, Martinique murmured, "Half a world away. It's scarcely far enough, is it?"

"But St. Croix—" Britt's reply came in a stranger's voice. "What does it mean? Is it to be a summer home for the two of them?"

Martinique was saved from answering by Philippe's hands raised again for silence. "And now you must hear our other reason for celebration."

The cheers died down. Britt felt the room spin. *This is it. Now the world will know, and my world will end.*

Philippe's resonant voice reached out to every corner of the vast, silent room. "The occasion of my distant cousin Margo's assumption of inheritance," he said in a dramatic cadence, "serves also to mark the announcement of a soon-to-be assumption of my own." There was a split-second pause. "The taking to myself of a wife."

A unanimous intake of breath split the charged

atmosphere. Philippe's grave face broke into a smile. "It is my very great privilege and pleasure and joy to present to you now my bride-to-be, late of Land's End and the future mistress of the Chateau de Laon— Mademoiselle Britt Ryan."

In an instant, the cheering crowd parted, and Britt in a state of shock saw Philippe striding toward her.

"Oh, my dear girl!" Martinique gasped breathlessly at her elbow. "I can't tell you how overjoyed I am."

Then Philippe was beside her, and with an arm encircling her waist, he led her swiftly back to the center of the room.

Numbly she watched as dozens of costumed waiters appeared out of nowhere bearing trays of sparkling crystal glasses filled with champagne. Edouard Rimbaud stepped forward from the crowd and proposed the toast, which was greeted with more cheers and thunderous applause and heartily drunk to amid much laughter and the joyous clinking of the fragile stemware.

Britt, still stunned, stared blankly up at Philippe. "I'm dreaming. That must be it."

He pulled her close. "Yes, my darling," he answered thickly. "But it's the dream of a lifetime, and one, thank God, from which neither of us need ever awaken."

"You took a terrible chance, you know."

Britt, speaking in the dawn light filtering into the garden room where Philippe held her in his arms, nestled closer to the heartbeat that was as vital to her as her own. "I might have said 'no' right there in front of all your friends."

"I wouldn't have blamed you if you had," Philippe murmured into her hair. "But I would have gone straight out and shot myself."

"Your friends' opinions of you matter so much?" she teased gently.

"Nothing matters but you. Tell me why in heaven's name it took me so long to discover that."

"There were complications," she answered lightly. And then in a more serious tone, "Don't you think it's time you explained how they were finally resolved?"

His lips moved on her cheek. "I'd rather kiss you again," which he proceeded to do with a passion that sent a spasm of longing up her spine. Reluctantly she broke free and pulled him toward the window seat. "Come. Sit down and tell me. I've been patient all evening."

He chuckled. "I thought you were being joyous and carefree and saucy and wonderful—but patient? That never showed once."

"That's only because you were so busy making me happy you didn't notice." Then unable to resist his nearness, she lifted her lips again for his kiss.

For a long while in the strengthening light of the dawn he held her, his hands moving possessively over the curves of her slender body and returning to frame the pixie face he had first glimpsed from his balloon.

"The maid from the meadow," he murmured hoarsely. "My lovely Britt."

"When can we go up again?" she whispered against his throat.

"In the balloon?" he sighed. "Winter's coming on, but maybe the gods will grant us one more day of perfect winds." His lips found the soft underside of her earlobe. "But I'm more interested in our wedding day."

Britt took a deep breath. "What beautiful words. I'd given up all hope of ever hearing them."

"Did you think me a terrible brute that day at the farmhouse?"

"Yes, and when Sydney told me you were forcing the magazine to send me here to cover the ball, I hated you." She paused. "But then—"

"Go on—it's our night for confessions."

"Then I saw you from my window overlooking the garden, and I knew I'd always love you no matter what you did."

His arms closed around her. "The same thing happened to me when you drove away from the farm that day."

"I've wondered," she said. "What did happen after I left?"

"I couldn't bear the sight of Margo so I walked in the orchard. Then I went back down to the river where you and I sailed in the punt. I spent some time in that little barn where we were sheltered from the rain." He lifted her chin and met the glow in her eyes. "You were in all those places, Britt. Everywhere I looked, I saw you. I felt as if some part of me had gone away with you, and I felt—" He hesitated. "I hoped and prayed after a while it might draw you back to me."

"I would never have come back on my own accord."

"I realized that. Then I went back to the house. Margo was furious. When the Rimbauds, tactful as always, left us to ourselves, she lit into me for all she was worth. I let her voice all her threats again, and then I told her I didn't care what she did."

"But you did care!"

He shook his head. "No—only about you. I told Margo she could charge me in court or not, as she pleased. She could spread her filthy lies in every newspaper on the Continent if she liked, but I would never marry her, not under any circumstance."

"Philippe, how could you risk that? You love the chateau so."

"I love you more. I nearly lost you before I discovered that losing anything else was meaningless in comparison."

They kissed again, fresh wonder at the power of love enfolding Britt anew.

When they parted, Britt said, "But I still don't understand what made Margo change her mind." She started suddenly. "She isn't— She wouldn't!"

"Go ahead with her plan?" His arm tightened about her reassuringly. "No, no. There'd have been no ball tonight if that had been the case. She agreed two days ago to drop all threats. Then the only remaining problem was how to persuade you to return to me."

But Britt was still puzzling over Margo's about-face. "You still haven't told me what caused Margo to change her mind. You must have discovered a powerful weapon of your own to use against her."

He shook his head. "For one thing, the sport went out of her challenge when she was convinced that I meant what I said—that I'd never give in to her."

He took a breath. "But the main reason she capitulated was the one you thought of when she first threatened us. Margo's ruthless, but she's clever too, and as you guessed, when she added up the odds, she realized she'd be damaged as much as I by any allegations she took to court. If only I'd acted more quickly. Think what could have been saved."

Britt nestled closer. "But think what I would have missed tonight. That lovely ball in my honor." She ran her hand over the velvet of her skirt. "This most beautiful of dresses."

"You haven't mentioned the necklace."

Her fingers went to it. "It's magnificent."

"It's your engagement gift." Then he added casually, "It was given first to Eugenie Monserrat three hundred years ago. Every Dolman bride since has worn it."

Britt sat up straight. "Do you mean it's real? These stones are really emeralds? These are diamonds?"

He laughed. "Of course."

"Oh, Philippe! I had no idea. I thought—" She ran the tip of her tongue across her lips. "Paste, that's what I thought. And glass."

"But do you like it?"

She fell back limply. "How could I not? Even when I thought it was only costume jewelry I loved it." A dismayed look controlled her delicate features. "Oh, Philippe, I don't belong here. I can't be mistress of the Chateau de Laon. Diamonds and emeralds appear the same to me as paste and glass. I'm too ordinary a person to fit into your life. Why, this necklace is worth more than my father could have earned in two lifetimes. I haven't the grace or the appreciation or any of the attributes you must have in a wife. I'll be an eternal embarrassment to you."

"Do you love me?" he said quietly.

She came swiftly into his arms. "You know I do. I have for so long that nothing which happened before I loved you seems to have any reality at all."

His fingers moved through the black tendrils curling at the nape of her neck. "Then you're all I'll ever need or want in a wife, my darling."

"There aren't any words I'd rather hear," she cried, "but love won't make me a gracious hostess. I'll make no end of blunders. This one with the necklace is only the first."

"You lectured me on love once," he answered with a bemused smile. "You told me love has a life of its own apart from the flesh—" He paused, searching his memory for the words. "Apart from the vagaries of the senses, you said. Now let me add to your definition: love can surmount all obstacles." He kissed her.

"You've made a believer out of me and nothing can move me now from that belief. Together we can overcome everything." His lips found hers again. "Tell me you have that kind of faith too, Britt."

"I want to," she whispered. "I can't live without you."

"Nor I without you. Besides," he teased, "you plighted me your troth tonight before those hundreds of persons. You can't renege now."

"I don't want to! But I'm afraid, Philippe."

He pulled her against his chest. "We haven't room in our lives for fear, Britt. Fear cripples. We're free to live in this world, you and I, and we're going to live gloriously. If problems arise, we can solve them together."

She sighed. "You make it sound so easy."

"It is actually. Think. Twenty-four hours ago would you have dreamed we'd be here together planning our future?"

"Never."

"Then you see? Anything is possible. Believe that. Believe in me."

Britt felt her doubts slipping from her as Philippe's arms wrapped her more closely. "Oh, darling, I do love you. But tell me," she said after a moment. "Margo—is she happy?"

"As happy as she's capable of being, I suppose," Philippe answered.

"I can't believe she's leaving France. What about all her friends, the social life she values so highly?"

"She'll still have it, only on a grander scale. She'll be an international socialite, and nothing could please her more. The estate in St. Croix is really a palace. I never cared for living there, so it was no great wrench for me to deed the place to her. Probably she'll spend half the year there entertaining; then the other half on the

Continent letting her friends repay her courtesies. It's exactly the kind of life she's suited for."

"So you did have to bribe her a little," said Britt, making an effort not to sound too disappointed.

"Not at all," Philippe replied crisply. "I didn't tell her until tonight just before the ball that I was giving her the castle. My only prior concession was allowing her to be present for the masquerade, and I thought that only fair since it was she who planned the whole thing."

"She knew you were going to announce our engagement?"

"Certainly. I told Martinique too." He squeezed her hand. "I had to have someone stand guard over you in case at the last minute you decided to bolt."

"I tried to. You were a devil to take away my camera."

He laughed. "I couldn't very well lead my fiancée to the fore bearing that thing, could I?"

"You ought to have had to!" she replied indignantly. "Making such a fuss at *La Revue*. Poor Sydney almost suffered a relapse. And what's he to do now? Not a single picture was taken at the ball."

"That's just as it should be," said Philippe with a contented sigh. "Once upon a time I let a photographer into my home and see what came of it. Never again!"

Britt smiled. "I don't care if I never see another camera, but that doesn't help poor Sydney. He was furious that I didn't get you to sign the release. What if he loses his job?"

"Don't worry. The moment I was notified you'd arrived at the chateau, I sent word to *La Revue* that the whole mixup had been settled to my complete satisfaction and that the release would be in tomorrow's mail. You can rest assured everyone is happy in Paris this morning."

Laughter from a late group of revelers drifted in from the hallway.

"Everyone's happy here, too." Britt lifted a contented face to Philippe's luminous gaze. "Most especially Philippe of the house of Dolman and plain Britt Ryan, late of Land's End."